# SUPERBIRD

## A THOMAS IRONCUTTER NOVEL
## BOOK 4

### DAVID ACHORD

SEVERED PRESS

# SUPERBIRD: A THOMAS IRONCUTTER NOVEL

**ISBN:  978-1-922551-29-0**

# CHAPTER 1

"No moon," Yuri said in his native tongue.

Anton pointed ambiguously and replied in English. "Plenty of streetlights."

He was correct. The nearby streetlights provided enough ambient lighting so the men would only need to use their flashlights when necessary.

There were three of them. Two had arrived at the Nashville International Airport this morning. Their forged passports listed them as being natives of Estonia, which was only off by a little over six hundred miles and a different country. When asked the purpose of their visit by the customs agent, they advised they were in Nashville to attend their nephew's wedding. The third man had been in the country for the past two days and was waiting for them when they arrived at the hotel on Donelson Pike.

"If you need a name to address me by, call me Andre," he said by way of introduction. Andre had many aliases.

"How long will this take?" one of the men asked. His real name was Yuri. Like the other man he arrived with, he was in his forties, tough, hardened, former Spetsnaz. He was suffering from jet lag and was not in a pleasant mood.

"We do it tonight," Andre replied. "A four-hour job, at the most."

"Who are we killing?" Anton asked.

Andre, a smaller man with thin lips, smiled slightly. "Nothing so dire. We are going to rob a grave," he said.

The two men swapped a glance, wondering why they'd been hired to travel all the way from Russia simply to rob a grave. When they were recruited by this same man, he was secretive about the mission, only saying it was low risk and could be accomplished in a single night. They were also promised a sizeable payment upon completion of the mission.

They watched curiously as the man pulled a piece of paper out of his pocket and unfolded it. Unfolding it revealed a hand map. He pointed at it and explained.

"This is the location of the cemetery where the grave is located. I have already procured transportation and equipment. We will leave here after midnight. I have bought all of you American clothing to wear. Leave your passports and any other identification in the room. We will go to the location and dig a hole alongside the grave, whereupon we will retrieve an item from the grave. A simple task, no?"

"What is this item?" Anton asked.

"The employer advised it is an item with an inscription engraved on it," Andre said. "Now, as I was saying, we will retrieve the item and I will deliver it to our employer. You will be paid when we return to the hotel."

"I have one or two questions," Yuri said. Andre nodded impatiently.

"What if we are seen?"

"This is why you were hired. You will utilize your skills acquired from your days as Spetsnaz, yes?" Andre said. The two men were indeed former Spetsnaz and had been imprisoned after being convicted of committing a contract killing. The little man had visited them one day and offered not only the money, but a government pardon for their crime.

"In answer to your next question, if either or both of you are somehow apprehended, you will claim to be homeless and refuse to speak to the police. The laws here are different from our home country. If you do not speak, they can do nothing to you. Sit tight and wait. Our employer will make the necessary arrangements to free you. It goes without saying that secrecy is vital. Our goal is to get in and get out without being discovered."

"We will not be discovered," Yuri proclaimed.

The grave was not hard to find. It was roughly fifty yards from the front entrance and had a large boulder sitting on top of it. Anton, he was the kind of man who never blindly accepted what he was told, crouched down by the headstone, and used his pocket flashlight to confirm the name. It only took a moment before he stood and gave Yuri a curt nod.

"The boulder presents a problem," Yuri said.

"This is why we will dig down on the side of the grave and access it in that manner. You two dig, I will keep watch," Andre said.

Yuri and Anton swapped a glance in the dark. Neither man liked Andre. They had discussed it on the plane ride. There was something about him they did not trust. They had decided to complete the mission but keep a watchful eye on him.

"Of course, little man," Yuri said. "Manual labor would be far too taxing for you."

Anton grunted a chuckle before taking a shovel and started digging. They worked a hole down the side of the grave. It was slow, laborious work and they were soon drenched in sweat. Even so, these tough, hardened men only paused once in their digging to drink some water and once when a car drove into the cemetery and parked. Yuri walked up to it and knocked on the window, asking for money. The amorous couple were so frightened, they did not bother to put their clothes back on before fleeing.

When they'd reached the side of the wooden coffin, Anton handed down a battery powered Sawzall from their ratty canvass bag to Yuri. The saw was loud, but it could not be helped. It was the quickest way to cut into the side of the coffin. Anton knew what to do if anybody became curious. The noise of the saw died, and Yuri hopped out of the hole.

"Bad air," he gasped between coughs.

"We must hurry," Andre admonished.

"Relax, little man," Yuri said. "The work is done. Get a flashlight. Go down into the hole and find this, whatever it is."

Andre smiled now, revealing small, pointy teeth. "Do you know what happens when you dance on the edge of the abyss?"

Yuri frowned in the darkness. Before he could react, a snub-nosed revolver appeared in the little man's hand. He fired once at Yuri, striking him in the chest. He turned quickly and shot Anton twice. He then turned back to Yuri. If he were a man who felt the need to explain, he would have told Yuri he bought the gun, for far more than it was worth, from a man standing on the corner near the hotel and that he and his friend were expendable; they were never going to be paid, they'd never see home again. Even though he was shot in the chest, Yuri turned to run. Andre quickly aimed and shot him in the back of the head. Satisfied that both men were dead, he took Yuri's advice and swapped his revolver for a small flashlight he had in his pocket.

Andre deftly dropped down into the hole and used the light to peer inside the coffin. The first thing he saw was a skeleton wearing an old brittle dress. He started to reach inside, but he stopped when he heard the sound of a car approaching. He had to climb out of the hole to see, and what he saw was not good.

A police car had entered through the front gate. The road was angled in respect to his current location, and it allowed him to see there was someone occupying the passenger seat. So, the car was occupied by two people: two police officers. He briefly thought of killing both officers, but he only had two bullets left in the revolver. Too risky, he thought.

He disappeared into the darkness and ran silently, quickly. Andre could run for hours if he had to.

# CHAPTER 2

"Alright, Rook, I'm about to teach you something they don't teach in the academy, so keep quiet and listen."

Officer Abigail "Abby" Severns refrained from rolling her eyes. She was worried her training officer would see the mannerism, even though it was dark inside the vehicle. He was clever and had street smarts, she had to give him that, but he was also an arrogant, insufferable prick. He kept the dashboard lights off, and the in-car computer was dimmed to its lowest setting. He had explained, numerous times, that night vision was diminished by artificial lighting.

"We're coming up on the oldest official cemetery in Nashville, the City Cemetery," he said. "There's Indian graves all over that are older, but this is the first official Nashville cemetery. Have you ever been here?"

"No, sir," Abby replied. She thought she heard some popping noises and glanced at Tomey to see if he had heard it to. If he had, he didn't acknowledge it. She rolled down her window as Tomey turned the patrol car into the entrance from Fourth Avenue South.

"There's a lot of history here," he said. "It was created in 1822 and currently there are about twenty-thousand people buried here. Did you know the person who coined the term Old Glory is buried here?"

"I think I may have heard that," she replied and turned her spotlight on. She wished he'd be quiet so she could perhaps hear the noise again.

Tomey continued. "You Generation-Z types have no appreciation for history. Are you wondering why we're here?"

"I assume the cemetery is closed at night so we're looking for trespassers," she said as she moved her spotlight from gravestone to gravestone.

"That's correct. Now we're getting to the part they don't teach you in the academy. If there's anybody hanging out in here, we're going to run them off, and then we're going to park and check the inside of our eyelids for a few."

Abby did a double take. "Are you sure, sir? I mean, that doesn't seem very tactical." Or ethical, she thought.

"That's why we're going to spell each other. I'll sleep for thirty minutes and then you catch thirty minutes. That's how officers take care of each other."

Abby withheld any comment. Sleeping while on duty was tantamount to sacrilege in her mind, but she knew better than to voice her opinion. Field Training Officer Tomey made it clear on the first night he was superior to any rookie cop and his opinion was the only one that mattered. So, instead of arguing, she focused out of her window. The spotlights gliding past the tombstones were casting eerie images. Suddenly, Abby straightened.

"Stop!" she shouted, much louder than she meant to.

Officer Tomey slammed on the brakes, jerking the cruiser to a halt.

"What the hell?" he asked, but he was staring at the empty space in the passenger seat. Officer Severns had bolted from the car and took off at a run.

"Damn rookie," he grumbled as he got on the radio. "One-sixteen, put us out at the City Cemetery on Fourth and Oak."

"Ten-four, can you advise on your traffic?" the dispatcher asked.

Tomey uttered a low, guttural profanity as he slapped the bottom of his flashlight to get it to work. He was rewarded with a bright flash of light, right into his eyes. He keyed up his shoulder mike while he blinked feverishly.

"I'll let you know in just a second," he growled, worked his uniform pants out of his butt crack, and then jogged in the direction his rookie went.

He found her within seconds. Her back was to him, and she had her flashlight pointed toward something lying on the ground beside a sizeable boulder. It only took him a second to realize it was a human and the blood gushing out of a hole in its head was a good indicator they'd stumbled into a crime. He fought to control his breath as he panned his flashlight in a quick three-sixty.

"Did you see anyone else, Rook?" he asked.

She pointed with her flashlight toward a second body.

"I think he's been shot too. I'll get the first aid kit."

"Hold on, Rookie," he said and made a quick assessment of both supine men. He then sighed deeply.

"No need for the first aid kit," he said and activated his portable mike. "Dispatch, we have two shooting victims here." He paused a minute and dropped to a knee by one of the bodies and checked for a carotid pulse. He did the same with the second victim.

"DRT, Rook. You know what that means? Dead Right There." He straightened, which took a bit of effort, and then lit up the victims with his flashlight. "You see that, Rook? Fresh blood. They've been shot within the past couple of minutes."

"I'm pretty sure I heard the gunshots while we were driving down Fourth Avenue," she said.

Tomey gave her a hard stare for a moment before activating his microphone.

"All responding units, be advised the suspect may still be in the area. Let's get a perimeter set up and have K-9 and aviation respond."

"Should we start a search?" she asked.

Tomey shook his head. "We're going to protect the scene. We don't go running around in the dark looking for an armed suspect if we can help it. We'll let the dog do that. He's much better at it than us." He cocked his head and pointed up. "You hear that? Aviation is already in the area."

As he said it, Officer Severns heard the distinct noise of the helicopter's rotors, and within seconds, the entire cemetery was lit up by its search light. The young rookie officer was anxious but ecstatic. This moment is what she lived for, the reason why she had wanted to be a police officer. Tomey confirmed it.

"Well, Rook, it looks like you've got your first murder, and it's a double murder at that," he said and gazed at her. He saw the gleam of excitement in her eyes. It reminded him back to when he was a young eager rookie.

Happier times.

He shook off the thoughts and focused on the present. "Alright, Rook, let's see if you've been paying attention to your training. Tell me what we do next?"

# CHAPTER 3

It was nine on a Sunday morning and already there was a distinct odor of fried baloney in the air. No surprise, baloney was a common food staple in jails everywhere. I know that from first-hand experience. I used to like a good bologna sandwich with a slice of cheese, extra mayo, and mustard, but not anymore. Back when I was locked up on a false murder charge, I ate so many of the damn things that I swore I would never eat bologna again. Not even if I was paid.

The smell was causing my queasy stomach to churn. I blamed Marti. My birthday party was yesterday. We had a variety of food and a keg of beer, but Marti also made a batch of Jell-O shots of various confections. And, because I was the birthday boy, I was encouraged to sample several of them.

I knew better, but I participated anyway. My stomach grumbled again. This time from deep down. The kind of deep down where you hoped a clean restroom was nearby. This day had started out badly and it did not seem like it was going to get any better.

After waiting almost thirty minutes, I was led to the visiting area and told to sit in an ugly red plastic chair, facing a thick glass fortified with wire mesh.

"The inmate will be here shortly," the deputy said. "When he gets here, the timer begins. It's a busy day, so you'll only have ten minutes."

He did not wait to see if I had any questions, which I didn't. A minute later Flaky was led into the room on the opposite side of the glass by a beefy deputy who could have been the brother of the one who escorted me in.

His orange jumpsuit hung loosely, like someone intentionally issued him a set three sizes too large. He hadn't trimmed his beard in a while either. When he saw me, his face lit up in a loose grin. He sat and waited until the deputy walked away. Since he was still cuffed, he had to use both hands to pick up the phone. I picked up the phone on my side.

"How's it going?" I asked.

Flaky shrugged. "Oh, you know. All jails are about the same," he said.

"Murder, huh?" I asked.

Flaky shrugged. He'd called me yesterday, on my forty-fifth birthday I might add, and informed me he'd been arrested. I caught the major details on the morning news report while I was washing ibuprofen down with coffee. He had been charged in the nearby city of Murfreesboro with killing a man who was a member of a rival outlaw biker club.

"Are they treating you okay?" I asked.

"Yeah, sure. You don't cause trouble, they don't give you grief. They won't let me be a trusty though. On account of the murder charge, I guess."

I nodded in understanding. When I first met Flaky, we were locked up together in the Davidson County Jail. Flaky was a trustee and I was in solitary. He befriended me and we'd been friends ever since. Although he looked like a bona fide psycho, I considered him a trusted friend.

"How about your lawyer? Have you met with him?" I asked.

"Yeah, he's young, like he's fresh out of law school."

"What's his name?"

"Tilford, Wes Tilford," he replied.

"Alright, I'll look up his info and give him a call. In any case of this magnitude, the defense is always afforded financing to hire a private investigator."

"Yeah, okay," he said.

"Have you said anything to the cops?"

Flaky grinned. "You know me better than that."

"Alright, good. I'll have this young attorney kicking ass and taking names."

I expected a chuckle, or something. Instead, Flaky frowned, as if he was thinking something over. After several seconds, he spoke.

"Listen, Thomas. I shouldn't have called you. It was a mistake."

"No problem, brother. You know I'll help you out. It's what I do."

Flaky shook his head. "I appreciate it, I really do, but I want you to stay out of this. Trust me, it's for the best."

"Why, what's the problem?" I asked.

"It's complicated. There are some of his biker brothers who are mad and looking for payback. I don't want you to get caught up in it."

It was my turn to frown. "Are you sure?"

"I appreciate it, Thomas, but trust me, this is one you want to stay away from. Like I said, it's complicated."

I knew there was no arguing about it. Flaky was always upfront with me and he never minced words. I sighed and found myself rubbing my stomach.

"Alright, brother, it's your call," I said. "I'll put some money in your commissary. You need anything else?"

Flaky shook his head. "Nah, appreciate it. It's good to see you, bro."

"You too," I said, although it wasn't good seeing him under these circumstances.

Flaky stood and hung up the phone. He looked back over his shoulder and gave me a nod before disappearing through the security door.

I retrieved my personal items out of the lock box and then stopped by and put enough into Flaky's commissary so he could buy whatever he needed. Back in the lobby, I tried to act casual as I made a beeline toward the men's room.

I hated using strange restrooms, but my stomach was not giving me an option. After, I washed my hands and splashed some water on my face. Looking in the mirror, I could see the bags under my eyes. I looked awful and felt as bad as I looked. Cursing Marti and her birthday shots, I headed toward the parking lot.

Exiting the building, I took a deep breath of fresh air before heading toward my car. The lot was full. Sunday was a big day for visitation. I overheard a little girl asking an obese woman if they were picking up daddy to go to church. The woman told her to shut up and behave. I avoided shaking my head in disgust and instead focused on my car. I had not even stepped off the sidewalk when a man's loud voice caused me to break stride.

"Look at this shit, would you?"

I turned to see two men standing a few feet down the sidewalk, both smoking cigarettes. I thought my stomach had settled, but when I recognized the man who spoke, it started churning again.

He looked the same; still overweight, still bald, still with the same slight underbite. He even had the same crooked glasses. Hell, I think he was even wearing the same stained tie he had on when I first met him. I should have kept walking, but I couldn't help myself.

"Why, hello, Georgie," I said.

I first encountered Detective George Thompson a year ago when I was hired to investigate the murder of a truck driver by the name of Lester Gwinnette. Thompson was the lead detective, and he'd really screwed up the case. I was able to convince the sheriff, his boss, that the suicide was in fact a murder. George looked like a fool and has hated me ever since.

"What are you doing here?" his tone indicated he wasn't simply asking; he was demanding.

"I'm seeing a client," I answered.

"Who?"

I started to tell him if he wanted to know, he should go check the visitor's log, but he probably didn't know they kept one.

"Frank Garrison," I said. "Why do you ask?"

"What for?"

"He's a client. You have one more question before your allotment runs out."

His scowl deepened. "Oh, yeah? I'll decide when I'm through asking questions."

"Oh, Georgie, Georgie, Georgie," I said with a shake of the head. I had a litany of smartassed responses, but it was time to go. I left him standing there with his friend, or whoever he was.

Once I got seated in my car, I activated my cell phone and after a little searching, found a phone number for Flaky's attorney. A male who sounded like he was fourteen answered the phone.

"Thomas Ironcutter calling for Wes Tilford."

"This is Wes Tilford," the man replied.

"Hello, Wes. I'm a private investigator and a friend of Frank Garrison. I just visited him at the jail, and I wondered if you and I could meet up to discuss his case."

"Who is this again?" he asked.

"Thomas Ironcutter." I said it real slow so he wouldn't have to ask it again.

"And you visited an inmate?"

"Yes, Frank Garrison, your client. You *are* Wes Tilford the attorney, correct?"

"Uh, yes that's correct. So, you visited with Frank Garrison," he said.

I looked at my phone, as if it'd give me a clue. "Have I caught you at a bad time, Mister Tilford?"

"Oh, no," he answered. "I'm just a little discombobulated at the moment. So, you're a friend of Frank."

I held off on a sarcastic comeback. My grumbling stomach was intensifying, and I needed to remain calm.

"Yes, I'm a friend of Frank. I am also a private investigator, and I am offering my services. Would you happen to be interested, or would that discombobulate you even further?"

"Oh, you're a private investigator."

"Yes, I said that. Should I repeat it a few more times so it will sink in?"

I heard the scratching of a pencil on paper. "Thomas Ironcutter. Got it. What can I do for you, Mister Ironcutter?"

My patience had come to an end. "What the hell, man, are you high or something?"

There was a moment's pause before he spoke again. "I beg your pardon?"

"Let me spell it out for you, you half-witted fool. I am a private investigator. You are Frank's defense attorney. He is being charged with murder. You will need the services of a private investigator if you hope to adequately represent your client against this murder charge. I am offering my services. Does that make it clear enough for you, or do you need to go dunk your head in the toilet and eliminate some of that discombobulation?"

"There's no need to be rude," he said, his voice sounding offended.

I took a deep breath. "Do you have my number on your caller I.D.?" I asked.

"I do indeed," he said after a second.

"Good. Now, listen closely. We have spoken for a solid five minutes now and have accomplished absolutely nothing. I don't know if you're having a bad day or what, but when you get your head out of your ass, give me a call."

I disconnected, tossed the phone into the passenger seat, and fumbled for a cigar out of my travel humidor.

"Let me guess, that was Garrison's attorney."

I looked out of my open car window. It was the man who had been smoking with Thompson. He was a younger black man, early thirties perhaps, medium skinned with pleasant features, and a muscular build hidden underneath a tan sport coat.

"Do you know him?" I asked.

He nodded. "I went to school with his older brother. Wes is fresh out of law school and has no idea what he's doing."

I narrowed my eyes at him. "A rookie attorney taking a murder case? You've got to be kidding me."

"Nope. Judge Weber assigned it to him. He's a little senile and has no business being on the bench anymore, but he keeps getting reelected."

"Hmm," I said and looked around. "Where's your buddy at?"

"Who, George?" he asked with a grin. "After he told me what a lowlife scumbag you were, he went back inside."

I chuckled. "Old Georgie doesn't like me too much."

"I got that impression," he said, and then stuck his hand out. "I'm Ricardo McAdoo."

"Thomas Ironcutter," I replied and shook his hand. "Let me get out and enjoy this cigar. Would you like one?"

Ricardo's eyes widened slightly. "Are you offering?"

I got another one out, exited my Mustang, and clipped the ends before handing him one. Lighting mine, I handed the lighter to him.

"Thanks," he said.

"Don't mention it," I replied and then threw my fishing line out to see if I would get a bite. "Are you familiar with Flaky's case?"

He took a long puff before looking at me. "Frank Garrison? Yep, it's my case."

"No kidding?"

"I kid you not," he said with a grin.

"I admit I don't know much about the case, but I can't see Flaky doing this. He's not a murderer."

McAdoo gave a short chortle. "Are you kidding? He looks like Charles Manson's bastard son."

I gave a slight shrug. "He's a little wild looking, I'll give you that, but he's no killer."

"How well do you know him?" he asked.

"He was a trusty in the Davidson County Jail when I was locked up," I said.

"Oh, yeah? What were you locked up for?" he asked.

"Murder," I answered.

He looked at me oddly. It was slowly replaced by recognition. "Ah, I remember you now. Falsely accused of murdering your wife, who in fact was killed by some crazy-ass rogue FBI agent, correct?"

"Yeah. He was the same man who killed a truck driver that your buddy Georgie wrote up as a suicide."

"Interesting," he said and took a thoughtful drag off his cigar. He then eyed me through a cloud of smoke.

"Why do you think your boy is innocent?" he asked.

I gave a slight shrug. "I've been friends with him for a little while. He's no angel, but he's a standup guy. I'm proud to call him a friend."

"That's all you need to be convinced he's not a murderer?"

I shrugged again. "I'm going to poke around, see if I can find out anything that'd prove his innocence. I hope you don't mind."

McAdoo chuckled. "I don't mind at all. My case is solid."

"Do tell," I said.

He laughed. "Alright, since you gave me an excellent cigar, I'll extend you this courtesy. The victim is a man by the name of Ivan Greenwood. He went by the moniker of Turk and was in a local biker club. He was found four days ago in his apartment, shot in the back of the head." He paused and worked his cigar. "We have your boy's prints in the apartment, and we have a witness who picked him out of a photo lineup. As for the rest, you'll find out when his lawyer files for discovery."

"Interesting," I said.

"Is there anything you'd like to tell me?" McAdoo asked.

I shrugged. "The first I learned of the case was yesterday when Flaky called me."

McAdoo frowned, but nodded and reached for his wallet. "Why don't we swap business cards? If you come up with something, maybe you'd be courteous enough to give me a call."

I agreed and reached for my own wallet. Swapping cards and shaking hands, I finally got on the road. I already decided as soon as I got home, I was going back to bed.

# CHAPTER 4

Parking my SUV, I headed inside and went directly to the kitchen. I had lots of leftovers from the party but opted for a bowl of granola cereal with skim milk in the hopes it would settle my stomach. As I ate, I looked around the house. It was still in disarray from the party, but I didn't have the energy or desire to clean up. Instead, I put the bowl and spoon in the sink, took off my shoes, and parked my butt in my easy chair. It was comfortable enough that I began nodding off within seconds. Unfortunately, my phone rang at about that moment where blissful slumber was approaching. Sherman Goldman greeted me in a cheerful voice.

"How is your schedule for the next day or so?" he asked.

I knew what that meant. He had some work for me.

"I've got a few things going on, but I'm free enough. What do you have?"

"We have encountered a problem in our investment."

My first structured payment on the lawsuit had recently come in. It was a substantial amount of money and was being wasted sitting in a low interest yielding savings account. Sherman convinced me to devote a portion of it into a real estate investment trust, commonly known as a REIT. The REIT directors, one of whom was Sherman, had purchased several residential properties in a depressed area of Murfreesboro. The plan was to tear down the old houses and create a multiplex of apartments, offices, and retail businesses. The politicians and Chamber of Commerce were all on board and the expected return on investment was projected to be over nine percent. Much higher than the interest on my savings account.

I knew Sherman well enough. He wasn't a drama queen. If he said there was a problem, there was a problem.

"What is it?" I asked.

"The it in question is a rather cantankerous gentleman by the name of Don Slocum. He is the remaining holdout, refuses to sell, and thus far has evaded all attempts of civil process service."

"We're going to sue him?" I asked.

"Yes, I'm afraid we have to," Sherman replied. "Actually, the city of Murfreesboro is suing him, but we will also be principals in the lawsuit."

"I'm not following," I said. I was about to say he could fill me in during the next meeting, but Sherman decided to explain anyway.

"The city of Murfreesboro is going to force Mister Slocum to sell under the tenets of eminent domain. They in turn will sell the property to us so that we may begin development. It's a legal precedent defined in Kelo versus the City of New London. It's a remarkably interesting legal theory that is going to be used to our advantage. You should read up on it, Thomas."

"Okay, sure. I'll look it up right now," I said, not meaning it for a minute.

If Sherman caught my sarcasm, he didn't show it. "Yes, very good. In the meantime, we need to get those papers properly served on Mister Slocum as soon as possible. Someone with your abilities could most assuredly succeed where others have failed."

I had to hand it to him, the man had a way with flattery. I suppose I should've thought of things like this before I invested in the REIT, but I didn't, and now I was committed. I usually received a fee when serving papers, but I knew this time, it would be expected of me.

"Alright, I'll come by and get the papers tomorrow. Be warned though, if he's as slippery as you're suggesting, it may take a few days."

"I have unwavering faith in you, Thomas. Cheerio."

The line disconnected before I could give an appropriate reply.

I set my phone in my lap and had my eyes closed for maybe thirty seconds when it rang again. I was tempted not to answer, but the caller I.D. showed it was my fat redneck buddy, Bubba.

"What's going on, Bubba?" I greeted.

"Are you home?" he asked.

"Yep."

"Can I come over? I got something I want to show you," he said.

I stifled a moan. All I wanted to do was take a peaceful, uninterrupted nap.

"When?" I asked.

"I'm about fifteen minutes away."

"Yeah, okay," I found myself saying.

Bubba was prompt and within minutes I heard the exhaust of the tow truck's big diesel engine. I poured us both a tall glass of sweet tea and met him outside as he parked beside my shop. There was an old rusty car strapped down on the back of the rollback. It was grimy, rusty, and missing a few parts. I handed over the glass of tea.

"What've you got there?" I asked, gesturing toward the junk car.

Bubba grinned. "Let's see how good you are. Look it over and tell me what you think it is."

The iced tea refreshed me slightly, so I indulged him and walked around the rollback, and surveyed the wreckage. Like I said, there were several body parts missing, but I recognized the outline. I finished my tea quickly and nodded in appreciation.

"Looks like a Plymouth Roadrunner."

"Check out the engine," Bubba urged.

I climbed on the rollback. The hood was intact, but the racing latches were missing. It opened with a groan. Peering inside, I recognized the big block engine almost immediately.

"A 426 Hemi to boot. Nice catch. How much did you pay?"

Bubba's grin got even bigger.

"You're right about the engine, and you're almost right about the car."

I frowned and stared back at the car. "It sure looks like a Roadrunner, what's left of it anyway."

"It's a Superbird," Bubba said.

I had sucked a cube of ice into my mouth when he spoke and almost choked. Bubba was grinning like a fat baby that'd just crapped himself. I stared back at the piece of junk he was gushing over.

"No kidding?" I asked.

"A 1970 Plymouth Superbird," he proudly proclaimed. "I've already checked the VIN and I found the build ticket under the headliner. I don't know how much you know about Superbirds, but there were less than two thousand built, and this one is number eighty-eight." He swept a hand at it. "That's the original engine and all the numbers match up."

I nodded in appreciation. "Wow, that's a good catch if you got it at a good price. How much?"

He kept grinning. "They had no idea it was a Superbird, and they only thought they were selling the engine and tranny. I paid a thousand for it. It drained my savings account, and my wife is going to kill me."

I nodded again. "You could probably turn around and sell it for," I thought about it a moment. "Hmm, at least five thousand, maybe more. I think your wife will like that."

"Yeah, I could, but I got a business proposition for you."

He studied me nervously, watching to see what my reaction was. I had been looking for business opportunities since my first structured payment. After paying off some bills, I had plenty left over. But then Sherman talked me into the REIT. I still had some liquidity, but not nearly as much and the investment was long term; my return on investment was not going to happen for a few years.

"Okay, let's hear it," I said.

"I say let's restore it. If we do it right, we could easily get a hundred grand out of it. Maybe more."

"Yeah, maybe," I agreed. "But it would have to be a Concours grade restoration. That would involve a lot of time and money."

Bubba frowned. "How much time and money?"

"It'd be in the thousands, and with only the two of us working on it, I'd say at least a year of hard work."

Bubba's frown deepened and he started chewing on his lower lip. "Um, well, what do you suggest?"

I stared at the old car for a full minute before replying. "Alright, it looks like mostly original parts, but there are several parts missing. If we can refurbish the drivetrain, fix the secondary systems, and make sure we have all factory parts," I paused a minute and thought. "If the engine isn't seized up, I think we can do all that in a couple of months and easily sell it for twenty grand."

Bubba's grin threatened to devour his entire face. "That's what I'm talking about! You wanna do it?"

I hopped down and tried to keep my grimy hands away from my clothes. "What're you thinking? You want to go in as partners?"

"Fifty-fifty. Oh, and we'll need to use your shop," he said.

I thought for another moment. I liked the car, and it would be a fun project. Bubba was a pleasant fellow in his southern redneck way, and he was a good mechanic.

"Alright, I'm game."

Bubba stuck out a meaty paw. "Put it here, partner." He pumped my hand with the enthusiasm of a kid milking their first cow. "Partners!" he repeated. His enthusiasm was infectious and I found myself grinning.

I changed into some work clothes and cleaned out a space in my shop for the Superbird.

"I have a good feeling about this one, Thomas," Bubba said. He couldn't stop grinning, and I had to admit, his attitude was contagious.

# CHAPTER 5

Bubba left after getting the car moved into the shop, saying he needed to go home and spend the rest of the day with his family. Long after he left, I sat and stared at the old car, remembering back the first time I saw a Superbird. I was ten or eleven. A man had brought his pride and joy to dad's garage for an oil change. It was blue, like Richard Petty's race car. I heard later he'd totaled it.

Going inside, I straightened up a little around the house and went to bed early. Tommy Boy chose that moment to play. He was like that sometimes. He'd wait for me to turn the lights off and go to bed and then he'd run around the house, chasing his toys, and knocking things over. He was an enormous pain in my ass from time to time.

Despite his antics, I fell asleep within minutes and awoke early the next morning feeling well rested. I went on a three-mile run and ate a healthy breakfast before showering and heading to Sherman's office. The legal papers were waiting on me with the receptionist. I typed in the address to Don Slocum's residence on my map app and headed to Murfreesboro, arriving precisely twenty-four minutes later.

The house may have been nice once, but years of neglect had taken its toll. It reminded me of a passage from To Kill a Mockingbird; you never really know a man until you stand in his shoes and walk around in them. Just standing on the Radley porch was enough.

Only in this case it was Don Slocum's porch.

When I parked at the curb in front of the house, I noticed several things: the weeds, the peeling paint, and the rotting soffits. When I'd reached the porch, I spotted the mailbox mounted on the wall by the front door. The lid had been welded shut, preventing the postal carrier from making proper delivery. All were clues indicating the gentleman residing inside was going to be a contrary SOB. People like this were often difficult to serve papers on, but I was undeterred and gave a shave-and-a-haircut rap on the door as I noticed a decal affixed to the door of a Vietnam combat ribbon.

The door was opened by an older man with a four-year growth of beard and matching white hair that had not yet been combed this week. He was wearing a coffee-stained tee shirt and soiled jeans that probably should have been thrown away last year. He also had a 44-magnum stuck in his waistband. He bobbed his head up and down as he stared, trying to get a good focus through a grimy pair of bifocals.

"What the hell do you want?" he snarled in a southern drawl.

This is where it got tricky. I had my phone sticking a little way out of the breast pocket of my sport jacket, recording everything. I needed to show I had identified Don and properly served him.

"Hello, Don, my name is Thomas Ironcutter," I said.

He squinted and bobbed his head a few additional times before speaking.

"Your name ain't familiar and I don't recognize you," he retorted.

I frowned as well. "Maybe I'm wrong, didn't I see you down at the VFW?"

He scoffed. "Not lately."

"Yeah, I haven't been there in a while either. They kicked me out," I said.

In fact, I'd never been to the VFW in Murfreesboro, but I'd recognized the decal and took a chance. He was still giving me a skeptical stare, but I had his interest now.

"What'd they kick you out for?" he asked.

I looked around as if somebody might be eavesdropping, then lowered my voice and leaned closer, which caused me to catch a whiff of his rancid breath. I kept myself from grimacing and continued with my ploy.

"Let's just say I was accused of improprieties with a certain lady who hangs out there."

His eyes lit up. "Ain't no ladies hang out there. They're all boozehound hussies."

I nodded in seeming agreement. "Yes, indeed."

He chortled, which turned to a cough. "Well, what is it that you wanted?" he asked.

"I have some paperwork for you," I said and reached into the inside pocket of my sport jacket. I pulled out a thick set of papers that were folded. I did not bother opening them and extended my arm. He started to reach for them but stopped.

"What kind of papers?" he asked; his wariness was back now.

"They're official papers from the City of Murfreesboro," I said.

His eyes narrowed and he jerked his arm back. "Are those court papers?"

"Yes, sir, I believe they are."

"I ain't accepting them. I don't have to if I don't want to." He seemed to remember he was armed, and his hand found its way to the pistol grip. His wariness had segued into anger.

"Now you listen to me. You get your ass off my porch, and you take them papers with you, or else!"

He emphasized his threat by tugging the pistol loose from his waistband. I dropped the papers. His eyes followed them as they fell to the porch. It was the break I needed. I reached forward and snatched the pistol out of his hand. He was momentarily shocked, but then tried to grab it back. I used my other hand to push him. He stumbled and he almost fell.

"You give that back!" he demanded.

I opened the cylinder and unloaded the bullets before inspecting the weapon.

"Mister Slocum, this revolver is filthy. Are you sure you're a veteran?"

"Two tours in 'Nam, youngster," he retorted.

"Well, a squared away veteran would know to keep their weapon spotless at all times. Here." I left the cylinder open and handed the revolver back to him but held onto the bullets. He noticed.

"Give those back to me too."

"Nope, not yet. Let me ask you something, Don. Why are you so reluctant to sell? I know for a fact they're offering you a lot more than this house is worth."

"You wouldn't understand," he said.

"Try me."

He huffed and glowered for a moment, but then explained. "This house was built by my grandfather back in 1900. I was born in the same bedroom my father was born in. You can tell your people I ain't leaving. It's my house and I don't have to sell it if I don't want to. I don't care what the court says."

He then took a deep breath and suddenly looked like he was about to cry. "Besides, I don't have anywhere else to go."

He stared at his gun a moment and scowled at me before stepping back inside and slamming the door shut. I tossed the bullets in the yard and then left before he found some inside and reloaded. I then drove down the road, found a place to park, and viewed the video. Satisfied, I texted Sherman.

Don Slocum has been served. All legal and recorded.

He responded a minute later.

Excellent.

Satisfied my work was done, I was excited about going home and getting started on the Superbird. I was about to call Bubba and discuss what we wanted to do first when my phone rang.

"Hello, Thomas, this is Wes Tilford."

Wes Tilford, Flaky's appointed attorney. When I spoke to him yesterday, it didn't go too well. Let's see if he'd gotten his head out of his ass yet.

"Hello, Wes. What can I do for you?"

"Would it be possible to meet and discuss Mister Garrison's case?" he asked.

"I'm currently in Murfreesboro. We can meet now if that would be convenient."

"Oh, yeah, that'd be great," he said.

"Give me the address to your office and I'll meet you there," I suggested.

He stammered now. "I uh, I don't actually have an office, yet. I was heading home. Would you mind meeting me there?"

He gave an address to an apartment near the Middle Tennessee State campus, only five minutes away. Parking my car, I took a moment to look around. It was an old set of apartments, dated and tired looking. The cars in the parking lot indicated a mixture of college students and poor folks. I found apartment 212 easily. Wes answered after my perfunctory knock, opened the door, and appraised me like I was a door-to-door vacuum cleaner salesman. I appraised him as well.

"You must be Thomas Ironcutter," he said.

"And you must be Wes Tilford," I replied.

I guessed him at twenty-five, average looking, maybe five-ten with a slender build and brown hair that was done up in one of those man buns that some men seemed to think was sexually appealing or something. He was still wearing a cheap gray suit but had removed his jacket, and as he stood there, he loosened his tie.

"Come in," he invited and opened the door wider. He did not offer to shake hands, simply stood there, and waited for me to enter. I walked into a small foyer that led to the den. I walked partway in and waited. Wes shut the door and then stood there rather awkwardly.

"I've got water and diet Pepsi. I have coffee too, but I'll have to brew it," he offered.

"I'm good, thanks. Where can we sit?"

"Oh, here." He walked over to a second-hand couch, scooped some dirty clothes off, and gestured at it while he sat in a matching chair. Both pieces of furniture looked like they'd seen better days. He had a coffee table, but it was stacked with various types of paperwork and a couple of empty pizza boxes.

"Excuse the mess, the maid doesn't come until Friday," he said with a chuckle.

"How is Flaky's case proceeding?" I asked.

"Not too well," he said.

"How can I help?"

He paused a moment and worked his mouth once or twice before speaking.

"There is a witness. She's a retired teacher who lives across the street from the victim's residence. Her statement is she saw Flaky knocking on the door earlier that morning. She didn't hear a gunshot, but a short time later saw a man leaving on the victim's motorcycle. She's not sure who because he was wearing a helmet. She's the one who picked Flaky out of a photographic lineup."

"No problem. Give me her information and I'll do it today or first thing tomorrow."

Wes nodded, but then sighed and rubbed his face.

"You look like someone kicked your dog. Is there something else?"

"Yeah, there is. Frank, or Flaky, whatever you want to call him, has really messed me up."

"How so?"

He pondered my question for a moment before holding up a finger.

"Let me do something right quick."

He then retrieved a laptop from his briefcase, opened it and began clicking and typing. After a minute, I heard a printer come to life and realized it was sitting on the kitchen table. He got up and retrieved whatever he had printed and brought it back to the den. He handed it to me before sitting.

"This is a non-disclosure agreement. I need you to read and sign it."

I stared at him a moment. Realizing he was serious, I read over the NDA. It was a boilerplate template that was vague and probably could not be enforced. I signed an obscure professional wrestler's name to it and slid it over to him. Nodding in satisfaction, he finally told me what was bugging him.

"I visited Flaky this morning. He told me where the victim's motorcycle was located."

"Where?" I asked.

"At a property storage business," he said and hooked a thumb in a vague direction. "It's only a couple of miles from here."

"Okay, let's go take a look," I suggested.

He looked at me like I was crazy. "You don't understand. If I come into contact with this motorcycle, I am ethically bound to turn it over to the police. They will know where it came from, and I will be forced to testify to that fact. If I do that, I have failed to adequately represent my client. If I don't, I am committing a criminal act and probably violating two or three canons of ethics. I'm damned either way."

"Catch Twenty-Two," I said.

"What's that?"

"It's a novel by Joseph Heller. The main character is a bombardier in World War Two. He goes to the doctor and tells him he can't fly because only a crazy person would willingly fly in a plane that the enemy is actively trying to shoot down. The doctor tells him since he knows it's crazy to do that, he can't ground him because he understands the insanity of it, even though continuing to fly is insane. But, if he did not realize how crazy it was, that was an indicator that a person should not be flying, but that person would never ask not to fly and therefore he could not ground him. Catch Twenty-Two."

"I don't get it," Wes lamented.

I wanted to throw my hands in the air and ask him why he was so dense. Instead, I took a slow, deep breath. "Forget it. What if I told you I had a way out of this for you?"

He scoffed. "I don't see how."

"There is. Let's start by going to make sure the bike is still there." I stood and motioned him toward the door.

He insisted on driving, which I regretted. His car, a Toyota Camry that was at least fifteen years old, was filthy. Any man who did not treat his car with care was not worthy of my respect. I would have said as much, but I don't think it would've mattered.

He drove to a location which, surprisingly, was not far from Don Slocum's house. The business was not one of those newer storage businesses with a secured gate and security cameras. Nope, it was old. Probably rented for cheap and probably why Flaky chose it in the first place.

I directed Wes to drive around the block a couple of times. When I was satisfied there was no active surveillance from the cops or any cameras I had missed, we entered the property and parked several units away. Reaching the unit number Flaky had told him, we looked to see the garage door secured by a single padlock.

"How are we going to get into it?" Wes asked.

I had already anticipated this and retrieved a lock-picking set from my detective's kit before we left. I got the padlock opened easily. We went inside and closed the door behind us. Wes found a switch and turned on a single overhead light.

The motorcycle was the only thing in the room, besides a crap ton of dust, which caused me to sneeze a couple of times. Recovering, I checked out the bike. It was a nice one, a customized Harley bagger, blood red with metallic black accents. A full-coverage helmet rested on the seat. When I picked it up a set of keys fell out. I opened the gas cap and peered in. It looked half full.

"So far, so good," I said.

Wes stared in incredulity and his level of anxiety was palpable. "What are you talking about? I'm still screwed, no matter what I do. I knew it was a mistake to call you."

"Relax," I admonished.

"Easier said than done," he griped. "Do you have any ideas or not?"

"In fact, I do. Do you have any attorney friends? Perhaps someone who owes you a favor?"

Wes bit his lip in thought, staring at the bike like it was a bomb with a timer counting down. After a moment he looked over at me.

"I have a buddy I went to law school with. I helped him with a case recently, so I guess he owes me a favor."

"Good. Give him a call and tell him you want to hire him as your attorney."

"I don't understand," he said.

"You're going to hire him. Then, you're going to give him this bike with instructions to turn it over to the cops."

He'd been staring at me in confusion, but slowly he began to understand.

"I think I see where you're going. I hire him as my attorney. I hand over the bike to him. He turns the bike over to the police, but he is now under the lawyer-client confidentiality blanket and cannot be forced to divulge where he got the bike from. I have fulfilled my legal obligation without repercussion and without damning my client."

"Yep, you got it," I said.

His eyes widened. "Holy hell, I think that'll work," he gushed.

I prodded him to make the call, and we met with his buddy an hour later at a car lot that was no longer in business. I wiped down the bike, eliminating any latent fingerprints I may have left as Wes gave instructions and paid him a dollar to make himself an official client. I tossed the helmet in the back seat. We drove away while his buddy was making the call.

"This is really going to work," Wes said as he drove. "How did you think of that?"

"There was a murder case in Nashville several years ago with a similar set of circumstances involving a motorcycle. Two lawyers came up with the idea. I'm friends with one of them and he told me about it one evening after a couple of beers."

"Interesting," he said and that was it. No expression of gratitude, no nothing.

"Why did you keep the helmet?" he asked.

"DNA," I answered. He glanced at me in confusion, but I didn't bother explaining.

I directed him to the house of the witness, and he watched while I interviewed her. Her name was Ethel Herring. She was a pleasant older woman who answered all my questions with a friendly smile. It only took me a few minutes to get what I needed and thanked her for her time. He waited until we got back to the car before speaking.

"What about it; did you see any holes in her story?"

"That lady is a rock-solid witness. The only thing you should ask her during cross examination is to confirm she did not actually see the murder, nor did she even know about the murder until the police informed her."

Wes scoffed. "She's old. I can have her confused and contradicting herself within minutes of cross."

"The jury will love her and she'll make you look like a fool. Don't mess with her."

I'd known women like Ethel. A typical southern belle, she could make mincemeat out of you with nothing more than a few cutting words. And smile sweetly the entire time. And then offer you a glass of sweet tea to drown your dejection. Nope, you didn't mess with women like that.

I explained all this during the ride back to his apartment, but I don't think the lesson sunk in. After leaving Wes, I finally headed home.

# CHAPTER 6

It took a little muscle and manipulation, but I managed to push the Superbird into place and activated the motor for the two-post lift.

"Let's see what we have here," I muttered as the audible ratcheting noise of the motor banged out a steady rhythm.

I saw a lot of surface rust, but nothing that could not be taken off with a grinder or perhaps soda blasting it. All the rubber items were dry and cracked, no surprise there, and would need to be replaced. Same with the tires, brakes, and shocks, maybe the u-joints, but that appeared to be all it needed underneath.

I grunted in satisfaction. No damage or bent frame, which meant a considerable saving in costs. I gave Bubba a call and told him of my findings.

"We can soda blast the undercarriage of the rust, and if the engine is still good, most of our labor will be on the body."

"What do you think of a full restore?" he asked.

I blew air out. "A full Concours restoration will be tedious and time consuming. Two or three years, at least. I'd suggest we restore in stages, and after each stage, we put it on the market and see if anyone bites."

"What if nobody wants to pay us a decent amount?" he asked.

"Then we'll keep going until we have a full restore and auction it off at Barrett Jackson."

Bubba chuckled. "I like the sound of that."

We agreed in principle and talked some more before hanging up. I knew he wanted to go for a full restore, but with our work schedules, it'd take a hell of a long time to do it right.

I looked around for my jack stands and realized I was using them for the '37 Coupe. I thought I had another pair, but if I did, they were hidden under junk somewhere. I had a lot of tools and spare parts, but my shop had also become a provisional storage shed. It was cramped in here. I still had moving boxes from my old house that I'd not even unpacked. I'd been avoiding them because most of the stuff would've reminded me of my deceased wife, but it was time to go through them and either throw it all out or donate to Goodwill. There were also several tote bins belonging to Percy. I decided to give him a call. He answered on the fourth ring.

"Hey buddy, you got a minute?"

"Yeah, what's up?" he asked.

I explained and asked if he still needed me to store his files with me.

He chuckled slightly. "You know, I had forgotten about them. I'll come get them as soon as we get back from our vacation."

I thanked him and disconnected the call. After hanging up, I focused back on the Superbird and began taking pictures. I was going to create a file showing the vehicle in its present state and documenting our restoration work. Not many grease monkeys bothered with this, but I found that it went a long way in justifying the sale price to a potential customer.

Sitting down at my desk, I got on my laptop and created a new file. While I waited for the pictures to download, I thought about Anna. I'd had a wonderful time at my birthday party. It seemed like everyone did. Marti had made a large batch of Jell-O shots. In addition to the beer I was drinking, she'd fed me several of the shots. I'd gotten sloshed. After everyone had left, she'd spent the night. I remembered waking up the next morning and walking into the den. Anna was sitting at my desk on the laptop. She gave me a cool stare before speaking.

"I've written up a report on Taco," she had said. "If you don't mind, proofread it and then email it."

I agreed. Taco was Taco Smith, a lowlife attorney who sought out independently owned retail businesses and sent in a disabled man under the guise of a customer who would find handicap violations. Taco would sue the business and then offer to drop the lawsuit if they paid him a few thousand. On the face of it, it sounded like a noble endeavor, but he was making false allegations against the businesses, like the public restroom was locked or inaccessible to his so-called client. We were able to prove it was nothing more than a scam.

"Consider it done," I said.

She then stood and gave me a cool stare. "Percy and I have decided to go on a trip and we're taking Gracie. We'll be back in a few days."

She walked out without further commentary. It was odd, like she was mad at me about something. I briefly wondered if it had something to do with Marti, but I dismissed it. Anna and I were friends and business partners, nothing more. I made a mental note to ask her about it when she and Percy returned home.

I was in the middle of editing the photos of the car when my phone rang. I did not recognize the number, hoped it wasn't a spam call, and answered. The voice on the other end was a man with a distinct accent. If I had to guess, I'd say Eastern European.

"Hello, I am attempting to contact a representative of Ironcutter Investigations."

His tone and demeanor made me believe this was a potential client, I answered professionally. "This is Thomas Ironcutter, how may I help you?"

"Ah, Mister Ironcutter, I am encouraged already. I am in urgent need of private investigative services. I have reviewed your website and it declares you are a former detective with the local police department. Is this correct?"

"Yes, sir. It is."

"Excellent. I would like to meet with you as soon as possible to discuss a case."

"Certainly. How about tomorrow morning, say, eight o'clock?"

"Please forgive my abruptness, but this is an urgent matter. Would it be possible to meet with you today? Perhaps within the next hour?"

Normally, I would have balked, but there was something in his voice that told me this was a man who was ready to hire me and had the money to do it. Even though my recent lawsuit settlement was generous, more than generous, my creation of an investment portfolio had stretched my finances. In short, I needed some spending money.

"Where are you currently located?" I asked.

"I am in Nashville. I can meet you wherever you need to."

I thought it over for two seconds before providing him the address to Mick's Place.

# CHAPTER 7

I had cleaned up and changed into presentable clothes, a pair of khaki slacks and a starched blue button-down shirt. I would have completed my ensemble with a sports jacket, but it was too hot, and I did not want it to smell like smoke.

I hurried, and despite the heavy Nashville traffic I arrived at Mick's several minutes early. When I walked in, my buddy Mick was waiting for me. There were a couple of customers, including two men I'd never seen before.

"Are you drinking anything?" Mick asked when I walked up to the bar.

"I'll have coffee."

"Humph, what kind of heresy is this? Are you even going to smoke? You have a fresh box of Kristoffs in your locker. You ought to try one."

"How do I have a fresh box of cigars?" I queried.

"The rep was in here earlier. I would've been remiss if I had not gotten you a box."

I gave him a look. "Gee, thanks."

Mick sometimes had a habit of purchasing cigars for me without my prior approval. I should've known better than give him my credit card number. I started to complain, but then again, I liked that brand of cigars and had been meaning to order a fresh box. But I wasn't going to admit that to this fat Irishman smirking at me.

"Oh, and that man over there is here for you. I don't know why you're sitting here chitchatting and keeping him waiting." He leaned forward and gave me a disgusted look. "Very unprofessional."

Mick finished his sentence with a scoff and walked off. Shaking my head, I turned toward a table in the far corner of the bar. An older man was sitting there staring expectantly. He was wearing a black suit, a white shirt with a tabbed collar, a blood red tie knotted perfectly in a half-Windsor, and thicker than normal wire frame glasses. He had a glass of water and an unlit cigar sitting on the table in front of him. Sophisticated looking.

He stood as I approached. He was not a big man, maybe five-nine, and it was hard to judge his physique under his suit, but he seemed fit. It was also difficult to judge his age; he could have been forty or seventy. I introduced myself.

"Hello, I'm Thomas Ironcutter."

"I am pleased to meet you, Mister Ironcutter. Will you join me?"

"Certainly," I said and sat. He sat as well.

"What can I do for you, Mister...?"

He placed his hands flat on the table. "Please forgive me, but at this time I would prefer to remain anonymous. I hope this does not offend you."

Before I could answer, Mick brought over one of my newly purchased cigars. "I already clipped it for you. You're welcome." He walked away without awaiting a response.

The man waited with a stoic expression. I took my time lighting the cigar and took a drag. It had an agreeable, spicy flavor.

"While I'm not concerned with your identity, it would be problematic to create a contract, don't you think?"

"I was thinking perhaps an oral contract would be adequate," he replied. "And I am prepared to pay in advance."

He reached down toward his feet and came up with a black canvas bag, similar in appearance to a piece of cheap carry-on luggage.

"Would ten thousand be sufficient for a week of your time?"

I stared at him a moment, wondering if he were joking. He stared back impassively. I put my cigar in the ashtray before unzipping the bag and peering inside. There were ten stacks of banded c-notes. I zipped the bag up. Retrieving my cigar, I took a drag and let the smoke slowly seep out.

"I hope your job is legal," I said. "If it isn't, we can't do business."

What he did not know, at least I didn't think he knew, was sometimes I did indeed do jobs that were, how to put it nicely, fell into the gray spectrum of legality. But I was not going to admit that. For all I knew, I was being set up. It wouldn't be the first time it's been attempted.

His reaction was a slight smile. "Perhaps an explanation of the case is in order."

"Yes, by all means."

"Yesterday, during the middle of the night, two men were killed while they were in the act of robbing a grave."

He reached down again and came up with an attaché case. Opening it, he retrieved some papers and handed them to me. The top page was a printout from a local news station's website. It detailed the discovery of the dead men. The others were similar printouts from the other local TV stations. I normally watched the news every morning, but I missed this one.

"Grave robbers," I remarked. "And somebody killed them."

"Yes, and the murderer is still at large." He paused a moment, as if deciding what he was going to tell me next.

"I am going to explain further with a brief oratory of religious history. Are you familiar with the Knights Templar?"

"A little. Most of what I know about them I learned from TV documentaries. They were a military branch of the Catholic church if I remember correctly."

"Yes. Officially, they were founded in the year 1119. Over time they became a powerful organization, and as the old saying goes, power corrupts. King Phillip the Fourth had become deeply indebted to them, so he had many of them arrested on untruthful charges of heresy. Those unfortunate men were tortured and burned at the stake. Eventually, at the king's urging, Pope Clement the Fifth had the Templars officially disbanded."

"Those documentaries I watched on TV suggested the surviving Templars went underground," I said.

"Indeed, they did," he answered. "It is believed their descendants survive to this day, operating clandestinely, behind the scenes, influencing world events." He offered a deprecating shrug. "I personally believe their movement and cause died out years ago, but when they were in power, they accumulated a number of valuable artifacts."

"Like the ark of the covenant," I suggested.

He gave the same thin smile. "Yes, many books and movies have been created around this story, no?"

"Yeah, and some of them are highly entertaining. So, is that what this case is? Was the ark of the covenant buried in the grave?"

The man chuckled. "Nothing so grandiose, but it is believed that a valuable artifact was indeed buried in this particular grave. Before you ask, I do not know specifically what the artifact is, only that it is rare and unique."

He paused a moment, as if weighing the subject matter before speaking. "I am an agent for a business entity that I will not name. We have been hired to recover the artifact."

"Who hired you?"

He offered that same small smile. "I cannot divulge that information."

"What exactly do you want me to do?" I asked. "Find the murderer or the artifact?"

"The artifact," he answered quickly. Maybe a little too quickly.

"Finding the murderer may lead to the artifact," I suggested.

For the first time, I saw a slight hint of anxiety creep across his face, but as quickly as it was there, it disappeared. He nodded slightly.

"Yes, finding the murderer may lead to recovery of the artifact, but I want you to pursue another avenue of investigation."

"Such as?"

He licked his lips slightly. "This is why I am hiring you specifically. I have read your history. There was an attempt to frame you for a murder by corrupt policemen. And, in addition, you were instrumental in identifying two policemen who were serial murderers."

I nodded slightly. Unfortunately, my life seemed to be on every search engine on the internet. Type in my name and you would get most of my biography. We stared at each other in silence. It took me a few seconds, but I suddenly understood.

"You believe the artifact may have been taken by one of the officers who responded to the scene of the murders," I said.

He held his palms out at my epiphany. It was then I noticed his hands had seen better days. There were multiple scars on his palms, and his pinky fingers were nothing more than little scarred stubs.

I nodded slowly. Most of the rank and file of our local police were honorable men and women. But yeah, I'd dealt with more than one corrupt cop in my time.

"Alright, I'll explore that avenue, but if one were to apply Occam's Razor, the murderer is the thief."

"I understand your logic," he said. "The simplest explanation is that the murderer purloined the artifact before fleeing."

I nodded in agreement. "Yes. Now, with that in mind, the police will be actively searching for the suspect. Do you have any information about him?"

He held his hands out again, which I assumed meant he had no idea who the murderer was.

I worked my cigar. Something told me he was withholding information from me, and I needed to decide if it was a dealbreaker or not.

"So, you were hired to find this artifact. Did these murder victims work with you?"

"Your mind is sharp, Thomas. To be specific, they worked *for* me. I am the one who hired them. They were to retrieve the artifact and bring it to me." He gestured at the bag. "That was to be their payment."

"I see," I said, although I was a little confused. There was a lot about this that was confusing. He continued.

"Somebody else has apparently involved themselves in this matter. I have my suspicions and my people are working on it. In the meantime, I feel it is prudent of me to investigate all other possibilities, including the possibility of theft by a policeman. Do you accept this assignment?"

I sipped my coffee. "Two men were already murdered because of this artifact, and the murderer remains at large. That is cause for concern."

He offered another thin smile. "When I conducted my research on you, I perceived you are a man of dauntless resolve. Meeting you in person has confirmed this perception. You are a big man with scarred knuckles and a nose that appears to have been broken at one time. No, Thomas, I do not think you are a man who is easily intimidated, but I realize the circumstances of this case may give you cause for concern. Hence, the payment."

I grunted slightly. "You sure have a way with words."

After a moment, I looked again through the papers. One had a picture of the grave. There was a large boulder on top of it.

"That's an unusual grave decoration," I remarked.

"Indeed," the man replied. "The decedent's husband had it placed there. Almost as if he wanted to ensure no one dug up the grave." He pointed a finger that had no fingernail at the picture.

"The date of the decedent's death is 1847," he said, and then leaned forward and lowered his voice. "Both the husband and wife were descendants of the Templar. There were many secrets buried along with the woman in this grave."

"I must admit, this is an unusual case."

"It intrigues you," he said with a hint of a mocking stare.

"Yes, it does. If I were to accept this case, I want you to know up front that I cannot guarantee a successful resolution."

"I understand. Do we have an agreement then?" he asked.

"Let's see what I can do in a week, assess my progress, and go from there," I said.

"Excellent, Mister Ironcutter. I have faith in your abilities." He stood and gathered his briefcase.

"Do you have a contact number?" I asked.

He retrieved a cheap looking phone out of the inner pocket of his jacket.

"This is, what I believe you call a burner phone. No voicemail, and only a limited number of minutes. I will call you in three days. Will that suffice?"

"I guess it'll have to," I said.

He stared at me a moment through those thick glasses before nodding and walking out.

Mick was shouting before the door had completely closed. "Yo, Dago, come on over here!"

# CHAPTER 8

"What kind of job does he have for you?" Mick asked. He had been trying his hardest to listen in on the conversation, but a few regulars at the bar kept him distracted with their banter.

"He had a foreign look to him," Ebbie said from his usual seat at the bar. "Very odd, if you ask me."

Wally, who was also sitting in his usual seat, nodded in agreement.

"So, sit down and talk to us, Dago. What kind of job is it?" Mick pressed.

I walked up to the bar and sat in a stool beside Ebbie. "There was a double murder at the Nashville Cemetery last night. He wants me to look into it," I said.

"Ah yes, the Nashville City Cemetery," Ebbie said. "I know it well. I wrote a series of articles about it for the Banner back in '79."

Wally rolled his eyes. I eyed Ebbie as I picked up the fresh beer Mick had poured for me. Ebenezer Farquhar was a professor emeritus at a local university. He was something of a history expert with an excellent memory and had even authored a few critically acclaimed books. He could be interesting to talk to, but he was also somewhat of a blowhard. I fumbled through the papers and found the picture of the grave in question.

"Alright, Ebbie, what do you know about this grave?" I asked.

Ebbie picked up the printout and gave a knowing nod. "Ah, yes, now that particular grave is a bit of a mystery. The occupant is a lady by the name of Sadie Rosemont Sartain. She was married to Methuselah Sartain for approximately six months before she died of consumption. That's what they called Tuberculosis back then. She was twenty-one at the time of her death. So sad." He took a swallow of beer before continuing.

"Her husband had her buried in the city cemetery. A few weeks or months go by, I don't remember which, but anyway, he had her grave dug up and reinterred on the other side of the cemetery."

"Why'd he do that?" Mick asked.

"Unknown," Ebbie replied. "She had originally been buried in a plot next to a relative. However, like I said, Methuselah had her remains disinterred and reburied in another plot. A year later, he had a large boulder placed on top. You see, at that time he was the secretary of the building commission and had various resources at his disposal. He utilized convicts from the local prison and an eight-mule team to haul the boulder to the cemetery and place it on top of the grave. He then had a metal tripod-looking confection mounted on top of the boulder and it held a bell. The reason for that is still a mystery."

"What happened then?" Mick asked.

Ebbie shrugged. "Shortly after doing this, he resigned his commission and moved from Nashville. He relocated to New Orleans where he proved to be a successful businessman. According to the local lore, he was involved in some type of cult down there."

"Nice story," I said. "How much of it is true?"

Ebbie merely shrugged, downed his beer, and requested another. I finished my beer and stood.

"Alright, I've got work to do," I said and looked pointedly at Mick. "Give me a call the next time you think I need another box of cigars."

"Humph," he replied.

I could have stayed and perhaps had another beer, but it wasn't every day that a client plunked down ten thousand in cold hard cash, so procrastination was not an option.

I exited the parking lot and headed to the Nashville City Cemetery.

# CHAPTER 9

The cemetery was located on Fourth Avenue South, not far from downtown. I parked near the entrance, killed the engine, and asked the little woman inside my phone the time for sunset. She told me I had about an hour of daylight left.

I sat in my car a couple of minutes and scanned the area. Satisfied I was alone, I got out and easily found the grave in question. There were many unique headstones throughout, but only one grave had a large boulder sitting on top of it. It was nothing special, a big fricking rock, aged and rough, a little over four feet in height. There was an iron fixture mounted on top of it consisting of three iron posts joined at the top with some decorative trim and a fist-sized weathered brass bell suspended by a chain in the middle.

The grave robber's hole along the side of it had already been filled in and tamped down. I smiled to myself in wry amusement; if the artifact was still in the grave, the mysterious Mister X was going to have to hire a new team to dig it back up.

I knew the cops had searched the area, but I was going to do the same before it got too dark to see. Professors and their textbooks specified a variety of search methods: the spiral search pattern, the strip pattern, the grid pattern, the zone pattern, and the wheel pattern, among others. They all looked great in a textbook, but I'd rarely seen them used in practical applications. Cops used their own methods. Some were better than others.

I opted for a rough spiral pattern. I started at the grave and began slowly working my way out, panning the ground with my tac-lite, even though it was not yet dark out. It was a futile effort. I found nothing. If any type of physical evidence was left behind, it was gone now.

I decided to take a break and think about it. There was a bench nearby; I made myself comfortable and looked around. I found cemeteries to have a peaceful ambience, and this one was no different from others. The old ones, like this one, were the best. There were some unique headstones and mausoleums which added to the ambience. Like Ebbie had said, this place was full of history. There were politicians, academics, soldiers, sailors, explorers, even convicts from the old state prison were buried here. Each grave had a person who had a story. The things they had experienced was beyond my imagination.

Gazing at Sadie's grave, I wondered what kind of life she lived. She died far too young, which was sad. I wondered how it had affected her husband, Methuselah. If I had to guess, I'd say he moved away because everything in the city reminded him of her.

I stifled the urge to smoke another cigar and headed to my car. I had a kit in the trunk I always carried with me. It had a plethora of goodies. Recording equipment, photography equipment, eavesdropping equipment, lockpicking equipment, you name it. This evening I was going to employ a surveillance camera that was disguised as a birdhouse. Finding a tree about twenty feet away from the Sartain grave, I mounted the birdhouse at about a foot above my head. Using the app on my phone, I checked the alignment of the lens and made the proper adjustments with the little brass screws. It was battery powered and motion activated. It was advertised as having enough battery power for thirty days. I'd never tested it to that length of time, but I'd successfully used it in the past and was confident with it.

Finishing up, I walked back toward the parking area and got in my Mustang. I still found it odd that my client was not overly concerned about the murderers. I had to admit, I had a nagging suspicion that in fact he may have been the person who had killed the three men. If that were true, what was his game? Was the only thing he needed me for to prove or disprove a cop took the artifact? Was that worth ten thousand?

The 351 Boss engine started up with a pleasant growl and I headed toward the interstate. My phone rang while I was sitting at a traffic light. I would not have answered, but it was my little buddy Ronald calling.

I answered with a little annoyance. "I hope this is important."

# CHAPTER 10

"What're you doing, Mister Fancy Pants?" Ronald greeted.

My buddy, Ronald. When I first met him, I could hardly get more than a sentence or two out of him. He'd come a long way since then.

"You're certainly in a good mood," I replied.

"Yeah, Marti came by. We went out and ate breakfast together. It was cool. A lot of men were looking at us and couldn't believe I had a beautiful woman with me."

"That sounds nice," I said. It did not escape me that I had not been invited and she had not called me back. I racked my brain trying to remember if I had angered her too but came up with nothing. So, both she and Anna were not speaking to me. Wonderful.

"Your GPS shows you at the city cemetery. What are you doing?" Ronald asked.

He had, among other things, access to the GPS on my phone. It was irritating, but it'd proven useful in the past when I'd gotten myself into a spot of trouble, so I tolerated it.

"I'm working on a case," I said and gave him a brief rundown.

"Sounds like a weird case," he said. "Oh, Marti has a case too."

"She does?"

"Yeah. A woman thinks her wife is cheating on her, so she hired Marti to get the evidence. I'm helping her with the research."

"I hope she's paying you," I said, wondering why Marti was suddenly taking on PI work and had not said a word to me about it.

"What's this favor you're asking?" I asked.

"Well, it's kind of complicated, but I have a friend, well, not really a friend, although we're friends on the internet…"

"Ronald, what kind of favor?" I pressed. Sometimes he easily got off track.

"Oh, yeah. Well, she's discovered some kind of bank fraud scheme and she wants to talk to you about it."

"How does she know about me?" I asked.

"Oh, I've told her about you and how we work cases together. She's probably done a lot of research on you too. That's how she is."

"Alright, no problem. How about I meet with her tomorrow evening sometime?"

"Um, well, that's the thing. She doesn't live here, and she said she's travelled a long way, so she'd like to meet as soon as possible."

"Okay, we can talk over the phone," I suggested.

"Yeah, I suggested that as well, but she wants to meet you in person. Tonight."

I couldn't help myself and groaned out loud.

"What's wrong?" Ronald asked.

I fought off a yawn before speaking. "I'm still a little worn out from the birthday party."

Ronald chuckled. "Yeah, you tied one on. Marti got a good laugh out of it."

"I'm sure she did," I said.

I remembered her grinning every time she fed me a shot. I also remembered the wild sex we had later. Sort of. I wondered if she got a good laugh out of that too.

"Hey, did Marti say anything about an argument or disagreement? Maybe Anna said something?"

"Um, no to both. Why? Did something happen?" he asked.

"No, nothing I'm aware of. Alright, getting back to your friend, I guess I could meet her. What time and where?"

"She said she'll meet you at midnight in Centennial Park."

I frowned. "What?"

"Um, yeah," Ronald said and tried to explain. "She's got this really paranoid thing going on, so she wants to meet at the park. She thinks she's safer that way."

I continued frowning. "Yeah, okay. Are you coming with me?" I asked.

"No, I can't. I got some stuff going on and I think she only wants to meet with you."

The stuff he was referring to was probably one of the online role-playing games he was hooked on. He'd play them on his computer for hours upon hours.

"What am I supposed to do, walk around the park until I somehow find her?"

Ronald snickered. "No, silly. She said she'd meet you by the monument near the pond. Do you know where that is?"

I did. It was a stone monument honoring the founder of Nashville, James Robertson. It was in front of the pond, which was called Lake Watauga. I'm sure there was some historical story attached to all of it, but my brain was not in the mood to remember.

"Alright. Meet her at the monument at midnight. Got it. What does she look like?"

"I don't know," Ronald replied. "I've never seen her. She goes by Valkyrie. That's her online name. I have no idea what her real name is."

I felt like groaning again but held it in. "Alright, Ronald, but you owe me big time for this."

Ronald snickered again. "Whatever. Call me later and let me know how it went."

I could not help but be a little confused about this meeting. If she had uncovered something illegal, why did she not simply report it to the FBI?

Technically, Centennial Park closed at dark, but there were always people there. Surprisingly, I only saw two cars parked by the Parthenon. Probably young lovers. I parked away from them and walked over to the monument. I checked the time on my phone. It was a quarter til midnight. Looking around, I spotted a swinging seat across from it. I walked over to it, sat, and waited. I decided I'd give her until five after midnight. If she was late, tough shit.

"Thomas."

The voice was quiet, barely above a whisper. I must have dozed off but now I was instantly awake. Looking around, I saw a figure standing under the shadows of a tree, which made her almost invisible.

"Yeah, right here," I said and stood. I waited a moment, but she didn't move. I walked over to her, stopping when I was ten feet away. She'd picked a good spot. The trees kept her features shadowed.

"I'm Thomas. What can I do for you?"

Instead of answering, she challenged me with a question.

"What is the online name of our mutual friend?"

I frowned and thought for a moment. "Mentat-314."

I saw her give a slight nod and she stepped out of the shadows. She was tall, maybe six feet, lanky, wearing jeans and a snug fitting black tee shirt. She was wearing a dark ball cap, but I could see pale blonde hair peeking out. Although it was dark and her features were hidden under the brim of the ball cap, her complexion appeared fair, like she didn't get out in the sun, and I guessed her to be in her mid to late twenties.

I stayed alert. After all, I did not know this woman, did not know if she was armed and had a grudge against me, or if she had an accomplice lurking nearby and was waiting for the opportunity to ambush me.

We stood there in silence a moment, staring at each other. I guess she was waiting for me to start it off.

"You're Valkyrie, I assume?" I asked.

"Yes."

"I have to admit, this is an odd way of meeting."

"I have to be careful," she said. She had a heavy accent; Eastern European or Russian if I had to guess. I immediately thought of my client. Coincidence? I didn't mention it.

"Okay, fair enough, I guess. What can I do for you?" I asked.

"I have something to give you," she said and stepped closer.

She held out a hand which had something in it. I reached out with my non-shooting hand and took it. Looking at it, I saw they were two cylindrical tubes of lip balm.

"Chapstick?" I asked.

"No. They are disguised storage drives."

I looked them over closely and opened the top of one of them revealing a USB connector. "Neat. What do they contain?"

"They contain data of a program designed to siphon funds from a bank. Two international banks, to be specific. So far, the group has managed to divert almost a million US dollars into their personal accounts."

"Impressive," I said. "It must be a clever scheme."

"It is, and that's just the beginning," she said. "The programming they created is so deeply embedded within the banks' systems they'll be able to siphon off more than fifty million in the next ten years. If they want more, they can do it, but it increases the risk of being caught. The way they have it set up now, they will never be discovered."

"And you want them caught," I surmised.

"There are four of them, and I want them to rot in prison," she replied.

I chuckled. "Okay, it sounds like a personal vendetta."

"Yes," she said and did not elaborate. She gestured at the drives. "Are you going to give them to the federal police? Mentat said you are personal friends with several members of the federal police."

"I have a few acquaintances with the FBI. They will undoubtedly want to interview you. It'll be confidential."

"No!"

She almost shouted it. Even in the dark, I could see her expression tighten but she quickly composed herself. "If it is discovered who I am, I will be killed. Or worse."

"That's a harsh allegation," I said. I couldn't tell if she was being serious or melodramatic. She seemed to understand what I was thinking.

"Think whatever you want, but my identity must remain anonymous."

"Alright, I'll not tell them anything other than I was given these to hand over to them." I gestured with my hand containing the thumb drives. "Valkyrie, I'm no computer expert, but won't they be able to do something with these, like learn your computer's IP address or something?"

"No, I have made sure that will not happen," she said. "Mentat vouched for you. I have travelled a long way based on that. Did I make a mistake?"

I slowly shook my head. "If you want anonymity, you'll have it. You can count on it."

She seemed satisfied by this response and then changed the subject. "I cannot pay you for this service, but Mentat said you would not require payment."

I grunted. Leave it to Ronald to decide when I would and would not require a fee.

"No, I won't need payment." I stared at the drives in my hand. "I'll get these in the right hands, but can you tell me why you came to me instead of going directly to a law enforcement agency in your own country?"

"It would seem easier, but where I come from, the government is full of corruption," she replied. "I have been told that in America the corruption is small. Is that true?"

I thought about the events in my life and the corrupt cops I had encountered. One tried to have me convicted of murdering my wife and another one tried to kill me. If not for Mick, he would have. But I also knew a lot of damn good cops.

"It's mostly true. I'm fairly good at figuring out the good ones from the bad ones."

"Then I have come to the right person," she said.

"I get the impression you live in Eastern Europe." I waited for a response, but she said nothing. "Well, if you do, you've travelled a long way simply to hand these over to me."

"There are other reasons that have brought me here. I knew Mentat lived here as well and he has often bragged of you, so…" she did not finish the sentence and instead stared at me a moment. "Mentat says you are his best friend."

"I'd like to think I am," I replied. She stared a moment longer before speaking again.

"I am going now. Please do not try to follow me."

"Okay, I won't. Is there any way I can contact you?" I asked.

"I will contact you, if it is necessary." She stared a moment longer, and it seemed like she had more to say, but then a car turned onto the road that led up to where my Mustang was parked. It seemed to unnerve her.

"Goodbye, Thomas," she said, and before I knew it, she was running away.

I watched her run almost the entire distance of the park before disappearing into the darkness. She ran with a graceful gait, like a gazelle, with the perfect form of someone who was accustomed to running. I grunted to myself. I had no doubt she was a cross-country runner, maybe even ran competitively.

I dropped the two data drives into my pocket, stretched, and enjoyed the night air. I watched as a car slowly drove by my car. It was a late model sports car, maybe a Camaro, bright green with a spoiler on the back. It stopped near my car and the driver's door began to open. I emerged from the shadows and began walking toward it, approaching from the rear. They must have seen me because they slammed the door closed and barked the tires as they took off.

My first impulse was to chase it down and demand to know what they were up to, but I was simply too tired to get involved in some silly confrontation. All I wanted to do was go home and sleep.

I put the car from my mind and thought of Valkyrie as I drove. She seemed to be an interesting person. She did not live in Nashville, and I wondered how far she had travelled simply to hand over the storage drives. I made a mental note to set my alarm for seven in the morning and I'd give the FBI a call.

When I arrived home, Tommy Boy was complaining loudly. I didn't understand, he had food and fresh water. Hell, I'd even cleaned out his litter box. Locking up, I went immediately to bed. Tommy Boy jumped up and nestled on the pillow beside me. His incessant meowing stopped, and he began purring contentedly. I guess he was simply lonely.

I was too. All I ever did these days was think about Simone. Not my deceased wife, only Simone. We had a connection, and I honestly saw myself spending the rest of my life with her. I would have had to make behavioral changes, sure. Like cigars. She didn't like them and I'm certain she would have eventually demanded that I quit. Same with other things, like taking on shady cases. She would not have allowed that.

I would have willfully complied with a smile, not a single regret.

# CHAPTER 11

I'd slept like a rock and awoke before my alarm went off. After cleaning up, I enjoyed some fresh coffee while sitting at my desk. The morning news was on, but I kept getting distracted by the two storage drives. I admit, I was a little tempted to plug them into my laptop and check them out, but then I reminded myself not to get involved in whatever it was. Nashville was seven hours behind Lyon, France, so unless she was taking an afternoon nap, my phone call was not going to wake her. She answered after the third ring.

"Special Agent Delmonico."

"Hello, Hope. How is my favorite FBI agent this morning?" I asked.

She responded with a bit of warm laughter. "I'm good. Working eighty-hour weeks, but I'm good. How are you, Thomas?"

"That's a lot of hours. I think you should quit and move back to Nashville."

She laughed again and I wanted to think I detected a hint of sadness. "Thanks to you, we have an excellent human trafficking case. If all goes to plan, we'll have a dozen indictments by the end of the week, and then we're looking at a few years of follow-ups and court. Everyone on the team is excited. This is a big case."

"Well, dang. Sounds like I won't be seeing you anytime soon. Oh well, my loss," I lamented.

"Don't tell me that's the only reason you called."

"What, I can't call simply to hear your sexy voice?" I asked.

She laughed again.

"Okay, you got me. I do have another reason for calling," I said and gave her a brief summation of my meeting with Valkyrie, the allegations she'd made, and the existence of the storage drives.

"Have you opened the drives?" she asked.

"No, I haven't. Honestly, I've got a lot on my plate right now and if I open them, I feel like I'd be opening Pandora's box. So, since you're too busy over there in France, I suppose I'll give your old boss Reuben Chandler a call."

There was a moment's pause before she responded. "Do me a favor and let me give Carter a call instead."

"Carter Pike?" I asked.

"Yeah. He's a former accountant, so he'd be good for this. Besides, he recently had a case blow up on him in court, and some of the higher-ups in DC have voiced their concern, so he needs something good to get him back in stride again."

"Okay, no problem. Have him call me."

We talked for another ten minutes before she had to go back to work. I ate a light breakfast with my coffee and told myself I needed to get busy on the case I had already been paid for. So, I booted up my computer in between bites and logged on. I'd had an idea while talking to Hope. Clicking on the police department's website, I found the number to the central precinct and called. The lady that answered was pleasant when I identified myself as a researcher for the Goldman law firm. It wasn't exactly a lie, but the Goldman name was well-known in Nashville. Me, I was known, but depending on who you asked, I was either a good guy or a troublemaker.

Asking her about the murders, she advised me the first two officers on the scene were Richard Tomey and Abigail Severns. She went on to say that neither had a department voicemail and she was not inclined to give me their home phone number. However, she provided me with their email addresses. After thanking her, I hung up and sent each of them an email requesting to meet. I did not know Severns, but I knew Tomey. He was a decent enough guy, a little on the loud side and liked to brag, but he was okay.

I then had an idea and called my sort-of friend, Detective Jay Sansing. Jay had been a detective in the Office of Professional Accountability when I first met him. He was currently a member of the Major Crimes Unit, which I considered a significant career improvement. Unlike the two patrol officers, Jay had his own office and phone. He didn't answer though, so I left a voicemail.

I heard the familiar exhaust of Bubba's tow truck approaching, so I got up and met him outside. When he got out, he pointed at some body parts strapped down in back.

"I got a buddy who works at a salvage yard in Cookeville. When I told him about the Bird, he found some parts," he pointed again. "What do you think?"

He had a trunk lid with hinges, the unique Superbird spoiler, and two bumpers that still had most of the chrome on them.

"I'd say you owe him a case of beer, if he didn't gouge you on the price," I said.

Bubba chuckled and pulled a folded-up piece of paper out of his pocket.

"He didn't tell the boss man what they were, so I got 'em cheap," he proclaimed.

"Awesome. Let's get to work." I started to say something else but realized something was wrong. My surveillance camera at the head of my driveway did not activate a signal to my phone. I opened the app on my phone and checked it. It appeared to be working.

"I'll be right back," I told Bubba and walked down my drive.

I had motion activated surveillance cameras mounted around my property, including one in a tree pointed toward my drive. When activated, I would receive a distinctive ping on my phone. I could then activate the app and view a live feed from the camera. Most of the time it was foraging deer or an occasional coyote.

It only took a minute to find the cut cable on the camera.

# CHAPTER 12

My phone rang as I was inspecting the cable. It was Special Agent Carter Pike. I'd had problems with FBI agents in the past, but not with Hope or her partner, Carter. He was a pleasant man, nondescript but competent.

After greeting him, I gave him a rundown about Valkyrie's case, and he agreed it would be something worth investigating. Carter said he was going to be out of the office most of the day and had no problem coming by my house to retrieve the storage drives. I then called Ronald and told him about the cut cable.

"I need you to go through the logs and try to figure out exactly when the cable was cut," I told him.

"Yeah, no problem," he replied. "Could an animal have gnawed on it?"

"Nope. It was definitely done with a pair of wire cutters," I said.

"Do you have anybody in mind?"

I sighed. "The list of possible suspects is a long one."

That caused Ronald to chuckle. When I got back to the house, Bubba had unloaded all the parts and had them arranged on the floor. He gestured toward the car.

"The rascal is dirty and grimy. Do you have a pressure washer?"

I had a small one buried under my worktable behind a lot of junk. It took almost five minutes to get to it. We pushed the car outside and I got it set up. Bubba started washing it while I tended to my cut camera cable. It didn't take long to repair it and get it working again. I fixed some iced tea and spelled Bubba on the pressure washer.

The car was indeed dirty. The undercarriage and engine housing had years of accumulated grime. We were only halfway done when a black Ford SUV approached and parked.

Special Agent Carter Pike parked and got out. Like I mentioned before, he was a nondescript man; average height, average weight, the kind of guy who did not stand out in a crowd. Today, he was wearing the standard FBI uniform, a charcoal gray suit with a starched white shirt, a blue tie to correspond to the current president's political party, and black wingtips. I liked him because he was a modest man, the opposite of an egotistical prick, which most law enforcement agencies seemed to have an abundance of.

"Good morning, Thomas," he greeted.

"Good morning. I'd shake your hand but I'm a little dirty. Follow me."

I led him inside and pointed out the storage drives that were sitting on my desk. He picked them up and scrutinized them.

"Fair warning, I've not opened them, so I have no idea if there is a virus or malware on them," I said.

"Yeah, we can work around that," he replied. "Tell me about this Valkyrie woman."

I spent the next five minutes going over the details. I did not tell him everything about her because frankly, he did not need to know everything. It might become relevant later, but not right now.

"She's adamant about remaining anonymous, which is why she used me as a cutout."

Carter nodded in thought and looked over his notes a moment before gazing hopefully. "I really need to interview her, Thomas."

"Like I said earlier, I don't know her true identity and I have no direct way of contacting her. As far as I know, she's long gone from Nashville. If she contacts me, I'll gladly pass along the request."

Carter nodded in acceptance and jotted an additional note. For some reason, I did not think Valkyrie had left Nashville, although I could not explain why. I kept that to myself as Carter finished his notes and tapped his notepad with his pen a few seconds before speaking.

"Alright, I've made cases with less information than this. I'll head back to the office and get our forensics people to have a look at these."

"I do have a question. Suppose she's a Russian spy and those drives have a super virus or something. How do you prevent that from messing things up?"

"The techs have protocols in place. They'll do a forensic analysis with a standalone computer first. If they're clean, we'll then look at what she has." He then cracked a smile. "I've got to hand it to you, nothing's ever boring with you. Oh, by the way, I happen to be friends with a certain TV celebrity who is a car collector and has a soft spot for old Caddies. I told him about yours and he might be interested in buying it."

"My sixty-one convertible? Nah, I'll keep that one forever." I thought for a second. "Hey, why don't you take a picture of my thirty-seven Coupe and send it to him? I've only started working on it, but he might like it. I'll sell it if the money's right."

Carter readily agreed to do so. He pulled a stainless-steel card case out of his inner jacket pocket and produced a couple of business cards. "My cell phone number is on it. If you see this Valkyrie lady again, give her one and tell her to please call me."

"Will do," I said. I'd already told him she did not want to speak to anyone else, but he was a detective, and a good detective was persistent and did not simply give up when they were told no. I understood this.

"I'll let you know what we have in a couple of days," he said.

I smiled slightly. "I'll admit, I'm curious, but honestly, I'd rather be left out of it. I've got a lot going on and I'd rather not be involved in this stuff. It's out of my bailiwick anyway."

Carter returned my smile. "I guess I understand. Oh, by the way, do you know Detective Jay Sansing?"

"Yes, I do. What's he done?"

Carter chuckled. "Oh, nothing nefarious. He called this morning. He's working a case involving two unidentified murder victims."

"Yeah, the grave robbers."

"It's an odd case. The two victims have tattoos common from Russian prisons. Each also have a tattoo on their forearm which is popular among members of the Spetsnaz. He put a call in to see if the FBI could help identifying them."

"Interesting," I said.

Jay had mentioned nothing of the tattoos, but he was under no obligation to keep me apprised of any developments in the case. Still, it irked me.

We walked over to the old Coupe, and he used his phone to snap a few pics. He promised to let me know what his celebrity friend thought and waved as he drove away.

Bubba and I ate a quick lunch and had made respectable progress on the Superbird before calling it for the day. I went inside and got some leftovers from the party along with a couple of beers and took them out to the picnic table. Bubba downed his beer in two swallows.

"Damn, that was good," he declared.

I chuckled and directed him to go get himself another one. He did so, found some cheese dip for our chips, and plopped down at the table.

"What do you think so far?" he asked between mouthfuls of nachos.

"I thought there'd be a lot more rust, but we're lucky, that'll work to our advantage. Let's hope our luck holds out with the engine."

"Yeah, I can't wait to hear that baby running," he said and then made a head nod toward my driveway. "I'm a little surprised at how busy you are. Do you work with the FBI a lot?"

"Some," I said. "We have a little bit of a love hate relationship. The agent that came by earlier seems like a decent guy. I passed along some information to him."

Bubba nodded and set his beer bottle down. "There's something I've been meaning to tell you ever since we became partners."

"What's that?"

"I'm currently on parole," he divulged.

I gazed at him in surprise. "I didn't know that."

"Armed robbery," he said before I asked. "I was labeled the getaway driver by the cops and prosecutor."

"What happened?" I asked.

"It was a few years ago. Me and a buddy were out drinking after work. Jaeger and beer, a wicked combination." He scrunched up his face at the memory. "Anyway, we ran out of beer and decided to run down to the store and buy some more. My buddy went in the store and grabbed a case out of the cooler. He decided the line was too long, so he was going to leave without paying for it. One of the employees tried to stop him and my buddy punched him. He fell and hit his head. My buddy Roach hopped in the car and didn't feel like he needed to mention what he did. When I saw the blue lights, I thought it was going to be a DUI stop, so I tried to outrun them. It was one of the dumbest things I'd ever done. I wrecked, the officers thumped us in the head a couple of times with their nightsticks, and we got arrested. I had a public defender who wasn't particularly good at his job and ended up getting five years."

Bubba sighed. "I guess I'm lucky. I only served eight months in prison before I got out on parole. I flatten my sentence in March of next year."

"You didn't know what happened inside the market?" I asked.

Bubba gave an adamant shake of his head. "No, sir. Roach told them as much, but it didn't matter." He stared somberly at me. "I guess I should've told you before we became business partners."

"Don't worry about it, Bubba, I..." I stopped mid-sentence and stared at my Mustang. A little bell was going off inside my head.

"What's wrong, Thomas?" Bubba asked.

I didn't answer. Instead, I walked over to the Mustang and dropped to the ground. I'm too big to crawl fully under a lowriding muscle car, so could only lay beside it and peek under it. I found it easily. I reached out and tugged on it. As I suspected, it was magnetically mounted. After a hard tug, it came free.

I guess the disabled surveillance camera gave it away. Normally, I would have thought the person in the Camaro at the park was simply curious about my Mustang. Even after they took off the way they did, I might've simply scared them. But the paranoia in my brain started working and decided it was no coincidence. Whoever was in that car had known I was at Centennial Park. Someone was actively surveilling me.

"What's that?" Bubba asked.

"It's a tracking device," I answered. "This particular model has a magnetic mount. It's a good one. One of the higher end models."

"Is it yours?"

"Nope." I walked over to my Ford Explorer and found a duplicate tracker. Same for my old Ford pickup and my Cadillac.

Laying them on the picnic table in front of us, I pointed at them. "Bubba, that's several hundred dollars' worth of electronic gizmos. Someone has gone to a lot of trouble to track my movements."

Bubba picked up one of them and frowned as he looked it over. "Why?"

"That's a good question."

He looked around. "You know something? If they went to this kind of trouble, they probably have cameras on your home too."

I looked at him in surprise. I was feeling rather stupid at that moment. After all, I was a former cop with a hefty amount of training and experience. I felt like I was good enough to not only teach surveillance and counter-surveillance techniques, but I was good enough to keep from something like this happening to me. Only it had, and I wasn't.

I cracked my knuckles in anger. Like Bubba said, if they went through that much trouble, it was conceivable they put some surveillance cameras somewhere around here.

"Bubba, I need to have a look around my property."

Bubba nodded somberly. "Gotcha. I've got to run home and grab a bite to eat before work anyway. I've got the evening shift for the rest of the month."

After he left, I walked to the entrance of my driveway and found it rather easily. A small surveillance camera mounted to a tree across the street. Battery operated. It was mine now.

I spent the next two hours painstakingly searching my property, but that was the only device I located. Three tracking devices and one surveillance camera. Someone had spent around a thousand dollars to keep tabs on me. I called Ronald and asked if it were conceivable that someone could hack into my surveillance cameras. He assured me they could not because he was managing them, and nobody could dupe him like that.

I spent the rest of the afternoon and evening around the house. I finally had it all cleaned up and after eating more leftovers, I sat in my chair, entertaining myself with a TV show on Netflix while randomly surfing the internet. At eleven I was about to turn in when my phone rang. The caller I.D. showed a Metro government number.

"I'm calling for Thomas Ironcutter," the woman's voice said.

"This is Thomas," I replied.

"Hello, Mister Ironcutter. This is Officer Abigail Severns. You sent an email asking me to contact you."

I instantly came fully awake. "Good evening, Officer. Thank you for calling me."

"What can I do for you?" she asked. She was being courteous, but I could hear a hint of impatience in her voice.

"I have been hired by a client to investigate certain facets of the double murder at the Nashville Cemetery."

"Okay," she replied.

"Would it be possible to meet with you in person and talk about it?" I asked.

There was a long pause before she answered. "Not tonight, but I get off work at seven and I have court tomorrow. I'll be at the courthouse at eight. We could meet then and there, but I'll only have a few minutes to talk."

"That'll be fine. Meet me at the cafeteria and I'll buy you a cup of coffee," I said.

She agreed and hung up. I could tell she was wary and possibly a little annoyed that I simply did not ask her what I wanted over the phone, but a good detective knew body language during the interview could tell you a lot more than what was being said. I set my alarm before going to bed. Tommy Boy took pity on me and left me alone.

# CHAPTER 13

I was early, but the courthouse was already bustling with people. After standing in line for a solid fifteen minutes waiting to pass through the metal detectors, I made my way through the crowd to the cafeteria's entrance and began searching the crowd for Officer Severns. I didn't have to wait long.

"Mister Ironcutter?"

I turned to the voice. Officer Abigail Severns was cute, early twenties, about five-four and somewhere around a hundred-forty. It was hard to tell due to the bullet proof vest under her uniform. Her physical stature was on the petite side, but she had pronounced shoulders and the muscles in her arms were well defined. Her light brown hair was tied back in a bun, and she had alert hazel blue eyes. She stared expectantly.

"Hi, call me Thomas, please," I said.

"And please call me Abby. I was going to get a quick bite of breakfast before court. We can talk then, if you like, but I can't accept any gratuities, so buying me coffee is out," she said with a small smile.

"I understand, I guess. Let's get in line."

There were only a couple of people ahead of us. We ordered; she chose hot tea and a bagel. I ordered a large coffee and the two of us walked to a nearby table.

"My training officer knows you," she said once we were seated. "When I said I was going to meet with you, he spent practically the rest of the shift telling me some wild stories."

"The entire shift?" I asked. "I didn't know I'd done enough that would take eight hours to talk about. I left a message with him as well."

She laughed as she took a bite. "Well, we had a few calls for service and an arrest, so maybe only for four of the eight hours, but they were some colorful stories."

"I hope they were amusing."

"Labeling them as amusing would be an understatement. They were most definitely interesting. I believe what has happened in your life after you were a police officer was the most perplexing. It's not everyone that can say an assistant chief-of-police tried to frame you for murder and the true culprit turned out to be a rogue FBI agent."

"True enough," I said and thought back to that time. The FBI agent in question was now dead, but former assistant chief Raymond Perry was still alive. After the lawsuit, he hastily put in his retirement papers and moved out of state. The District Attorney's office declined to prosecute him and never gave me a reason why. On occasion, I'd toyed with the idea of finding where he currently lived and paying him a little visit which would consist of a close encounter between his nose and my knuckles. I suddenly realized Abby was talking.

"So, you seem to have led a rather interesting life."

I don't know what she'd said before that, so I responded with a small smile and a nod.

"You said you're a private investigator now?" she asked.

"I am, and that's why I want to talk to you. My client is interested in certain aspects of this double murder at the cemetery."

She thought about it a moment before commenting. "I'm not sure what I can tell you. My training officer and I were the first ones at the scene of the murders, but I didn't do much. We secured the scene and called in support, that was about it."

"It's my understanding you believe the shootings had happened within minutes of you entering the cemetery."

Abby nodded. "Probably within seconds. Even Tomey believes that. The blood was still coming out of the victims' gunshot wounds, and when I checked them for a pulse, they were still warm. In fact, they looked like they were sweating, presumably from the physical exertion of digging the hole." She shrugged as if to emphasize she was merely speculating and went back to her bagel.

"Were any of them conscious? Did any of them say anything?"

"No, and no," she replied and dabbed her lips with a napkin. "Are you trying to figure out who shot them?"

"Actually, no."

She arched an eyebrow in surprise. "You're not?"

"Nope. I'm sure the detectives will figure it out. My client has hired me for something else entirely."

Her eyebrows furrowed in puzzlement. I gave what I hoped to be a disarming smile.

"I'll give a brief explanation. The two men were under the belief that a rare and valuable artifact was buried with the lady in her grave back in the 1830s. They were hired to rob the grave and retrieve the artifact, and while attempting this, they were shot. My client believes whoever shot them was attempting to steal the artifact but before they could do so, you and Tomey drove into the cemetery, preventing them from getting it."

"Which explains why they were fresh kills," Abby said.

"Yes," I said in agreement. "So, you two drive into the cemetery and the murderer or murderers flee empty handed."

"Do you know what the artifact is?" she asked.

"I have no idea, only that it's old and may have some kind of relationship with the Knights Templar." I waited to see if she had any other questions before proceeding. "I've been hired to attempt to locate this artifact. Specifically, to attempt to find out if an officer at the scene took it."

Abby stared somberly. "This client believes a police officer may have stolen this, what did you call it, an artifact?"

"Yes," I answered.

"But you don't have any idea what it is?"

"I do not."

She stared at me as she finished her tea. "Do you think I may have taken it?"

I responded quickly. "Nope, not for a minute."

"Why not?"

I paused a moment and stared back. "My answer might sound a little on the arrogant side."

She gave a short chortle. "I work with a man who is the epitome of arrogance. You're not even close. So, let's hear it."

"Alright, I'll try to answer. When you've been a cop for a while, and you're a good cop, you'll develop what is commonly called a cop's intuition. You encounter a lot of people when you're on the job and you have to be able to size them up within a couple of minutes."

"Alright, tell me how you do that?" she asked.

"Assess their demeanor, body language, and overall behavior. Sometimes your assessment takes longer than a couple of minutes, it may even take more than one interaction."

"Does it work?"

"It does for me, most of the time. I'll give you an example. Back when I was a rookie cop, like you, there was this one fellow rookie I went through the academy with. From the get-go, I was wary of him. He was the same age as me, likeable, and seemed capable, but he scored low on the first major exam, as did a few others. He suggested a method of cheating during the ensuing tests so that nobody would fail."

"He was only thinking of himself," Abby said. "If he got caught, the rest would be caught too."

"Yep. I knew immediately he was a bad egg and kept my distance from him. He went on to graduate, barely."

"What kind of cop was he on the streets?" she asked.

"He got caught shaking down street corner drug dealers," I said.

"Oh, wow. What happened to him?" she asked.

"He was set up, arrested, convicted, and served time. I heard he moved to Texas when he was released."

"So, do you think I'm a good officer?" she asked with a challenging grin.

"I do."

"Really?"

"Yep. You're a rookie and still have a lot to learn, but yeah, I do."

Her grin broadened. "Thank you. I have a credo I live by. Carry out your duties with respect for the Lord, with honesty and pure motives."

I was about to finish my coffee but stopped. "Alright, I know that's scripture, but I'm not placing it."

"The book of Chronicles," she said. "My father was a Presbyterian preacher."

"Ah, he had a positive influence in your life I'm guessing," I said.

"He did," she said. Her smile disappeared and her face darkened slightly. "He died of cancer not too long ago."

"I'm sorry to hear that."

"Thank you," she said. "I'll never do anything that would shame him or my family. So, you're correct, I'd never steal." She leaned forward in her seat. "Before you ask, nobody in my presence took anything from that grave either. I was there the entire time, and if they had tried it, I would have personally reported them."

I chuckled. "I believe you. Did you get a look inside it?" I asked.

She frowned. "Inside the grave? No."

"How about the crime scene tech? Did they get down in the hole and look in the grave?"

She shook her head. "She took some pictures, but the only person who got down in the hole was a fireman. He's the one who went down and put a strap around the man's torso. That's how they were able to lift him out. Then the fireman crawled up and looked around like he was the hero of the day. He then strutted over to me and asked me out on a date." She rolled her eyes. "It was stupid. We had two dead men and an active crime scene, and all he could think about was asking me out."

"Did you go?" I asked.

She scoffed. "Not hardly. Anyway, he glanced at the hole that had been cut into the side of the coffin, but that was it. He didn't take anything out." She thought a moment. "Oh, I overheard him talking to the female detective that came to the scene. Kettleworth. Do you know her?"

"I'm afraid I do," I replied. I refrained from telling her what I thought about Kettleworth as a person and her skills as a detective.

"Yeah, well, I heard him tell her that all he saw was a skeleton wearing an old dress."

"Interesting," I said.

She was about to say something but stopped when a couple of male officers close to her age stopped by the table and spoke to her. They unabashedly flirted while occasionally giving me sidelong glances. She listened attentively while they bragged about a foot chase and arrest of a burglary suspect. After they left, she turned to me.

"I'm sorry about that."

"Not a problem. A woman like you is bound to get a lot of attention," I said.

She frowned slightly. "What do you mean by that?"

"I'm not implying anything sexist. You're a young, beautiful, professional woman who is working in a male dominated profession. You're going to get a lot of attention, both positive and negative."

She stared a moment before smiling at my explanation and then changed the subject. "Tomey also said you used to be a detective in the homicide unit."

"That's where I worked before I resigned."

I could see she was about to ask something, but her phone chimed. She pulled it out of the case on her duty belt and tapped the screen. She then explained. "I set an alarm so I wouldn't miss court. I'm sorry, I have to go. I don't feel like I've helped you any."

"You've helped me more than you realize. I won't take up any more of your time." I stood. She stood with me. I reached for my wallet and pulled out a business card. "If you can think of anything, please give me a call."

"Sure," she said and glanced at my card briefly before putting it in her breast pocket. She then stuck out her hand. "It was nice meeting you."

She hurried off while I stood there. She walked with a purpose, shoulders square and a determined stride. She reminded me of a soldier. I forced myself to stop staring at her backside and headed for the exit.

I thought over our conversation as I walked. Even though I was no closer to finding this mysterious artifact, I was satisfied she was not a thief, and I was additionally convinced she was being truthful when she said she would have reported anyone who tried to steal anything from that grave.

I chuckled slightly to myself. If Officer Severns knew about some of my occasional shady practices, she probably would have nothing to do with me. As I walked, I took note of the multitude of corporate women out and about. It was a warm day and many of them were wearing colorful summer dresses. I could have sat on one of the benches in the shade and enjoyed the scenery all day, but I had other things to do. Ronald called as I exited the parking garage.

"What's up, Buttercup," he greeted.

"Back at you," I replied. "What are you up to?"

"I narrowed the timeline down to your wires being cut. It was the night before last at about midnight. There is a brief image of a person dressed like a ninja darting from one tree to the next and then the power goes off."

I drummed the steering wheel and waited for the light to turn green. "No facial recognition?"

"Nope," he answered. "They were covering their face with a scarf or something. Who do you think did it?"

"Hell, Ronald, the list is long. Alright, anything else? Have you heard from Valkyrie?"

"I don't have anything else at the moment and no, I haven't heard from Valkyrie."

"Did you know she travelled from Europe?" I asked.

"Um, no, not really. We were in a chat room not too long ago and she said she had to come to Nashville on business. That's when she peppered me with questions about you and asked to meet with you."

Interesting, I thought. "Alright. If you talk to her or chat with her online, ask her to give me a call."

"Okay, you got it. Whatever happened with her case?"

"I turned it over to the FBI, like she requested," I said. He asked a couple of additional questions before disconnecting the call.

I had a lot to do back at the house, including a double-check of my entire security system and perhaps look at ways of beefing it up, but first I needed to go to the Nashville City Cemetery.

# CHAPTER 14

My luck was holding. There was nobody around. It was a weekday morning, and I knew people sometimes came here to eat lunch or have romantic interludes, so I wasted no time. First, I hustled over to the surveillance camera, changed the battery, and swapped out the video card. I then walked over to the grave and looked around. Satisfied that nothing had changed, I sat at a nearby park bench, lit a cigar, and played through the previous twenty-four hours of recording via my phone app.

There were a few short videos of people walking around, but they were all during the day and the only people who seemed unusually interested in the Sartain grave was a skinny young man with a Tennessee Titans ball cap pulled down low. The man had walked from the parking lot, stopped, and stared at the grave for several minutes. He had his back to the camera, but eventually he turned and looked around the rest of the cemetery. Seeing his face, I straightened and peered closer to my phone's screen. The person was not a man, it was a woman. It was dark the first time I saw her, but I recognized her immediately.

"Why, hello, Valkyrie," I murmured. To say I was surprised would be an understatement, but before I had formed an opinion of why she was here, a man's voice interrupted my thoughts.

"That is one fine smelling cigar you got there, sir."

I turned toward the voice to see a man standing about twenty feet away. His clothing and general demeanor indicated to me he was homeless. He looked to be in his fifties, but he could have been younger. His face was drawn, and weather beaten, and his gray hair was mostly hidden by an old ball cap featuring the logo of Red Man chewing tobacco. I could see a rough linear scar along his forehead slightly above his eyebrows.

It has been my experience that homeless people are a peculiar breed. Some were the scum of the earth, but some were the salt of the earth. The latter category of people had interesting stories and a unique outlook on life.

"Yes, it is," I said. "Are you a cigar aficionado?"

"Well, sir, I used to be, but I've fallen on hard times and cannot afford anything other than an occasional cheap cigar from the local store."

I nodded thoughtfully and pulled out a leather case for my cigars from my jacket pocket. When I pulled it out, my jacket came open, revealing my sidearm holstered on my hip. The homeless man spotted it immediately. If he had been entertaining any notion of mugging me, he now knew it would not end well. If he was alarmed, his demeanor did not show it. Instead, he closed his eyes slightly and inhaled.

"Yes, sir, that is one beautiful smelling cigar."

"Well, let's see what we have here," I said. I pulled one out of my case, clipped the end, and handed it to him. "I'm not in the habit of giving away expensive cigars, but you look like a man who would appreciate a fine Dominican blend."

He took it, admired it with reverence before sitting on the ground and using the lighter I offered. Once it was lit, he took one long draw and savored it for several seconds before letting the smoke out.

"That's delicious. I've almost forgotten what a good cigar tastes like," he said.

I nodded in agreement and pocketed my lighter. He looked at me solemnly, warily.

"If you don't mind me asking, are you a cop?"

"No," I replied.

He nodded in relief. He'd probably been on the wrong side of the law more than once.

"Do you live around here?" I asked.

"I usually stay at the mission," he said. "But they don't let you in there if you've been drinking, so I got me a little spot over by the railroad tracks."

"What do you do for money?"

"I get work out of a temp labor agency. They didn't have nothing for me today, so I thought I'd walk over here and hang out. This place is peaceful."

"Yes, it is." I paused a moment. "Did you hear what happened here Saturday night?"

"I heard some men got killed," he said and pointed toward the grave. "Right over there, I think."

"Yeah, that's what I heard too," I said and plunged ahead. "I'm looking into it."

He frowned. "I thought you said you weren't a cop."

"I'm not. I'm a private investigator."

"Oh. Like on one of those TV shows," he said.

I chuckled. "Nothing nearly so glamorous or exciting."

"Are you investigating the murders?" he asked.

"In a manner of speaking," I replied. "The police are looking for the murder suspect, I'm trying to figure out what those men were after. By the way, my name's Thomas Ironcutter."

The man instantly stuck out his hand. "Larry T. Boles. The T is for Thomas. Larry T-Thomas Boles, that's me." Once we shook hands, the man seemed like he was glad to have someone to talk to.

"I used to be a man of importance," he said, and his face took on a sad expression. "Not so much anymore."

"Yeah?"

"Yes, sir, I was. Unfortunately, dipsomania took control of my life. Oh, and I tried to kill my wife's lover a few years back. The outcome of the trial was not in my favor, and I had to spend some time in prison."

"That's usually how it ends up," I said. "I imagine she divorced you while you were locked up."

"She certainly did. I am as yet undecided if I should forgive her or not."

I chuckled. "My wife cheated on me as well. It did not end favorably for her."

"What happened?" he asked.

"Her lover killed her."

He stared a moment, probably wondering if I was bullshitting him or not. Finally, he offered a nod.

"His act was to your ultimate benefit," he asserted.

"I don't know about that," I replied.

Logically, and in retrospect, Larry T-Thomas Boles was probably correct, but I never wanted Marcia to die. I most certainly would have divorced her, but she didn't deserve to die. In her own way, she was a good person and probably would have been a great mom to her unborn child.

"Would you happen to have anything to drink, Thomas?" Larry asked.

"I normally carry a flask with me, but I left it home today," I said.

Larry frowned. "Ah, well. I find panhandling distasteful, but if I want a drink, I am going to have to do it."

I chuckled at the subtle hint. Reaching for my wallet, I pulled out a twenty and a business card.

"I have a job for you, if you're interested," I said.

His eyes lit up in interest. "What kind of job?"

I gestured at the grave. "The men who were murdered were attempting to rob that grave. If you don't mind, kind of keep an eye on it. If you see anyone suspicious, get a good look at them, maybe get the tag off the car they're driving. If that happens, give me a call. All I ask is you don't make up a story in the hopes of getting more money."

My newfound friend nodded somberly and shook my hand before taking the money and card.

"Larry T-Thomas Boles is your man," he declared.

# CHAPTER 15

After arriving home, I changed out of my nice clothes and went to work on fixing the cut camera cable. I had not bothered using conduit when I originally installed the camera, which I guess was a mistake, but it made me wonder how they cut the power without giving themselves a good shock.

I found two game trail cameras in my shop gathering dust on a shelf. After putting in new batteries and ensuring they still worked, I set them up. One was focused on my house; the other was pointed on the camera that focused on my driveway. They were battery operated and needed no power lines.

Finishing up, I walked back to my house and fixed lunch. I was devouring a ham and cheese sandwich with the last of the nacho chips when my phone rang. The caller I.D. classified it as an unknown number. I had an idea of who it was, but I answered with my standard Salutation.

"Good morning, Mister Ironcutter," the voice said.

As I suspected, it was my mysterious client, Mister X. "I'm glad you called. I have a couple of updates for you."

"Please proceed," he instructed.

I gave him a rundown of my interview of Officer Severns. "In short, I am convinced no police personnel got into the grave and stole the artifact."

I did not tell him about my surveillance camera on the grave and Valkyrie's presence. I thought I'd hold back that morsel until it yielded something. There were several seconds of silence, so long that I thought the call had disconnected.

"Are you there?" I asked.

"Mister Ironcutter, this is unacceptable." He spoke deliberately, in a low, menacing tone. I took a slow, deep breath before responding.

"I disagree, but I do not want you to feel you've been cheated. I will itemize a bill for you and refund what I have not earned."

"No!" he shouted. "You will earn your payment and you will find which of those police officers have stolen the artifact!"

"Do not yell at me," I admonished.

I heard him taking several deep breaths before speaking. "I apologize for my outburst."

"No problem. How are you so certain this so-called artifact is not still in the grave?" I posed.

He did not have an answer for that. Instead, he focused back on the officers.

"What was the name of the officer you interviewed?"

"Abigail Severns," I said.

"And she denied everything, how convenient."

"Look, I know cops. I can figure out which ones are dirty. She's not a dirty cop. She'd never steal anything."

He grunted. "What about the other officer? The senior officer?" he asked.

"Officer Tomey. I've not yet interviewed him."

"Tell me about him. What is his first name?" he asked.

"Richard Tomey. He's a veteran officer. I used to work with him. He's stubborn and arrogant, but he's not a thief. I'll speak to him soon, but I doubt he has anything else to add."

There was another long pause before he spoke.

"Very well. Continue your investigation, Mister Ironcutter. I will call you again in two days."

He disconnected the call without waiting for a response from me. I wanted to tell him there was nothing else to investigate. I sat there, waiting for an idea to come to me. The man was convinced this so-called artifact was in Sadie Sartain's grave, although he never fully explained why. It made me think of something and even though his number was blocked, I tried the redial function. Surprisingly, he answered.

"Methuselah Sartain," I said.

"What's that?" he asked.

"Methuselah Sartain," I repeated. "Sadie's husband. How do you know that this artifact is not in his grave?"

I heard him breathing, but he did not respond.

"You've already desecrated his grave, haven't you?"

"No, I have not," he said. "In fact, I am uncertain where he is interred. You have given me something to think about. I believe, based on your suggestion, I would like for you to focus your investigation on Methuselah Sartain."

"I can do that," I said. After all, the man had paid me ten grand and I probably had only performed a thousand or two of actual work. "I tell you what. Let me do some research and see what I can find. Call me back in a couple of hours."

I disconnected the call and leaned back in my chair, but only for a second before grabbing my laptop. There were several websites that had information on dead people. Ancestry sites and grave registry sites were the best. I had them bookmarked, but a couple of them needed me to renew my subscription before allowing me to proceed with my search.

Having completed that task, I began searching. I found Methuselah on a grave registry site. It appeared he was interred in a Catholic cemetery shortly after the Civil War down in New Orleans. It wasn't hard to find, which made me wonder why my client did not already have this information. I printed it off and walked out to my shop. I was a couple of hours into working on the Superbird when he called back.

"Excellent," he said, after I had explained.

"It was on the internet, why didn't you look it up?" I asked.

"Oh, Mister Ironcutter, I already have. I merely wanted to see how proficient your skills are."

"A test? That's rather juvenile, don't you think?"

He chuckled. "So, it is. I would like for you to travel to New Orleans, Mister Ironcutter. I would like for you to inspect the grave and report your findings. I have left some paperwork with your friend at the cigar business."

"Well, I don't know. I have some things I need to do around here," I said. "Why don't you go ahead and tell me what this artifact is and why is it so damned important?"

I could hear him breathing deeply and I thought for a moment he was not going to answer me.

"There is a story that has been handed down through the generations that after the alleged resurrection of Yeshua, or Jesus as he is commonly known, Pontius Pilate had some important information recorded in inscriptions on a piece of metal. He did this to, how do you Americans say it? To cover his ass. The information he recorded is believed to have damning information of him and therefore of the Christian faith."

"What kind of damning information?" I asked.

"Sadly, I do not know. Several years ago, a scroll was found gathering dust in an obscure Italian monastery. The scribe was apparently old or perhaps had a health disorder because the writing was so poor it was almost unreadable. It mentioned the artifact and how moving the inscription is. It is said to be a piece of brass metal."

"Nobody knows what it looks like or what it says?" I asked.

"The writing was almost ineligible, and the scribe seemed to have problems with his words."

"Sounds like he was drunk," I remarked.

"Entirely possible, I suppose. Whatever his impediment, his rambling has led to various speculations. In short, nobody knows for certain, but the verbiage in the scroll implies the information will have a significant effect on Christian history. Some believe the effect could be catastrophic and they will do whatever it takes to gain possession of it."

"Who?" I asked.

"Are you a religious man, Thomas?" he asked.

"I guess I'm what you'd call a fallen Catholic," I admitted.

It was true. Although I still read a passage or two before bed on occasion, I had not attended mass or taken communion in several years.

He gave a low chuckle. "A Catholic you say? Would it surprise you to learn my employer's rival is the Vatican?"

"The Vatican?"

"Yes. The Pope and the elite men who run the Catholic religion. They want this artifact. Not to share it with the world, but to hide it from the world. Like I mentioned, it is believed the inscription on the artifact could have devastating consequences to the Christian faith. I do not know, personally, but there are men in high places who want it."

I scoffed. I didn't see how mere words written on a piece of metal could be so important, but I kept my opinion to myself. He seemed to sense my trepidation.

"What are your thoughts, Mister Ironcutter?"

"My thoughts? I feel like there is something else going on here far more dire than the mere location of an old artifact, and my thoughts are telling me that you are a person who I should have nothing to do with."

He surprised me with a laugh. "My visage seems to have that effect on people, but I can assure you my sole intention is to recover the artifact for my employer. If I am successful, I will return home, be rewarded handsomely, and you will most likely never see me again. Now then, let's discuss Methuselah Sartain."

"Yes, let's do that. How did you determine he ended up with the artifact?"

"The monk gave the name of the Templar who had once had possession of the artifact. Methuselah Sartain is a descendant of that particular Templar. The paperwork I have left with your friend should provide you with all the pertinent information. Please follow up on it."

He disconnected, leaving me talking to dead air. I punched a button and called Mick. He answered with his usual politeness.

"What're you doing, Dago?" he asked in his usual snide tone. I decided to have some fun with him.

"Oh, man, let me tell you. I just finished eating a delicious home-cooked meal from your wife and now she's giving me a foot rub."

"Yeah, you're a real comedian. That odd looking man came by here earlier and left you a package. When are you coming to get it?"

I shook my head. The man had dropped off the package before he'd even contacted me. He was a step ahead of me and had led me along to Methuselah before I had even thought about it. Kudos to him, but I wasn't ready to admit he was smarter than me.

"I guess I'll come down there when Kim gets finished," I said and threw in a few more barbs for good measure before hanging up.

I arrived at Mick's Place an hour later. My fat Irish friend had a beer waiting on me. I noticed Marti wasn't working. Mick set a large manila envelope in front of me.

"There's some paperwork about a church in New Orleans in there," he said. I should have known he'd look in it. "Are you going on a road trip or something?"

"Yeah, in a day or two," I said and casually looked around. "How's things going around here?"

"Marti ain't working if that's what you're asking," Mick replied with a smirk. "She's been taking some days off. I swear to the Almighty, you can't get dependable help these days. But what can I do? She's got big tits and the customers love her."

Mick walked down to the other end of the bar to refill a customer's empty beer glass, still grumbling the whole time. I took advantage of the moment of silence to look over the paperwork the mysterious little man had left for me. It was some information about the church and adjoining cemetery. It had been in New Orleans for at least two hundred years. Curiosity led me to open Google Earth on my phone and have a look at the place. I saw a church, one or two smaller buildings behind it, and the cemetery. It was located on the southside of New Orleans, named after a saint, and appeared to be a typical New Orleans cemetery, filled with mausoleums. Clicking on the website, I saw that it was opened in the early eighteen-hundreds, and although it wasn't the oldest cemetery in New Orleans, it was steeped in history. The website also said that tourists were welcome.

I ordered another beer and read some more before closing my laptop. I thought about it while I socialized with some of the other customers, including a busty brunette whom I had never seen in the place before. She had come in with Marley and Mel, a thirty-something couple who were frequent customers. Neither smoked cigars but they enjoyed smoking hookah, which Mick allowed for some silly reason.

Her name was Felicity, a single mother of two who, within two minutes of meeting her, proclaimed her ex-husband to have been a tyrannical, emotionally abusive loser of a man who she was going to take back to court because he wasn't paying enough in child support.

I thought about my case while she showed everyone her newest tattoo, a Chinese symbol on the back of her neck. I idly wondered how she could afford a tattoo if the child support was so woefully inadequate, decided I didn't care, but continued to act interested, although any interest I initially had was steadily draining away the longer she babbled.

I had to admit to myself the case was beginning to intrigue me. What kind of inscription could possibly be so powerful? I already knew I was going to New Orleans to inspect Methuselah Sartain's grave. It was probably going to be a wasted effort, but I did not know that until I tried. I finished my beer as Felicity continued talking and watched through the windows as a dirty truck with oversized tires slowly circled the parking lot before parking. A man exited and stared balefully toward the business before marching in with his chest puffed out. He stood immediately inside the door and fixated on the table I was sitting at.

"What the fuck is this?" he demanded as he strode toward us.

"Oh shit," Felicity muttered. Her friends murmured the same thing.

"He a friend of yours?" I asked as he strode over.

"It's her boyfriend," Marley said under his breath.

He gave his best menacing stare at all of us before his eyes rested on Felicity. He pointed a finger at her. "I'll deal with you in a minute." His finger then realigned itself at me. "Who in the hell are you?"

He was standing close, and I was sitting. I didn't like that. He was also tall, taller than me and I stood six-three. I knew Mick would back my play no matter what, but I was a little too old to be engaging in barroom brawls. Besides, Felicity wasn't worth it, not by a long shot.

"Me? I'm nobody, I was just leaving," I said, pushed my chair back, and stood.

"You're damn right you are," he growled. "Let me give you a little present on your way out."

I saw it coming. It was a haymaker with his right fist. I had no doubt he'd successfully pulled this type of move before, probably more than once. Ducking under a punch was sometimes difficult for me because my opponents were seldom taller than me, but not with him.

I ducked under his haymaker and sent him into sleepy time with an uppercut to his chin. I grabbed his shirt collar and managed to slow his fall so he wouldn't crack his skull on the concrete floor and ripped his shirt in the process.

"Oh my God!" Felicity shouted and jumped up so quickly her chair fell over. Mel and Marley sat motionless with their jaws hanging open.

I crouched and frisked him quickly. Finding a lock blade knife in his pants pocket and a cheap handgun tucked in his waistband, I grabbed both and stood. Mick came around from the back of the bar, a lead slap palmed in his hand. He seemed to breathe a sigh of relief when I stood and handed him the weapons.

He took them and stared down at the man. "I've never seen him in here before, but it'll be his last visit, I guarantee that."

"I believe it's past my bedtime," I said. He gave me a curt nod. I knew he'd take care of the rest.

I heard running footsteps as I neared my SUV. Turning, I saw it was Felicity. No doubt she was going to give me a piece of her mind for beating up her boyfriend.

"Oh my God, nobody has ever come to my rescue like that!" she exclaimed and grabbed me in a hug, pressing her breasts tightly against me.

"It's not like that," I said, but she didn't listen.

After a moment she let go and peered briefly through the plate glass windows. Mick and a couple others had helped numb nuts into a sitting position on the floor. He still seemed addled and was gingerly touching his chin. Felicity focused back on me. There was a glint in her eye.

"I need to go back in there and take care of that mess, but let's you and I get together sometime, alright? I'll tell Mel to give you my number."

She hugged me again and added to it by grabbing my backside with one hand and squeezing. She gave me one last lingering stare before hurrying back inside. I got in my car and hastily exited the parking lot.

I'd met a few women like Felicity in my time. Dysfunctional, always having drama in their lives, they were walking catastrophes. Women like her always seemed to find a man who used the wrong head to do his thinking. She'd use him as much as she could before he'd smarten up.

"Not me," I muttered and hurried home.

# CHAPTER 16

I went to bed early and headed out at five in the morning in an effort to avoid the rush hour traffic, but it was still a long, boring drive to New Orleans. To make it worse, there was a lot of construction work being performed on the interstate starting at Tuscaloosa and going through Birmingham.

I arrived at a little after two in the afternoon and headed straight for the church. Unlike most Catholic churches, this one was rather humble in size. It was stone, built in a gothic style of architecture, and probably could only seat about a hundred people at the most. The cemetery was located behind it and was far more impressive. I walked over to the main entrance and stared at it in awe. It easily covered five acres or more and was filled with all sorts of ornate mausoleums.

It was incredible. It was intimidating. It was doing something to me that I could not explain.

"It's amazing, isn't it?"

I turned toward the voice to see a man who looked old enough to be Methuselah's brother. He was wearing a black cassock and a simple gold cross hung from a simple gold chain. My powerful detective skills told me he was a priest.

"It sure is something," I agreed.

He pointed to an ambiguous spot toward the right with his wooden cane. "That's where I'll be buried one day, perhaps soon."

"It looks like a good place to be buried."

"Yes, it is," he said. After a moment he pointed again. A more specific point this time, to a simple bench seat under a large old tree draped in Spanish moss.

"I usually like to sit there during the day, when there is a pleasant breeze and it's not too hot or too cold and watch the tourists."

I nodded in understanding, or agreement, or maybe I nodded for no reason at all, I'm not sure. I could not place his accent either, but I was certain he was not a Louisiana native.

"How would I go about finding a specific grave?" I asked.

"There is a plat in the office, but it is locked at the moment. The key bearer is a young upstart priest who is counting the days when he can take over. He left for lunch two hours ago and has not yet returned. He does that sometimes."

"Sounds like I'll have to do it the old-fashioned way then. I guess I better get started," I said.

"Is it an old grave?" he asked.

"Yes, it is. The man's name is Methuselah Sartain and he died in 1865."

I saw him frown and his lips pursed under his thick gray beard. "I know of this grave."

My eyes widened. "You do?"

"It is a mausoleum actually." He pointed again with his cane. "Follow that path. Turn left at the fourth cross-path. The mausoleum is the ninth or tenth one. You should have no problem spotting it. When you are finished, come join me. I'll be at my bench."

I thanked him and started walking. I didn't know why he wanted me to join him after. Perhaps he was lonely for company, or perhaps his profession gave him the power to spot a fallen Catholic.

The mausoleums were stacked together, like concrete tiny homes with a carved cross on the top of each one. The Sartain mausoleum also had a wrought iron enclosure mounted to the right side. It reminded me of a crude bird cage. There was a fist-sized bell hanging from a chain in it, brass with a heavy coating of patina and writing on it. In other words, it was identical in appearance to the bell on top of Sadie's grave.

The matching bell was indeed interesting, but there was one aspect of Methuselah Sartain's mausoleum that was beyond interesting. One could say it was downright puzzling. It had been forced open.

# CHAPTER 17

I warily looked around, wondering if I was being watched. I didn't see anyone, but a dozen people could've been crouched down behind the numerous mausoleums, and I would not have seen them. I took photos with my phone, including a few close-ups of that bell, and then used the flashlight app to walk inside.

The top of the crypt had been pushed open, which was impressive. It had to weigh a few hundred pounds. I'm not a small man and I keep myself in shape, and I would've had a hard time getting it to budge.

The coffin had also been forced open. I'd seen more than one dead body in my lifetime. All shapes, sizes, and states of decay. Even so, it unnerved me a little bit. I used the light on my app to peer in.

The late Methuselah Sartain appeared to have been buried in a ballroom tuxedo, complete with a fancy red silk scarf that was surprisingly still intact, and a cane with a brass handle. His remains had been disturbed; he was no longer lying on his back. Instead, it looked like he'd been turned to one side, as if the culprit or culprits had searched underneath him for something specific. If I were a grave robber, I would have taken the fancy walking cane. And maybe the scarf. I took a few pictures before conducting a careful inspection without touching anything, but I found nothing.

I had no idea if the thief found what they were looking for. The only thing I was certain of at that moment was the sound of the hammer on a pistol being cocked. I slowly turned to see an older black man with a large pistol. And he was pointing it at me.

"Easy, Mister," I said.

"What you doing in here, boy?" he asked in a heavy Creole accent.

"I was doing some research on this man. It appears somebody has desecrated his tomb, and if you are wondering, I assure you I did not do it."

He scoffed but did not take his eyes off me. He was wearing a black ball cap with gold lettering that proclaimed he was a Vietnam vet. If that wasn't enough, he was wearing a leather vest adorned with little pins and medals referencing his military service.

"You broke in last night," he accused. "Yeah, you did it, I know you did, and I figured you'd be back."

I shook my head slowly. "Last night I was home in my bed, but if you think I did it, by all means call the police."

He narrowed his eyes at me. "You don't sound like you're from around here. Where're you from, boy?"

I eyed him a moment before answering. "I'm from Nashville. I've been on the road all day and got here less than an hour ago, and I'm no one's boy."

"Why're you here then?" he asked.

I gestured at the coffin. "The late Mister Sartain once lived in Nashville. His wife is buried there. I am a private investigator and have been hired to conduct research on the two of them. Now, would you mind lowering that weapon before it goes off?"

He stared with steady brown eyes. "It'll only go off if I make it go off." He continued staring but after a moment he slowly lowered his revolver.

"Why'd somebody hire you to research a man that's been dead for over a hundred years?" he asked.

"That would be confidential information and not something I'm going to disclose," I replied.

He narrowed his eyes slightly. "Come on out here in the sunlight where I can get a good look at you."

He backed out of the doorway and directed me to follow with a wave of his gun.

"Who are you?" he asked.

"My name is Thomas Ironcutter, and like I said, I'm a private investigator."

"And you ain't going to say why you're investigating this man," he said.

"That's right. Why don't we go talk to the old priest who gave me directions to this crypt? He should be sitting on his favorite bench, waiting on me."

He arched an eyebrow now. "You know Father Anthony?"

"I met him for the first time about twenty minutes ago."

He thought about my answer, and I watched him chew it over. My phone rang. I ignored it. He motioned with his pistol.

"Alright, let's go have a talk with Father Anthony. If he don't agree with what you're saying, I believe I'll take you up on that suggestion and make that call to the police."

Father Anthony looked up as we approached, and I saw the hint of a smile form. "I see you two have met," he said.

"You know him, huh?" the man asked.

"Yes, I do, Mister Everly," he replied and focused on me. "Mister Everly is the caretaker here. He is passionate about his job. As you can imagine, when the desecration to the mausoleum was discovered, Mister Everly took it personally."

"Did you set me up so he could point a gun at my head?" I asked.

Father Anthony looked taken aback and focused on Everly. "Mister Everly, that was uncalled for!" he admonished.

"How are you so certain he ain't the one who did it?" Everly rejoined.

Father Anthony gave a patient smile. "Mister Everly, whoever broke into the mausoleum had plenty of time to find whatever they were looking for. If this man was the perpetrator, why has he returned to the scene of the crime and why did he ask me the location of the mausoleum?"

Mister Everly took turns staring at both of us for several seconds before grunting and walking off.

"Please let me apologize for Mister Everly's actions with the weapon. He is a good man and a valued member of our church. Sometimes, he is overprotective. Please, come sit with me and let us talk about Methuselah Sartain."

# CHAPTER 18

I sat and talked with Father Anthony the rest of the afternoon. He was originally from Italy and an interesting man with a lifetime of stories. My phone rang a few times, but the prefix number indicated the call was originating from a Metro government phone. I ignored it. When the call ended, another one began within seconds. The caller ID showed it was from Jay Sansing's personal phone. I reluctantly answered it.

"Why are you bugging me?" I asked.

"I'm sorry to bother you, Thomas, but we have an urgent matter we need to talk to you about. Where are you?"

When he used the plural instead of the singular, I was suddenly suspicious.

"If you must know, I am currently in New Orleans. What's the urgent matter?"

"Uh, hold on for a minute," he said. I waited for a few seconds and debated on whether to hang up on him.

"Uh, Thomas, can you prove you're currently in New Orleans?"

"That's a stupid question. Is there a reason why I may need to?"

"We really need for you to come back to Nashville as soon as possible," he said.

"Why?" I asked.

"I am not at liberty to say over the phone," he replied.

"Well then, I'm a little busy down here and I'll come back to Nashville when my business is concluded."

I put my phone away and turned to see Father Anthony staring at me in concern.

"Is everything okay, Thomas?" he asked.

I shrugged. "It's nothing that can't wait."

The sun was setting, and it seemed as though Father Anthony was getting tired. I stood and offered my hand. Father Anthony shook it and said he'd pray for me tonight. Getting back into my Ford, I realized I was famished. I was in New Orleans and decided I wanted some good Cajun food. I found a place on Tchoupitoulas Street that sounded promising. Its advertisement boasted of great Cajun cuisine and live entertainment. A couple of Yelp reviews called it a dive bar, which sounded perfect to me.

The reviewers were right on the money, the place was the epitome of a dive bar. The interior was dark and the Formica top on the bar was marred with hundreds of burn marks from the cigarettes of drunken patrons. It was clean though and the a/c was keeping the place at a pleasant temperature. The bartender was a blonde about my age, huge breasts, tight revealing top, and a face heavy with makeup. I imagined an image of Marti in twenty years and wondered if this was how she was going to end up.

"Hi, sugar. I haven't ever seen you around here before," she said with a friendly grin. She still had nice teeth, or maybe they were dentures. I wasn't going to ask.

"Yeah, I'm just a tourist. I'm hoping for some good food and music," I said.

"If you like Dixieland jazz, this is the place. Our food is decent enough. I'd recommend the jambalaya."

"Alright, I'll do that. What about cigar smoking?" I asked.

She answered by grinning again and lighting a cigarette. Now it was my turn to smile. I looked over her shoulder at the taps. There weren't many choices.

"Is the Budweiser nice and cold?"

"I'll bet my ass on it," she replied. Now her grin was a little mischievous.

"I'll take one then."

There was currently only one other person sitting at the bar. He was fixated on one of the several TVs that was showing an LSU baseball game. He did not look like the type of person that'd complain about a little cigar smoke. I pulled one out, clipped it, and lit it. I'd taken my first draw off it when my busty bartender returned, a glass of beer in hand.

"Ooh, that smells good," she said.

"Most women don't like the smell of cigars."

"I'm not most women, honey," she said with a big smile. "If you're a tourist, why ain't you down in the quarter?" she asked.

"I don't care for big crowds," I said and took a sip. She didn't have anything to worry about losing her ass, the beer was deliciously cold.

"Well?" she asked.

"It's wonderful. What time does the band start?"

"We have a solo act starting in a few minutes and the house band starts around nine or ten."

"Great," I said and fished a credit card out of my wallet. "Start me a tab, please ma'am and I'll take some of that jambalaya you're bragging about."

She took my card and gave it a once over. "Thomas Ironcutter, why that's a nice name."

"Thank you, what's yours?" I asked.

"Margo." She held out her hand and we shook. I couldn't help but notice a tattoo on both arms and another was peeking out of the low vee-necked top she was wearing.

"Margo, you remind me of a friend of mine," I said. "Her name's Marti and she's a bartender in Nashville."

I half expected her jaw to drop and exclaim Marti was her long-lost daughter. Instead, she surprised me.

"Does she have big tits too?" she asked, and then burst out in laughter.

I laughed with her. "I like you already, Margo."

The jambalaya was only about six out of ten, but the cold beer made up for it. While I was eating, a couple of regulars sat at the bar next to me. Margo introduced me to them, and they did not seem to mind a tourist in their hangout. One of them was a lovely looking petite redhead who made it clear her male companion was only a drinking buddy. We had a pleasant conversation until the band started and it got too noisy. Then it was reduced to snippets of chat in between songs.

I was having an enjoyable time and could have stayed all night, especially with Little Red giving me multiple flirtatious smiles, but I was simply too tired. At midnight, I signaled Margo to tab me out. Red's smile turned sad when she realized what I was doing but gave me a friendly hug and shouted something. I had no idea what she said, it was too noisy, but I smiled and nodded before making my way to the door.

# CHAPTER 19

I found a decent hotel nearby, got a room, and barely remembered crawling between the sheets before the alarm on my phone went off at seven the next morning. The hotel had a breakfast buffet and plenty of coffee, which was exactly what I needed. There were only two other people present when I walked in, an older married couple, so it was pleasantly quiet.

I thought about my client while I ate. He had not called and when I tried calling him, the number was no longer in service. His lack of communication made me suspicious, as in I was beginning to strongly suspect he was the person who had desecrated Methuselah Sartain's mausoleum. If he didn't do it, he might've hired someone. And, if he was indeed the culprit, why did he send me down here? It made me wonder if he wanted to get me out of Nashville for some reason.

After breakfast, I decided to take a break and visit the National World War Two Museum I'd heard so much about. It was incredible and I stayed there for hours. As I was exiting, I saw a small group of older men and realized they were veterans. I caught the eye of one of them and nodded my gratitude before exiting.

After, I went back to the church and invited Father Anthony to join me for dinner. He readily agreed and directed me to a bistro near the church. It turned out he was a regular customer, and everyone enjoyed his company.

We shared an after-dinner coffee and were soon engaged in a deep conversation about the Catholic faith. I found his views to be pragmatic. He was candid about the darker chapters in the history of Catholicism. He called them blemishes but made no apologies for them.

"Have you ever been to the Vatican?" I asked.

"I have. I once lived there and worked under the auspices of the Holy See."

"That must have been a wonderful experience," I said. He gave a slight nod but did not answer.

"I've heard the library is extensive," I said, wondering what happened to cause him to go from the Vatican to this small church in New Orleans.

He nodded at my question. "It is vast. One could spend a lifetime in that library and never read all the books." He chuckled. "Of course, one would also need to read a variety of languages."

"How's your knowledge about lost religious artifacts?" I asked.

I could see Father Anthony smile through his thick beard. "Like the Ark of the Covenant?"

"Yeah, something like that. Apparently, Methuselah Sartain was in possession of some type of religious artifact. All I know about it is it is a piece of brass with an important inscription on it."

"Sounds intriguing," he said and sipped some coffee. "There are many, many lost artifacts and relics. Several could match your description." He held up a finger. "But, keep in mind, for every authentic religious relic, there are fake ones. Probably even more so."

"Yeah, no doubt."

"Do you have any additional details?" he asked.

"Nope, only that it's metal and has an inscription on it. It was believed that the artifact was buried with his wife, but it wasn't."

"Do you know what the inscription is?" he asked.

"Not a clue."

"Interesting," he said. He pondered it a moment before speaking. "The surname, Sartain, is it French in origin?"

"I'm not certain. I suppose I should do a little research on the man," I said.

"What about his wife? What is her maiden name?"

"Another good question, Father. It's Rosemont. I suppose I'll need to research her ancestry as well."

Father Anthony nodded. "Their lineage may offer some insight. There are many documentations of family lineages in the Vatican library. Did you know that most of those internet sites regarding a person's ancestry is run by the Mormons?"

"I've heard that."

He gave a hint of a smile. "The Mormons are so different from us Catholics, and yet we are so much alike." He stood slowly. "It is time for evening prayers. It was a pleasure talking with you, Thomas. I hope you come visit again before I become a permanent resident of the cemetery."

I left Father Anthony and went back to the hotel. I stretched out on the bed and relaxed, contemplating what I should do next. I could visit the government archives tomorrow and conduct some further research on Methuselah, but I felt like I was being manipulated by my client and it was leaving a bad taste in my mouth. I decided I was done in New Orleans and would head back to Nashville in the morning. And, as for this case, I was not going to devote any further effort into it until I had a nice long conversation with my client.

Somewhere during this deep thought process, I fell asleep, but was awakened by my phone ringing. The first thing I looked at was the digital clock on the nightstand. It read a little after two. Picking up the phone, I focused on the caller ID. It was Ronald.

"I need to talk to you!" He sounded agitated, panicked.

"What's up, bud?" I asked.

"Someone has set your shop on fire!" he shouted.

# CHAPTER 20

I'm certain I gripped the steering wheel so tightly my knuckles stayed white the entire trip back from New Orleans. I kept pushing on the accelerator and had to consciously force myself to slow down. After all, the damage was done and there was nothing I could have done differently by arriving a few minutes earlier.

I could swear I smelled the smoke a quarter mile before I got home. My house was not visible from the road. I liked it that way. My drive curved through several old trees before it came into view and the garage was behind the house. When I rounded the last curve, the damage came into view.

I wanted in my heart to believe it was going to be minimal. Perhaps it was nothing more than a little fire and smoke damage, but all that was left was a muddled pile of charred debris. I parked my SUV and sat there for a few minutes, staring in disbelief. The fire trucks were long gone. The only indicator of their visit were pools of standing water and several sets of tire ruts in my yard.

If one looked closely, you could see what was left of my prized possessions. Before leaving for New Orleans, I'd managed to move stuff around to make room for the Mustang. So, there they were. The Mustang, the two Cadillacs, and the Superbird. All burnt to a crisp. My old trusty Ford truck, which was parked at the side of the garage, also destroyed. It was awful to look at and my stomach was in knots.

Eventually, I got out and walked around, surveying the damage. My house was mostly intact, but the back of the house, the side nearest to the garage, had some smoke and heat damage, and the roofing shingles were all blackened and curled up. Stuffed in the door jamb was a business card from a Fire Marshall from the Nashville Fire Department. A note was scribbled on the back requesting I call him as soon as I made it back home.

I did as he requested. He asked me to stay put and he'd be there in twenty minutes. I fought down any kind of rude retort and disconnected the call. I walked inside, fed Tommy Boy, and poured a glass of iced tea. I allowed myself to brood only for a minute, and then my detective instincts took over. I changed into some work clothes, retrieved my digital camera out of my kit, and began photographing everything.

After I took several dozen photographs, I worked my way into the garage to see if there was anything at all that was salvageable.

Nothing. Nothing at all. The cars, my tools, everything was burnt to shit. I wondered if Percy knew all his files were gone as well. I tried calling him, but it went to voicemail.

"Hey, Percy, when you get this message, give me a call, please. It's extremely important."

I hung up and tried calling Anna. It also went to voicemail.

I was sitting at my picnic table when a white SUV drove down the driveway. It had the familiar markings of the Nashville Fire Department on the side of the doors and a light bar on top. The driver parked well away from the fire damage and got out. He looked like he was in his fifties with curly salt and pepper hair, and a slight paunch. He took a moment to light a cigarette before walking over.

"Are you Thomas Ironcutter?" he asked. I nodded. He looked me over. "You look like you've been rummaging around in there. Did you find anything?"

"No evidence, if that's what you mean."

He nodded and gestured at one of the folding chairs sitting outside. "Do you mind if I sit?"

"Not at all. If you're inclined, I've got a pitcher of sweet tea in the fridge. Help yourself."

"I believe I will. Thank you," he said and walked in the back door. He came out a moment later with a tall glass and sat.

"What flammables did you have stored in there?" he asked.

"I had two five-gallon gas cans, both mostly full, and there were the assorted automotive cleaning products. I kept them all properly stored in a wall locker, lids on tight and all that."

He nodded and took a drag off his cigarette. "What about shop rags?"

"Yeah, I kept the used rags in one of those steel safety cans. Have you determined a cause yet?"

"I can tell you it was deliberately set. There are multiple points of origin, and my old arson investigator's nose smells an accelerant. Regular gas would be my guess, but I'm going to send samples off to the lab anyway. Alright, I have two questions." He pointed at the surveillance camera mounted on the eave. "Does it work?"

"Yeah. I'll see about getting a copy downloaded. My buddy has already viewed it. He says you can see what looks like a slender man lurking around about two this morning. He said it looks like he was wearing a ski mask, or something similar, and carrying something. Probably a gas can."

"Figures. Well, I'll still need a copy."

"Sure," I said. "What's your second question?"

"I need to eliminate you as a suspect. Any thoughts on that?"

"That's the easy part. I was in New Orleans when this nonsense happened. I have all my receipts sitting in my briefcase, which is still in my car. It includes a hotel receipt and a bar tab that is timestamped at about midnight the night before. The bartender, a friendly gal by the name of Margo, will no doubt remember me if you were to give her a call. Do you want to look them over?"

He nodded. I went to my automobile, got them out, and laid them out on the picnic table. He took pictures of them with his cell phone.

"What about insurance?" he asked.

"I have it, but it won't cover everything. I had a total of five cars. Two old Cadillacs, a Mustang convertible, a Pontiac, and Ford pickup truck. Only three of them were insured, and don't even get me started on the replacement costs of all my tools. Nope, I'm going to take a hit in the wallet on this one, even with the payout."

"Sorry to hear that," he said.

I gave a curt nod in acknowledgement.

He stubbed his cigarette out and lit another. "I believe we've eliminated you as a suspect. So, do you have any possible suspects in mind?"

"Nobody I can think of at the moment."

It was not exactly the truth. I had several possible suspects in mind, but I wasn't going to tell him. At least, not yet. I don't know how I was going to do it, but I was going to find out who was responsible for this and take care of them in a way the American judicial system would most certainly frown upon. I finished my tea and stood. My muscles were tight and fatigued. I stretched and worked out a kink.

"Listen, I drove all night and I've got to get an insurance agent out here before I can get some sleep. So, if there's nothing else…"

He stood. "Alright, I'll get out of your hair. My email address is on my card. I'd appreciate that video as soon as possible."

After he left, I called the insurance company and left a voicemail. As I sat there, my phone pinged, indicating a car had turned into my drive. Ronald appeared a few seconds later. Parking, he got out and stared at the charred remains in slack-jawed fascination.

"Man, it looks even worse in real life," he exclaimed.

I stared at him. Tact was not a strong point for him. "Did you download the video?"

"Yeah. I even tried to enhance it, but it's no good. All it shows is a man wearing all black. He's not a big guy though. A little bigger than me, but nowhere near your size or Percy's size." He handed over a thumb drive. "The data size is too large to email you, so here it is."

"Thanks, buddy," I said.

"What happens now?" he asked.

"We'll need to make copies for the arson investigator and the insurance agent."

"I can do that," he volunteered.

"Good, thanks."

Ronald continued staring at the garage with a glum expression. "Man, those cars were like your most prized possessions."

"Yep."

"You spent over a year on the Cadillac alone," he said.

"Yep."

"Wow," he mumbled. "Are you going to replace them?"

"I don't know yet," I said.

I would've rather taken a beating from five grown men than lose my cars like this and I did not know if I had it in me to do it again. I tended to get too emotionally attached to them. My phone pinged again, and my dejected mood was about to get worse. Bubba and his familiar tow truck came into view. He parked and shut off the loud diesel, and then sat there for several seconds before he got out and slowly walked over.

"I saw it on the news and knew it was your shop. It's all gone, ain't it?" he moaned.

"I'm afraid so, Bubba."

He nodded slowly. The look on his face was of extreme heartbreak and he started tearing up. "Have you got anything to drink?"

I went inside and poured a large glass of iced tea but didn't immediately go back outside. In addition to the ten thousand my client had paid me, I had another few thousand safely tucked away in a hidden floor safe. It was for emergencies, and I guess this counted. I opened the safe and counted out two thousand. I peeked out the window to see that he had composed himself before walking back outside. I handed him a glass of tea and the money. He looked at in surprise.

"Reimbursement for the car," I said. "Whoever did this is someone who has a grudge against me, not you. There's no need for you to suffer for it as well."

He eyed the money. "Are you sure? I mean, the wife is going to be happy, but I don't want to impose on you like this."

"I'm sure."

He eyed the money a moment longer before folding it in half and pocketing it.

"I sure appreciate it. To be honest, money was going to be a little tight this month. Now my wife won't have anything to nag me about. Are you going to rebuild the shop?"

"Yeah, eventually. Once all this gets sorted out," I replied.

"Can I help?" he asked.

I looked at him in surprise. He clarified. "Well, I would kind of like to be paid a little bit. I need to do some kind of side work to help with the bills, and besides, maybe I can find another car for us to partner up on and we'll need a good shop to restore it."

He gave a hopeful grin, which made the day a little better.

"I can do that," I said.

I was fatigued but I knew I was not going to be able to sleep yet. And besides, I knew as soon as I closed my eyes, my phone would ring. Sure enough, as soon as that thought passed through my brain, it began ringing. First was the insurance agent, a nasally sounding lady who said she'd send their claims adjustor out right away.

Next was Percy. He took the news stoically. He was not the type of person to go into a tirade, but I imagined he was stewing inside.

"There's no need to cut your trip short," I said.

"Actually, we're planning on coming back in the morning," he said.

"The house smells like smoke. Tell Anna everything will need to be washed, maybe more than once."

To my surprise, Anna got on the phone.

"Are you and Tommy Boy okay?" she asked.

"Yeah, I was out of town when it happened and Tommy Boy was safe in the house," I said and hesitated a moment. "Are you okay? I feel like you're upset with me about something."

"I'm going to move in with Percy," she suddenly said.

"Oh, yeah? That's great. You two make a good couple," I said.

"That's not what you said at the party," she huffed.

So, that's what had her upset. My drunk ass made some kind of flippant remark that hurt her feelings. I probably thought I was being humorous, but the opposite happened. Stupid of me. I wanted to ask what I said, but then thought maybe I should leave it alone, let it die.

"I'm not making any excuses, but with all those shots Marti was feeding me, I was three sheets in the wind before I knew it. If I said something hurtful, I sincerely apologize."

"It's okay," she said after a long moment.

"I hope so," I said. "Not only are you my partner, but I also consider you my friend and I would not intentionally do anything to hurt you."

"Percy and I are your friends too," she said.

"I hope so."

I gave them the standard have a safe trip back offering before hanging up. My grumbling stomach reminded me that I'd not eaten since yesterday evening. I fixed a sandwich and ate slowly as I stared out the kitchen window at the destruction. My shop was like my second home. Sometimes, I'd hang out in there doing mostly nothing. It was a comfort zone for me.

I didn't know how long before I could rebuild, but I was not going to look at the mess any longer than necessary. I got on the internet, found a waste disposal service, and ordered a construction debris box to be delivered. I was going to start cleaning up as soon as possible.

"You're not going to beat me," I muttered to whoever it was that set the fire.

I found Tommy Boy hiding in my closet. I could tell he was upset, and it took some coaxing to get him to come out. After petting him for a few minutes he seemed better and followed me to the kitchen where I fed him.

I began doing laundry, thinking, and muttering to myself. My thoughts were singular and focused on one topic only – who set the fire. I gave no thought whatsoever to the desecration of both graves and the mysterious fricking artifact. I didn't care about that. I did, however, wonder if my client was the arsonist. If he was, that begged the next question; why? Why would he have set my garage on fire? There was no logical answer, at least none that I was aware of.

I tentatively ruled him out. For the moment. I was convinced whoever did it was the same person who had been following me and had put the tracking devices on my car. The more I thought about it, the more I was convinced the person in the green Camaro was responsible for everything.

If, and when, I found that person, there was going to be hell to pay.

# CHAPTER 21

I hardly remembered going to bed. I think it was right after I had put on a clean pair of sheets, but I got a good night's sleep and was up promptly at six. I got cleaned up and was in a good mood, until I looked out the kitchen window. I emitted a deep sigh and caught Tommy Boy sitting by his food bowl, staring expectantly.

"Alright, buddy," I said and fixed him breakfast.

My phone began ringing as I was eating a cinnamon flavored bagel with a pot of Black Rifle coffee. The blend was called Murdered Out. It contained a lot of caffeine, and I had the feeling I was going to need it. I set up a meeting time with the claims adjustor and was standing outside wallowing in misery as I eyed the damage. It didn't look any better from yesterday. I was having a conversation with myself when Detective Jay Sansing called.

"Are you still in New Orleans?" he asked.

"Nope. I'm home. What do you need?" I asked.

"I'll be over there in a few minutes," he replied and hung up before I could respond.

"That's damned weird," I muttered.

I was immediately suspicious. If he needed something or had a question, he could have said it over the phone. The caffeine was doing its job and it only took a couple of seconds for my brain to analyze the phone call and figure out what he was up to. I quickly called Ronald. He was groggy from sleep.

"Alright, buddy, wake up. I'm going to need your help. I'm fairly certain I'm about to have a search warrant served on me."

"What? Why?"

"It has to be something to do with the murder of the grave robbers," I said. "Or it could be something else entirely. Whatever it is, it's going to happen soon. Probably within the next thirty minutes."

I heard him gasp, but he recovered quickly. "Okay, I'll get the cameras on live feed and turn the sound on. You need to activate Broken Arrow on both your phone and laptop. Do you remember that app?"

I did. It was a self-destruct program that Ronald had installed after a similar situation several months ago in which I was beaten and arrested by the SWAT team. "Yep, I'll turn them both on right now."

"Good. I'll activate the code from my end, if needed," he said.

"Thanks, Ronald. Monitor the cameras. I could be totally wrong about this, but I'll give the word if necessary."

"I've got you online now," he said.

"Alright. I've got a few things to do before they get here, and I don't have much time."

I hung up and got to work. It only took a minute to ensure my phone and laptop were synced up. The ultra-strong coffee had me going at full speed. I grabbed some files and other paperwork I didn't want them to have access to, along with some other items, stuffed it all in my detective's kit, and hurried through the woods to my neighbor's house. Buford was in the back yard watering his rose bushes and stared at me in bemusement as I walked up. I explained and dropped the bag in his garage before jogging back through the woods. I'd managed to get back to my house and was sitting in a lawn chair as the police vehicles appeared in my driveway.

I waved at the surveillance camera. "Here they come. This definitely isn't a social call. Go ahead and activate it."

I glanced at my phone as they sped down my driveway. The self-destruct application began doing its job. I smiled in satisfaction. All of my files were synced up to one of Ronald's VPN servers, so I wasn't going to lose any data. But they wouldn't know that.

There were four cars, two unmarked, two marked. The driver of the lead patrol car was going fast. He waited until the last second before slamming on his brakes and jerking his steering wheel, causing his car to slide sideways. He jumped out with his duty weapon drawn and pointed at me. I'm sure he thought he looked cool and macho.

"Get your ass on the ground!" he shouted.

The other patrol officer had also jumped out of his cruiser during this exchange. Not wanting to be left out of the action, he drew his respective duty weapon and began shouting his own orders. "Get your hands up!"

It was all being recorded, so I slowly stood, letting my phone drop to the ground. "You two idiots need to make up your mind. Do you want my hands in the air or do you want me to get my ass on the ground?"

They stood there, squared off with me, and continued shouting their conflicting orders. I raised my hands. One of them approached and looked like he was going to throw me to the ground. He holstered his weapon and grabbed me in a one-armed takedown move when Jay was suddenly by my side. He was wearing his usual ensemble, a starched light blue button-down shirt, blue paisley tie, and slate gray slacks. His weapon and badge were fastened to a black leather belt, which matched his polished black shoes. I wouldn't say it out loud, but he had a professional look to him.

"What the hell are you doing, Officer?" he demanded.

"We're taking down an armed felon!" the officer replied with a look of irritation for Jay interfering with him. He started to grab me again, but Jay grabbed his arm.

"Stand down! Who in the hell told you this man is an armed felon?"

Both officers now appeared confused. One of them pointed to the other detective, who was only now getting out of her car. Detective Linda Kettleworth. She was wearing a jade green pants suit that was not complimentary to her ample figure. I guess what stood out to me more than anything was the Clint Eastwood style shoulder holster, which was against department regulations and had been for several years. Department policy required belt holsters, but fat people didn't like them.

"Armed felon, huh? What do you think about that, Detective?" I asked Jay.

I could see the consternation in his expression, but he took a deep breath and got himself under control. "Officers, holster your weapons." When they hesitated, he shouted at them. "Now, damn it!"

They slowly did so. Jay waited until Kettleworth came closer before angrily speaking. "Why did you tell these two officers we're arresting an armed felon?"

Kettleworth smirked. "Oh, they must have misunderstood me. I told them he had a murder arrest on his record and was known to be armed. Both are true, as you know."

Jay gritted his teeth and then faced the two uniformed men. "Officers, you have been duped. We are merely executing a search warrant. There is no arrest warrant outstanding for Mister Ironcutter. If you'll remember, we had a briefing before leaving the office, and none of this was discussed."

One of the officers scoffed. "Yeah, no biggie."

"What do you mean by that?" Jay demanded. "Let me tell you what I just witnessed. I witnessed two officers point loaded weapons at an innocent civilian, and you were about to put your hands on him and make an illegal arrest. Do you know what happened the last time some officers did the same thing to this man? Two of them lost their jobs and Mister Ironcutter successfully sued the police department for a large amount of money."

Jay paused to take a breath. I was going to point out that my previous charges had been expunged, but Kettleworth decided she needed to chime in.

"This is a waste of time. We have a search warrant to execute."

Jay started to say something, but I interrupted. "What is this search warrant all about?"

Jay faced me. "It has to do with Officer Richard Tomey."

"What about him?" I asked.

"He's been murdered."

# CHAPTER 22

I stared at Jay, half expecting him to start laughing, but I knew he wouldn't joke about something like that. "Murdered? What happened?"

"When he didn't show up for roll call, his sergeant went to his house and found him. That was two days ago. We've managed to keep it quiet, but the chief held a press conference this morning."

"Alright, I can understand that. So, why am I considered a suspect and what kind of evidence do you think you can discover?"

"We'll discuss all of that down at headquarters, Ironcutter," Kettleworth said.

"I might consider it at another time, but not today. As you can see, I have my hands full with an arson case."

"You don't have a choice, Ironcutter," she rejoined.

I turned to Jay. "Perhaps I heard incorrectly when you said there is no arrest warrant. Is there a warrant for my arrest, Detective?"

"There might be," Kettleworth chimed.

Jay shook his head. "There is no warrant for your arrest, Thomas." He turned to Kettleworth. "Linda, Thomas knows as much about the law and criminal procedure as we do. Perhaps even more. You're not helping the situation by playing games."

She glared at the two of us before focusing on the patrol officers and shaking her head like she was dealing with incompetent fools. She reminded me of a hypothetical assertion known as the Dunning-Kruger effect. Simply put, stupid people often do not realize how stupid they are. Jay watched her actions without comment and focused again on me.

"As you well know, his murder is our number one priority. And the reason we are here is because we believe there is a nexus between his murder and the double murder of the two grave robbers."

"So, in a continuation of this theme, my client is a suspect, and you believe I have information or evidence linking him to the murders."

Jay held his hands out in silent agreement of my reasoning.

"I've already told you everything I know about the man. I do not have any evidence or information that would indicate otherwise."

"Nevertheless, it is an avenue of investigation that we must explore," he said. "If I may add, there is also a theory that has been put forth suggesting you are colluding with your client. A lack of evidence will dispel that theory, wouldn't you agree?"

"Am I going to get to see this search warrant?" I asked.

Kettleworth was holding some papers in her hand, which I assumed was the search warrant. She looked down at them before offering them with an outstretched arm. As I reached out for them, she opened her hand and let them drop to the ground.

"Oops," she said with a smirk. One of the uniformed officers chuckled.

I picked them up and began reading. It was a valid warrant, signed by a judge and dated today, so they'd covered themselves. I read most of the affidavit before Kettleworth yanked the papers out of my hand.

"Alright, that's enough. You'll get your copy when we're through here." She looked down and spotted my phone lying on the ground. "Ah, the first piece of evidence." She reached down and picked it up. Looking at me, she gave another smirk.

"You might get it back, one day, maybe. Well then, let's get started." She motioned to the two uniformed officers. They dutifully followed her through the back door of my house. Jay pointed at the remains of the garage.

"I want to ask you about this arson," he said.

"You're just now asking about it?"

"I only heard about it this morning; I'm sure it's pretty devastating to you."

"That's an understatement," I replied.

"Is it in any way related to Tomey's murder, or the murder of the grave robbers?"

"Are you asking me if my client is the person who set my garage on fire? I don't think so, but it's certainly possible. I'll ask him if I ever speak to him again. I'm sure he'll give me an honest answer." If he caught my sarcasm, it didn't show. "How long are you assholes going to be here?"

"We'll have to be thorough," he said.

"You're not going to find anything."

Before he could respond, there was a shout from within my house.

"Ironcutter!" Detective Kettleworth came storming out of my house carrying my laptop. She waddled over to us as quickly as her obesity and ill-fitting shoes allowed her to and held out my laptop as if it were diseased.

"What the hell is wrong with your computer?" she demanded.

I glanced at the screen. It was lit up in a blur of pixelated snow.

"Oh my," I lamented.

Jay stared at the screen for only a moment before realizing what was happening.

"Oh shit," he muttered.

"Oh shit? What do you mean, oh shit?" Kettleworth demanded.

The look on Jay's face was priceless. "Thomas, this was totally unnecessary."

I didn't respond. Kettleworth stared at him, then at me, then back at him. "What did he do?"

"What did you do, activate some type of self-destruct program?" he accused.

I stared back in mock innocence. "Whatever do you mean?"

Detective Linda Gayle Kettleworth tried desperately to make all fifty-seven of her IQ points figure out what Jay was referring to but failed to do so.

"What do you mean?" she asked.

"It would appear that every piece of data on this computer has been eradicated. Something tells me even the forensics techs won't be able to recover anything."

He was right.

Low-IQ Linda stared in incredulity. "You mean he's destroyed evidence?"

"It appears so."

Her features turned ugly, and she pointed her finger at me. "I'm going to have you arrested for tampering with evidence."

I glanced over at Jay. "You want to explain, or should I?"

He let out a sigh. "Yes, we could charge him, but it'd never stick in court. His attorneys would rip us to shreds and then he'd sue again."

"You can count on it," I said.

She pointed at the computer. "That didn't happen by itself. He had to have done it."

"Well, I have a confession to make." Both of them looked at me in surprise, probably thinking I was going to admit to the murder. "You see, lately I've developed a proclivity of viewing inappropriate online content. What can I say? I'm a sucker for midget porn." I gestured at the screen. "I guess I picked up a nasty computer virus."

Kettleworth frowned in confusion. Jay shook his head in exasperation. They'd find out later that my phone was in the same condition, but it was going to be my secret for now. A car coming down the driveway distracted us. I gestured at it.

"That should be the claims adjustor for the insurance company. You two go ahead and waste your time looking for fictitious evidence and then get the hell out of here. I've got other things to do."

"Alright, Thomas. We'll talk more later," Jay said and guided his dumbass partner back inside my house.

The claims adjustor was an affable man in his thirties. He seemed indifferent about the police searching my house and said he wanted to take some photographs. He then asked if there was an ongoing investigation. I gave him the name and number of the arson investigator, which he dutifully jotted down.

"Well, it looks like a total loss. I'm going to put in the report that you need a new roof on your house as well," he said.

"I appreciate that."

"Are you going to rebuild?" he asked.

"I believe I will, yes."

He gave a thoughtful nod. "If you do and you want us to be your insurance provider, you'll have to install a fire-retardant system. I'll email you some documents that have the requirements."

"If I rebuild, I'd like to get started on it as soon as possible. When can I expect a check?" I asked.

"The first thing I have to do is call this arson investigator and have him confirm you are not a suspect. Then, the home office will decide on a number. I'll present it to you, and between me and you, they'll lowball you. Get a number in your head and be ready to make a counter proposal."

"I understand and I appreciate the advice," I said.

He smiled. "Just don't tell anyone I told you that."

He asked a few more questions before finishing up and leaving. I was going to fix myself a glass of tea but discovered my doors locked. It was a petty act. My travel humidor was in my Ford. I grabbed myself a cigar and sat under a shade tree, stewing over my run of misfortune. After an hour, Jay came outside and asked for the key fob to the Ford. He searched it thoroughly and found nothing. He walked over and stood before me. I stared at him before eyeing one of the uniforms go out to the car and retrieving a cardboard box. I frowned in puzzlement.

"What the hell are you guys taking?" I asked.

"We'll be seizing your firearms for ballistics testing," he said.

"That's already been done once. The information is on file," I replied.

"We'll have to do it again. If you were in my spot, you'd do the same, right? Are they all here?"

"Of course, they are." It was a lie, and he probably knew it, but I wasn't concerned. I wouldn't admit it, but he was right about retesting the weapons. That's what I would have done. "How much longer?"

"We're almost finished. Maybe another hour. We've been directed to spray your home, clothing, and shoes with Luminol." He pointed down at my shoes. "Including those. I think we can do without the clothing you're wearing."

I didn't argue, pulled my shoes off, and handed them to him. They were looking for blood, so I assumed Tomey's crime scene must have been messy. It was a prudent measure. Luminol was a presumptive test for blood and could even react on bloodstains that'd been present for a long period of time and weren't visible to the naked eye. If they found even a hint of a bloodstain on anything, they'd swab it for purposes of a DNA analysis. I watched as Kettleworth walked out to my Ford and began spraying the interior. She then stood and waited. I would have told her that it needed to be dark in order to see any reaction but kept it to myself. After a moment she shut the door and walked back inside.

"How was he killed?" I asked.

Jay frowned. "I'm sorry, Thomas, there's a lot of details of the murder I cannot discuss right now."

I understood, but I didn't like it. "Okay, if you say so."

"Thank you for understanding."

I gestured around. "This is a waste of your time and resources. I hope you're smart enough to know that."

"I would normally agree with you, Thomas, but to be honest, the only hint of a motive or possible suspect lies with your client and his search for this alleged artifact."

"Yeah, well, when someone infers there might be bloodstains from Tomey on my shoes or clothing, that means someone is suggesting I was at the crime scene, and that is a suspicion derived from not one scintilla of actual evidence. I know what's going on. This harebrained idea has the stench of Poston on it."

Jay shrugged but did not say anything. Kettleworth soon walked out and joined us. Jay handed over the shoes.

"Anything you want to tell us, Ironcutter? You should talk to us now. You know if we find a trace of blood, you're going to jail for murder."

I scoffed. "That's not how it works. You should probably get with a real detective and have them explain it to you."

Her face reddened and turned ugly, or should I say uglier. "You won't be such a smartass when you're locked up with gangbangers that decide to take their turns with you."

"You don't even realize what a fool you sound like," I said.

"You think this whole thing is a joke, don't you," she accused.

"I think a lot of things. I think the murder of Richard Tomey is a tragedy. Thinking you are a competent, professional detective is the joke."

Her face reddened even more. She stared balefully. "I'm more of a detective than you ever were. You resigned under a cloud, remember?"

"Oh, I remember. I remember it all," I said. "I remember how a couple of corrupt cops tried to frame me for murder. I remember how I made them look like fools. And I'll remember this."

"Is that a threat, Ironcutter?" she said.

"You bet your big fat ass it is."

I thought she was going to explode, literally. She even took a step toward me, like she was going to attack me. I was going to let her. Jay intervened, preventing what would have been a huge payday for me. He took her by the elbow and led her back inside my house, where they remained for another hour.

When they walked back out, they walked directly toward me. I could tell that Kettleworth had regained her composure. Jay probably had a long talk with her. She marched up and summarily dropped papers at my feet.

"There's your copy of the search warrant," she said with a smile.

"Alright, Thomas. We're finished," Jay said. He started to turn away but stopped as if he had a sudden thought. It was a common tactic used by a TV show character called Columbo.

"Oh, by the way. Did I understand correctly you were in New Orleans the past couple of days?"

"I was in New Orleans at the time of Richard's murder," I said.

"Can you prove that?" Kettleworth asked.

"I can if I have to, and at the moment I don't have to," I said.

She pointed a finger at me. "Go ahead and keep acting like this is all a big joke, but you've tangled with the wrong detective this time," she warned.

"Oh dear. You actually think you're a detective."

She thought she was giving me the death stare, but it only made her look comical. "You know, Ironcutter, you think you're clever. But all you've done today is confirm you're a bona fide suspect in Tomey's murder."

"You're wrong, but I suspect that's a normal way of life for you. Alright, I'm tired of this nonsense. If you're done, I imagine you need to get back to the office." I made a shooing motion with my hand. "Go in haste."

Linda continued to scowl. Jay gave a perfunctory nod and turned to the patrol officers.

"Head on back to headquarters. We'll be there shortly."

The two patrol officers needed no further prompting, got in their cars, and sped off. The two detectives were close behind. Kettleworth gave me one last nasty sneer before backing into my yard and turning around.

After they left, I picked up the search warrant and read the list of seized items. I then walked inside and looked around. I grew angrier with every step. My belongings were thrown everywhere. My clothes were scattered, all my books were pulled off the shelves and thrown onto the floor, my chair was turned over, and generally everything was trashed.

Their pièce de resistance of their trespass upon my property were my hats. Four Stetson brand fedoras. I'd had them for years and they fit my head perfectly. If I was not wearing one of them, they lived on the top shelf in the coat closet. Now, they were lying on the floor, and it was obvious someone had stomped on them.

I glanced up at one of my cameras. I hoped like hell all this had been recorded. When I spotted the kitchen camera, my eyes narrowed. It had been messed with. Standing on a kitchen chair, I could see where somebody had disabled it.

I had a few hand tools in a drawer and used them to fix the camera. After, I found a piece of notebook paper and wrote a message to Ronald and held it in front of the camera for a minute. It said I was fine, I had no phone, and to come by first thing in the morning.

I caught a feint odor of the Luminol, causing me to wonder how much they'd used. I suddenly thought of Tommy Boy. I found him in the hallway closet. As soon as I opened the door, he started in on me.

"I'm sorry, buddy. Rest assured they're going to pay for this."

I placated him with a can of food and watched him eat for a minute before heading into my room and pulling all the bedding off. My sheets were damp and had a chemical smell. I put them in the wash and then worked on my books. I had them all put back in their proper order on the shelves when the washer chimed. The wet bedding went into the dryer and the first load of clothes went into the wash. Wash, dry, repeat. It was going to take all night.

For some reason, they also dumped the kitchen drawers, scattering the utensils on the floor. Whatever the dishwasher didn't hold went into the sink. I lost track of time until I glanced out the window and realized it was dark out. I decided to take a break and fixed myself a tumbler of Scotch. Throwing in an ice-cold whiskey rock, I walked outside.

Seating myself on the front porch, I took a swallow and rocked slowly, trying to decompress while contemplating this quagmire I was in. Had they stepped over the line? Yes. Could I sue them for it? In other words, did I have a cause of action? That was the question. The probable cause for the warrant was thin, but good enough for a judge to sign it. But the terms of the settlement of my lawsuit specified there would be no retaliation of any kind. Could their actions be considered retaliatory? I'd call William and discuss it with him tomorrow.

I sipped my Scotch and started thinking about that damned gypsy curse. The amriya. When the gypsy girl, Kalina was her name, had told me about it, I shrugged it off as nonsense, but now it didn't seem so preposterous anymore. And if things couldn't have gotten worse, a man suddenly appeared out of the shadows in my front yard, and he didn't look friendly.

# CHAPTER 23

I jumped to my feet. Another figure emerged, and then a third. They walked closer and the porch light finally lit them up. They were all rough looking men, and then I realized they were wearing denim cuts.

Bikers. Outlaw bikers.

"Good evening, gentlemen," I said and took a small step backwards.

I was no stranger to fighting, but three on one was tough odds, and these were tough looking dudes. At any other time, I would have introduced them to my Springfield, which was an excellent equalizer.

But tonight, thanks to Sansing and Kettleworth, I was unarmed. I started talking as I thought out my possible options.

"What brings you men out tonight?" I asked in as friendly a tone as I could muster.

"Your name's Ironcutter, isn't it?" the first one asked, although it wasn't a question, more of a confirmation.

"Yeah, that's right," I said.

"We're here to talk to you about Flaky," he said.

He was the one who walked out first, presumably the leader of this trio of shitheads. He was of average height, late thirties, and wearing a beard that'd not been trimmed since puberty. There was a little musculature in his arms, more like a working man rather than a weightlifter or martial artist, but still, I didn't underestimate him.

"What about him?" I asked.

"You and he are buddies, right?"

"Yeah, that's right," I said.

"You're going to tell us all about him," he said.

"He's currently at the Rutherford County Jail, facing a murder charge."

One of the other men spoke up. "Yeah, he killed one of our brothers."

He spoke in kind of a growl. He was a big dude, almost as big as Bull. Mid-thirties, same kind of beard as his buddy, but definitely more meat on him. Mostly fat though. The third guy was short and wiry. He looked like he needed a fix.

If I were armed, I would've already given them an ultimatum, but they had me at a disadvantage. I kept talking, hoping the situation would resolve itself, but they kept moving closer and it didn't seem likely this was going to be resolved peacefully. Nevertheless, I kept talking.

"Yeah, Turk, right? Which club are you men?"

"Satan's Dogs," the leader said with a smirk.

"Oh, yeah, I've heard of you guys." I'd never heard of them. "Are you and the Baroques affiliated?"

The big one spat on the ground. The leader spoke.

"I wouldn't say that. In fact, since they killed one of our brothers, you might say we're enemies at the moment. You know what that means? It means you're our enemy."

"Yeah, well, in my world I'd actually have to do something bad to a person to become their enemy. I've not done that. Not yet anyway. You don't want me as an enemy. Now, tell me what the hell you boys want." I suddenly thought of something. "Wait a minute. Are you gentlemen responsible for burning down my shop?"

The leader frowned, and then slowly shook his head. "It wasn't us, bud. Sounds like you have more enemies out there than us."

I believed him. I mean, why would they go to the trouble and then deny doing it?

"Alright, I believe you. As far as Flaky goes, I don't know anything about his involvement with Turk's murder."

The leader spat. "Do you think we should take your word for it?"

"At the moment, all I have is my word. It'll have to do," I said. It wasn't going to placate them, and I knew it.

The leader leered at me. "I'll tell you what. The four of us are going to go in your house and have a nice long conversation. You're going to tell us all about Flaky and the Baroques."

"And if you tell us everything, we won't hurt you too bad," the big one said with his own leering grin.

In fact, all three were grinning now. It was like a pack of hyenas had their prey cornered and they were excited about the anticipated outcome. It didn't take long to size things up. These boys were here to get information they believed I had, and they intended to hurt me to get it. The way I saw it, I could try to run, or I could fight. I was already in a foul mood. My cars were toast and my former co-workers had once again treated me like shit. And now these knuckleheads had come to my home, uninvited, and were threatening to hurt me.

"Well, boys, this sounds serious," I said as I walked to the edge of my porch.

The big guy started making more threats as I bent my knees slightly. Their leader sensed, a little too late, what I was going to do. His eyes lit up in surprise as I sprung off the porch toward him and landed a solid right hook to his jaw. His head snapped around and he slunk to the ground like a sack of wet flour.

I felt a hard blow to my head, slightly above my ear. I saw stars and stumbled. The big man took another swing as I got my footing. I managed to duck the blow and put a solid right into his gut. He grunted and I felt spittle hit my forehead. I followed up with a left right combo to his face. He took both punches and grunted again. I busted his lower lip open, but he didn't go down. I put another right hook on his big head, and I thought I saw his knees wobble.

I was beginning to believe I might have a chance, but that third guy sprang into action. He was a cagey little shit. Instead of taking me head on, he dove at my legs and wrapped his arms around them. I was about to deliver a hammer blow to the back of his neck, but the big one was not out of the fight. I sensed movement and looked up to see a meaty fist coming at me. It caught me square in the nose before I could react.

There are grown men in the world who have never been punched in the nose. I'm not talking about a bitch slap; I'm talking about a rock-hard punch that lands solidly. The first time hurts like hell and you're likely to see Tweety Bird flying around before going down in a heap. I'd taken some solid hits in the nose over the years. I was sixteen the first time it was broken, and it was my father who did it.

The big man succeeded in breaking it again. It hurt, it had me addled, and then the little guy punched me in the nads. I fell to the ground as I desperately tried to protect my groin. I heard a chuckle and looked up. The big guy was grinning sadistically. He needed a dentist. I was going to tell him at the first opportunity. He had squared up and tried to kick me in the face. I dodged it, and even managed to get a good punch on the little guy at the same time. He brought his foot back for another kick when suddenly a gunshot pierced the night air.

# CHAPTER 24

The big man grabbed his left butt cheek and howled in pain. The smaller biker still had my legs wrapped up and was still giving me painful punches. Big boy was hopping up and down, cursing loudly, and had momentarily forgotten about me. I took the opportunity to grab the little guy by his long stringy hair and pulled his head back. I then pummeled his face until I felt his grip slacken. I pushed him off, launched a knee into his chin, and scrambled backward in a crawl until I could get on my feet. I then ran. No, that's not accurate. I then stumbled into the darkness for several yards before taking cover behind a tree.

The big man was grimacing in pain. He looked like a constipated Eskimo. He stared menacingly toward the general direction of the gunshot. "Who's the bastard that shot me? Show yourself!"

"You boys better get the hell out of here before you get yourselves killed," I warned. The truth was, I had no idea who had shot the big man. For all I knew, they were trying to shoot me and missed. Even so, I played it up.

"One word from me and you're all dead men," I growled.

The first man, the apparent leader, was sitting up now, holding his jaw. The little man was still conscious, but he was lying on the ground moaning in pain. I was growing impatient with them.

"Yo, big man," I called out.

He scowled into the dark in my direction. "Yeah, what?"

"You're wasting your time here. I don't know anything about Turk's murder, and that's the damned truth. Now get your friends on their feet and get going. If you don't get to an emergency room soon, you're going to have a bad time. You might even bleed out and die."

The big man was still glaring at me, and for a moment I thought he was crazy enough to come charging after me, but their leader was on his feet now.

"Help me with Zango," he directed. Big boy obeyed and the two men helped their friend Zango to his feet. They each grabbed an arm and began helping him walk down the drive. After a couple of steps, he stopped and turned.

"You got the better of us, I'll admit that." He took a moment to spit blood out of his mouth before continuing. "But this ain't over."

"Damn right," the big one said.

"It better be, or else next time I won't be so nice," I warned.

The leader stared toward me, grunted, and spat again before the three of them walked down my drive toward the road. I stayed behind the tree and waited, although I wasn't sure exactly what I was waiting for and had no idea how long I was going to stay there. I was feeling both dumb and impotent. The cops had taken all my firearms, but then I remembered I had a backup handgun, a Glock model G43X, in one of my detective's kits.

I worked my way through the dark and the trees and headed to Buford's house. He was certainly already in bed, and it was possible he'd think I was an intruder and shoot me, but I had to take a chance. When I knocked on the door, his dog began barking.

"Buford, it's Thomas!" I yelled. After a few seconds, a light came on. It took him a minute or two before he came to the door, and he was not happy.

"What the hell?" he proclaimed and then stared me up and down. "Is that your blood all over you?"

I gave him a synopsis of everything that'd happened and asked to retrieve my two kits. He grumbled and complained about being awakened so late at night, but he acquiesced and opened his garage door. Thanking him profusely, I retrieved the Glock, checked its load, and proceeded back to my house. When I emerged from the woods, I saw a police car sitting in my drive.

"Great," I muttered.

I set my bags and gun down behind a tree and walked out into the light. The first officer I saw was a young man in his twenties who looked physically fit and wearing a high-and-tight haircut. There was another officer with him, and I was surprised to see that it was Officer Severns. When she saw me, her jaw dropped open in surprise. She walked up and used her tac-light to look me up and down. I couldn't see my face, but the front of my shirt was soaked in blood.

"What happened to you?" she asked.

"After the search warrant, three men came by and attacked me."

"Where are they now?" she asked.

"Long gone. What brings you guys here?"

"Dispatch received an anonymous call," the male officer said. I glanced at his name tag. It identified him as Clark. Both had the black band across their badges, signifying their mourning of the death of Officer Tomey.

"Wait," Abby exclaimed. "What search warrant?"

"There are a few detectives in the department who believe I am involved in the death of Tomey."

"Are you?" Officer Clark asked.

I fixed him with a cold stare and spat blood on the ground in front of him. "That's an incredibly stupid question." I waited for him to make another comment, but he broke eye contact and turned to Abby.

"Take a report and let's get out of here," he directed and walked back to the patrol car. Abby watched him until he got in and slammed the door shut and got on his cell phone.

"Are you on evening shift now?" I asked her.

"Yeah, after Tomey's murder, they moved me," she said. "You look pretty banged up. I think you need to go to the hospital."

"I might go in the morning. It depends on how I feel when I wake up," I said.

It was probably prudent that I get some medical care, but the first thing I intended to do in the morning was call the Goldmans and get something done. Abby continued to stare me up and down. She then pursed her lips and shook her head at my obstinacy.

"Alright, I think you should but if you're going to be stubborn, the least I can do is take an incident report," she said.

I started to tell her not to worry about it. After all, I wasn't going to prosecute, but then I thought about how I was treated during the search warrant and how the report might add some leverage if this escalated into another lawsuit.

"Alright, let's do that," I said.

"Give me a minute and I'll go get the laptop," she said.

"I'll be in the kitchen."

She came inside a minute later and looked around at the calamity with a frown.

"Are you normally this messy?" she asked.

"This is the aftermath of your co-workers trashing the place looking for mysterious evidence that would somehow link me to Tomey's murder."

She continued looking around a minute longer before fixing me with a stare. I guess she was trying to determine if I really did have something to do with the death of her former training officer.

"I'd say your nose is broken," she remarked.

"Yeah, most likely. It's not the first time it's been broken."

"I can see that. It also looks like you have a baseball growing on the side of your head."

"Yeah, I caught a punch there too."

"You might have a concussion," she surmised.

I tried to smile. "I'm too hardheaded to have a concussion. A little ice will help."

"Are you in pain?"

"A little bit." That was an understatement. In addition to my head and nose, my family jewels were throbbing unmercifully. I resisted the urge to reach down and rub myself.

Without being asked, I pulled my license out of my wallet and handed it to her. She thanked me and used the info on it to fill in the blanks on the report. Completing that task, she asked for me to give her the details of the attack and a description of the three suspects. I provided a narrative of the events, but I might've added that one of them had a handgun and apparently shot his friend in the ass by accident. A hint of a smile crossed her face, but she had no comment and finished the report. She then handed me a card with various information, including the incident number of the report.

"I guess the only other question I have is who called 911?" she asked and pointed around. "I mean, your house is a little isolated, so it wasn't like a neighbor saw something."

"Correct on all counts and I have no idea who might've called. Perhaps it was someone driving by, and they heard the gunshot."

She nodded, not buying it but not pushing it. It seemed like she had something to say, thought better of it, and stood.

"Do you feel safe staying here alone?" she asked.

I offered another smile. "I'll be fine."

She nodded, as if nodding to a child. She probably thought, given my current state, that I was incapable of caring for myself. Honestly, I was tempted to invite her to stay and protect me, but I had no business making a pass at a woman half my age. Besides, even if she were willing, I wasn't up for it.

"Let me ask you something. Do you know what happened to Tomey?" I asked.

"We're not supposed to talk about it," she said, paused, and seemed to reach an internal decision.

"The rumor is, he was tied up and tortured, but other than that, I don't know anything. The autopsy showed he died of a heart attack, presumably as a result of the torture."

I frowned. The details left me with even more questions, but she did not know anything else.

"You should clean yourself up and get a good night's rest," she suggested.

"Yeah, I intend to. And, for the record, I had nothing to do with Tomey's murder. I hope you believe that."

She hesitated a moment longer, and then nodded curtly. "Okay, try to get some sleep."

"I will. Be safe," I replied.

I watched their taillights disappear before hustling back to where I dropped my kits and handgun. While she may have had good reason to believe I was helpless, I liked to believe I had held my own against the three bikers. Sure, they would have beaten me down if not for the big one getting shot, but all three of them will be aching tomorrow, maybe not as much as me, but they'll know they'd been in a fight. Now I was armed, and if they came back, they'd be dead before they hit the ground.

I glanced at the clock on the stove. It was almost midnight. I got a zip-lock baggie, put some ice in it, and walked into the bathroom. I had blood all over me. I was about to strip and get in the shower when there was a soft knock at the front door.

"You've got to be kidding me," I growled and headed toward the door.

I held my Glock with one hand as I stood off to the side and opened the door with the other. To my surprise, Valkyrie was standing there.

# CHAPTER 25

"Hello."

"Yeah, hello. This is a surprise," I said.

She was wearing those designer jeans that have holes purposely cut in them and a black tee shirt. Her hair was still braided, but she wasn't wearing a hoodie or a hat tonight and I could see that her hair was a beautiful flaxen blonde. I had to admit, standing there in the glow of the light, she was rather pleasing to the eye. Her features were smooth, flawless.

"May I come inside?"

"Are you alone?" I asked.

She nodded. I held the door open for her. Before going inside, I looked out and saw a white Chevy Malibu. I'm sure it was a rental. I peered around to see if someone was lurking around. Shutting the door behind us, I turned the deadbolt and turned toward her. She faced me.

"I waited for the police to leave. Are they coming back?"

"I don't think so," I said.

"Are you alone?"

I made a head nod toward Tommy Boy.

"Just me and the cat," I said.

"Mentat said you have a woman for a roommate."

I grunted and held the baggie of ice against my nose. It hurt and I had no doubt I would have two black eyes in the morning. I shifted the bag to the knot on the side of my head.

"That would be Anna. She's on vacation with her boyfriend. And Mentat's real name is Ronald."

"Your nose needs moving," she said.

"Moving?"

"It is off."

"Do you mean it needs straightening?" I asked. She nodded. "Yeah, I was about to go into the bathroom and do that. It's going to hurt like hell, so if you hear me screaming, pay it no mind."

I walked into my bathroom and started by daintily rinsing some of the dried blood from my face and then prepared myself. Valkyrie walked in and watched as I put my hands on the sides of my nose, gritted my teeth, and pushed the bridge back into alignment. I grunted in pain when I did it, but at least I didn't scream.

The action caused my nose to start bleeding again. I shoved toilet tissue into each nostril and then turned the shower on.

"I need to get cleaned up," I said, hinting for her to give me some privacy.

"Get undressed, I will check you for other injuries."

I started to protest, but she repeated her demand. Sighing, I acquiesced and stripped to my skivvies. I happened to be wearing a fresh pair of Tommy Hilfiger's, so I wasn't too embarrassed, and tried to be subtle as I sucked my gut in. She looked me over carefully and then pulled my underwear down. If the sight of my manhood excited her, she hid it well.

"I saw the little man punch you here, no?"

"Yes, several times," I said, wondering what the hell she was going to do next.

She peered closely. "I do not see any swelling, are you in pain here?"

"If I wasn't, the little soldier would be saluting right now."

She looked up in confusion.

"Forget it, I'll be okay."

She made no comment and stared at my manhood a second or two longer before standing. I quickly pulled my drawers up.

"You have bumps and scrapes, but I do not see any serious injuries. You will have soreness and bruising, especially there," she said, pointing south. "It could have been worse. It is a good thing I decided to visit, no?"

Understanding dawned on me. "Wait a minute. You're the one who shot the big guy?"

"Yes, they would have hurt you badly if I did not," she said.

"Well, um, thank you. Where is your gun?"

She pulled it out of the back of her waistband and held it for me to see. It was a compact 380 semiauto. She put it back before I could reach for it and gestured at the running shower. I wondered where she'd gotten it.

"Clean yourself. I will protect you," she said.

I started to laugh before realizing she was being serious. "Alright, if you don't mind, wait for me out in the den, unless you're going to get in with me."

She eyed me a moment and a hint of a smile formed before she walked out of the bathroom, closing the door behind her.

By the time I finished showering, I was starting to ache all over. I dressed in a tee shirt and a pair of loose-fitting Nike gym shorts before walking into the den. Valkyrie was sitting on the couch with Tommy

Boy on the opposite end, staring at her. I went to the kitchen and retrieved my glass of Scotch before joining her in the den.

"I have questions," I said.

"My real name is Eva Abramovich, and I am from Ukraine," she said.

"Well, that answers two of my questions, Eva from Ukraine, but it seems rather odd to me that you travelled all the way from Ukraine to Tennessee simply to hand off a couple of thumb drives. Help me understand if you don't mind."

She stared evenly at me. "There is another reason for me being here."

"I'd love to hear why," I replied.

Eva said nothing for a moment. I could see her expression tighten, as if engaged in a mental battle, and it took several seconds before she spoke.

"There is a man who has ruined my life. He is here now. At least, he was. That is why I am here. I want to find him."

"Okay, I can possibly help you with that. I'll need as much information about him that you have. A recent photo would also be helpful."

She shook her head slightly. "I can give you the information, but you do not need a photo. You have already met him."

I sat forward in my chair, causing my family jewels to shoot stabs of pain up into my guts, but I ignored it because I knew instantly who she was talking about. The mysterious Mister X.

"Tell me everything about him."

"What would you like to know?" she asked.

"Start by telling me his name."

"The name he is using is Mishka Abramovich, but I do not know if that is his real name. He has used many other names in the past."

"He uses aliases? Why?" I asked.

"I asked him once. He said it is the nature of his work but would not say what he meant by that."

"How do you know him?"

"I am married to him," she said quietly, and after a moment, explained. "I was a dumb teenage girl. I was poor and lived in a town full of poor people. My friends and I joined a dating website where pretty young girls are looking for marriage to rich older men. I was picked by Mishka."

The look on her face was heartbreaking. If I knew her better, and I didn't feel so rough, I would have gotten up and given her a hug.

"He is much older than me."

"How old?" I asked.

"I am not certain. At first, I was not interested in him, but he has a gift with words, and I must admit, I was excited that he had money. He said many wonderful things and made many promises. I thought, in time, I could learn to love him. He turned out to be a cold, abusive man."

She squeezed her eyes shut. "I do not know who he works for, but he is always travelling, doing jobs. He sent me to university to learn computers, but I am not allowed to work. I always had a love for running, so he allowed me to participate on the track team. That led to a spot on the Olympics."

"Is he part of the bank fraud scheme?" I asked.

She nodded. "He and three others. They claim to be cousins. They are all evil people."

"Do you think he killed those two men who robbed the grave?"

"It is possible," she answered.

"Do you know where he currently is?"

She shook her head. I sat down in my chair and spread my legs to help ease my discomfort. Even though Eva was an attractive woman, the aching in my groin precluded any sexual thoughts. I took the baggie of ice and gently placed it on my lap, not knowing if it'd help or not. I took in everything she said, wondering how it all affected me.

"Does he know you're here in Tennessee?" I asked.

"I do not think so."

"So, what's next for you?"

"I think I want to find out what he is doing here before I go back home."

I gave her a brief summation of my interaction with him, although I got the impression she already knew. I told her of the grave in Nashville, the murders of the two grave robbers, and the murder of Officer Tomey. I don't remember if I told her about New Orleans, as somewhere during all that I fell asleep.

# CHAPTER 26

When I awoke, the sun was coming up and I was in my easy chair with a blanket over my legs and Tommy Boy on my lap, sleeping contentedly. The bag of ice had melted and was lying on the floor. I picked the blanket up by the edges and gently lifted. Tommy Boy barely opened his eyes as I awkwardly stood, walked him over to the couch, and softly put him down.

I was stiff from the fight, and I mentally tallied the places in my body that ached. Head, nose, knuckles, groin. Valkyrie, better known as Eva, was gone. The clock said it was almost six. I could have used a few more hours of sleep, but I had a lot to do. I got cleaned up and did some slow stretching to try to work the kinks out.

I wanted to canvass the houses nearby and see if there were any security cameras that may have recorded street traffic, but one glance in the mirror told me otherwise. The bump on the side of my head was mostly gone, but my nose was swollen, and I now had two black eyes. Nope, my appearance would not have been conducive to cooperation from strangers. I'd call Percy as soon as Ronald arrived and see if he would help me out.

I washed down some Ibuprofen with a glass of water and began making breakfast. Ronald drove up as I sat down to eat. He walked in and plopped a laptop down on the table beside my plate.

"You're up early," I remarked.

"I was worried," he said and gestured toward the laptop. "You can use this until you get another one. Oh, I've checked your cloud. All your files are still intact and have not been viewed by anyone else. So, we're good on that end."

"Good. Do you have your phone with you?"

He snorted. "Of course." He pulled it off his belt clip, unlocked it, and handed it to me. I called Percy and explained. He readily agreed to help out. I then called Mick, who sounded like I'd woken him, and told him about the fire.

"If you don't mind, keep your ears open. It was on the news, but my name and address weren't mentioned."

"Yeah, I follow you," he said with a yawn. "Anybody starts talking about it and knows it was your property, they might've had something to do with it."

"Yeah, exactly."

"Say, you don't think it's somebody that's been putting the wood to Marti and they're jealous of you, do you?" he pondered.

He was trying to bait me, but I didn't bite. "It could be anybody."

"Alright, I'll conduct a subtle interrogation of everyone I think may be a suspect and get back to you."

"I would prefer you just listen in on people's conversations. You're good at that."

"Are you saying I'm a nosy busybody?"

"Yep," I answered.

"Yeah, well, kiss my ass. You'll be eating your words when I find out who did it."

He hung up before I could respond. I then called Sherman and gave him a summation of yesterday's events. He listened quietly. Someone who did not know Sherman might've accused him of drifting off to sleep while I talked, but I knew the old man was absorbing everything I said and analyzing it with that razor sharp brain of his.

"What about those three bikers?" he asked when I had finished. "Do you think they were lying in wait to ambush you? And you were left with no phone to call nine-one-one?"

"Yeah, could be."

I heard a tsking noise from him. "I believe I might be able to use this to our advantage. As far as the search warrant, that is a valid means of police work, but their execution and subsequent actions could be called into question. Let me make a few phone calls and see if I can stir up the pot."

"Okay. I won't have a new phone until later today, so give me a call this evening," I said.

Sherman agreed before hanging up. I then called Commander Sory Bartlett. It went to voicemail. I left an eloquent message.

"Since there was no gunplay involved in Tomey's murder, seizing my weapons went beyond the scope of the search warrant, as did trashing my house. Unless you idiots think I was involved in the murders of the grave robbers, which was not mentioned in the affidavit, but if that is the case, your detectives should have inquired about my alibi. I'll give you a freebie. The night they were killed was my birthday. I was having a party at my house. A dozen people were present, including Percy. You know him, he's a police detective. And, I had a guest spend the night."

I felt my blood pressure increasing, which was causing my headache to worsen. I took a slow, deep breath before continuing.

"You can make this right if you want to. In the meantime, I've contacted my attorney and he is prepared to move forward with a harassment lawsuit. Check with the chief about the terms of settlement of my last lawsuit. It specifically states there shall be no type of retaliatory action. The way your minions destroyed my house was nothing more than spite. One would think you people learned your lesson."

I disconnected the call and faced Ronald. "Should I go ahead and buy a new phone and laptop?"

He shrugged. "I can reformat them once you get them back, but if you're asking for my advice, I say go ahead and upgrade."

I nodded and gently dabbed at my runny nose with a tissue. Ronald was staring curiously.

"That looks painful," he said.

"It is."

"I've never been in a fight. Well, I have, but it was one-sided. Marcellus Johnson beat me up when I was in the ninth grade. I got him back though."

"You did? How?"

"I hacked the high school's computer and changed all his grades to F. When he got his report card, he didn't even complain, just dropped out. I saw him a couple of years ago, he was working on the back of a garbage truck."

I chuckled. Ronald walked around the house. "Yeah, they trashed the place."

"How much was recorded before they disabled the camera?"

"Not everything, but enough. It was one of the cops in uniform who disabled the camera, but it was the woman who told him to do it. I've got it recorded."

"Good. Do me a favor. I have a digital camera over there in that bag. Walk around the house and take a few pictures."

I watched him work while I ate breakfast. He muttered to himself as he took each picture, and I found myself smiling at his behavior. I reminded myself that I often did the exact same thing. Ronald worked his way through the house before ending up back in the den. He gestured at the shelf on the far wall.

"At least they didn't touch your books," he said.

"They did. I've already put them back."

"Did you take pictures first?" he asked.

I shook my head. "Honestly, I was so pissed I didn't think about it at the time."

"Pity," he muttered, and then stared. "I should get some closeups of your face. It looks awful. Is your beanbag dark and bruised? We should take pictures of it too," he said.

"You're not taking pictures of my beanbag," I huffed.

Ronald snickered. "Okay, face only."

I sat still while Ronald snapped away and stared out of my kitchen window. It was still a little surreal to me, but the charred remains were pure reality. Glancing over, I caught Ronald staring. It looked like he was about to cry. I frowned.

"What's wrong, buddy?" I asked.

"Those three men could have killed you," he said.

"Ah, it wasn't going to end up like that. They probably would have slapped me around a little, that's all."

"But what if something happens to you? You're always getting into situations like these. You're my best friend. If you're killed, I won't have anyone."

His lower lip was quivering so hard I thought there might've been an earthquake going on. I reached out and gave his shoulder a squeeze.

"You have other friends besides me. Percy and Anna really like you. So does Marti."

"Yeah, but they don't understand me the way you do. I can talk to you and tell you things I'd never tell them. You're the one who helped me overcome my agoraphobia, mostly. And my depression, and my suicidal thoughts. You've helped me with all of that."

He wiped away some tears, and I felt myself becoming emotional as well.

"Look, buddy. I think I've demonstrated by now I'm a pretty tough old bastard and hard to kill. But I'll have a long talk with Percy and Anna and make sure they'll always be there for you."

He stifled a sob as he stared at me with big round eyes. "Really?"

"Absolutely." I got up and fetched a couple of tissues for him. He nodded gratefully, wiped his face, and blew his nose so loud it woke Tommy Boy. It took him a moment to compose himself, but after a few minutes, he was back to his old self.

"They'll be back tomorrow, I think. We can invite them over and crank up the grill if you want."

Ronald nodded. "Yeah, that'd be cool. I hope they had a good trip. Do you think they'll get married?" he asked.

I laughed, which hurt my nose. "I'm surprised they haven't already tied the knot. Oh, by the way, getting back to that other topic, if the impossible happens and I die before my time, you are my sole beneficiary in my will." Ronald stared blankly. "You get everything. I've never told anyone, but there is a floor safe hidden under my bed. Do you remember the date my wife died?"

"Uh, I think so," he said.

"That's the combination. Don't tell anybody about it."

"Okay," he said and his eyes widened. "Why did you tell me that? Do you have cancer or something?"

"No buddy, I'm in good health," I said with a reassuring smile. He nodded, but I think he still had doubts. I stood. "Alright, enough of this morbid talk. Let's go to the computer store."

Ronald drove while I used his phone to read my emails and check the status of the debris bin. They promised to have it delivered to my house within a couple of hours.

Once at the store, Ronald bounced around the store ogling all the computers and accessories. He picked out what I needed, including a newer model router, and picked a few items for himself. We were back at my house an hour later. He peppered me with questions about Eva as we got everything set up.

"I watched you two on the cameras. She looks hot. How does she look in person?" he asked.

"She's tall and lean. Athletic with pretty blue eyes and light blonde hair. She told me she used to be a long-distance runner."

"She really shot that guy in the butt?" he asked.

"Yep."

His eyes were wide. "I want to meet her," he gushed.

"If I ever see her again, I'll tell her. I don't know how to get in contact with her. Hey, look her up on the old internet. Her name's Eva, she's from the Ukraine, and she used to run track."

Ronald bit his lower lip in thought, but then started clicking away on my new laptop. He found her as I was cleaning up the kitchen. I walked over and looked at his screen.

"Eva Abramovich. She was on the Olympic track team a few years ago," he exclaimed.

I looked at the picture of her. She was obviously younger, skinnier. Personally, I thought she looked a hell of a lot better now than back then.

"Now you know who Valkyrie is. Keep in mind she might not want you to know this."

Ronald looked crestfallen but nodded his head. "Yeah, probably."

"Don't worry, I'll remind her what a great guy you are. She already knows it, but you know how women are, you have to remind them occasionally."

Ronald responded with a big grin. "Alright, what do you need me to help you with?"

"Why don't you start by calling the phone company. I think it'd be prudent of me to have a landline finally installed."

"Yeah, that's long overdue," he remarked.

He was right. Back when I had resigned from the police department and first started out as a PI, I operated on a shoestring budget. Having a cell phone and a house phone seemed redundant, but last night was a good example of why I needed both. Besides, I could afford it now.

I walked out to the burnt remains of my garage while Ronald made the arrangements with the telephone company. It did not look like anything was disturbed. I guess they didn't want to dirty themselves searching for possible evidence when it would be much more fun to trash my house.

Everything was burned and beyond hope. The temperature of the fire undoubtedly ruined the hardening of the hand tools, and the power tools could not be fixed. I probably could have restored the cars, but it looked futile. I stood in silence staring at the mess when I heard a car coming down my drive. When I walked outside, I recognized Detective Sansing's vehicle.

# CHAPTER 27

Detective Sansing. That's how I thought of him now. In the formal sense. No longer as Jay, my friend, but Detective Sansing, someone I was merely acquainted with.

I stood and waited as he parked and got out. He opened the back door to his unmarked car and came out with a familiar looking cardboard box and my rifles slung over his shoulder. He walked over to me and stopped.

"I couldn't get your phone and computer back, but here's the rest," he said. "I know you don't want to hear it, but I'm sorry about all this."

I gestured at the weapons. "Poston didn't simply let you walk out with those, so what happened?"

Jay gave a small, grim smile. "Bartlett called an emergency meeting about thirty minutes ago. The chief was present."

"Oh, this sounds good already," I said.

"The chief regaled us with a story about how the mayor and your lawyer are close personal friends and apparently they'd had a phone conversation this morning. I think you know how it went from there. The chief informed the commander that our actions opened the door to another lawsuit."

"He's right," I said while giving him a pointed stare.

"Well, I was told to gather up everything except your phone and laptop and bring it back immediately. I was then excused. As soon as I closed the door, I could hear the Commander tearing into Kettleworth."

"You should have stayed in the meeting. I guarantee she blamed everything on you," I said.

"Commander Bartlett knows me better than that. Between you and me, Kettleworth hadn't even logged them into the property room. They were still sitting in the trunk of her car," he said, and then scoffed. "She violates department SOP frequently."

I gave a curt nod of understanding. "She's not a good detective, you know. She may have seniority over you, but you should avoid working with her." I waved a hand toward my house. "But let's talk about you. You did nothing while she and those two uniforms trashed it. You knew it was out of line, but you did nothing. That doesn't make you much better."

He stared at the ground and did not offer a response. I motioned for him to follow me inside and he dutifully followed. Once inside, I took the box from his hands, set it on the kitchen table, and gave the handguns a cursory inspection. Jay gently laid the two rifles on the table and stood back.

I was going to give them all a thorough inspection to make sure they'd not been damaged or tampered with, but at the moment my head was hurting too much. I sat and worked two more Ibuprofen out of the bottle. Ronald poured a fresh glass of water. I nodded my thanks before washing them down. Ronald stared back and forth between Jay and me. He did not know Jay well, which meant he was not going to speak unless spoken to. Jay cleared his throat.

"May I have a glass of water?"

"Yeah, help yourself," I grumbled.

Jay poured himself a glass, which caused Ronald to jump up and get a can of Coke out of the fridge for himself. Jay drank a swallow and stood there, fidgeting.

"For Christ's sake, you two, sit down," I directed. "You're making my headache worse."

Ronald giggled. Jay took the hint and sat. I caught him staring at me.

"What?"

"What happened to you?" he asked.

"He got jumped last night after you big tough police tore up his house and left," Ronald said.

I glanced at Ronald in surprise. It was the most aggressive thing I'd heard him say in a while.

"Who jumped you?" Jay asked.

"Some biker boys who think I have information that I don't," I said. "You assholes left me without any weapon to defend myself and without a phone to call 911."

"He's lucky he didn't get killed," Ronald said.

"Did you file a report?" he asked.

"I absolutely did. I was sure to include in my statement how you and your colleagues left me helpless."

Jay was pale at the implications. He excused himself, stepped outside, and was on his cell phone before the door swung shut.

It gave me a slight feeling of satisfaction, but I still felt like crap. I wanted nothing more than to grab a cold beer and park my butt in one of my rocking chairs for the rest of the day, but I still had more to do.

"Ronald, do you happen to know Bull's phone number? I don't have it memorized."

He found an old contact list from my cloud account. I'd called Bull a couple of times since Flaky's arrest, and so far, he had not returned any of my messages. Surprisingly, he answered this time.

"It's Thomas," I greeted.

"Oh, hey. Been meaning to call you back. How've you been?"

"I've been a little worried about Flaky. He told me to stay away from his case."

"He did? Well, that's a good idea," Bull replied. "There's a lot of shit going on and he probably doesn't want you getting caught up in it."

"Yeah, that's awfully nice of him. He's probably going to get a life sentence and I'm supposed to sit on my hands and not help him."

Bull didn't respond, but I could hear him breathing.

"There's a problem though," I said.

"What's that?" he asked.

"I got a visit from three Satan's Dogs last night, and it wasn't a friendly visit."

"Yeah? Who were they?"

"One was named Zango, a little stringy guy. One was average sized with a filthy beard, he seemed like the leader, and the third one was almost as big as you. They wanted information about the Baroques."

"What'd you tell them?"

"Nothing. They jumped me. The big guy could take a punch, but when he got shot in the ass he screamed like a little girl."

Bull emitted a belly laugh. "You shot him, huh?"

"I didn't, but that doesn't matter. Before they left, they promised a return visit. What are they after, Bull?"

"Hang on a second," he said and muted his phone. After a couple of minutes, he came back on.

"You still there?"

"Yep," I said. "You got an answer for me?"

"Don't worry about anything, we're going to take care of it."

"What about Flaky?" I asked.

"Don't worry about him either. He's going to be fine. Haven't you heard? Their star witness died yesterday." He laughed again before hanging up.

I trampled through my memory until I came up with Wes Tilford's number and called him.

"Yeah, she was found yesterday by her niece," he said. "They're doing an autopsy, but it looks like a heart attack."

"What does that do for the case?" I asked. "Did they obtain a sworn statement from her?"

"Um, I don't know," he said.

I sighed in exasperation. A sworn statement could be submitted as evidence in court. If they recorded the photo lineup identification, it could be used as well.

"That is something you should find out," I suggested.

"Yeah, yeah, I need to look into that. Listen, I need to get to court," he said.

I don't know if he was sincere or merely attempting to avoid my nagging. I told him to call me back when he had more information. He gave me a halfhearted assurance that he would and hung up. And even though I had two people telling me to stay out of it, I called the Rutherford Sheriff's Department and requested Detective McAdoo. I was transferred, and after a couple of rings, he picked up.

"My gut told me you'd be calling," he said by way of greeting.

"I can't help but worry for my friend. Is it true the eyewitness was found deceased?"

"Unfortunately, it's true. She was a nice lady. A retired teacher."

"I have to ask, is there anything suspicious about her death?"

"Doesn't look like it. Her niece called her the evening before. She said she wasn't feeling well and was going to bed early. The niece came by the next morning. When Ethel didn't answer, the niece used her key to make entry, and found her lying on the bathroom floor beside the toilet." He paused a moment. It sounded like he took a sip of coffee. "Now, don't get your hopes up, the DA said we're still going forward with prosecution."

"Alright, I appreciate you talking to me. Maybe I can return the favor sometime," I said.

Detective McAdoo got a good laugh out of that and hung up. I handed the phone back to Ronald, leaned back in my chair, and gently rubbed my eyes.

"Are you okay?" he asked.

"I've been better, but I've certainly been worse," I said.

"Your eyes are getting blacker," he said.

"Yeah, it'll take a few days before it goes away." I debated on taking a few more Ibuprofen but decided against it. Abby suggested a visit to the ER and that's probably what I needed, but at the moment I only wanted to sit and relax.

Jay walked back inside. "Alright, I told Commander Bartlett what happened to you. He's going to direct the precinct commander to increase the patrol in your zone."

I rolled my eyes. I knew from experience that an increase of patrol meant nothing. Jay sensed what I was thinking.

"Well, if there's nothing else, I'll be going," he said and made his way to the door.

I held a finger up. "Wait a minute. Get your notepad out."

He stared in puzzlement but retrieved a notepad out of his jacket pocket. "What've you got?"

"My client's name is Mishka Abramovich, and no, I've not been keeping this from you. I only learned of it recently."

Jay's eyes widened and scribbled furiously as I spelled out the name. I didn't tell him how I learned the name, nor did I mention Eva. He began peppering me with more questions, which irritated me, and I shooed him out.

The dumpster bin arrived as Ronald was leaving. I showed him where I wanted it dropped. Once he did so, he left without comment, for which I was thankful. The last thing I wanted to do was shoot the breeze with some stranger.

I wiped down my Springfield 45 and holstered it on my waist. The best thing I could've done for myself would've been to park myself in my chair and rest, but that wasn't in my nature. I drove to the hardware store where I purchased some work gloves, a pack of disposable respirator masks, and some other items. I opted for lunch from a drive-thru before heading home and beginning the slow, arduous task of throwing debris into the dumpster.

# CHAPTER 28

It took two solid days of work to clean the mess up. I suppose I could've hired some itinerant workers off the street and had it done by dinner on the first day, but it was something I needed to do alone. The first day was rough. I was still sore from the fight. Even so, I pushed through the pain and worked all day.

At the end of the day, while I was sitting in my chair aching all over, my stubbornness finally wore off. I called Bubba and asked him if he still wanted some part-time work. He showed up early the next morning and with his help, we got a sizeable amount of clean up accomplished.

The damage went beyond the garage. There was a layer of soot on everything and the roof shingles looked awful. The claims adjustor's prediction was spot on. The settlement offer was far below what it should have been. It took a bit of haggling and a three-way phone call involving Sherman before an adequate payout was reached. It was not as much as I felt the total damages would cost, but it would have to do.

Bubba had a neighbor who had a pressure washing business. He came over and had the brickwork and the concrete pad cleaned in two hours. I fixed us a big tray of snacks and carried them to the picnic table. Bubba and I sat there and watched. We chatted about cars and stuff while we ate. I told him I wasn't going to attempt to salvage anything and scrap it all. At one point, Bubba gestured toward the spot where the garage once was.

"Are you going to do anything different when you rebuild it?" Bubba asked.

"You know what? I've been thinking about it, and I've decided I'm going to make it bigger."

His eyes widened in surprise. "You are?"

"Yep," I said and pointed at the concrete pad, which was now cleaned of soot and grime. "I'm going to have the building contractor put down another concrete pad beside that one. Twice the size."

"Wow," he said.

"Yep, double the footage. Life is short, Bubba. I've always enjoyed working on cars and it's not like I need to save money to buy a new house for the wife or send my kids to college."

Bubba laughed. "You're a lucky man. I still think we could've saved some of your tools."

I shook my head. "The intense heat of the fire most likely compromised their hardness. I suppose I could've turned in the ones that had a lifetime warranty, but I don't want to go through the hassle. Nope, it's not worth it. I'm buying everything new."

Bubba chortled. "Man, oh man. A brand-new shop with all new tools. It's a wet dream come true."

I laughed now. "That's the idea. I'm going to make lemonade out of this pile of horse shit. Don't worry, when we get this built, we'll find another car to restore."

I explained to him the process of rebuilding it, how I was going to lay it out, and all the tools I intended to buy.

"The insurance agent already told me if I was going to rebuild, I'd have to install a sprinkler system, but I guess it'd be the prudent thing to do. That means I'll have to install heat, so the pipes won't freeze, but that's okay. Having a warm shop to work in during the winter will be nice."

We chatted for the next hour, debating on the types and brands of tools I wanted.

"You've got to find a way to get around paying retail," Bubba remarked. "Buying by bulk might make it cheaper. Maybe find a friend who has a commercial account who'd be willing to work with you."

"Yeah, I was thinking about that. I'll figure something out. Hold on, I've got an idea."

I went inside and got my laptop, along with a couple more beers, and the two of us created a wish list of the various tools I wanted. Eventually, Bubba asked me about my ongoing case.

"I've not heard from my client, so I guess I'm done with it," I said. I finished my beer and tossed the bottle in the trash can. Bubba did the same. "I've turned down two potential cases this week. I guess I should call them back and see if they still want to hire me. It's time to get some cash flow going."

Bubba nodded his agreement and pulled two more bottles out of the cooler at our feet.

I thought about the murder of Richard Tomey. I'd not heard from Jay, nor anyone else with the department. I hadn't seen anything on the news either, which made me wonder what kind of progress they'd made, if any. For that matter, there had also been nothing about the two grave robbers. I was tempted to call Percy and get some inside information, but I did not want to take advantage of our friendship in that manner.

I don't know if there was some kind of psychic force at play but thinking about the murders must have done something. The distinct tone on my phone alerted me to activity at the head of my driveway. A moment later, a vehicle appeared. I recognized Percy's unmarked car, and he wasn't alone. As they got closer, I could see he had Sansing with him. Both men got out and walked over.

"They asked me to help," Percy said by way of an explanation.

I pointed at Jay. "Did he tell you they trashed my house and seized items that went beyond the scope of the warrant?"

Jay spoke up. "Thomas, I apologize for that. I can assure you if I am ever in a similar situation involving you, I won't allow anything like that to happen again."

I grunted and motioned for them to sit. "Either of you want a beer?"

"We're on duty," Percy said. "I'm guessing you know why we're here."

"Tomey's case is at a dead end and you two are trying to learn more about my mysterious client," I replied.

Percy nodded. "We ran the name you provided through Customs. A man using that name came into the country via France on June Fifth. There is no record of him using his passport since. It's assumed he is still in the country."

Jay pulled a piece of paper out of a manila folder and handed it to me. It was a printout of a passport photograph.

"Is that the man you know as Mishka Abramovich?" he asked.

It only took me a moment of looking at the pic. "Yes, it is. Was he travelling alone?"

"We believe he was," Percy said.

"Well, if he's still around, he's either buying new clothes or he's got someone doing his laundry," I remarked.

Percy gave a small smile while Jay took a note of my brilliant insight.

"You have never mentioned the results of the toxicology tests," I said.

Percy glanced at Jay, deferring to him, and letting me know he was only along for the ride. Jay cleared his throat.

"There was evidence of," he paused and looked at his notes, "Methohexital. Have you heard of it?"

"Can't say that I have," I said.

"Yeah, me neither. I had to look it up. It's a fast-acting barbituric derivative. It's short acting, which leads us to believe Tomey's assailant only wanted him incapacitated for a few minutes. The medical examiner found a small puncture wound on his neck, right at the carotid artery."

"It was a skillful move," Percy said. "If Richard were injected anywhere else, the sedative would not have had an immediate effect."

"The suspect wanted him incapacitated long enough to secure him, tie him up or whatever, but he wanted him awake to torture him," I surmised.

Jay nodded in agreement. "We have a working hypothesis that he was ambushed in his home, drugged, and interrogated about something. The torture was a means of attempting to extract the information from him."

"So, the question is, what was Richard interrogated about?" Percy asked. When he asked the question, he was staring steadily, mentally conveying that I needed to tell what I knew.

I pondered on it a moment. "If my client was the person who did this, no doubt he would've accused him of stealing the artifact and wanted Tomey to give it up."

"But you don't think he did it," Jay asked.

"I'm not saying that. If I were in your shoes, I would consider him a viable suspect as well, but there's no proof. The only thing I can say for a certainty is that Tomey didn't steal anything from that grave. Neither did his rookie. I sincerely doubt she's ever stolen anything in her life."

Jay stared a moment before speaking. "I'd have to say I agree with your assessment of Officer Severns. We've interviewed her extensively and there are no red flags at all. But how are you so certain about Tomey?"

"Officer Severns, being the rookie, was tasked with guarding the crime scene and recording the names of everyone who entered the scene. That means she had eyes on the grave at all times. If anybody, including Tomey, had taken something, she would have seen it and reported him."

Jay considered it and slowly nodded. "I can see that. She has that air of unwavering honesty."

I nodded in agreement.

"Have you ever found out what this artifact is?" he asked.

"Nope. My client claims he's not even sure what it is, only that it has some sort of religious significance and was once owned by the Knights Templar, which makes it valuable."

There was silence for a moment, but then Percy spoke up. "Thomas, who do you think shot the grave robbers?"

I thought for a moment, choosing my words. "My client is certainly a viable person of interest in that as well. He has a possible motive, and it's not difficult to buy a gun on the street, but how in the world did he obtain that drug? It would be hard to come by, right?"

"You make a good point," Jay conceded.

"Also, he claims there is a rival organization that is also seeking this artifact. He further stated they are more aggressive and would not hesitate to commit murder if it helps them reach their objective."

"Do you know who this rival organization is?" Percy asked.

"He claims it is a group within the Catholic organization," I said.

Jay's eyes widened. "The Catholics? Like the Pope?"

"That was my impression," I said.

"Do you believe that?" Jay asked.

I shrugged. "For all I know, that's who he's working for, and if he is, I could see how they would have a lot of connections and could have access to resources such as a disabling drug."

We talked for several more minutes. I tentatively agreed to call if I had any further contact with Mishka. I watched them drive off before rejoining Bubba. He handed me another beer.

"You know, you probably shouldn't drive," I said.

He glanced at me and frowned. "Yeah, maybe not. I'll get my wife to come get me."

Bubba's wife showed up at five. She wasn't happy, but she was pleasant to me when he introduced us. I was gracious and polite and threw out multiple compliments about Bubba. That seemed to placate her a little.

After they left, I took a hot shower, shaved, and stared at myself in the mirror. The swelling and bruising on my face had subsided somewhat, and the family jewels didn't hurt anymore, which was good. I'd not seen nor heard from Marti in several days. I guess our friends with benefit arrangement had run its course. That was fine. She was fun to be with, but I knew it was never going to go any further.

I dressed in a pair of shorts and a mismatched Under Armour sleeveless tee shirt. I wasn't expecting guests, otherwise I might've dressed more appropriately. Maybe.

I made sure Tommy Boy was fed and then had a look in the fridge. I had a lot of stuff, but most of it were leftovers from my birthday party and were probably expired. I spent a few minutes throwing out the old food and took another look. There wasn't much left. I settled for eggs and turkey sausage. I had one tomato that appeared to be still good, so I sliced it up, sprinkled it with salt, and added it to my plate. Beer was not a complimentary beverage, and I did not want any caffeine, so I settled on a glass of ice water.

Finishing up, I took my trash out and decided to have a beer for dessert. I was sitting in one of the folding chairs Bubba and I were sitting in earlier, enjoying the balmy night and the lightning bugs, when I saw headlights coming down my drive. I wasn't too concerned. If it was someone who had bad intentions, I had my Springfield 45 holstered on my hips and would not hesitate to use it.

When the driver parked and got out, I was surprised to see it was Eva. She was wearing tight black shorts and a sleeveless tee shirt surprisingly similar to mine. I had to admit, those long legs and blonde hair made her look enticing. The little soldier certainly noticed and started sending my brain dirty messages. She walked up and stood before me.

"Hello."

"This is a surprise," I said. "I figured you'd gone back home."

"I went to New York City. I have always wanted to see it," she said and paused a minute. "I thought about asking you to go with me."

It was a nice thing to say, but for some reason I didn't think she was sincere.

"Did you have an enjoyable trip?"

"It was, but now I am back," she said.

"Okay, I'll bite. Why are you back?"

"I want to find out what Mishka is doing. What are you drinking?"

"Beer. Would you like one? I have some stronger stuff inside if you don't like beer."

"Do you have vodka?" she asked.

"I believe I do. What kind of mixer would you like with it?" I asked.

She shook her head. "Straight, no mixer."

I found a bottle of Kettle One and poured her the equivalent of a shot. She took the tumbler from my hand, inspected the contents, and took a small sip. Nodding in appreciation, she downed it in one swallow.

"May I have another, please?" she promised with a mischievous smile.

I smiled, went back inside, and brought the entire bottle out this time. She nodded appreciatively and refilled her glass.

"That was excellent. How do you Americans say, it hit the spot. I will drink slower now," she said.

I laughed and tipped my beer to her. She took a small sip and looked around. "You have started cleaning."

"Yes, I have. I am going to rebuild as soon as possible,' I said.

"Will you keep working on old cars?"

"Yeah, it's something I like to do. What is your passion?" I asked.

"Computers."

I nodded. "I should have known that. It's Ronald's passion too. Ronald has issues with social skills. The internet opened up the world to him."

"Me too. I was an introverted child and found comfort in computers. I found that I had a talent for coding."

"Who taught you?" I asked.

She hesitated a moment before answering. "I am mostly self-taught. What about you, Thomas? What do you have a talent for besides cars?"

I chuckled. "Definitely not coding. I can use a computer, but I'm not anywhere near the level of you and Ronald. So, not much I guess."

"What about your skills as an investigator?"

I shrugged. "Yeah, I suppose so."

Eva laughed lightheartedly. "You are too modest, Thomas."

"If I were good, I'd have already figured out who set my garage on fire."

"Who do you think did it?" she asked.

"I have to admit, I've considered Mishka as a viable suspect."

"No," she replied quickly, maybe too quickly. She saw me staring, broke eye contact, and stared at her shoes. After taking a sip of her vodka, she offered an explanation.

"Mishka rarely acts rashly. If he were to burn your garage, it would be to achieve an objective, and it would have been apparent by now."

"Yeah, if you say so."

She gave a light laugh. "If it makes you feel any better, I am confident he did not do it."

"Well, there you go. A suspect I can cross off my list."

She laughed again. Soon the subject changed to other things, and we talked throughout the night. I found myself enjoying her company. She was an interesting, well-spoken person and a wealth of knowledge. If the vodka was making her drunk, I sure couldn't see it. At one point I asked her when she was going back home.

"I do not know. I do not have anything to go back to other than Mishka's home."

"If I can be nosey, what are you doing for money?"

She grinned. That familiar mischievous grin. "I am spending Mishka's money. He probably suspects I am doing this, but he cannot prove it."

"Where is he?" I asked. "I have not seen nor heard from him in several days."

"He is currently in Miami," she said, causing me to wonder how she knew that. "It is my understanding he is meeting with people who are associated with the Cuban government."

"Alright, I have to ask. How do you know he's in Miami? Do you know what hotel, or anything like that?" I asked.

"I do not, but he is coming back to Nashville. That is why I am here." She had been looking in the dark, but now gazed at me. "I need a place to stay."

"Uh, well, you can stay here. My roommate has recently moved out, so her bed is available."

"Thank you, Thomas. It will only be for a day, two days at the most."

She retrieved two pieces of luggage from the car and followed me inside. I locked everything up and set my alarm, something I'd been doing ever since the fire. I explained it to Eva and suggested we could go eat breakfast in the morning.

I went to bed then. I was inclined to invite Eva to join me but felt it may be inappropriate. After all, she was much younger than me and married. I was almost asleep when I sensed her walking into my room. I opened my eyes to see her standing a few feet away from my bed. She was still wearing the same clothes but had taken her shoes off.

"Thomas, can I sleep here without us doing anything? I am lonely."

"Um, yeah, sure," I said.

I pulled the blankets aside. She crawled in and snuggled up beside me as I pulled the blankets over her. If she noticed the little soldier standing at full attention, she made no mention of it and was soon breathing deeply.

# CHAPTER 29

Nashville history is a little fuzzy, but it is believed there have been a total of five police headquarters over the years. The first headquarters was in the courthouse, and as the city grew, so did the police department. The first independent police headquarters building was built at the intersection of Second Avenue and Gay Street. In the ensuing years, HQ was relocated three different times, all of which were on the same street. The headquarters I had worked out of was called the Criminal Justice Center, which not only housed the police headquarters, but also the county jail.

The only positive thing I could say about the place was its proximity to the courts, a mere walk across the street. A casual stroll taking no more than five minutes. There were constant issues with the place. Poor heating in the winter, poor cooling in the summer, always in a state of repair, always dirty. Don't even get me started on the restrooms.

The new HQ was the antithesis of the old Criminal Justice Center. It was a modern, 110,000 square feet structure with a ground floor, three stories and a decent sized parking lot. When I walked into the lobby, I had to admit, it had a pleasant atmosphere. The interior was painted with shades of cool grays, and it even had a nice smell. Tax dollars well spent. I checked in with the security guard and waited. Sure, I could've called, but I wanted to see the place.

Within a minute, Jay emerged from a secured door, spotted me, and crossed the lobby.

"Hey, Thomas. I admit, I'm surprised to see you here," he said.

"Yeah, I was driving by and thought I'd stop in. I have some information you could probably use."

"Alright, what do you have?" he asked.

"Mishka is currently in Miami."

He stared at me like I was playing a cruel joke. "Are you certain?"

"Fairly certain. I only found out last night. The source is somewhat credible." I glanced at the clock on the wall. "Alright, I've got to get going. If he makes contact, I'll let you know." I gestured around with my hand. "You'll have to take me on a tour of this place sometime. It looks nice."

He had more questions, but I ignored him and walked out.

When Eva and I had awakened this morning, I took her to a nice bistro for breakfast. While we ate, we continued our amiable conversation from last night and she asked about Ronald.

"He's a great guy. You two should meet in person," I said.

It took a little urging before she agreed. I called Ronald ahead of time and he was gushing in excitement. As I suspected, they hit it off immediately. When he led her to the basement where his cyberspace lair was located, she became as excited as he was. I was soon nothing more than a spectator as they sat in front of Ronald's multiple monitors and began opening up various programs.

I suggested the two of them hang out while I went out to run errands and Ronald could bring her over later. I even offered to fix dinner for the three of us. They glanced at each other, grinned, and readily agreed.

My first stop was headquarters. I had to admit, I was curious and wanted to see the place, but as soon as I walked in the lobby, I started feeling anxious, boxed in, visualizing getting thrown to the floor and handcuffed. So, I gave Jay the information and got the hell out of there. The rest of the day consisted of me running errands before ending up at the grocery store. I stocked up with enough food for two, including lots of fruit and vegetables. Yeah, I know she told me she was only going to stay one or two days, but one never knew. My final stop was my favorite liquor store. I bought a bottle of Balvenie Scotch for me and Finlandia vodka for Eva. Ronald called as I walked in the door.

"Guess what?" he said.

"You're selling everything and moving to Ukraine with Eva," I answered.

He giggled. "Nope. I showed Eva my app I have on your phone, and we've been following you everywhere."

I gritted my teeth slightly. If Eva was suspicious, she may be wondering what I was doing at police headquarters. If she knew I was relaying information to the police that she'd told me, she might get upset. If she asked me about it, I wasn't going to lie, I'd be truthful and hope that she understood.

"I should have dinner ready in two hours. Fresh salad, vegetable soup for you, and Rigatoni with white Bolognese for Eva and me."

I heard a whisper before Ronald spoke. "Eva would rather have soup."

I chuckled. "No problem. I'll fix enough for both of you, and I have fresh bread from the deli."

The recipe I had for the Rigatoni was for a four-person serving. I fixed it anyway. If they could not be persuaded to eat any, I'd be reheating leftovers for a couple days, but I didn't mind.

Ronald and I had sweet tea to drink, Eva opted for iced water. I now understood why she was so lithe.

"I'd like to know more of your track and field career," I said between bites.

"I was a long-distance runner. I started as a child. I was good, better than most, but in the Olympics, there were ten other women who were better than me," she said with a laugh. "My coach believed the other runners were blood doping, but it could not be proven. Since I refused to do it, my career as a track star was over, but running will always be a passion of mine."

Soon, the subject turned back again to computer programming, where I became a polite listener. When it got dark, Ronald said he needed to get back home. After he left, Eva stood and walked to the edge of the porch.

"I noticed a path through your trees the other night."

"Yeah, I have five acres that's full of trees. I created a trail through them. I use it for morning walks or to jog."

"How long is it?" she asked.

"The way the trail is configured, one lap is a touch over a half mile."

She looked up at the sky. "There is a full moon tonight. It's pretty."

"Here in America, a full moon in June is called a strawberry moon," I said.

"Why is that?"

"The strawberries are blooming this month. I don't know where any strawberry fields are around here, but I imagine it's nice."

"Let's go for a run," she suddenly suggested.

I arched an eyebrow in surprise. "Right now?"

She responded with an inviting smile. "Yes, right now. The night air is pleasant, and the moon will light the pathway."

I would have rather sat on the porch and drank a glass of Scotch. Don't get me wrong, I jogged on a regular basis, but I strongly suspected I was outclassed. I thought about it a moment, and figured, why not.

"Sure, but you have to take it easy on me," I said.

Her only answer was a broadening smile.

I went to my bedroom, found my running shoes, and put on some shorts and an old tee shirt. I donned a fanny pack that I kept my handgun in and adjusted the strap before walking to the den. Eva came out of the guest bedroom wearing a pair of black spandex shorts that track stars commonly wore, and a plain white tee shirt. We went outside where the trail started and began stretching.

"Can I tell you a secret?" she asked.

"What's that?" I huffed out as I tried to stretch my hamstrings.

"When I was a young teenage girl and had no breasts, I would tuck my hair into my hat and run at night with my shirt off. Anybody that saw me thought I was a boy. It would arouse me greatly."

"I believe I'd like to see that sometime," I said with a chuckle.

Eva responded with that same inviting smile before pulling off her shirt and tossing it at me. She was not wearing a bra. Her breasts were small but perfectly shaped. I only got a glimpse of them before she took off.

I tried to keep up. Imagine a clumsy Rottweiler trying to chase down a gazelle. She finally stopped after six laps. When I caught up with her, it took all the inner strength I had not to drop down on the ground. I was sweating profusely and gasping for air. Eva's breathing was moderate and even. Her only evidence of physical activity was a sheen of sweat covering her upper torso and glistening in the moonlight.

Even in my fatigued state I found myself becoming aroused. Eva probably saw it. She did not seem to mind the copious amounts of sweat dripping off me, stepped close, and embraced me. We kissed deeply. I'd like to think she wanted more. No doubt I wanted more, but I gently, reluctantly, moved her back.

"You're a married woman," I said.

"Yes," she agreed. She stared intensely for a moment before kissing me again. This time it was soft, tender, not as intense as the first one.

"Why don't we sit on the porch and cool down? I can fix a pitcher of ice water," I suggested.

"Do you have any vodka left?" she asked.

"In fact, I bought a bottle this afternoon. It is currently sitting in the freezer."

This brought a smile to her face. "I will put my shirt back on."

We talked into the night. Mostly, she wanted to hear my life story. I obliged her until I started yawning. We showered separately but ended up in the same bed. She cuddled against me and softly stroked my chest.

"You're killing me," I muttered.

"How is your nose?" she asked.

"It was hurting a little when we were jogging, but it's fine now." I didn't tell her when I was in the shower it bled a little.

"I am leaving tomorrow," she suddenly said.

"Where are you going? Home?"

"No. I am going to Miami to find out what Mishka is doing."

I nodded in the dark. "You want me to go with you?" I found myself asking.

"That would be nice, but no. I need you here in case he eludes me and comes back to Nashville."

"Okay, but how do I get in touch with you?"

She was silent a moment, as if coming to a decision. "I will give you my phone number, but please memorize it and do not record it in your contact list."

"Yeah, no problem. Also, Ronald put a messenger app on my phone that he says does not record any data."

"Perfect," she said and snuggled closer. "I like you, Thomas."

I kissed her on top of her forehead. "So, what's next for you after Miami?"

She murmured something I could not understand. I asked her what she said, but she was silent. It was then I realized her breathing had changed and she was sound asleep.

# CHAPTER 30

I was awakened by the sound of the shower. I wanted to get in with her but resisted temptation. Instead, I cleaned up in the spare bathroom, dressed casually, and began preparing breakfast. She walked in wearing my bathrobe, which was far too large for her.

"What time does your flight leave?" I asked.

"Not until later today." She paused a moment before speaking. "May I stay here until then?"

"Of course," I replied a little quicker than I meant to. I admonished myself and motioned toward the stove. "I get the impression you don't eat meat, but I have eggs, buttermilk biscuits, and homemade grits. I also have milk, orange juice, and coffee. You pick."

"Two biscuits, orange juice, and coffee, please," she said.

My phone rang as I was loading our plates. I glanced at the caller I.D. and frowned slightly.

"You'll want to hear this," I said and answered. It was Special Agent Carter Pike. I put it on speaker.

"Hello, Thomas. I hope I've not called too early," he said.

"Not at all. How's it going?" I asked.

"I'm following up on this information you gave me. It looks like this is something significant."

"Excellent. Will you be able to make a case out of it?"

He chuckled. "That's putting it mildly. A joint task force has been created and the bankers in question were contacted Friday. It's turning into a sizeable operation. The good part about this is the bankers are ecstatic the FBI has discovered this. It's great PR for us."

"I'm glad to hear it," I said.

"Which brings me to the reason why I am calling. The attorneys at the DOJ are adamant that we conduct a formal interview of this mysterious informant."

Eva's features darkened in concern, and she shook her head.

"I'm afraid that's not possible, Carter," I said. "I don't know exactly where she is, but I'm fairly certain she left the country the same morning I gave you the flash drives."

"Alright, I need as much information about her as you can give me," he said.

"Uh, I only saw her at night. She was a short, thick woman. She looked like she was in her forties, or older, with a ruddy complexion." I grinned at Eva. She smirked. I chuckled out loud. "She reminded me of a character in a movie. Can't remember the name, but it was an old babushka type Russian character. That's about all I can say about her."

"Hmm, that's not much. Are you certain about her age? What about her accent?"

"Heavy accent. I'm not sure about the age. Hell, in this day and age, I'm not even sure about the gender."

Carter sighed. "Alright, if that's all you have, it'll have to do. I am probably going to be told to have you meet with a forensic artist and attempt to create a composite drawing."

"I don't know when I'll be able to do that, Carter. I don't know if you've heard, but an arsonist burned down my garage."

"Oh, wow, I didn't know that," he said.

"Yeah, it's all a big mess and the investigation has been taking a lot of my time."

He asked me about the cars. When I told him I'd lost them all, he let out a deeper sigh.

"Man, that's got to hurt. Okay, I'll leave you alone, but please give me a call as soon as you're available," he said.

"You got it," I replied before hanging up and focusing on Eva.

"Sounds like good news on that end," I said.

"You have quite the imagination in describing me," she replied. I grinned.

She sipped her orange juice before smiling slightly. "What are you going to do today?"

"Since I'm no longer working on Mishka's case, I'm free to enjoy the weekend. I think I might go play some golf."

"I have never played golf," she said. "It seems like a silly game."

I laughed. "It is, indeed."

She then gazed at me with a questioning expression. "Did you ever find out what the item is that Mishka is searching for?"

"He gave me this description of a piece of metal, possibly brass, with an inscription etched in it. It wasn't in Sadie Sartain's grave and if it was interred with Methuselah Sartain, it is long gone."

She frowned in confusion and listened intently as I told her of my trip to New Orleans and the discovery of the break in of the mausoleum.

"I had time to look around thoroughly. If there was any kind of artifact, it was taken by whoever broke in."

Her attention was fixed on me, her breakfast all but forgotten. It made me have a little tingling sensation in the back of my mind. Was she interested in the artifact too?

"What if there was never an artifact in Methuselah's mausoleum?" she asked.

I shrugged. "Then that possibly means Mishka is chasing a red herring," I said.

She frowned in puzzlement. "I do not understand."

"It's an old saying. It roughly means he is following a false lead."

My pinging phone interrupted our conversation. Looking at the live feed on my phone, I observed a familiar car coming down my driveway. I cursed under my breath.

"Who is it, Thomas?" she asked.

"Cops. Stay here. I don't want them to know you exist," I said.

Eva nodded and I hurried outside. I stood in my drive, causing them to stop several feet away from my house. Poston and Kettleworth exited the vehicle.

"What the hell are you two doing are?" I demanded.

"We have more questions, Ironcutter," Kettleworth replied.

"I'll not be answering any of your questions," I said.

Kettleworth scowled and Poston smirked, like he thought I was afraid of him. He then pointed at the Chevy Malibu, Eva's rental car. "That doesn't look like anything you'd drive around in, Ironcutter. Do you have company?"

Without waiting for a response, he pulled out his ink pen, wrote down the tag number and then tried to start walking toward my house. I stepped in front of him. We were mere inches away. Poston, being a few inches shorter than me, stared up with a taunting glare. Kettleworth walked up and stood beside him with her own challenging stare.

I'd laugh under any other circumstances. These two wouldn't stand a chance against me, yet here they were, puffing up on me in my own yard like little banty roosters. I slowly, deliberately took my phone out of my pocket and activated the recorder.

"Detectives Poston and Kettleworth. You do not have a warrant and are therefore trespassing on my property. I am lawfully ordering the two of you to leave, or else I will be placing you under citizen's arrest."

I then stuck my phone within inches of Poston's face. I'd hoped he would try something so I could knock his ass out. He continued staring. I moved the phone to Kettleworth.

"You better get that phone out of my face," she ordered.

"Or else what?" I asked.

She started to attempt to grab the phone out of my hand, but Poston intervened.

"Forget it, he's not worth it," he said.

I watched and continued to record as the two of them retreated to their car. As they were leaving, Poston smirked and pointed his fingers at me like it was a pistol and pulled the trigger. Poston held his smirk for a couple of seconds before turning the car around and heading down the driveway. I continued recording until the car disappeared around the curve in the drive. Satisfied they had left my property, I went back inside and explained to Eva who they were and what they were after.

"I don't want them causing you any trouble," I said.

"They are gone now, and I will be leaving," she said.

I frowned and slowly shook my head. "I don't think they're really gone. Poston has run the tag by now and knows it's a rental vehicle. My guess is they're parked somewhere nearby, waiting on you to leave so they can stop you and question you."

"I can handle them," she said.

"Yeah, I believe you can, but they might do something stupid, like detain you, and you'll miss your flight. I have a better idea."

Buford was agreeable, although I had to bribe him with a big plate of leftover Rigatoni. Eva's flight was at three, which nowadays meant she needed to be at the airport no later than one. At noon, Buford climbed in the Malibu and drove off. I waited five minutes and left in my SUV with Eva crouched down in the back. As I suspected, a patrol car had Buford pulled over less than a mile from my house. I drove by without looking at them and took Eva to the airport. Stopping at the drop-off lane, I got out with her and retrieved her luggage.

Facing her, I gave her a reassuring smile. "Come back soon, okay?"

She leaned in and gave me a tender kiss on the lips. She then grabbed her luggage and soon disappeared through the automatic doors leading inside. The kiss surprised me. I liked it, but for some reason, I found myself wondering if she had an ulterior motive. I shrugged it off to unfounded paranoia.

It only took a minute to drive over to the rental car agency. Buford walked out of the door as I parked. He was smirking when he got in.

"How'd it go?" I asked.

"Did you know police officers get mad when you call them a bunch of communist cocksuckers?"

# CHAPTER 31

I spent the rest of Saturday evening at Mick's Place, and I let them talk me into playing golf with them Sunday. It was sunny and hot, but I played decently and had an enjoyable day, despite Mick and Wally's constant barbs. We had a couple of beers at the clubhouse afterward, but I begged off on relocating to Mick's and went home.

My attorney buddy, Hal Garrison called in the evening and asked if I would serve a half dozen subpoenas for him. I agreed and promised I'd have them served by the end of the week.

"That'll buy a few extra tools," I muttered after hanging up.

My first structured payment from the lawsuit was, how shall I put it, plentiful. I'd used it to pay off my mortgage, bought the new Ford Explorer, the old Cadillac Coupe, and a few other goodies. And then I let Sherman talk me into investing a sizeable chunk into the REIT. It was a good deal, but the return on investment would not even begin for two years. The next structured payment from the lawsuit was not due for three years, and even though I was going to get an insurance payout for the arson, it was not going to cover everything I planned on buying to rebuild the shop. So, if I needed to serve a few subpoenas to get a little spending money in my wallet, I was happy to do so. A decent case or three would help as well.

Sherman had all but guaranteed an eight to ten percent return on the REIT investment. He intended to fully retire on his birthday and made a passing comment about my work status.

"With the amount of money you'll be making, along with the structured payouts, you won't need to work," he had said.

He was right. Once the return on investment began, I'd be set. The question is, did I really want to retire? My first instinct was to tell myself no. But, as Ronald pointed out, I'd had too many close calls and I wasn't getting any younger. Perhaps Sherman was right, and I needed to consider retiring from PI work. I smiled at the thought. I could spend my days fooling around with old cars, maybe take a few golf trips to fancy resorts. It was something to think about.

I fixed a ham and cheese sandwich along with a tall glass of iced water before sitting and listening to my voicemail messages. Unfortunately, all I had were spam calls, a mixture of extended car warranty offers and offers to buy my house. I deleted them all and turned my attention to my emails.

I had three that were solicitations to join various private investigator associations. I eschewed those types of organizations. All they did was take your money every year and give you a certificate of membership. I guess it was something they thought I could hang on the wall and feel important. They didn't help my business in any form or fashion.

There were three that were inquiries about hiring me. One started their email by stating they were disabled and on a fixed income. I stopped reading after that phrase and deleted it. It's been my experience whenever someone used buzzwords like fixed income or some other phrase designed to elicit sympathy meant they expected a substantial discount, or perhaps I should even work their case for free. I didn't give these people the time of day.

The final two were potentially viable cases. One of them wanted me to locate their birth mother. The other one advised they had been defrauded out of several thousand dollars and they wanted me to find the perpetrator. I sent them both a response, advising them of my rates and invited them to make an appointment for a sit down.

After completing that, I refilled my glass of water and began working on an eloquent email to Commander Sory Bartlett, the head of Metro's Criminal Investigations Division. I advised him of Poston and Kettleworth's latest ongoing antics, and then attached the video. I had to edit it down so I could email it, but it should have been enough. I ended by demanding he order his two flunkies to cease and desist the harassment, otherwise I'd sue them - again.

Even though it was Sunday evening, Bartlett surprised me by responding ten minutes later, advising he would look into it. It was the most I could hope for. After all, my client might have possibly murdered a police officer and they would no doubt use that as a rationalization for their actions.

I closed my mailbox and felt like I needed to decompress, so I started browsing the internet looking at tools I wanted and began compiling a wish list. Before I knew it, a couple of hours had passed. I stood, stretched, poured another glass of water, and decided I was going to call Flaky's attorney, Wes Tilford. I'd not heard from him lately and that annoyed me. He answered after a couple of rings. I could hear music in the background.

"Hello, Wes. It's Thomas Ironcutter."

There was a moment's hesitation before he responded. "Oh, yeah, hey. What's up?"

"I'm checking up on Flaky's case. Any new developments?" I asked.

"Not really. I mean, I got the paperwork from the discovery motion, but I've only started to work on it. You heard about the witness dying of a heart attack, right?"

"Yeah," I replied. He seemed to have forgotten the two of us had already discussed the death of Ethel Herring. The discovery motion was more concerning though. He should have completed that task days ago.

"Do you have any pretrial motions in the works?" I asked.

"Yeah, I'm working on it," he said. It was a vague response, and I got the hint he had done little, if anything. I wanted to explode on him, but I kept my temper in check.

"Alright. I'm available if you need any help," I said.

"Yeah, okay. I may take you up on that," he said and disconnected the call. I glanced at my phone's screen. The call lasted less than five minutes.

"You little shit," I muttered.

The man had gotten me worked up. I'd planned on relaxing in my chair and doing some reading before bed, but I knew that wasn't going to happen. It was not yet ten o'clock. Mick closed his bar at eleven on Saturday nights, but I wasn't in the mood to go down there and hang out for only a few minutes.

Since I was done with Mishka's case, I decided to drive over to the cemetery and retrieve my surveillance camera. I made sure Tommy Boy had food and water before I left.

There were no cars in the parking lot, and I didn't see anyone loitering. I parked and walked over to the birdhouse. My original intention was to pack it up and take it home, but as I stared at it, I decided to leave it in place a little longer. Damned if I know why.

I swapped out the battery and card with no problem and stuffed them in my pocket. Task completed, I stretched and looked around. It was a quiet night, and the cemetery was in a peaceful slumber. Instead of going back home, I decided it would be nice to sit here a while and relax.

I sat on one of the benches, made myself comfortable, and lit a cigar. Getting it going with a few puffs, I leaned back and stared out at the silent gravestones. Life was rough for most of the people buried there. Like Sadie. She died at a young age due to a disease that could now be treated. Each grave had a story, and when I thought about it, it made my problems seem a little smaller in comparison.

It helped a little, but not completely. The arson angered me beyond words and the stigma of being a person of interest in the murder of a man I once worked with certainly did not make me feel good about myself. The treatment from my former co-workers added to it.

I reached for my phone and texted Eva. Maybe she could make some kind of breakthrough in determining whether or not Mishka was involved in Tomey's murder. I then texted Bull and asked him about the status of their rival bikers. He called me a couple of minutes later.

"Been meaning to call you," he said.

"Yeah, I'm sure."

He missed my sarcasm. "We had a sit down with the Satan's Dogs yesterday. A lot of things were talked about, and we've reached a truce. They also agreed not to mess with any of our associates, and that includes you."

"What's going on with them and Turk's murder?" I asked.

"Ah, I can't really get into that."

"Really, Bull? After all we've been through? All I want to do is help our friend. Flaky is your best friend, right?"

Bull grunted and muttered something under his breath before speaking. "It's like this. There's a lot of shit going on that you don't want to know about. The Dogs had a misunderstanding about some things, but they're square now. Oh, and their prez admitted you pack a good punch. The other boy thinks you need to tell him who shot him in the ass though." He said it with a chuckle.

I let out a sigh. "Alright, if this is all I'm going to get, I guess it'll have to do."

"Listen, all of us appreciate your willingness to go to bat for Flaky, but we've got it taken care of."

"He could be convicted, you know," I said.

Bull grunted again. "I suppose it's possible. If it happens, he won't be forgotten. The Baroques always take care of their own."

"Alright, big man, if you say so. If anything changes, give me a call."

Bull grunted his agreement and hung up. I sighed and relit my cigar. As I did so, I saw a man walking down Oak Street and when he passed under a streetlight, I realized I recognized him.

"Yo, Larry!" I shouted. "Larry T-Thomas Boles!"

When he looked over, I gave a wave. He stopped and squinted in confusion but walked over anyway. When he got closer, recognition dawned on his face.

"Why, it is my good friend, uh," he stammered. He reeked of alcohol. Maybe that's why he forgot my name.

"Thomas," I reminded.

"Yeah, yeah. Thomas," he said, and then inhaled deeply. "Ah, another fine smelling cigar. Might you have an extra?"

I guess I knew that was coming. I prepped one for him and handed it over along with my lighter. He lit it and inhaled greedily, which made him cough.

"Be gentle with it," I said with a chuckle and took the lighter back before it made its way into his pocket. "How've you been, Larry?"

"About the same," Larry replied. He seemed lost in thought for a few seconds before snapping his fingers.

"I have almost forgot, I found something that you may want to know about."

"Yeah? What'd you find?" I asked.

"A van," he said.

I stared in confusion. "A van?"

"Yep, a van."

"Ah, okay," I said, not knowing where he was going with this.

Larry puffed on his cigar. I thought he was finished talking about the van, but after a minute he gestured down the road with the cigar.

"It's the van those graverobbers used," he said.

I stared in bemusement. "Really?"

"Yup. I saw all three of them in it with my own two eyes. You want me to show it to you?"

I frowned to myself as I followed Larry. He said there were three men. That seemed to imply the murderer was working with the other two men. Mishka made no mention of hiring a third grave robber, and my gut was telling me he was the third man, even though he made no mention of him accompanying the two men when they executed their mission.

I had questions without answers, and that was irritating the hell out of me.

Larry walked down Oak Street to a plain white Chevy Express work van parked in a gravel lot. I guessed it was about five years old. There were a couple of nicks and dents along the sides, but otherwise there was nothing remarkable about it. I walked closer and used the light on my phone to peer inside. There were a couple of blankets in there, along with an empty whiskey bottle and other trash. I turned to Larry and eyed him.

"Have you been in it? Sleeping in it maybe?" I asked.

"Well, yeah, but not much," Larry replied. "That ain't a problem, is it?"

I grunted. "Can you describe the men?"

Larry shrugged. "Uh, well, they were average looking white men. Maybe around my age. There wasn't nothing special about them. One of them was about your size, the other wasn't as tall, maybe more like my size, but he had a thick chest. The third one was short. Definitely short. Not midget or leprechaun short, but short."

"Would you be able to identify them if you saw them again?"

Larry's response was another shrug of the shoulders. "I dunno. It was dark when I saw them."

And you were probably drunk, I thought. I took some pictures with my phone, and then called Jay Sansing.

"I hope I woke your ass up," I said when he answered.

I heard him yawn. "Yes, you did. As you might imagine, we've been putting in long hours. Is this something important or are you drunk and thought this would be a funny way of getting back at me?"

"I'm looking at a van that was supposedly used by the dead grave robbers," I said. I heard some stirring, like he was sitting up in bed.

"Are you sure?" he asked.

"Nope," I replied. "Maybe if I give you the tag, you can run it and see if there's anything to it."

There was more noise, like he was fumbling around for something to write on. "Alright, give me the tag."

I read it off to him. There was more fumbling around before I heard the distinct noise of police radio traffic, indicating he'd turned on his portable radio. Jay called the dispatcher, who answered promptly. He provided the tag, and after a minute, I heard the dispatcher read off the information. The van was apparently registered to the HVAC business nearby. I wondered why it was parked in the gravel lot and how Larry was able to sleep in it without the business owners being aware of it.

Jay sighed. "Looks like a false alarm. If there's nothing else, I'm going to go back to sleep."

"Get her to read off the last four digits of the VIN," I suggested.

He cleared his throat and seemed to ponder my request for a moment before directing the dispatcher. She complied. I listened to her read it off while I peered at the VIN.

"Well?" Jay asked when she'd finished.

"It's not a match. Let me read it off to you."

I heard his pen scratching as I read it off and then he repeated it to the dispatcher. After a few seconds, she informed him the van had been reported stolen. He asked her when it was reported, and she replied with a date that coincided with the double murder. She then asked his location.

"Stand by please," he said and then practically shouted into his phone. "Where are you?"

After I told him, he ordered me, and then begged me to stay where I was. A patrol officer arrived within a minute. I pointed out the van in question and explained everything to him. An on-duty detective soon drove up and had me repeat everything. Jay drove up a few minutes later and I repeated the details once again.

Satisfied they had what they needed, and they weren't going to arrest Larry, I waited until they were busy talking amongst themselves before slipping back to my SUV and drove home. Jay called a few minutes later as I turned into my driveway.

"I appreciate this, Thomas," he said.

"I doubt you'll get any prints or DNA, but it's a small piece in the puzzle," I said.

"Yeah. The business it was stolen from has security cameras and the owner said he provided a copy to the auto theft detective. We're working on it now. Maybe we'll get lucky."

"Maybe," I said. "Oh, Larry, the homeless guy, said he saw three men and they were together."

"Yeah, we spoke to him here. We're taking him to HQ for a formal interview and we'll find him a place to sleep it off."

"Good thinking."

"Alright, thanks again," he said before disconnecting.

I was still irked with him and his co-workers, but I kept reminding myself this wasn't about me, it was about apprehending a cop killer. I glanced at the empty space where my shop used to be as I walked inside.

While sitting in the cemetery, I'd made some decisions. My conversation with Bull did not alleviate my concerns with Flaky's welfare and I wasn't going to sit idly by while my friend got hung with a murder conviction. It was late now, and I wanted to get an early start in the morning. Getting tucked in, I absently rolled over on my side, causing my nose to press against the pillow and shooting a stabbing pain up into my brain. I got myself perfectly centered in the bed, lying on my back with my arms to my side, and willed myself to stay still. I think I fell asleep within minutes.

# CHAPTER 32

I was banging on Wes Tilford's door promptly at eight the next morning. When he answered, I could tell he'd been out drinking most of the night. I know the look. I've looked the same on more than one occasion, but I wasn't going to let him know that. I looked him over.

"You look like shit warmed over," I said. "Here."

I stuck my arm out and handed him a cup of coffee. He stared at it dumbfounded with bloodshot eyes for a second before his brain registered what it was.

"Where'd you get that?" he asked.

"McDonald's drive-thru. Great coffee at a decent price," I said and held up my own cup for emphasis.

"Um, thanks, but I'm more of a cappuccino man."

I scoffed. "I'm shocked."

"Why are you here?" he asked and then he focused on me. "What happened to you? Were you in a car wreck?"

I ignored his question, brushed by him, and walked in, stopping in the den. It smelled like a combination of stale beer and trash that'd been left untended for too long. I sipped my coffee, but it was now lukewarm. Walking into the kitchen, I spotted a required commodity for all bachelors – a microwave. It was clean enough, so I put the cup in and set it for thirty seconds. Wes had followed me and stared.

"Why are you here?" he asked again.

I turned to him. "You and I are going to sit down and thoroughly read the discovery material. Since you got it so quickly, would I be correct in assuming they fast-tracked this case through the Grand Jury?"

He nodded. "They've already reached out with an offer. Murder in the second degree, with a sentencing recommendation of fifteen to twenty-five."

"What was your response?" I asked.

"I haven't discussed it with Mister Garrison yet," he said.

"When did they make the offer?" I asked.

"Uh, Wednesday," he answered.

I narrowed my eyes at him. "Today is Tuesday. They made the offer six days ago and you haven't discussed it with Flaky yet?"

Wes puffed up at my indignant tone. "I don't know who you think you are, but you're out of line coming into my house and talking to me like I'm a child."

He started to say more, but then suddenly grabbed his stomach and hurried down the hall, stepped through an open door, and slammed it shut. I then heard the distinct sound of the toilet seat being dropped.

I sighed and sat at his table, waiting. It was hard to ignore the obnoxious sounds emanating through the closed door and thin walls. I hoped he had the forethought to turn the bathroom's exhaust fan on. After a few minutes, I heard the toilet flush once, twice, and then a third time, soon followed by the sound of the shower running. I guess he'd made a mess of things. He finally made a reappearance, wearing baggy cargo shorts and a faded jersey bearing Greek letters. He reminded me of an over-age frat boy who refused to leave college for the real world.

"Sorry about that," he muttered as he sat beside me, his cup of coffee forgotten. I stood, reheated it in his microwave, and brought it to him. He nodded gratefully.

He sat there, staring at me, totally befuddled now. I waited. Finally, after a few long minutes, a look of understanding crept across his face.

"Oh, yeah. I have the discovery paperwork in my briefcase."

"Let's get started on it," I said. It was not a suggestion; it was a command.

He stared a moment in defiance before acquiescing. "I suppose I could use a second set of eyes."

He opened his briefcase and laid the paperwork on the table. We read the various documents and Wes began taking notes without me having to say anything. After thirty minutes, Wes stood and stretched.

"I think my stomach is settled down. I'm going to order something to eat."

"Good idea," I said.

He got on his phone and opened an app for one of the mobile food delivery services. After typing on his phone, he paused and glanced at me.

"You want me to order you anything?" he asked.

"If you don't have any coffee here, order a large cup," I said.

He nodded and did so. After a minute he went back to reading. I found the detective's report on his interview of Ethel Herring and the photographic lineup. I had to admit, I found no flaws. The interview and viewing of the lineup were recorded and the lineup array was excellent. That is, Flaky's photograph did not stand out from the others. I said as much to Wes.

"That's not good," he lamented.

The delivery came forty minutes later. I answered the door while Wes fumbled through his papers. As I suspected, my coffee was almost room temperature. I handed the bag of food to Wes before heading back to the microwave.

This was the gist of our activity for the next two hours before he tossed down his legal pad, slumped back in his chair, and rubbed his eyes.

"I've got a few ideas for a motion, but their case is pretty solid," he said.

"Alright, do your lawyer stuff, but first, you need to go visit Flaky and discuss the plea offer. He'll reject it, but you should've done it last week."

"Yeah, you're probably right," he admitted. He picked up his cell phone and looked at the time.

"Ah, if I'm going to do it, we should probably get going. I have plans for later this afternoon."

"Keg party?" I asked. He stared in puzzlement. "Forget it. Alright, I'll go with you. Let's get going. But first, why don't you change into some clothes that a professional lawyer would wear."

He looked down at his attire, nodded, and went into a bedroom. He emerged ten minutes later wearing an off-the-rack suit with the jacket sleeves about two inches too long.

"You should get it tailored," I suggested.

"Yeah, my mother said the same thing, but money's a little tight right now."

We rode together to the Rutherford County Jail and waited in the visitor's lobby until our names were called. When Flaky emerged and sat, he picked up the phone and gestured at me. I took the phone on our side.

"What the hell happened to you?" he asked.

"I had a run in with a couple of Satan's Dogs," I replied.

"Oh shit, brother. I told you to stay out of this case."

"I think Bull has it straightened out, and I'm going to help you out, whether you like it or not," I said. "Here, your attorney needs to talk to you."

I handed the phone over and listened as Wes explained the plea offer. As I expected, Flaky shook his head and had a few expletives to add. The conversation lasted another minute, but there was not much left to talk about. Wes concluded the meeting and promised to be in touch.

"Well, it looks like this one is going to trial," he grumbled as we walked out.

I sensed he was uncomfortable with the prospect of a jury trial.

"You need to file an immediate motion for the judge to appoint co-counsel."

He glanced at me. I detected a rising level of stress. "You think so?"

"Definitely. A murder case requires a lot of work. I'm surprised it hasn't already been done."

I waited until we got back to my car before speaking again.

"Wes, I'm going to talk to you man-to-man. Your work product on Flaky's case has been subpar, and I'm being nice when I say that. You need to get your head out of your ass and start acting like a professional lawyer."

"Yeah, okay," he said.

I pointedly stared. "Your tone indicates you don't think much of my advice."

He snorted. "You think?"

"Yeah, I think. Let me put it another way. You can accept it as both a threat and a warning; if Flaky is convicted due to your bumbling ineptitude, I'll do everything I can to get you disbarred."

He stared at me in disbelief. I stared back for a moment before starting my car. Neither of us spoke as I drove him back to his shitty apartment. When I parked, he got out and hesitated a moment.

"I see no reason for us to have any further contact with each other."

He closed the door without waiting for a response and walked away. I watched him as he disappeared through the door without looking back.

"Idiot," I muttered and headed home.

# CHAPTER 33

It was early afternoon when I returned home. I'd picked up some Chinese carryout on the way and ate it at my kitchen table as I watched TV, flipping back and forth between CNN, CNBC, and Fox News. After, I changed into some shorts and a tee shirt, grabbed a beer, and walked out back.

Bubba and I had mostly everything cleaned up from the fire. We'd even sold the cars and had them hauled away. The only thing left was the concrete floor where the shop once sat. I was committed to rebuilding and was anxious to get it started. After taking several measurements around the existing concrete pad, I went inside, fortified myself with a fresh beer, and sat at my desk. A half hour and one beer later and I had completed a decently drawn sketch of what I wanted on some graph paper.

My first inclination was to rebuild it myself. I had the knowledge and skills to do it, but I knew I would keep getting sidetracked with cases and other business. If I did it myself, it'd take several months, maybe a year or more, and I didn't want to wait that long.

Nope. I wasn't going to rebuild it myself. I wanted my shop rebuilt as soon as possible. After all, I had the money, and I wasn't getting any younger. Nope, I was going to hire a professional contractor and get it built as soon as possible.

"Yep, that's what I'm going to do," I muttered.

I opened my contact list and scrolled through it until I found a buddy named Fitz who used to be a cop. He was a damn good cop too, but after being shot in the line of duty, he decided he liked being a building contractor far better.

I called, we caught up with each other's respective lives for a couple of minutes, and then I got down to business and told him what I wanted.

"When do you want to get started?" he asked.

"Tomorrow," I replied. "I want it completely built before Labor Day."

Fitz let out a sigh. "Damn, Thomas, that'll be tough. I've got other jobs going on."

"I bet you can make it work if I pay extra."

I could hear his drumming fingers against a metal surface, perhaps the hood of his truck. I also heard noises in the background, causing me to think he was at a job site, which meant he wasn't bullshitting me, he had other jobs.

"Like I said, I can pay extra."

After a moment, he asked me what my dimensions were. I told him and advised half the concrete pad was already in place. He thought a moment longer before speaking.

"What do you think about a metal building?" he asked.

"Yeah, that'll work as long as it meets my requirements. I'm going to need to install a fire sprinkler system, so that means I'll need heat."

He thought for a few seconds. "Alright, I've got a kit for a two-car garage sitting in the back of my warehouse gathering dust. It was a custom order, and after I'd paid the manufacturer, the sorry SOB filed bankruptcy on me. Let me come by your house and see if it's something I could make work. How about I come by in about an hour?"

"I'll be here. I might even have a cold beer waiting for you," I said.

He chuckled and hung up. I nodded in satisfaction. I remembered Fitz was always a go-getter and I knew he could make it work.

I walked around the area, envisioning what the new shop was going to look like. At first, I was excited at the prospect of a new shop but looking at the bare concrete where my old shop once stood brought up bittersweet feelings. I had some fond memories from that shop. The one that seemed to stand out the most was one evening when Simone sat in a chair, drinking wine, and watching me as I changed the water pump in the Mustang.

I stared a few more minutes before getting a notepad and began writing down specific things I needed. I was contemplating getting a fresh beer when my phone rang.

"Good afternoon, Mister Ironcutter," he said.

I let out a slight scoff. "I was wondering if I'd ever hear from you again." I suspected this was probably going to be a long conversation, so I walked out front and sat on the porch.

"I apologize for my absence, I had an unrelated business emergency arise," he claimed, even though I doubt he expected me to believe him.

"Yeah, okay. Why are you calling?" I asked.

"I would like for you to first update me on the status of your investigation."

"I can keep it brief. The last time we spoke, you sent me to New Orleans."

"Indeed, I did. What did you find?" he asked.

"Someone got to Methuselah Sartain's mausoleum before I did. They broke into it and if there was any kind of artifact with his remains, they have it and they're long gone."

There was a long moment of silence before he spoke. "I see. This is most distressing news. Have you been able to identify the culprit?"

"No. I have my suspicions, but the bottom line is I am not interested in who did it," I said.

"Oh?"

"Yep. My investigation has run its course. There is nothing more for me to do except help try to solve a murder."

"Whose murder?" he asked.

"Officer Richard Tomey," I said.

"Ah, yes. The news reports mentioned the murder of a Nashville policeman, but I did not know it was Officer Tomey."

Tomey's murder had indeed made national news, so it could have been a logical explanation of him knowing about it, but I had my doubts.

"Do you have any suggestions of who I should investigate?" I asked.

"From the tone of your voice, you seem to be implying I had something to do with it."

"Did you?"

He made a tsking sound. "Let me be clear, I did not murder Officer Tomey."

"The cops said he was tortured, as if the culprit was trying to get information out of him. Perhaps the culprit was convinced Officer Tomey had stolen something out of an old grave and was questioning him about it."

"I admit, I would have liked for you to have questioned him. His death is unfortunate. Do you know if his residence was searched?"

"Yeah, the suspect or suspects ransacked his place."

"Do you think they found it?" he asked.

"Nope. Tomey did not steal the artifact. No police personnel at the scene took the artifact, I am certain of this."

"Yes, that may be true, but my sources inform me that the other party who is interested in this matter have not had any successful resolution either, which means the artifact is still unaccounted for."

"Well then, there are four possibilities," I said.

"Yes? Go on," he urged.

"Your competition has in fact recovered it and they're lying about it, you're lying, or there is a third party involved whom you are not aware of."

There was a moment's pause while he considered what I said. Or perhaps he was thinking up another good lie in order to further string me along.

"That is an interesting supposition," he finally said. "I have not thought of the possibility of a third party being involved in this. Thomas, do you think you could explore this possibility?"

"I'm not sure I want to," I said, and then had an idea. "I'll tell you what. I will continue my investigation if you agree to meet with the detectives investigating Officer Tomey's murder. They've been wanting to speak with you."

There was another long pause. Long enough that I thought maybe he had hung up.

"What is the fourth possibility you alluded to?" he asked.

"The fourth possibility is there is no artifact. It is merely a fanciful tale conjured up by a drunken priest, which leads me to a question. How did you come to believe the artifact was in the possession of Methuselah Sartain in the first place?"

"What I am about to say to you is strictly confidential," he said.

"Go on."

"My employer is a group of people who are descendants of the Knights Templar. In fact, you might say they are the modern-day Knights Templar."

"Like the Masons?" I asked.

"Oh, no, Mister Ironcutter. These are not men who meet at a clubhouse and drink beer, these are men and women who are actual descendants of the original Templars, as was Methuselah Sartain."

"Alright, so they really exist," I said.

"Indeed, they do. They are in possession of historical documents that have been passed down from generation to generation. I won't bore you with the details, but the priest mentions a man specifically by name. Research has found this man is a forefather of Methuselah. Further research has turned up that refers to members of the Templar who escaped the inquisitions. Methuselah's forefather was one of them. More information in the documents indicate there were several artifacts that were in their possession and have been handed down from father to son. The Sartain artifact is probably the most important one."

"More important than the Ark of the Covenant?" I asked.

He chuckled. "No, not quite that precious. But valuable, nonetheless. So, the artifact exists, and we must find it."

"We, huh?"

"Yes, we, Mister Ironcutter. You are a part of this now," he declared.

I grunted. "If you want me to continue to be a part of this, you will need to meet with the detectives. I can help provide you with legal representation if you feel you need it."

He paused before speaking. "I will be in touch."

I heard the click of the call being disconnected. I put my phone in my pocket and realized I had my beer bottle in a death grip. I willed myself to relax. The man irked me. I felt as though he were playing a game and I was going to be used as a scapegoat in the event he was caught. I had an idea and called Ronald.

"I just had a phone call and I want to know where the person is who called me," I said.

"Um, it'll take some time to set up. The computer I have dedicated to your stuff is offline. I'm upgrading it," he said.

I sighed. "Alright."

"Who called? Was it Mishka?"

"Yeah. He was supposedly in Miami, but I get the feeling he's back in Nashville," I said. "Well, it was a thought. I'm sure he'll turn up soon."

I considered calling Jay and arranging for Metro to put a wiretap on my phone, but I wasn't sure I was ready for that level of intrusion. Not yet, but I knew it may have to be done at some point though.

Fitz arrived thirty minutes early, which was a pleasant surprise. After opening a couple of beers, we got down to work. He took several measurements and a few pictures while we talked. I handed him my list of requirements and he studied it while he sipped his beer. After a moment he took a carpenter's pencil out from behind his ear and wrote something down on my list.

"Alright, the prefab kit I was referring to is a little small for what you want, but if I put up concrete block walls around the back and sides, I can make it work. I'll draw up a contract tonight with all the specifics, but here's a rough estimate of the cost."

He handed me the paper. There was a number written down at the top. I reached into my pocket and pulled out a check I'd already filled out and handed it to him.

"Here's your down payment," I said. He unfolded it and looked it over. I saw his eyes widen in pleasant surprise.

"Yep, I believe we can do business, Thomas," he said with a grin. "I'll have the contract drawn up tonight. It'll take a day or two for me to pull the permits, but I think we can go ahead and get started with the preliminary work."

We shook hands and he left. It was still warm out, but the temperature had dropped to the eighties once the sun had started going down, which made for a pleasant evening. I got a fresh beer and sat in a lawn chair. Ronald texted me a moment later.

The call came from Miami International Airport.

So, the man was still in Miami. Interesting. I considered texting Jay and relaying the information, but immediately squashed that idea. If I did, he'd tell the others, and that would lead them to believe I was in regular contact with the man. That would lead to unwanted attention from them.

My phone rang again. When I answered, it sounded like an older man.

"Hey, Sport. I'm calling about possibly hiring you for a job," he said.

"Alright, Sport. What kind of job might you have in mind?"

"I have a former son-in-law who has absconded with several thousand dollars in assets. I need to find him. Is that something in your bailiwick?"

"Yes, it is," I said. Locating people was indeed something within my skill set, but for some reason, I was getting a bad vibe from this potential client. Maybe I was still agitated about Mishka, so I tried to remain professional.

"If they're still in the United States and using their own name, I have a good success rate in locating them. I'll require any information you have about him, including information on any pending court cases."

"Yeah, I can do that. My daughter has all kinds of dirt on him. This man is a rat. Let me tell you…"

He launched into a long-winded diatribe about all the troubles the son-in-law had caused in his family's life. I waited until there was a lull and interrupted.

"I'm not interested in your family dynamics, Sport. If you want to hire me to find the man, I will. I don't need to know all the family drama."

"Oh, I absolutely want to hire you. This man needs to be in prison. Let me tell you what he did to my little girl."

I interrupted again. "Before we talk about anything else, we need to discuss my fee. My base fee is a thousand a week, plus expenses, and I require the first payment up front."

There was a long sigh, and I could hear a woman saying something in the background. "Well, Sport, let's talk. I'm disabled and on a fixed income. You need to work with me a little bit on that fee of yours."

I heard the woman in the background shouting that he should tell me he was a veteran. I guess she thought I gave veteran discounts. Funny, my electric company had never discounted my bill due to my veteran's status. It was my turn to sigh, and I had a sudden spark of a memory. "Did you recently email me regarding this case?"

"Yes, I did, and I didn't get a response," the man said.

"Yeah, there's a reason for that. I'm not going to take your case," I said.

"Why not, Sport?"

"Because my fee is non-negotiable, and when a person starts talking about being disabled or being on a fixed income, I know you can't afford me."

"Sport, a good businessman always leaves a little wiggle room on their rates for special or extenuating circumstances."

"I'll let you in on a little secret, Sport, you aren't special. Have a good day." I disconnected the call and cursed under my breath. My phone rang again. I answered and was about to unleash a torrent of invectives but stopped short.

"Hi, Thomas, it's Officer Severns. Abby."

I was surprised. She was not someone I ever expected to receive a phone call from. "Hey, Abby, what's going on?"

"If it's not too much trouble, I'd like to come by your house and talk to you for a minute. It won't take long," she said.

"Yeah, sure," I said, growing even more confused.

She said she'd be by in ten minutes. I didn't think there was anything nefarious going on, but I was definitely confused.

"I guess I'll find out in ten minutes," I said to myself, and walked inside.

I don't know why, but I hurried to the bathroom where I brushed my hair and teeth before changing out of the baggy shorts I was wearing and into a clean pair of khaki shorts. I'd gotten the beer bottles thrown into the trash as the marked patrol car entered the driveway.

It looked like she was riding with the same officer. Clark was his name. He was sitting in the passenger seat and seemed to be involved in an intense conversation on his phone. Abby got out and walked up. Her uniform was crisply pressed, and her boots had a polished spit shine. She looked sharp, professional.

"I hope I'm not bothering you," she said.

"Not at all. How's work going?" I asked.

She glanced back at the car and lowered her voice. "I'd take Tomey over him any day. Tomey may have been a big talker, but at least he was teaching me stuff. This one is constantly on the phone arguing with his girlfriend. I swear, he's at it the entire shift. When he isn't on the phone, he's complaining about what a rotten bitch she is." She then brought her hand up to her mouth. "Um, sorry, I meant what a rotten person she is."

I smiled. "I'm often guilty of bad language too."

She smiled back and nodded. "Anyway, the reason I'm here is about Tomey."

"His funeral is tomorrow, right?"

"Yeah, and the chief is expected to give a press conference about the status of his murder investigation. They are really pressuring the detectives to produce something. Today, I was at headquarters for four hours being interviewed." When she said the word 'interviewed' she used air quotes. "They asked me everything, including if I was having a sexual relationship with him. It was humiliating."

I waited to see if there was a question. There didn't seem to be. I cleared my throat.

"When a case languishes, it's not uncommon for detectives to broaden the scope of their investigation. They explore other possible motives and interview more people, ask pointed questions, you get the idea."

She considered what I said a moment before speaking. "They also asked me about you."

I frowned. "Who was interviewing you?"

"Detectives Poston and Kettleworth," she said.

My frown was replaced with a look of disgust and a slight shake of my head. "Yeah, I should've known. Look, during your law enforcement career, you are going to work with people who are good at their job and others who are not so good. The ones who are not so good often attempt to make up for their deficiencies in different ways."

"Like bad talking other people to try to make themselves look superior," she said.

"Exactly," I said, and a slight smile crossed my lips. "What does the bible say about that?"

"The book of James comes to mind. Do not speak evil against one another," she said.

"Yes indeed."

"They said some pretty bad things," she said.

"I'm a flawed human, no doubt about it, but I guess I've been guilty of saying bad things about others as well," I said.

"Detective Poston seems to have a particular disliking of you. Why is that?" she asked.

I gave a contemptuous chuckle. "Ian Poston and I used to work together. He is a vain and petty man."

"Because you're tall and handsome and he's short, and maybe not so handsome?" she asked.

I grinned. "That might be part of it. Mostly, it's because he has always thought of himself as the superior detective. He's decent, but he's definitely not superior. Back when we worked together, I would point it out on occasion."

"Really? Like how? Give me an example," she urged.

"Alright. One time he cleared a cold murder and then bragged about it for days. The problem was, he did not perform due diligence and the case got messed up. The commander then handed off the case to me. I was able to clean it up and present it to the DA for a successful prosecution."

"How did he mess it up?" she asked.

"When the case went cold, a reward was posted for information about the murder. A young man came forward and claimed he was an eyewitness. There were three men involved and he knew all of them. He had learned enough intimate details about the case so that his story seemed credible. The problem Poston had, he never corroborated anything. It turned out this so-called witness was locked up in juvenile detention when the murder occurred. There was no way he was an eyewitness."

"Oh, wow," she said.

"Yeah. This all came out in the media and Poston was convinced I fed them the information."

"Did you?" she asked with a slight grin.

"Nope. There were at least two news crews present in the courtroom during the preliminary hearing. Poston knew this, but he blamed me anyway."

"Alright, so what about Kettleworth?" she asked.

"We've never worked together on any cases, and I barely know her. When the rogue FBI agent was killed at my house, she responded to the scene and immediately branded me as a murder suspect before knowing all the facts. I was not in a good mood and voiced my opinion of her poor detective skills. She's disliked me ever since."

She was staring intensely now. "They didn't come right out and accuse you, but they strongly implied you are involved. Not only in Tomey's murder, but also the murders of the grave robbers."

I took a deep breath in order to keep from getting angry. "Abby, I'm no saint. Tomey was no saint, but he was a good man and a good officer. I would never knowingly or willingly hinder the prosecution of his murderer."

"What about destroying evidence?" she asked. "Detective Kettleworth said you destroyed incriminating files on your phone and laptop."

I chuckled. "Oh, I may have deleted some data, but it had nothing to do with Tomey's case. It's a little hard to explain, but I had a lot of sensitive information on other cases. Information that I would not trust Kettleworth or Poston with. Make no mistake, if either of those two could find something to use against me, they would."

She continued staring the entire time I spoke. I suppose she was assessing me. After I finished speaking, she glanced back at her partner, who was still on his phone.

"Alright, you've given me a lot to think about."

I could see from her expression she was stressing over something. I asked about it. She took a long moment before making eye contact.

"I want to be a good officer, but I'm getting told things I'm not sure I believe, and it feels like I'm getting manipulated and used."

"Let me guess, when you first started in this line of work, you thought in terms of law and order, black and white, it'd all be easy to figure out. Now you're starting to see it's a little more complex."

She smiled slightly. "Yeah, I guess so. Was it the same with you?"

"Oh yeah."

"What did you do about it?" she asked.

"I tried to do my job the way I thought it was supposed to be done and chose my friends carefully."

"Should I choose you as a friend, Thomas?" she asked.

I gazed at her in surprise. "I hope so. I would like that."

She stared. "Your face is looking better. You're getting back to handsome again."

Our conversation was interrupted by her partner honking the horn.

She jerked her head back to the car and jumped to her feet. "I better get going."

"Call anytime," I replied and watched as she hustled back to the patrol car. I could see her partner seeming to chastise her before they turned the car around and sped away.

# CHAPTER 34

"What's up, dickhead," Hal greeted when he answered.

"Good news, my little shyster buddy, all subpoenas have been served," I said.

"Wow, that was quick. I should probably pay you a bonus, but that'd be stupid of me."

"If you think you can get a payment deposited in my account before the end of the week, that'll be good enough."

"Consider it done," he said. "I might have a new case next week. A traffic fatality involving a man driving his employer's delivery truck. Supposedly, the truck had brake issues and the driver had brought it to the attention of the owner, who ignored his complaint. It could be a good one. I'll let you know if I can use you."

He thanked me again before hanging up. I went home, changed clothes, and began doing yardwork. I had the front yard mostly done when a white Jeep Wrangler appeared in my drive. The occupant parked and got out. It was Abby.

She was wearing jeans and a dark blue Polo shirt with a tee shirt underneath. It was over eighty degrees out, so the extra clothing seemed like a little much. She gave a slight wave as she walked up.

"Nice ride. Is that your personal vehicle?" I asked.

"Yeah, I bought it used, but it's in great shape." She looked at my half-finished yard. "I'm sorry, I called first, but when you didn't answer I thought I'd drive by and take a chance."

I nodded and stared. She had an odd expression. I wasn't sure what to make of it. Maybe she was enthralled by my sweat soaked tee shirt sticking to my body, or maybe not.

"I've been thinking about taking a break and getting a fresh glass of iced tea. Would you like some?"

"Sure," she answered.

"We can sit outside on the porch, if you like," I suggested.

"Okay."

Returning with two large glasses that were already soaked with condensation, I handed one to her. When I sat, Abby had a small piece of paper and pen in hand. She took the glass with her empty hand, took a sip, and set it down.

"That hits the spot. I've been meaning to come by and talk to you," she said. She then held up the piece of paper.

I'm wearing a wire.

I nodded in acknowledgement, although this took me by surprise. I halfway suspected they'd try something, but I never thought they'd use a rookie officer. If she had not tipped me off, I doubt I would have figured it out. I could only imagine the sales pitch used on her to get her to do this. It was probably a combination of intimidation and false promises. I motioned for her to hand the note over. She frowned but did so.

"What would you like to talk about?" I said as I slowly but deliberately tore the slip of paper into little pieces and stuck them in my pocket.

"Richard," she replied.

I nodded. "It's always hard when a police officer is murdered. I take it since he was your training officer, it's been especially difficult."

"Yes, it has." She took a swallow, and then stared pointedly at me. "Thomas, I feel like you know more than you're telling."

I nodded and thought of an appropriate answer for this charade. "I've only known you a short time, but I feel I can trust you, Abby. What would you like to know?"

"Could you talk to me in confidence and tell me what's really going on?"

Her gaze was steady, but I could tell she was uncomfortable. A bead of sweat ran down the side of her face. She frowned and swiped at it.

"As you already know, my client was in search of an artifact he believed was hidden in Sadie Sartain's grave. He has admitted hiring the two men to rob the grave but believes they were murdered before recovering the artifact. He specifically hired me to investigate the possibility a police officer had stolen the artifact while on the scene of the double murder."

It was a wordy explanation and not normally how I spoke, but I wanted to be clear so that maybe this nonsense would end.

"Ah, I understand why you met with me and questioned me now," she said.

"Yes, exactly. He had researched my background and felt that my past would give me an advantage with getting information from cops."

"What did you tell him?" she asked, although we'd already discussed this previously.

"I informed him that as a result of our talk, I was convinced that not only did you not take the artifact, but nobody else did either. At least, no cop or other personnel at the scene. I told him I was certain of this and that your integrity was beyond reproach."

Her gaze intensified and I could see her eyes were suddenly watering up. I looked away and she quickly wiped them.

"So, the esteemed detectives believe my client may have murdered Tomey," I said.

"They think it's a strong possibility," she said.

"And they believe I may be complicit, or that I somehow aided and abetted in the murder," I added. "Perhaps they even believe I have actively tried to hinder the investigation."

She was gripping her knees tightly. "If there's anything you know…"

"The answer is no to all three lines of thought."

"But you wiped your computer and cell phone," she said.

Instead of answering and having it on record that I destroyed data, I shrugged and deflected. "Abby, I've already provided all the pertinent information I have about my client to Detective Sansing. Even after their unprofessional behavior, I immediately called Sansing when I learned of the van. When I learned of my client's name, I personally went to headquarters and gave the information to Sansing. I liked Tomey. He was a co-worker of mine at one time. I want his killer apprehended as much as anyone else."

"Do you think your client murdered him?"

When she asked, it was almost like she was reading from a script. No doubt they'd had her memorize a list of questions to ask. I gave her a slight shrug.

"I honestly don't know. I've asked him, he's denied it."

"Where is he now?" she asked.

"I don't know. The one and only time we've met face-to-face was when he hired me. All subsequent conversations have been by phone."

It took about half a second before I realized I'd screwed up. My statement now gave them the probable cause to obtain a court order for a wiretap. If Poston was listening in, and I had no doubt he was, he'd have a court order drafted for a judge to sign by this time tomorrow. The only good thing about it; he was going to be up all night working on his verbiage for the affidavit. If Abby understood my faux pax, she didn't show it.

"Is there anyone else who may have reason to kill Richard?" she asked.

That one surprised me a little. I wondered who told her to think of that one. It indicated they might actually believe someone else may have been responsible. I thought about it a moment before answering.

"Possibly. Mishka mentioned that another group of people were also after this alleged artifact. I never said anything to Jay about it."

"Why not?" she asked.

"Because of the outrageousness of it. He claimed there is a group within the Catholic organization who are also actively seeking this artifact."

Her eyes widened. I held a hand up, like it puzzled me as well. "I know, it sounds crazy, and I have absolutely no proof of this, that's why I never said anything. I want you to understand something though, we are assuming the reason Tomey was murdered was because of this artifact. It may have nothing to do with it at all. The motive for his murder could be something totally unrelated. An old enemy, a crazy ex, anyone."

"But what if it does have to do with the artifact?" she asked.

"Then I will help catch the person who did it," I said.

We talked a few more minutes before she stood.

"I have to go. We should talk again soon," she said.

"Of course," I replied.

I walked her to her car and then watched her leave. I finished with the yardwork, hosed off the lawnmower, and returned it to Buford's garage. A new lawnmower was definitely on top of the list, and I made a mental note to go shopping tomorrow. Abby called me as I was getting out of the shower.

"I don't have it on anymore. I didn't want to do it, but they kept pressuring me until I agreed. I'm sorry," she said.

"Don't worry about it," I replied. "Everything I told you was the truth."

"I believe you. After I left you, they grilled me for almost an hour and want me to arrange another meeting with you."

"That'll be fine," I said, then smiled. "We'll meet when you're off duty, so they'll have to pay you overtime."

She chuckled slightly. "Yeah, that'll be cool."

"Oh, before I forget, they will more than likely get a wiretap on my phone within the next day or two, so keep that in mind whenever you call me."

I heard her gasp. "A wiretap? Do you really think they'll do that?"

"Kettleworth probably doesn't even know the procedure to do it, but Poston does, and he's convinced I'm complicit. So, yeah, I'm certain of it."

She thought it over before nodding in understanding. "Okay. What do we do next?"

"Go along with everything they ask you. Controlled phone calls, text messages, an offer to give me a full body massage. You get the idea."

She laughed now. "Yeah, okay."

"Seriously, they'll tell you to turn up the pressure on me to be more forthcoming. Do what they say."

"I don't like doing this. It feels dishonest and dirty," she said.

"Undercover work is all about deception."

She sighed. "Yeah, I guess. It looks a lot cooler on TV than it really is."

We agreed that if they wanted her to wear a wire again, she'd call me and invite me to lunch. After another minute or two of conversation, we hung up. I felt sorry for her. She was being put in a position she was not comfortable with, and it wasn't fair how they were treating this rookie cop. I had no doubt they told her how much it would do for her career if she could get me to admit to all kinds of evil acts.

The night was young, and I was alone. It was times like these that I missed Simone terribly. I had no desire to go out, but I did give a thought to giving Marti a call. Ultimately, I found a decent movie on TV and made myself comfortable in my easy chair. Tommy Boy waited expectantly until I put my old, well-worn throw blanket over my legs. He then jumped up and curled up on my lap. He fell asleep first. I had the stamina to at least stay awake until the movie was over.

# CHAPTER 35

After a hard morning run, I checked my trail cameras. There was nothing of importance, only a few deer and a lone coyote. I was hoping for a return visit from the arsonist. Until I could figure some other way of identifying them, this was my best chance.

But there was nothing.

I was on my second mug of coffee when it occurred to me that I had not yet looked at the video card from the cemetery's surveillance camera. Sitting at my desk, I plugged it into my laptop and opened it. What I saw threw me for a loop.

There was a person digging beside Sadie Sartain's grave. The night vision was excellent. I had no problem recognizing Larry T as in Thomas Boles. I also recognized the person standing there, watching Larry work, even though she was wearing a ball cap pulled low.

"What the hell is going on here?" I muttered.

It was Valkyrie, also known as Eva.

It took Larry a considerable amount of time to dig the hole, but he was a workhorse and only stopped to take an occasional water break. Luckily, I had a large memory card and it recorded everything from start to finish. I fast-forwarded to the part where Larry was down in the hole and Eva was standing over it. I could see a faint glow emanating from the hole, presumably from a flashlight. After several minutes, Larry emerged from the hole and stood beside Eva. It appeared they were talking but my video did not record sound. Larry went back down in the hole one final time. He was down there for several minutes before once again crawling out. After a brief conversation, Larry began refilling the hole. Finishing, he smoothed everything over. I guess that's why I didn't notice the ground had been disturbed when I retrieved the card. As I watched, the two of them then walked toward the parking lot and out of sight. There was no other activity the rest of the night.

This was an unusual turn. What was Eva doing? I had questions, many questions. I tried calling her with the number she'd provided, but it went straight to voicemail. I left a message, hoping she'd call back, but I was uncertain if she would be honest and forthcoming. That's when I immediately thought of Larry T-Thomas Boles. I smiled to myself. A good cigar and a few sips from my flask would get more honesty out of him than anyone. I had no way of calling him though. I was going to have to hunt him down. Hopping in my Explorer, I headed toward the cemetery.

Not finding him anywhere around the cemetery, I began slowly driving up and down the streets in the area. I struck out there as well, so I headed over to the Nashville Rescue Mission on Lafayette. A couple of loafers were sitting out front. They knew who Larry was, but nobody admitted to seeing him in the past couple of days.

The law-and-order part of my brain told me it was my duty to call Detective Jay Sansing and provide this information, but I was still pissed off at all of them and decided against it. I wasn't even inclined to call Percy. So, I kept driving around, expanding my search, block by block.

I had numerous phone calls while I was doing this. It was a good thing I had that accessory which allowed me to sync the phone to the car, allowing for hands-free talking. I answered each call in hopes it was Eva, but for some reason Wednesday seemed to be the day for the spam callers. It was the usual trash, along with one slightly amusing call from a person who purported themselves to be the president of the local FOP booster club and invited me to become a member. When I stated I was currently under house arrest and awaiting trial for buggery on the high seas, he hung up on me.

Surprisingly, Eva called back an hour later.

"Hello, Thomas," she greeted.

"Hello. Where are you?" I asked.

"I am in Nashville. I have been with a friend of yours. A man named Larry."

"Oh, yeah? What have you two been doing?"

"I hired him to dig up the grave," she said.

Her candor was unexpected. It made me wonder if she knew about the presence of my surveillance camera. "Alright, you've got my curiosity aroused. Why did you do it?"

"I wanted to see for myself if anything was there."

"What did you find?" I asked.

"You already know the answer to that question, yes?"

"Yes, I believe I do," I said and sighed.

"Are you upset, Thomas?" Eva asked.

"Upset? No, but I strongly suspect there is a lot you're not telling me."

"Thomas, there are things that I cannot tell you, I am sorry," she said, and then disconnected.

I wanted to know more. I wanted to say more, but it wasn't going to happen it seemed. This case was growing more and more frustrating. I had to admit to myself, if Eva was not a part of this, I wouldn't be so emotionally invested in this case.

"Damn it all," I growled.

Finding Larry did not seem important anymore. None of it seemed important anymore. Ten minutes later I was turning into the parking lot of Mick's Place.

# CHAPTER 36

Regret. That was the buzzword for the day.

I did two things the night before that I was now regretting. First, I drank too much. Marti was tending bar and she made sure I didn't go dry. Second, instead of getting a taxi, Marti drove me home, and ended up spending the night.

Now, I was feeling like crap. My head was throbbing, and my bedroom smelled like a combination of stale cigar smoke and sex. Marti was lying beside me, her nose buried in my ear, snoring like a beaver in heat.

I carefully worked my way free of her arms and the tangle of sheets and tiptoed my way to the restroom. After cleaning up, I went to the kitchen, prepped a pot of coffee, and dry-swallowed four Ibuprofen.

There was a trail of clothing leading from the den to my bedroom, a good indicator of how our night ended. I gathered them up and went to the utility room. Separating Marti's clothes from mine, I threw hers in the dryer with a few of those scented fabric softener sheets. I did not wash them because, frankly, I wanted her to leave as soon as possible. I couldn't say why exactly. I liked her, I cared about her, but she wasn't Simone and never would be. I was wondering if it would be that way with any woman I was with when I heard my plumbing kick in. She was showering, which was good.

I walked into the kitchen, sat, and rubbed the back of my neck. I'd scolded myself several times in the past for drinking too much, which was always followed by a mental promise to slow it down. It never seemed to work. Marti soon walked out of the bedroom, wearing nothing, and sat at the kitchen table with me. I poured her a cup of coffee and told her what I'd done with her clothes.

"Thanks. I don't like the day after smell that comes from working at Mick's, but the tips are good and I don't have to do lap dances anymore," she said with a wink.

I nodded and was about to comment about how much more she got in tips back when she was stripping but decided to remain quiet. She had an incredible body, enhanced by breast implants, and she was cute, but the late nights, the bars, the smoking, it was starting to show in her features.

"You tied one on last night," she remarked.

"Yeah, I'm paying for it now," I replied, wondering how I looked and if my face was also aging prematurely.

"You did it again, you know," she remarked.

I stared at her in confusion. "I did what?"

"We were getting it on, and I was about to have one hell of an orgasm, and then you called me Simone."

"I did that?" I asked.

She nodded. "It kind of ruined the moment. You did it on the night of your birthday too." She made a goofy expression. "Oh, Simone, I love you so much!"

She said it in a mocking tone, which did not endear me to her, but I wasn't going to argue.

"Sorry about that," I muttered.

"It's okay. I was mad about it the other night, but I'm over it."

She took a sip of coffee before standing and walking back to the utility room. She came back a minute later, dressed. She walked over, kissed me on top of the head, and caressed my hair for a second.

"You know, I'm more than just a fuck toy. If you ever want to simply talk, I'm here for you."

Her statement surprised me. I didn't think she cared about anything other than the sex and the free meals when I took her out.

"That's a kind gesture. I might take you up on it sometime. Thanks for being understanding," I said.

She smiled. "You need a haircut. Do you need a ride back to your car?"

"Nah, I know you have things to do. I'll get an Uber or something."

"Okay. I'll see you later. Call me."

She'd been gone less than a minute when my phone rang.

"Hello, Thomas, it's Abby."

"Good morning. How's it going?" I asked. I guessed her formalities were due to being recorded, so I played along.

"I was wondering if I could come by and talk?"

"Sure. I need to go pick up my car. If you can give me a ride, I'll buy you lunch."

She agreed and arrived within ten minutes. It made me suspect that they were parked nearby the whole time. My suspicions were confirmed when I spotted our tail two minutes into our ride.

"Why did you leave your car?" she asked as we rode.

"I'd had a few beers and chose not to drive," I said.

"Did you have your girlfriend come get you?" she asked.

"Something like that," I answered.

I wasn't sure why she asked, decided it didn't matter, and changed the subject to the reason she'd come over. After all, I had no doubt she was acting on the direction of Poston and Kettleworth. They probably had a script they made her memorize. If she didn't follow it, I had no doubt they'd tear into her during the debriefing.

"Have there been any updates on Tomey's murder case?" I asked.

"None that I know of. They're continuing to interview people. How about you? Have you learned anything?"

I shrugged, and then remembered the wire and gave a verbal response. "No, I haven't."

"How about that client, has he contacted you?"

"Nope. I don't even know if he's still around or long gone. I'm sure he's considered a person of interest, but I have no information that would prove one way or another."

I was certain the man would be calling any day now, but I wasn't going to voice it out loud. To do so would have provided additional probable cause that would convince a judge to authorize prolonging the phone tap.

I rubbed my temples. My headache had only slightly dissipated, and I wasn't in the mood to play this game. Not today. I provided directions and soon we were parked beside my Explorer. Abby noticed I was being unusually quiet and tried to start a conversation a couple of times before giving up. I unclasped my seatbelt and turned toward her.

"I apologize for not being good company. If you don't mind, I'd like to take a raincheck on lunch."

"Sure," she said. It was obvious she was disappointed, but I had no idea if it was because she didn't complete her mission of getting me to talk or if she actually wanted my company. I decided to help her out a little bit.

"Oh, I almost forgot to mention something," I said.

"You did? What?"

"Someone recently dug down into the Sartain grave again."

Her eyes widened at the information. "Really?"

"Yeah. After they did it, they filled the hole back in and smoothed it out. The casual observer would never spot it."

"Who do you think did it? Your client?" she asked.

"No, I think it was someone other than him," I said.

"Um, why do you think that?" she asked. It was a good question, but I wasn't going to tell her how I knew.

"Call it a hunch," I said.

"What were they looking for? The same thing your client is looking for?" she asked.

"That would be my guess. I doubt they found anything either."

She slowly nodded and frowned. "You're saying there's more than one person or persons looking for this treasure?"

"That's my hunch. For all I know, there could be multiple treasure seekers. I appreciate the ride. I promise to make it up to you. How about I give you a shout tomorrow?"

"Okay," she said.

I sat in my Ford and watched her drive off. The car that had been following us, a dark green Chevy Malibu, was stationary in a church parking lot a block away. If I were in a better mood, I would've led them on a merry ride down to Tunica and they could've wasted the day watching me play poker.

Instead, I went back home and fixed a couple of simple egg sandwiches, light on the salt and pepper, plenty of mayo. The meal settled my stomach and my headache had mostly subsided. Putting the dirty dishes in the washer, I wiped down the kitchen counter and then sat. I probably could have sat the rest of the day, but I knew I needed to get up and do some kind of physical activity. Work up a good sweat and all that.

I decided to take a walk around my property. Gracie, Anna's German Shepherd, used to join me on my walks and I enjoyed her company, but now I was alone. Maybe I should get a dog of my own. I checked everything as I walked, but nothing appeared to have been tampered with or out of the ordinary. I guess this vengeful enemy was satisfied with the fire and was done with me.

I was standing at the entrance of my driveway, contemplating the idea of putting up a security gate, when Abby's Jeep came into view. She slowed when she saw me. I thought she was going to drive off, but after a moment of apparent indecision, she turned in and stopped.

# CHAPTER 37

She rolled down her window and offered a nervous smile. "Hi."

"Fancy seeing you again so soon," I said.

"I was worried about you. You seemed sick," she said, and after a moment, she continued. "I'm not wearing a wire right now. I'm supposed to call you tomorrow and guilt you into taking me to lunch."

I nodded. "We can do that."

"If you're sick, we can wait."

I let out a sigh. "I have a small confession to make. I'm not really sick. I'm a little bit hungover."

"Oh."

"I was hanging out with friends last night and had a few too many. I'm feeling better now." My explanation was perhaps an attempt at minimization, and I only felt slightly better.

"That's why I don't drink," she said. "My father was a recovering alcoholic."

I wasn't sure if she was implying that I was an alcoholic too, but I nodded in understanding.

"So, what brings you back here?" I asked.

She bit her lip and dropped her head.

"What's wrong?" I asked.

"It's stupid. I'm sorry I'm bothering you. I should go."

"No, don't go. I'm glad to see you. I'm confused though; what's going on?"

She took a deep breath and let it out slowly before regarding me. "I just needed someone to talk to. Like I said. I'm being stupid."

"You're not being stupid," I quickly replied. "Come on, drive me to the house. We'll go inside where it's nice and cool."

She agreed. After parking, I led her inside. I could tell something was genuinely bothering her. This wasn't a ruse.

"Are you thirsty?" I asked. She nodded. "Make yourself comfortable and I'll fix some iced tea."

I poured two glasses and found her in the den, staring at my custom-made shelves that were lined with books.

"I saw these the other night. You said they'd dumped them all on the floor," she said.

"Yes, they did," I replied. "Kettleworth was the instigator, but Sansing is not without some responsibility."

"Why would they do something like that?" she asked.

I smiled at her naiveté. "She's not the first cop to trash somebody's residence under the guise of looking for evidence, but in this case she did it purely out of maliciousness. Don't ever be like her."

"I won't. Did you ever do it when you were a detective?" she asked.

"Not me personally, but I've assisted in search warrants where a few co-workers got carried away."

"Did you do anything about it?"

I shrugged. "There was a time when police officers didn't snitch out their own unless it was something serious. I'd intervene when I felt like it was feasible, maybe admonish them, but that was it."

"We have a policy now that says if I don't report an officer's wrongdoing, I'm considered guilty of the wrongdoing as well and will be punished for it."

"Not a bad policy," I said. "Sometimes the wrong people get into law enforcement. The blue wall of silence hid those people. Departments are slowly but steadily changing that mindset."

"I won't ever stand for it," she declared.

"Good. You want to hear a tip from an old dumb cop?"

She smiled. "Sure, but I hardly think you're dumb, and you're not that old."

I nodded at the compliment and gestured at the books. "If you're ever involved in serving a search warrant, use logic. For example, each of those books could hide something. A methodical search is far better than simply pulling them off the shelf and tossing them around.

"You may find yourself involved in searching the house of somebody who is nothing more than a lowlife thug. Even they deserve a modicum of respect. Don't go overboard and destroy stuff." I walked over to a book, pulled it from the shelf, opened it, and pulled out a folded sheet of paper.

"What's that?" she asked.

"I jotted down all my usernames and passwords as a backup. Kettleworth never found it because she was more focused on disrespecting me than finding evidence." I tucked the paper back in the book and replaced it.

"They never found it?" she asked.

"Nope."

"Pretty clever, but I bet I would've found it," she said with a grin.

"You probably would have. It wouldn't have done any good though."

"Yeah, she told me about that. You used some kind of malicious software to destroy all your data. She wanted me to get you to admit to that on record so she could charge you with it. Why'd you do that?"

"Why, I don't even know what you're talking about," I replied.

She smirked. "I'm not wearing a wire right now." She saw my look. "I know what you're about to say, you'll need to strip search me to confirm that."

I shrugged. She scoffed and turned back toward my books. I sat down and watched her while I drank my tea. After a moment, she pulled a random book out and began going through it.

"That one's a machinist's reference manual," I said.

"Is it interesting?" she asked with a wry smile.

"It is to me. You may find it dull reading."

She pointed at the sticky tabs that were on different pages. "What are these for?"

"I bookmarked some specific information."

She looked up. "Wouldn't it be easier just to look this stuff up on the internet?"

"Sometimes, but I like books," I replied.

She nodded in seeming understanding, put the book back and sat on the couch. I got up and refilled our glasses.

"Thanks," she said and looked around. "You've cleaned up the house pretty good. It was a wreck the last time I was here."

"I've got almost everything back to normal. There's still a faint odor of smoke though. I'll need to spend the day doing a deep clean, like washing down the walls and all that stuff."

"Yeah," she agreed.

Tommy Boy came out of the back room and looked us over.

"That's Tommy Boy."

"Hi, Tommy Boy," Abby said. "Is he named after you?"

"Oh, no. He was already named that by his original owner. She was one of my clients. After she died, I kind of adopted him, or he adopted me. I'm not sure which applies."

She smiled at my quip. Tommy Boy looked us over a few more seconds before wandering into the kitchen. After a moment, I could hear him eating. Abby drank her tea in silence. After several seconds of silence, I prodded her.

"So, what's bothering you? Trouble at work?"

She nodded her head again and her eyes clouded up. "I overheard a couple of officers talking about me yesterday."

"Unflattering remarks, I'm guessing?" I queried.

She nodded again. "One of them said I was a pretentious know-it-all and the others laughed."

I caught myself from chuckling. To me, it was a trivial matter, but obviously she was upset, and I wasn't going to make it worse.

"Do you know the context of the conversation or what he was referring to?"

"The day before that, he was talking about Tennessee's domestic violence laws and I corrected him on a couple of points," she said. "Oh, and a week before that, the same guy had asked me out. I told him he wasn't my type. Since then, he's been a little snippy toward me. He said a few other unflattering remarks that I won't repeat."

"You bruised his ego and he's lashing out," I said.

"Yeah, I guess so," she agreed. "It still hurts though. I want people to like me, but it seems like I can't make any friends. There are these two women on my shift. They're gay. No big deal, right? But they don't even speak to me. Do you know why? Because Clark told them I was a devout Christian."

"They think you're a homophobe based on your Christian beliefs," I surmised.

"Yeah, but I'm not. I tried to tell one of them, but she wouldn't listen." She blinked several times and dabbed at her eyes. "I just want them to like me."

"Not everyone is going to like you," I said. "There will be different reasons. Envy, jealousy, spite, bias, sexism, the list is endless. And have you ever heard of the term schadenfreude?"

"I can't say that I have," she said.

"It's German. It means deriving great pleasure at someone's misfortune."

She thought about it before nodding. "I bet Poston was full of schadenfreude when you were arrested for your wife's murder."

I gave a grim smile. "Yeah, probably. I know there are people out there who don't like me, they speak badly of me, they wish me endless misfortune. I've learned not to let it affect me. Don't let those kinds of people beat you down and harm your self-esteem. It's hard to do, but once you achieve that mindset, people like that become irrelevant."

"How long did it take you to get that kind of mindset?" Abby asked.

"It took a bit of doing," I admitted. "It started back when I was a teenager. I didn't have a good homelife and I escaped it by joining the Army. That was a huge maturation period in my life. I guess that's where it started."

She asked about my childhood, and I gave her the Reader's Digest version. I left out a lot of things, but she got the highlights.

"So, you're a preacher's daughter?" I asked, changing the subject before she started asking for more details.

"Yep. I have a brother that's two years older than me and a sister that's four years older. I was the baby of the family."

"I remember you telling me that your father died of cancer. How are your mom and siblings handling it?"

I saw her jaw muscles tighten. "Gina, that's my sister, is doing great. She's a veterinarian and has always been there for me. George is my brother. I guess you'd say he's been struggling through life for the past couple of years." She glanced at me. "He has an issue with addiction. We've tried to intervene, but nothing we do seems to help. He's currently living somewhere in California."

"I'm sorry to hear that. How's your mom? I imagine your father's death was pretty hard on her."

Abby scoffed. "She eloped six months after Dad died. Gina and I met him once before they got married. He's now living in our house."

"How do you like him?"

She scrunched up her face. "I don't understand what mom sees in him. He's old, almost seventy. Yesterday, he walked into the kitchen wearing nothing but boxers and a tee shirt that was probably as old as him." She made a face of disgust.

"I take it you don't like old people," I said with a chuckle.

"It's not that, it's his attitude. He thinks he knows everything, and if you disagree with him, he acts like you're an ignorant buffoon. He's one of those who constantly remarks how my generation is lazy and self-entitled. You know, one of those old people who brag that they walked three miles to school every morning after they'd fed the chickens."

"Sounds like he'd fit right in at Mick's," I remarked.

"What?"

I explained. "Mick's Place. It's the cigar bar where my car was parked. There's a bunch of gasbags who hang out in there."

She laughed. "You hang out there, right?"

I smiled. "Yes, I do. I'd like to think I'm not a gasbag, but I probably am."

"You shouldn't smoke and drink," she admonished.

"Yeah, you're probably right. We all have our weaknesses."

"I'm dyslexic," she suddenly blurted and then she stared at me with a little bit of embarrassment in her expression.

"You are?"

"Let me rephrase. I have a mild case of dyslexia, but it went undiagnosed until I was a sophomore in high school. So, as you can imagine, I lagged behind the other students. The teacher who discovered it was awesome. She created reading exercises for me to overcome it. My reading comprehension is much better now, but I don't think I'd ever read as much as you do. I prefer listening to audiobooks."

"Let me guess, the discovery of your dyslexia led you to become an overachiever in your attempt to catch up with everyone else."

She laughed again. "You are right more than you realize."

"It could be why you come across as a know-it-all to some people," I suggested.

Her smile vanished and she frowned in thought a moment. "Do you think so?"

"I don't know, but it could be."

She thought a moment longer. "I suppose." She frowned again. "Let me ask you something. Did I do the right thing by telling you I was wearing a wire?"

"I believe you did. There are others that would disagree, like Poston and Kettleworth. Even Bartlett, so never tell anyone what you did. It'll be our secret."

"Maybe I shouldn't have said anything," she said.

"Maybe, but if you had not told me and I found out later, we would not be friends."

She stared now. "Do you consider me a friend?"

I stared back. "Absolutely."

She thought it over a moment. "Let me ask you something. Have you ever had a female friend where there wasn't any sex involved?"

I gave a reassuring smile. "Yep. I don't know if you've met Percy's girlfriend, Anna. She and I are good friends. In fact, she was my roommate for a while until she recently moved in with him. And no, there was never any sex."

She continued staring, probably wondering if I was being truthful. "Did you ever think about it?"

"Yeah, I guess so, back when we first met. She's a beautiful girl, but we've never been anything more than friends."

"How'd that work out?"

"It's been good. We've even partnered up on some cases."

"Are you still partners?" she asked.

My smile faded. "Since she started dating Percy, she's kind of gone independent on me, but that's alright. I'm more of a one-man operation anyway."

"I can see that," she said. "You strike me as the kind of man who does his own thing."

I thought about it. "I suppose."

"So, we're friends, right?"

"I hope so," I replied. "But there's something I have to say. I have conditions."

"Like what?"

"When we have conversations like this, you know, confidential conversations, we don't discuss what we've talked about to anyone else. You may not realize it, but when you told me you were wearing a wire, it had a significant impact on me."

"I take it you have trust issues," she surmised.

"Yes, I do."

"You've been betrayed by people you've trusted, like your wife."

"Among others, yes," I said.

She nodded. "I understand. I want the same."

"You got it."

She grinned now. "Good. I want to ask you something else."

"What's that?"

She pointed over toward the kitchen. "You have a lot of cookware. Does that mean you know your way around the kitchen?"

"I do, although I don't cook as much as I used to. Have you had lunch yet?"

"Nope, and I'm starving."

It was my turn to grin. "Well then, let me see what I can cook up for us."

# CHAPTER 38

It was late when Abby left. I had fixed us turkey burgers for lunch, and we ended up spending the day together. I showed her around the property, the photos of all my cars, and talked a lot about police work. I then fixed dinner, an Italian classic, spaghetti with homemade sauce.

I was tired after she left, but instead of going to bed, I sat on the couch a while longer, relaxing and reminiscing. When I was her age, I too was an eager rookie cop, fresh out of the academy and not quite emotionally healed from my time in Iraq. I'd won a Silver Star over there. Gallantry in action, they said. The truth was, I don't know how gallant I was, but I do know I was scared to death.

The Army was a tremendous experience for me, but when it came time to reenlist, I was done. No more Army life. I had no idea what I was going to do as a civilian until I found out Metro was hiring. I put in an application, and the rest was history.

Back then I had an amiable personality, and for some reason people found me easy to talk to. My commanding officer in the Army said I had a leader's bearing, and people in law enforcement appreciated that. Being a decorated veteran certainly helped.

Abby was at a disadvantage. She was young and pretty, but she was straightlaced, not a flirt, and perhaps a little naïve. In fact, she was the opposite of someone like Marti, who used her looks to get men to do her bidding. And it sounded like she was a little outspoken in her opinions and beliefs. It didn't help that she was in an occupation dominated by alpha males either. If I was still working for the department, I'm certain I could help her out, but I wasn't.

I stood, stretched, and was about to turn in for the night when my phone pinged. Opening the app's camera viewer, I saw a car stopped at the head of my driveway. They had their high beams on, which made it difficult to see the shape of the vehicle or its occupants.

I grabbed my Springfield and did a quick check of the magazine along with a press-check. I had a tac-lite in a kitchen drawer. I turned off all the lights and grabbed it before carefully opening my back door. I didn't see anyone, so I quickly exited and then began walking in a zigzag between trees as I made my way toward the head of my driveway.

The car was stationary, but the mufflers were a little loud, indicating a sports car, or something similar. I made my way closer. If this was the

SOB who set my garage on fire, I was going to have an interaction with them that they were not going to enjoy.

I was getting close enough to charge the car, but as I crept around a big elm tree, I startled two deer. They ran away from me and across the road, alerting the driver. They hastily backed up and squealed the tires as they sped off. I ran in a full sprint now, but I was too late. The only thing I saw were the taillights disappearing around a curve in the road. However, I did get a good look at their shape and design.

I hustled back to my house and logged onto my computer. It didn't take long to find a matching design. It was a Chevy product, either a Corvette or Camaro, like that lime green Camaro I saw at Centennial Park.

I went back outside and walked around my property to ensure there wasn't anyone lurking about before sitting in one of the rocking chairs on my front porch. I had all the lights off and made sure my phone had a good charge. It was going to be a long night, but if they decided to pay me another visit in the night, I was going to be waiting on them.

I kept my handgun and tac-lite in my lap and napped off and on while I waited, hoping they'd come back, but my only visitor was a lone coyote. He barely gave me a glance as he trotted through the yard, stopping only long enough to urinate on a tree.

At five in the morning, I decided there'd be no return visit and went inside. I was too irritated to go to bed, so I fixed a pot of coffee and decided I'd go ahead and begin the day. As I drank my first cup of coffee, I knew I had to be more proactive if I was ever going to find out who set my shop on fire.

Sometimes, when you had no readily identifiable suspect, the best way to develop a case was by eliminating probable suspects. That was going to be my first step.

"Let's get started on that right now," I muttered as I headed for the shower.

# CHAPTER 39

The Satan's Dogs clubhouse was located on Old Nashville Highway outside of Lavergne. It was an older, rustic house that was poorly maintained, but they had a newer looking eight-foot-tall chain-link fence surrounding the property, along with a heavy metal gate blocking the drive. I saw a security camera mounted on a pole on the secure side of the fence and I had no doubt there were other cameras. The yard was littered with trash, and I could see a prefab metal detached garage out back, along with several bikes and a couple of cars. I parked down the road away from the property, but close enough that the front gate was in my field of view.

It was time to conduct surveillance on these assholes and find out if one of them owned a lime green Camaro. Before leaving the house, I made sure I had everything I needed, including snacks, water, and an empty milk jug. I didn't like doing surveillance work, but it was a necessary job, especially in my line of work. I dressed casually, with jeans, a gray short sleeved shirt, and a comfortable fitting pair of Tims. I'd been wearing Timberland boots long before Gen-Z'ers made them popular. The pair I was currently wearing were at least ten-years old, had only been resoled once, and still had plenty of life left in them.

Traffic was heavy but absent of any wrecks, allowing me to arrive within twenty minutes. Getting myself as comfortable as I could, I spent the rest of the day watching them with my binoculars and a freshly downloaded audio book. The book, a police mystery thriller, was rife with procedural errors, but I suffered through it. When I was done with it, I planned on giving it to Abby.

There was little movement throughout the day. At one point, a grungy looking sleazeball came outside and stood on the front porch a moment before unzipping his fly and urinating. Finishing, he shook himself vigorously before wiping his hand on his pants and walking back inside. Outlaw bikers weren't high on the societal spectrum, in fact, they prided themselves on being anti-society, but when Duke was running the Baroques, he never would have allowed that type of behavior.

I never saw a Camaro the entire day. In fact, except for the idiot urinating off the porch, there was no movement at all. Finally, at about six in the evening, a man walked out a side door and walked toward the back. It looked like the club's president, but he disappeared around the back before I could get a good look at him with the binos. After a moment, I heard the loud exhaust of a bike being started. The bike and rider emerged from behind the house and exited the gate. I held my phone to my ear and used my arm to shield my face as he drove by.

I caught enough of a glimpse to confirm it was the president. After a moment, I started up my SUV and began following at a discrete distance. His bike was a newer model fat boy with loud aftermarket pipes and ape hangers. I had to close the distance between us due to traffic and I knew if he were paying attention, he would soon spot me.

My surveillance mission was a bust. I had nothing. It was time to try something else. Something more direct. I accelerated, weaved through traffic, and drove up beside him. He glanced over and did a double take. I rolled down my window.

"I think you owe me a beer!" I shouted over the noise of his loud pipes.

He glared a moment before a smirk crept across his face. He then made a follow-me motion and sped away. He led me to a biker's dive bar located off the main drag in between the cities of Lavergne and Smyrna. He parked in an area of the lot reserved for bikes. I parked my Explorer at the far end of the parking lot.

"The way I see it, you owe *me* a beer," he retorted as I walked up. "My jaw hurt for a couple of days and Whopper is still walking with a limp."

Whopper must have been the big guy who Eva shot in the ass. I made a mental note of it as I no doubt would probably run into him again in the future.

"Whopper was about to kick my teeth in. I didn't shoot him, but he got what he deserved. He doesn't deserve shit. I'll buy you a beer though."

He grinned. "A free beer it is then."

When we walked into the bar, he was greeted by a few people, obviously a regular. I got a few silent stares, but since I was with him, I guess I wasn't considered an interloper. Not yet anyway. We bellied up to the bar and he motioned to the bartender, a fifty-something woman with cheaply dyed hair who looked like she'd been rode hard and hung up wet many times over the years.

"Budweiser draft, Mona," he said.

She nodded and gave me a bored questioning stare. I told her I'd have the same. She poured the beer into two glasses, leaving enough head on each that the foam was spilling over when she sat them down. He did not seem to notice or care. He took a large swallow and foam dripped down into his beard. I sipped mine. It was a little warmer than I preferred, but I didn't complain. I looked him over. He was in his thirties, rough looking, with a pockmarked face and a teardrop tattoo under his left eye. His arms were festooned with low quality tats, probably from prison.

"I never did get your name," I said.

"I go by Bang-Bang," he said. "And you're Thomas Ironcutter, an ex-cop who's now a fancy private eye."

He said it loud enough so the other patrons could hear that part about me being an ex-cop. I saw a couple of them giving me a hard stare through a dirty Budweiser mirror on the wall behind the bar.

"I'll have to admit, you throw a good punch. Even Whopper said so," he said. "But I gotta ask you, why are we talking?"

"I talked to Bull recently. He said y'all had a sit-down and worked things out," I said.

Bang-Bang scoffed, finished his beer in three sloppy swallows, and motioned for Mona to pour him another.

"Yeah, we talked. What else did he tell you?" he asked.

"He said there's been a truce worked out and there are some other things in the works."

He didn't answer. Mona approached and handed him a fresh glass, along with me, even though I still had most of my beer left. Bang-Bang grabbed a saltshaker and sprinkled his beer.

"Drink up, you're buying," he said. "You haven't exactly said why we're talking."

"A couple of things actually. First, do you remember the other night when I asked if you guys were the ones who burned down my shop?"

He glanced at me before his attention was distracted by a woman who had sat down at the bar with another man who looked like a biker wannabe. She was well endowed with a low-cut top designed to show them off. She was easily forty pounds overweight, with dyed purplish-blonde hair that was of slightly better quality than Mona's. She was trashy looking, which meant she fit right in. He ogled her a moment longer before focusing back on me.

"Yeah, I remember that. So, you had a shop huh?"

"Yes, I did. It was about the same size as that shop behind your clubhouse."

He gave me a hard stare when I said that. "You've been watching us?"

"I want to know which one of you drives a green Camaro."

His stare hardened. "I have a Camaro. A sixty-eight SS model. It ain't green though, it's red. Is that what you're looking for?"

"Nope. I'm looking for a newer model, something under three-years-old."

He shook his head. "It's not one of us then. You're barking up the wrong tree, bub," he said.

I'd been watching his body language the entire time and I had to admit to myself I believed him. I told him as much.

"I told you the same thing the night we met," he said.

"You did, and I believed you that night. But looking back at how the three of you came to my house with the intention of putting me in a hospital, I started to have doubts."

He clicked his teeth and glanced over at the blonde again. She saw him staring and casually flipped her hair. "We were just going to scare you a little. You're the one who decided to start fighting." He took another swallow of beer. "So, who has a beef with you?"

"I'm not sure. In my line of work, I've made a few people mad at me. I needed to eliminate you guys and I thought this would be the best way."

"Coming to me man-to-man, I like that." He took a swallow and waited until he caught the blonde's eye. When he did, he gave her a wink. I saw her in the mirror give a flirtatious grin.

"So, what was the other thing you wanted to talk about?" he asked.

"I'm not getting a straight answer with Flaky being accused of killing your friend. I was hoping maybe you could clue me in."

He grunted. "It's club business, dude, and you ain't in our club."

"Fair enough. Let me ask you, do you think Flaky killed Turk or is there a possibility someone else did it?"

His response was a noncommittal shrug, which made me realize it was futile to ask him anything else about Turk's murder. He was right. I wasn't a Satan's Dog, nor was I a Baroque. And that meant I wasn't in the loop. He motioned for Mona to bring him another. As I watched her pour them, I realized I wasn't going to get anything else out of the man. Not here, not now.

When Mona walked up with two more fresh beers, I put some money on the bar and stood. Bang-Bang saw it and frowned at me.

"You ain't sticking around? I'm a thirsty man."

I pointed to the third beer Mona had set in front of me. It was beside the second one, which was untouched.

"You can have those. Take care, Bang-Bang," I said.

Bang-Bang grunted. "Yeah, you too man." He was done with me as well.

I started heading toward the door, but I'd been sitting most of the day in my Explorer without a break, so I decided to hit the head before driving back to Nashville. Looking back, it probably wasn't the wisest decision.

I walked into the disgustingly filthy restroom and stood at a cracked urinal that held the remnants of multiple cigarette butts and chewing gum. I heard the door open behind me as I finished up. I spotted movement in my peripheral vision and assumed it was a patron who needed to use the facilities as well. I was wrong. He spoke to me as I was pulling my zipper up.

"How ya' doing, pig," he growled.

I saw sudden movement and instinctively ducked, which saved me. The beer bottle grazed the back of my head but didn't make solid contact. He swung so hard, the momentum carried his arm past my head and into the wall. It shattered the bottle on impact. I knew what was going to happen next. He was going to take that broken beer bottle and give my face a Freddy Kreuger makeover. I wasn't going to let that happen.

His eyes widened in a mixture of surprise and fear as my punch made solid contact with his chin. The impact knocked him backwards. He fell to the floor, his head hitting with a nasty thud. I waited to see what he'd do next, but he was out cold. He was a rough looking barfly, maybe around thirty or so, wearing work clothes that indicated he had a job at a nearby tire factory. He was one of the men who heard Bang-Bang mouthing off about me being an ex-cop. Perhaps that was enough reason for him to ambush me.

I was sorely tempted to stomp his face into a mud puddle, but I held back and got out of there. Bang-Bang had moved down a couple of stools and was now talking to the blonde, totally oblivious of me. Only one other man was paying attention to me, and when he saw me walking out, he set his beer down and hurried to the men's room.

I walked out to my Explorer as a group of bikers turned in. I recognized Whopper leading the pack. My nose was still not fully healed, which irked me. It would've been nice to return the favor. I knew I could take him. He was big, but slow, and I knew I had more skills. But his buddies may have been inclined to jump in and I didn't know if there was going to be a bar full of drunks about to pour into the parking lot looking to avenge the idiot I'd just knocked out.

Nope, it was time to go.

I walked across the parking lot and got into my Explorer unnoticed. Backing out of the parking space, I eased out of the parking lot, and then slowly but steadily accelerated, checking my mirror the whole time.

# CHAPTER 40

I didn't care to go home and stare at the spot where my shop once was, so I went to Mick's instead. The chunky man greeted me when I walked in.

"How're you doing, Dago?" he asked.

"Not too bad," I replied and sat at an open bar stool. Unlike that seedy shithole I met Bang-Bang in, Mick kept his place clean. The furniture was new, and the entire business had a cozy ambience. I liked it here and I definitely felt safer.

"How's the nose? It's looking better. I mean, you're still ugly as sin but it looks better."

Some of the regulars laughed at Mick's quip. I smiled along with them and lit up a cigar as Mick brought me a glass of Nashville Lager. It was cold and fresh. Better than the swill that Mona served.

"There was a woman in here last night asking about you," he said.

"Oh, yeah? Who was it?"

"You remember that gal who comes in with Marley and Melanie? Fellatio or something?"

The chuckleheads laughed again.

"Felicity," I corrected.

"Yeah, that's her. Anyway, she came in here last night with those two Hookah smoking hippies and asked about you."

I grunted. "Yeah, no thanks."

"Yeah, I can't say I blame you. That gal is goofier than a tapeworm in a hippy high on acid."

I wasn't sure I understood his metaphor, but then decided I didn't care. I took a swallow and savored the taste. Definitely better.

"Yeah, why would he fool with that goofy broad when he's laying the pipe to Marti."

I looked down the bar toward the voice. It was Hiram, the blowhard who claimed he was once a CIA spy.

"Don't talk like that. Marti is a sweet girl," Wally admonished, which surprised me. Wally was a braggart, but he was not a confrontational type of person. Coming to Marti's defense was out of character. I was about to agree with him, but Mick chimed in as well.

"Yeah, don't talk about Marti like that. She's our girl and deserves respect."

I chuckled to myself. Marti sure had them wrapped around her little finger. Me too, probably. My phone vibrated. I was receiving a text from Percy.

10-20?

He was using ten-code asking for my location. I texted back that I was smoking. There were no more texts. I suspected he knew my phone was being tapped and my clue was adequate for him to know where I was. Fifteen minutes later, I saw him driving into the parking lot. I walked outside.

"What's going on?" I asked.

"I just got out of a meeting. The FBI is formally joining the investigation tomorrow and are creating a task force. Poston and Kettleworth have made a big deal about your mysterious client and your possible involvement. My prediction is they're going to start scrutinizing everything about you. If I had to guess, there is going to be another search warrant coming your way, and perhaps even active surveillance."

"Let me guess, Poston keeps spouting off to anyone that'll listen that I'm a viable suspect."

"Only about three times an hour," Percy quipped.

"Alright, I appreciate you letting me know," I said. "I assume you know there may be something wrong with my phone."

He gave a slight nod. It was illegal for him to inform me of a wiretap. At the minimum, it would cost him his job. I hoped nobody ever discovered that Abby had tipped me off. I was going to educate her on wiretap laws at my first opportunity.

"I've got to get home, Anna expected me an hour ago," he said. "Oh, I've been so busy I've neglected talking to you. I knocked on every door of your neighbors the other day. Short answer, there is no video. Also, I have something you want." He reached into his car and pulled out some papers.

"You remember Ratajkowski?" he asked.

"Yeah, I haven't heard of him since he lost his job."

Ratajkowski was once a TBI agent. Percy and I had helped him out on a big case a few years back. Not too long after that, he'd gotten into a car wreck and was charged with DUI. It cost him his job.

"He's now a recovering alcoholic and works at the DMV. I bumped into him when I was getting some info on another case. He asked about you and if you still restored old cars. I told him about the shop, and you believe the suspect drives a late model Camaro. He compiled a list of all Camaros three-years-old or less registered in Tennessee."

I stared at the handful of papers. "He did that?"

"Yep. He said to tell you hello and you owe him a cup of coffee."

We said our goodbyes and I walked back inside. Getting a fresh beer, I began perusing the list. It didn't take long before I saw a name I recognized. Two beers and one cigar later, I had a plan. A devious plan. If caught, I'd be in a hell of a mess.

That wasn't going to stop me.

# CHAPTER 41

My plan was coarse, unrefined. It had a lot of what-ifs and other variables, and if I was caught, it could cost me. A lawsuit, a felony conviction, possible prison time, maybe all three. I was going to do it anyway and damn the consequences. I knew I'd never have enough proof to prosecute him, and besides, he had enough money to hire a legal team and get it thrown out of court. It was high risk, but the satisfaction I was going to have if I pulled it off was going to be sweet.

I was contemplating whether I wanted another beer or tab out and go home when my phone vibrated. To my surprise, it was a text from Bull asking where I was. When I replied I was at Mick's Place, he texted back, telling me to stay there, he wanted to have a few words with me. Fifteen minutes later, I heard the sounds of two Harleys roaring into the parking lot. It was Bull and another man who I had only met once. I believed he went by the nickname of Doobie. A twenty-something with a goatee, tats, and piercings in his eyebrows. They walked in, and upon seeing Marti, they both broke into shit-eating grins.

"Hell's bells, I didn't know you worked here," Bull said.

"Hey, Bull," Marti replied with little warmth. "Do you two want a beer?"

"Yeah, and put it on Ironcutter's tab," he replied.

"Nope," Marti retorted before I could speak. "Either you pay for it, or you can go drink somewhere else."

Bull glared and watched as Doobie pulled out his wallet and ordered a beer for himself. After a moment, he realized Marti wasn't going to be intimidated.

"Fine," he growled and pulled a sawbuck out of his pocket. Grabbing the bottle of Budweiser, he motioned for me to follow him outside.

There were some patio tables and chairs immediately outside the building. None were occupied at the moment. Bull picked one and sat. He looked like a big grizzly bear sitting there, and he motioned me to sit in the opposite chair. I did so, warily. The man had a temper, and unlike Whopper, I knew this big man was strong as an ox and a formidable fighter.

"Heard you had a talk with Bang-Bang this afternoon," he said.

"I did. Is that a problem?"

"It could be," he said. He paused a minute and drank his beer. It seemed like he was considering what he should say next. Knowing his level of intellect, it was probably difficult for him.

"The Baroques have been kind of whacked since Duke ghosted us and the strip club burned down. Flaky and I have managed to pull it all together, but now he's in jail and I'm going to be the next president. What do you think about that?"

I thought carefully about how I was going to phrase my response. "Before I answer, I want you to know I'm going to give you my honest opinion and you might not like it."

"Lay it on me," he said.

"Alright. You're not as smart as Duke, and you often let your temper get the better of you. You could be a good prez, but only if you keep your temper in check and find you a smart guy to be your vice president. Flaky, for example. He's smarter than most people think."

"Yeah, but he may be out of action for a while. Flaky said I ought to ask you for advice when I needed it. I'd like to do that from time to time if you don't mind."

That one surprised me. The two of us weren't enemies, but we weren't exactly bosom buddies either.

"We can do that, but I'm thinking we'd have to be careful about what we talk about. There are some activities you and your boys may be involved in that I don't want anything to do with or even know about."

"Yeah, I got you, but you've got to leave this shit with Flaky alone," he said.

"Hard to do, Bull. I consider Flaky a friend and I want to help him."

Bull tapped his beer glass with a meaty finger for a few seconds. I got the idea that his anger was growing. Finally, he took a deep breath and let it out.

"Alright, I'm staying cool here, and you telling me not to talk about certain things makes sense. So, I'm going to tell you a little imaginary story. It goes like this. Once upon a time, there were these two clubs. They had some things in common and some of them decided to join together and make one big club. But there were others who didn't think we should join together. One of them decided he was probably going to do something to his club's president, so something got done to him before he could do anything. Well, that particular president didn't know of the plans going on behind his back and thought that people were trying to hurt his club, so he and a couple of his buddies went looking for answers. You follow me so far?"

"I believe I do."

"Alright, so we had a little sit down and had a meeting of the minds. It's all been squared, but there are still issues going on that you don't want to be a part of."

"Sounds like maybe there's going to be a patch-over," I remarked.

Bull glanced in surprise. "Yeah."

I nodded. The Satan's Dogs were going to be patched over and become Baroques. Bull was telling me Turk was against it and had some sort of nefarious plan against Bang-Bang. Someone decided to kill Turk and Flaky had been arrested for it.

I stared at Bull, wondering if he was the one who killed Turk. After all, a while back Flaky took an auto theft charge for Bull and did some time while Bull remained free.

"What do you think of all that?" Bull asked.

I considered his question a moment before answering. "It's good to grow, but I'm not so sure you can trust those boys. So, Bang-Bang is going to relinquish his role as president?"

"He's going to be the veep. We've made some other con...concussions."

"Concessions," I corrected.

"Yeah, concessions. So, keeping on with this story, this other club has some problems and we're going to take care of them. That's part of the deal."

He didn't go into detail about what those problems were, and I was smart enough not to ask. We talked about bike related business stuff before he and Doobie left. I sat outside, enjoying the night, and watched as the crowd thinned until I was the only one left. Marti came outside with a beer for me and a mixed drink for herself. She stretched before sitting.

"You and Bull seemed to have a lot to talk about," she remarked.

"He's going to be the president of the Baroques and there's going to be a patch-over," I said.

She laughed without humor. "Lord help us all."

"I don't know Doobie too well. Is he anything like Bull?"

"He's an okay dude. His old lady is getting out on parole in a couple of months and he's undecided if this is a good thing or a bad thing."

"Why would it be bad?" I asked.

"Because he hooked up with another girl while she was in prison. Old lady number two is currently pregnant with his kid."

I laughed. It felt good. I hadn't had a good laugh in a while. When I realized I was probably expressing my own form of schadenfreude in regard to Doobie's situation, I stopped.

"What about you?" I asked. "Do you ever want kids?"

"One day," she answered. "I'd like to do some travelling first. You know, see the world and all that. Then I'll find a good man and settle down. Maybe."

I nodded in thought. Marti could probably make someone a good wife. I had no idea if she was seeing anyone besides me and I did not ask. She finished her drink and stood.

"I've got to do some cleaning up before closing. I'll see you tomorrow?"

The question had an implied message; she wasn't going home with me tonight. I took the hint and stood.

"I need to get home myself. I suppose I'll see you in a day or so."

I did not tell her that tomorrow night, I was going to be on a mission of vengeance. It might take me more than one night before I was successful, but it was going to happen.

# CHAPTER 42

I'd only met Eddie Barker one time. He was a rich trust fund baby who had probably never worked a day in his life. The kind of guy who wore custom tailored slacks and expensive loafers without socks. He was in his late thirties and his life consisted of choosing which party or social event to attend each night. He was also friends with Al, and according to the registration list provided by Ratajkowski, he owned a brand new, lime green, Chevy ZL-1 Camaro.

He lived in a nice condominium complex in a suburb of Nashville known as Green Hills. I watched him one evening as he left and followed him directly to Davidson Country Club. He parked in a handicap spot, I guess because he felt entitled. I drove around until it got dark and then parked a short distance down the road at a church.

I wore nondescript golf apparel and a full-brimmed ball cap pulled down low. If anyone saw me, they'd assume I was a golfer from the club. I'd played there a few times, and had even considered joining it, but they weren't my kind of people. Based on those previous visits, I knew their surveillance cameras were old and obsolete. The kind that only recorded in black and white at a low pixilation. I wasn't worried about them recording me, there was no way facial recognition could be possible. Whoever viewed it would only see a man carrying a water bottle, but there wasn't water in it.

Walking the short distance, I approached Eddie's car, all the while cognizant of any people walking around in the parking lot. Currently, there were none, which made it all too easy. It only took a minute to do the deed. I was almost back to the car I'd borrowed off the tow lot that Bubba worked at when I heard the distinct popping and crackling noise of the fire. I smiled in satisfaction as I drove away. I wasn't finished yet. Part two of this plan of revenge was coming up.

I was waiting for him when he finally arrived back at his condo via taxi. It was after midnight and based on the manner in which he stumbled out of the cab, I surmised he was drunk. After exiting the cab, he tossed some money at the driver and slammed the door. I heard him mutter an invective about the driver's ethnicity as he walked toward his condo. His chino slacks looked expensive, along with the untucked shirt.

"Rough night, huh?" I queried.

He slowed his walk and squinted in my direction. I emerged from the darkness and walked toward him, stopping when I was about ten feet away. It took his alcohol sodden brain a few seconds.

"I know you, don't I?"

"Yeah, we met at the country club a while back. It's a shame about your Camaro. Total loss, I'm guessing."

He frowned in puzzlement, and then understanding hit him. His expression turned to incredulity. "You're the one who set my car on fire?"

"I never said that. If I had to guess, I'd say the person who did it was probably getting even with you for setting their garage on fire."

His jaw dropped open, and he pointed at me. "You're Ironcutter. Tom or Thomas, something like that."

"Yeah, that's me."

He frowned. "I didn't have anything to do with that," he declared. His brain worked slowly, but after a few seconds, his frown turned to an angry scowl. "You set my car on fire!"

He almost shouted it. I grinned and winked. It had the desired effect.

"You bastard," he snarled and charged me. He probably thought he was going to take me by surprise, but I was expecting it. Closing the distance, he threw a haymaker with his right. I deftly sidestepped, and as he went stumbling by me, I gave him an openhanded slap to the back of the neck. It jolted the mass of nerves at the base of the skull, and he dropped face first to the asphalt. When he rolled over, I could see blood spurting out of his nose.

"Damn, it looks broken. I bet that hurt."

"Fuck you," he retorted and daintily held his nose. "That car cost over seventy grand. You're going to pay."

"Yeah, right. Your little escapade is costing me over a hundred grand, and it ruined five cars, two of which I cherished. Be thankful I don't give you the beating of your life."

He coughed and spit. "I didn't set your garage on fire, you idiot."

"When I mentioned my garage, you instantly knew who I am and why I'm here. You implicated yourself. I won't be able to prove it in court, but I know it was you."

His attitude was making me angry. I started walking toward him, my fists clenching. He instantly raised a hand in surrender.

"Don't get up," I warned and started to walk away.

"I didn't do it," he repeated.

"You can deny it all you want. I know better."

"You fool, what reason would I have to do that to you?"

I turned and walked back to him. "That is an excellent question. Why *did* you set my garage on fire?"

He laughed without humor before choking and coughing again. "Why indeed? Perhaps you scorned a woman who maybe had a few emotional issues going on."

I frowned, and it took me a moment to realize who he was referring to.

"Are you saying Al did it?" I asked. He nodded.

Al, also known as Allison Mars, was a vivacious thirty-eight-year-old blonde with big blue eyes and a body she kept taut with regular visits to the gym. We'd dated briefly. I liked her, but frankly, she was wound a little too tight for me and it had not worked out.

"I don't believe you," I declared.

"Believe what you want. Sure, I bought those tracking units and waited while she put them on your cars. I even drove her around a couple of times while we followed you, but I wasn't there when she set the fire."

"You knew about it," I accused.

He held a finger up. "After the fact. She called me after she did it. She was crying hysterically and worried she'd burned your entire house down."

I stared him down. He was unmoved. "Alright, let's say I believe you. Why did she do it?"

He shrugged. "She tended to become fixated on men she dated. You weren't the first one, so don't feel special. She took it hard when you dumped her. Her prior boyfriend did the same thing. He was lucky. All she did to him was slash his tires." He wiped his face and stared at his bloody hand before offering a shrug. "She hadn't been right since her husband was killed."

I stared in incomprehension. I knew she didn't take the break up well, but like I said, it was a brief romance. Nothing to get overly upset about. I never would have guessed she would have gone this far.

"I'm not sure I believe you. I'll take it up with her," I said and started to walk away again.

"You can't."

I stopped yet again and turned back to him. "Why is that?"

"She overdosed the day after she started the fire. They took her off life support yesterday. That event at the country club tonight? That was a celebration of life party in her honor."

I wanted to ask him more but couldn't risk it. For all I knew, one of his neighbors had seen our scuffle and called the police. I left him, hustled back to my car, and went directly to the tow lot. Swapping cars, I headed out and was home a short time later.

I'd already worked out my alibi with Ronald. If Eddie decided to report me to the police, Ronald had rigged a surveillance video showing the two of us sitting in my den, watching TV for the majority of the night.

The whole caper left me thirsty. I fixed a large glass of iced water and sat down in front of my laptop. I found Allison's obituary within a minute. It saddened me more than I thought it would. Sure, she destroyed my property, but I wished there was something I could have done that would have prevented it.

I sighed heavily and logged off. I was no longer feeling good about my act of vengeance. Sleep did not come easily.

# CHAPTER 43

It took the investigator three days before paying me a visit regarding Eddie's car fire. It was the same investigator who was assigned to my garage arson. He got out of his car, waved, and walked over to where I was standing.

"Good morning," I greeted.

"Good morning," he responded and gestured at the tradesmen currently framing the structure with the red primed steel beams. "It's coming along."

"Yes, it is," I agreed.

He lit up a cigarette. "Looks like you're increasing the square footage."

"I am. I'm putting a sprinkler system in it as well." I emphasized my statement by pointing at the ditch where the plumber was working.

"Smart move. So, let's get down to it. Eddie Barker's Camaro, did you do it?"

"Eddie Barker? The name sounds familiar, but I have no idea what you're talking about."

He gave a knowing smirk. "Alibi?"

I asked for a date and time frame. When he replied, I told him and gestured at my surveillance cameras. "I have an inside camera too. I'll download it. It'll show me home all night."

"Good enough. I hope it doesn't show you walking around in the buff," he said with a chuckle.

"I don't think so."

"Good, I ain't into that." We continued watching the workers. He took a hit off his cigarette and exhaled. "He had an interesting story."

"I can imagine," I said.

"Yeah, he said you had spurned a female friend of his and she got carried away. He said you took it out on him because you thought he did it."

"That's a heck of a story," I said.

"Yeah, it seemed awfully convenient that this woman he named is now deceased. Dead of an overdose. I actually knew her."

"Sounds like some sort of Shakespeare tragedy. Have you ever watched a Shakespeare play?"

"Other than Romeo and Juliet back in high school, I can't say that I have."

"I remember that one. Both of them died. Sad story."

"Yes, it is," he agreed. He finished his cigarette, stepped on the butt, and gestured at the garage. "I'd like to see the finished product."

"Stop by in about a month. It should be done by then."

"I believe I will," he said.

I made a show of downloading the video onto a thumb drive and handed it to him. A computer forensics specialist might be able to discover the fraud, but I was banking on both Ronald's skills and them not bothering to waste time on it.

He asked a couple of additional questions before finishing up. He got halfway to his car before stopping and turning.

"Do you remember Mindy McCready?"

"The country music star? Yeah, why?" I asked.

"She was another tragedy. My first wife was the spitting image of her. She killed herself too. Overdosed on heroin. Allison reminds me of both of them. Sometimes those demons can't be overcome."

He didn't wait for a response, and I watched as he left. He was right. Sometimes those demons could not be beaten. Would it have been different if I had tried to work out our differences and continued dating her? I doubted it. I wasn't a therapist; I couldn't fix what was hurting her. And besides, I had my own demons that I fought every day.

When I had read Al's obituary, I contacted a woman I knew was a friend with her. She said that although she did not want to speak ill of the dead, Al had been battling depression for a while, even before her husband was killed in action over in Afghanistan.

I'd said a silent prayer for her salvation, but that was all I could do. Frankly, I was finding it hard to forgive her act of arson. I suppose I would, in time.

I walked outside and watched the plumber as he tapped into my main line. He'd already dug a ditch and laid the pipe out. Running water lines into the garage meant that I was going to have to heat it as well. It wasn't going to be cheap, but my insurance company insisted. Looking at the progress being made was elevating my mood, but not by much.

"Looks like a big cluster-doodle."

I turned at the voice. It was Buford. He was standing there with his thumbs hooked in the straps of his bib overalls while his poodle watered the tree. As I watched, he spat a glob of tobacco juice on the ground and then gestured at his poodle. "If it weren't for Skippy, I imagine your house would have burned too."

"You're the one who called 911?" I asked.

"Yep. Skippy woke me up with his danged barking. I thought someone was breaking in and then I saw the flames."

"I didn't know that. Thanks Skippy," I said and petted him. Buford spat again.

"How long have you been chewing?" I asked.

He frowned a moment. "I started when they sent me over to Korea during the war. Been doing it ever since."

"And you're what, eighty?"

"Somewhere in there. Why are you asking?"

"You give me hope that tobacco doesn't really cause cancer," I said.

Buford responded with a grunt. Not many people still alive knew about Buford's war experience and how he'd won a slew of medals, including the Distinguished Service Cross. He was lucky enough to survive Korea and come back home in mostly one piece. He then took over the family's farm and his father's bootlegging operation. After his wife died and his only child married and moved to Australia, he retired from farming and began selling off parcels of land. I was lucky enough to get a five-acre tract that backed up to his property line. As far as I knew, his preacher and I were Buford's only remaining friends. The rest were dead.

"I guess they're making pretty good progress though. They should have it done before the weather turns," he said.

"That's the plan. What are you up to?" I asked.

"Just getting some exercise." He gestured at the work crew. "Is this a good outfit?"

"Yeah, I believe they are. The contractor is a friend of mine. He's a former cop."

He grunted and worked on his chew a moment before speaking. "Brother Milton wants me to contribute to remodeling the church and adding some rooms for daycare or something. I thought I might help out a little bit. What's your friend's name, anyway?"

I went inside and jotted down Fitz's information. When I handed it to him, Buford looked it over a moment before sticking it in his pocket. "You going to keep working on cars?"

"Yep."

"That truck of mine needs an oil change. I'd appreciate it if you could take care of it."

"Yeah, I can do that," I promised.

He gave a small nod, spat again, and walked off; his poodle obediently followed. If I knew Buford as well as I believed, he was going to finance most of that church remodeling himself. It would certainly ensure Brother Milton would give Buford one heck of a funeral when he died.

It was a pleasant day, so I took my laptop outside and sat at my picnic table. I had two online classes I needed to complete in order to retain my certification in traffic accident reconstruction. I'd not worked one of those cases in over a year, but I was prudent about keeping my various certifications current and active. The first recertification took almost an hour. After completing it, I stood and stretched before I decided to inspect the worker's progress. I walked around the garage, looking for mistakes. There weren't any that I could see. The steelworkers were doing a good job. Same with the plumber.

I was antsy. I needed to do something. I usually worked out when I felt like this, but thanks to Al, my weights and boxing equipment were burnt up. More items to add to the ever-growing list of things I needed to purchase. Maybe I'd simply join a gym.

I decided to go ahead and buy the oil and filter for Buford's old truck, and then had a sudden idea. I hooked up the trailer and headed to Home Depot. They had a zero-turn mower on sale. I looked it over for only a couple of minutes before purchasing it, along with a new gas can. I filled it at the local stop and rob before going home.

I went directly to Buford's, changed his oil, and then went ahead and cut his grass. He and his poodle watched while sitting under a shade tree. After, I went home, topped off the gas tank, and cut my own yard.

Sometimes, when I had some inner issue to work out, I could sit in my rocker and think things through, but most of the time my brain worked better when I was doing something physical and unrelated to the problem. Like riding around on a lawn mower. There is a phrase for it that I had difficulty remembering. Abstract thinking? Subconscious problem-solving? Gestalting? Not certain, doesn't matter. Whatever the name or phrase, it worked for me. Sometimes.

Today, I was drawing a blank.

After finishing with the yard, I parked it and let it cool before rinsing it off. I liked it. It was the best lawn mower I'd ever owned. I still needed a new weed eater though and admonished myself for forgetting to buy one while I was at Home Depot. I started to reach for my phone and create a list when it vibrated. I had an incoming text. It was from Anna.

Are you home? I have something I want to talk to you about.

I replied that I was and to come on by. She showed up twenty minutes later, driving her blue Nissan Cube. She jumped out and smiled, which lit up her whole face. She was wearing white shorts and a green top that fit her lithe body perfectly. Percy was a lucky man. Gracie jumped out and ran up to me with her tail wagging. I squatted and gave her a hug. She responded with a slobbery lick. She spotted the mower.

"I could smell the freshly cut grass before I turned in your driveway. Is it new?"

"Yep, about four hours old now," I said.

She sneezed twice in rapid succession. "Sorry, I get hay fever easily."

"That reminds me, I need to get a blower, or else I'll track the clippings inside. Let's go in."

I got us tea and we sat at the kitchen table while Gracie and Tommy Boy got reacquainted by chasing each other around the house. Anna seemed a little antsy. She'd only been sitting a moment when she jumped up and refilled her glass, even though it was still half full. I decided to throw out a probing question.

"How are you and Percy?"

"We're doing great. He's been working a lot of hours lately. A task force has been created on the officer's murder and the double murder at the cemetery, so Percy has been covering all the other cases. He said it'll all return to normal soon."

"Yeah, I hope so," I remarked.

"He's been working long hours, but when he gets home, we'll sit and talk until bedtime. He's an interesting man, even though he doesn't talk a lot."

"Yes, he is," I agreed. "How is his daughter?"

Her expression tightened slightly. "She's in Romania visiting family, but she's coming back in two days. Don't tell anyone this, but she is a strange girl. And she has money. Percy assumes she gets it from her mother's side of the family but he's not certain.

"We get along, but there's definitely an invisible wall between us. I've tried, but I honestly don't think she cares a wit to have any kind of friendship with me. Percy has talked to her about going to college, but I don't know what she's going to do."

"I'm sorry to hear that," I said, and sensed she wanted to change the subject. "What else has been happening in your life?"

"You know I've been helping Marti with her infidelity case," she said.

"Yeah, how's that going?" I asked.

"It turned ugly. When we turned over the information to the client, she went nuts. We thought we had her calmed down, but later on, she confronted her wife and put her in the hospital. She was arrested and we'll probably be subpoenaed to testify. Here's the part where you can say you told me so."

I shook my head. "I won't do that, but I certainly hope you learned from it."

"Yeah, I have. Anyway, since then I've been doing some work for Rochelle. She has a big divorce case coming up and I've been serving subpoenas."

"Yeah?" I replied. Rochelle Anderson was an attorney who specialized in divorces and high-dollar lawsuits. I'm certain she had a deep-seated hatred of all men.

"She's got a huge divorce case coming up. The man is worth millions, and he doesn't want to pay a fair settlement."

I chuckled now. I'm sure Rochelle's cut was going to be commiserate upon how much of a settlement she could obtain.

"So, here's what I wanted to talk to you about. She made me a job offer yesterday," she said.

"Oh, yeah?"

"My official title will be legal assistant, but she said if I sign a contract with her, she'll pay my way through paralegal school."

"That's a heck of an offer. What does Percy think about it?" I asked.

"He hates Rochelle. Years ago, she represented his wife in their divorce. Did you know that?"

"I do. She tried to make Percy look like he was an awful man. He's not."

"I know that," she said. "He's not too keen on the idea. He thinks I'll be indebted to her, and she'll use it to her advantage. What do you think?"

I thought about it a moment before answering. "My guess is she can be a hard person to work for. The terms of the contract would definitely need to be agreeable. What's the salary?"

"I'm not allowed to discuss it," she said and then casually held one of her hands up. There was a number written on her palm. It was an impressive number. I nodded in understanding. If someone had offered a salary like that to me back when I was her age, I would have been ecstatic. She seemed troubled though.

"So, what are you going to do?" I asked.

"If I weren't dating Percy, I would have already said yes, but I don't want to cause any problems between us."

We discussed her dilemma for several minutes. All I knew to say was to list the pros and cons of working for Rochelle and talk it over with Percy. I don't know if I helped her with her decision, but she seemed to take my advice under consideration. We talked some more and then I helped her load the rest of her belongings and gave her a hug before she left.

I stood outside and watched her drive away. I had enjoyed her visit but watching her leave left me a little sad. I had grown accustomed to her company. Sometimes, we'd sit up late at night and simply talk. Sometimes it would be a deep conversation, other nights it would be lighthearted stuff, like the time she regaled me with of all the ludicrous shenanigans at the strip club she and Marti used to work at.

Now she was gone. I was happy for her and Percy, but I missed her. If she still lived here, we would've already been engrossed in a deep conversation about Eva and Mishka. She might've even helped me figure everything out.

I took a hot shower before putting on a fresh pair of jeans and a tee shirt. Pouring a generous helping of Scotch into a tumbler, I walked outside to my front porch. I left the lights off to keep the insects at a minimum, or so I told myself.

I sat there for only a few minutes before going inside and locking up. I surfed channels on the TV, but when I found nothing that interested me, I went to bed. My mood was dark. I could not shake the feeling that something foreboding was on the horizon.

# CHAPTER 44

I woke up early, like three o'clock early. It happened sometimes. Probably from too much caffeine and nicotine, and not enough physical activity.

I stirred around the house, found nothing on TV, and decided to go for an early morning run. The cool morning air was pleasant and all I needed was a flashlight to see on the trail. After some calisthenics and cool down stretches, I sat at my desk and amused myself by browsing the internet.

My phone rang as I was looking at the DeWalt Tools website. I glanced at the clock and then the caller I.D. It was a little after four and the identity showed an unknown caller. Thinking it might be Eva, I answered.

"Hey, Thomas. It is I, Larry T-Thomas Boles."

He was slurring his words, an indicator of drunkenness. I guess he'd kept my business card, otherwise I had no idea how he got my number.

"What's going on, Larry?" I asked.

"I think I might have some information about that grave, and I wanted to talk to you about it," he said.

"Okay, let's hear it."

"I'd rather talk to you in person. Uh, I mean, it's important," he replied.

A personal meeting. A hint of a smile crossed my face. It probably meant he wanted to get some money out of me, but that was okay. I had been wanting to ask him about Eva and how she talked him into digging up the grave.

"Yeah, okay. When and where?" I asked.

We agreed to meet in thirty minutes at the cemetery. I hurriedly showered and dressed. I would've liked to fix some coffee and eat some breakfast, but I didn't have time.

There was little traffic at this time of the morning, and I made it to the cemetery in about ten minutes. Larry was sitting on a bench at the parking lot drinking out of a bottle. He was wearing the same clothes from the other night, and they were still stained with dirt. I parked and scanned the area before getting out.

"Yo, Larry," I said as I approached.

Larry greeted me by holding up his bottle. I sat beside him, leaving plenty of room in between us. The man reeked.

"Hello, T-Thomas Ironcutter," he slurred out. I glanced down at the bottle. It was almost empty.

"Have you been up all night?" I asked.

"Yeah, mostly," he replied. "I'm glad you came. I've been meaning to talk to you."

"What about?"

He hooked a thumb behind him. "You know that grave you've been interested in? Well, the other night, I got hired to dig it up."

"You did, huh? Why?" I asked.

"Well, they paid me a hundred dollars. That's decent money, you know."

I kept any hint of irritation out of my voice. "But why did they want the grave dug up? Do you know?"

"Because there was supposed to be something valuable down in there. That's what they said anyway."

"I see. Did you find anything?" I asked.

"Nah. There wasn't nothing but a skeleton wearing an old dress. It looked like it could've been a wedding gown, or something like that. There wasn't even a bible in there. I heard back then people got buried with a bible. I guess that isn't necessarily true."

"I guess not," I said in agreement. "Was there anything else that stood out?"

Larry thought a moment and shook his head. "Nope. I've never looked inside an old grave before, but it was about how I imagined it would be. Let me ask you something, I'm not going to get in trouble about this, am I?"

"It'd be best to keep it to yourself and not go around bragging about it."

He nodded. "Good thinking, loose lips sink ships."

"Yeah, that's the idea," I said.

I knew Eva was involved in this latest episode, but I didn't want to tip my hand. I phrased my next question so he would not suspect anything.

"Who in the world would hire you to do such a thing?" I asked.

He made a flippant wave of his free hand. "Just a man and woman. I'd never met them before."

I straightened and stared at Larry. "Two people?"

"Yes, Mister Ironcutter."

I turned sharply at the voice. It was Mishka, standing a couple of feet away, and pointing a handgun at me. The little bastard was good. Not many people were capable of sneaking up behind me. He was smiling smugly with those thin lips.

"I am so glad you decided to come. Please do not do anything foolish or I will be forced to shoot you. I will only wound you of course, but it will most assuredly be painful. Raise your hands slowly and keep them up until I give you further instructions."

It took only a second to weigh my options; try to go for my gun or try to make a run for it. I had no doubt if I tried either, I was going to be shot. I did as he said and raised my hands.

"What's this all about, Mishka?" I asked.

"Hold your questions for now, please," he said and gestured at Larry. "Mister Boles, Mister Ironcutter is probably armed with a semiautomatic handgun, which is holstered on his right hip. Please take it from him."

Larry nodded and leaned close. "Sorry," he mumbled as he reached over and unholstered my handgun.

"Stand now please, Mister Ironcutter, and allow Mister Boles to perform a thorough search of you," Mishka directed.

I didn't like it, but I did as I was told. Larry found the lock blade knife in my pocket. Now I was completely unarmed. If I had an opportunity, I'd grab the little man's gun hand and punch his lights out, but my instincts told me he wouldn't be stupid enough to get too close to me.

"He's clean, boss," Larry said when he'd finished.

"Very good. Let's get started, shall we? Mister Boles, you will lead us. Mister Ironcutter, you follow. Let me remind you, if you try anything, I will be forced to shoot you, and if I do that, I will be forced to shoot Mister Boles as well."

"Point taken. Why are you doing this?" I asked.

"All in due time," he replied. "We have a lot to talk about. Perhaps this can work out to the advantage of all three of us."

I happened to glance at Larry, who nodded vigorously. "There's going to be a big reward coming our way."

It was obvious he had Larry beguiled, which meant the chances of convincing him to side with me was going to be slim. I was in a pickle. I gestured with a hand.

"Well then, lead the way, Judas."

If Larry caught the reference, he didn't show it. Instead, he began walking through the cemetery in a southwesterly direction. I'd always had an innate sense of direction and I was intimately familiar with the geographics of Nashville. When we started walking, I knew we were heading toward the old ruins of Fort Negley. Knowing my exact location could help tremendously if I were able to make a run for it.

The cemetery's property line ended at an old chain link fence that was in various stages of neglect. A portion of it had been torn away. Larry walked through it and onto a dim path through an overgrowth of bushes and weeds, along with an occasional tree. It was still dark out, but the sky was beginning to lighten. After a five-minute walk, the trail ended at an old shed made up of graying wood and a rusted metal roof.

"Here it is, boss," Larry said.

Mishka had been following along about ten feet behind me. When Larry and I had stopped, he continued walking and I heard him getting close. I was about to turn around and make a play when I felt a sudden prick in the side of my neck. I jerked away from him, took a few steps, and turned toward him. I held a hand up to my neck and touched the spot that felt like I was bitten by a large mosquito. Mishka was holding the gun in one hand and something that looked like a syringe in the other. I frowned in confusion and I felt the blood drain from my face.

"What the hell did you just do?" I demanded.

Within seconds, my vision began blurring. I tried to back away, to escape, but my knees buckled. The last thing I was aware of was Mishka staring at me impassively.

# CHAPTER 45

A few years back, there was a popular show on cable TV featuring a serial killer with a unique technique of disabling his target. He'd use some type of subterfuge to get close to them and quickly stick a syringe in their neck. His target was almost immediately rendered incapacitated with whatever kind of sedative was in the syringe. I didn't think it was realistic.

I was wrong.

When I came to, my chin was resting on my chest, and it felt like I had been drooling. It took several seconds before my neck muscles responded, allowing me to force my head up. Everything was blurry and I blinked several times in an effort to focus. I found myself sitting in an old but sturdy wooden chair. The kind they used to have in school rooms. I tried to rub my face but couldn't move my arms. Looking down, I saw why. They were secured to the chair with a number of thick zip-ties, as were my legs. Looking around, it appeared I was inside an old building constructed with wooden slats. It wasn't large, which gave me the impression it was a shed. No doubt it was the shed we had walked to before Mishka stuck that syringe in me.

I could make out Mishka and Larry. Mishka was seated across from me in a similar chair and Larry was standing off to the side. He was still drunk, but he appeared nervous, and his face was glistening with an oily sweat.

I won't say I panicked, but I started forcefully trying to free myself. My muscles seemed numb and weren't functioning at a hundred percent, but it didn't stop me from trying. Mishka stood, walked over, and rested a hand on my shoulder.

"You will find your attempts to free yourself futile, Thomas. Save your energy, you will need it for what is to come."

"What the hell is going on?" I demanded. There was anger in my tone, but I was a little frightened as well.

"I injected you with a sedative," he said and held up the little syringe type of device with a needle sticking out. "It is a handy little tool I have used on occasion. The particular sedative I used causes short-term unconsciousness. Fifty milligrams would be considered a standard dosage, but I had a little difficulty with the fat police officer, and since you are a big man with a lot of muscle, I chose to up the dosage with you. Even so, you have only been unconscious for," he paused a moment and glanced at his wristwatch, "for only thirty-two minutes. You seem to have a high tolerance."

"Gee, thanks," I slurred. My tongue was numb, making it rather difficult to enunciate my words. He sensed what I was thinking.

"The effects of the sedative take a bit to wear off. You'll be back to normal soon."

I responded with a grunt.

"You are now wondering why I have done this to you, correct?" he asked.

"Yeah."

"I need information, Thomas."

I answered slowly, deliberately. "I have no idea where your bullshit artifact is".

His eyes seemed to magnify as he focused on me through his glasses with an emotionless, appraising stare. "It is possible you are telling the truth. We shall see. For the moment, we are going to wait until the effects of the sedative have diminished. While we are waiting, perhaps you would like to ask some questions of your own."

He stared at me expectantly.

"Alright, who do you work for?"

He smiled slightly. "Your question is difficult to answer. It is a business consortium comprised of both government and individual people. The decisions they make control world events." He silently worked his mouth a moment and then placed both his hands on mine.

"It is believed that this artifact could change the world as we know it."

"How?" I asked.

Mishka removed his hands from mine and shrugged. "I do not yet know."

"What about you? What's your story?" I asked. "What's your real name?"

He gave a small smile. "I have used my current name for some time now. As for my background, that is a story for another time. Suffice it to say, I came from humble origins and my younger years were difficult, one might even say horrendous." He paused a moment and his features darkened. I guessed he might have been thinking of an unpleasant memory. It only lasted a second.

"Now, enough about me, your speech is clearing up, which is indicative of the sedative wearing off. Let us get started, shall we?" He turned to Larry. "Did you purchase the items I requested?"

Larry nodded vigorously and pulled a small plastic grocery bag out of his pocket. He handed the bag to Mishka, who pulled out the contents. There wasn't much, a cellophane package and a plastic package of rubber bands. When I recognized the items sealed in the cellophane package, I got goosebumps. It was a five-pack of single edged razor blades. Mishka saw me staring at the items and gave me a somber expression.

"It pains me to have to do this, Thomas, but you have left me with no other options. You see, I am going to ask you a series of questions, and I must be certain you are telling me the truth."

"What are you about to do, boss?" Larry asked.

I glanced over at him. Despite his intoxication, Larry was nervous, and his sweating had increased exponentially. As a result, his body odor was pervading the shed. Or maybe it was me. I was sweating too. Mishka looked fresh as a daisy. Larry repeated his question.

Mishka glanced at him in annoyance. "It is a necessary action, Mister Boles."

Larry stared in drunken consternation as Mishka removed the razor blades from the packaging and inspected the edge of each one. When a flicker of a smile crossed Mishka's face, sweat started running down my forehead and into my eyes. I blinked repeatedly but it wasn't helping.

"I don't know about this, boss," Larry said.

Mishka seemed to ignore his trepidation. He casually took his suit jacket off and draped it across the back of his chair before taking out his gun from his waistband and shooting Larry in the chest. Larry T-Thomas Boles gasped in pain and clutched at the entrance wound before dropping onto the dirty floor.

I let out an involuntary gasp and stared down at Larry in surprise. He convulsed slightly and his breathing only lasted a few seconds before he let out a final sigh. It was then I noticed my phone, or should I say, what was left of my phone. It was lying on the ground, smashed, which meant the GPS was no long working. I then slowly looked up to see Mishka staring without emotion.

"There was no need for that," I said.

"Necessary," Mishka replied. He then pulled his chair over close to mine and sat.

"The rubber bands will slow down the flow of blood and prevent it from squirting on me. I would normally take more precautions, such as wearing protective gear, but I am somewhat pressed for time."

He tore open the bag of rubber bands and proceeded to wrap several around my left wrist. He then paused and gave me a somber stare before picking up one of the razor blades.

"Believe me when I tell you I am speaking from experience; the pain will be agonizing. Do not feel less of a man if you scream and beg."

"I have no doubt I'll scream, but I won't tell you anything," I said.

Mishka gave a thin, tight smile. "Oh, but you will, Thomas. You will."

He stared pointedly for a moment as he thumbed the edge of one of the razor blades. He then grabbed my hand and forcibly extended my pinkie finger. He made a cut down the middle, destroying a perfectly good tented arch pattern. It hurt more than I thought it would. Think of a paper cut multiplied by a factor of ten. I gasped and gritted my teeth, but at least managed not to scream. He gave a small, sadistic smile.

"Excellent, Thomas. I wanted to see if you had a stout constitution and you have not disappointed me. Let us now begin with the questions. The first question is about the artifact. Where is it?"

I was trying hard to think up a smartassed response. Bravery in the face of torture, that sort of thing, but all I could think of was how much more pain the little man was about to inflict on me. As these thoughts went through my mind, he suddenly made another cut. I let out something audible, not sure if it could be called a scream, but it was close. I tried desperately to kick my legs free, knowing the effort was futile but trying anyway.

Mishka waited for me to answer. When I didn't, he poked at the two slices with the corner of the razor, causing waves of pain to shoot up my arm. I was beginning to become nauseous, but something else also happened. I had a sudden, amazing epiphany. A blinding burst of insight. I had the answer to the riddle.

A neuroscientist could no doubt explain what happened. All I know is the excruciating pain had somehow activated my brain. It analyzed the information I had stored away and formulated an answer.

I'd discovered the artifact. It was right before me the whole time. It was right in front of Mishka the entire time as well. In fact, there were two of them.

The problem was, how long could I hold out without telling Mishka? Once I divulged the information, I knew he'd kill me and leave me lying beside Larry T-Thomas Boles. We probably would not be discovered for weeks. By that time, the summer heat and insects would literally destroy all exposed flesh. Definitely a closed casket funeral.

For some reason, I started thinking about an old case. A man died of a heart attack while fishing on the banks of Percy Priest Lake. He wasn't discovered for three days. By then, every inch of exposed skin was covered in maggots. It wasn't a pretty sight. Didn't smell too good either. I wondered if that was how I was going to end up.

I had been scrunching my eyes shut, but now I opened them and stared at Mishka. He stared back expectantly.

"Well, Thomas?"

I don't know how I did it, but I made direct eye contact, smiled, and let out a chuckle. He stared back and even arched an eyebrow.

"Do you find this amusing, Mister Ironcutter?" he asked.

"Amusing? That's not the word I'd use. No, it's not amusing. On the contrary, it hurts like hell, but you'll never get anything out of me. I know it now."

Mishka gave a small, patient smile, like he was dealing with a slow-witted child.

"One of my colleagues was fond of using a similar technique to extract information, but he did not cut the fingers. He cut on the scrotum and penis. I always thought that method to be rather sadistic and there were undertones of repressed homosexuality."

He shook his head in mock sadness. "Your stubbornness is forcing my hand, Mister Ironcutter. It pains me, but I believe this will have to be my next course of action. What do you think?"

"I think you're going to kill me no matter what, but I think I'll be able to resist you long enough and that help will come before you kill me."

Mishka shook his head slowly. "There is nobody coming to rescue you, Thomas," he said, and then made another cut to my pinkie. This time I yelled out in pain and tears welled up in my eyes. I could barely make out a small, sadistic smile forming on his lips. He was about to say something else but was interrupted.

"Stop."

The voice was like a sudden intrusion. We both turned in surprise at the source. Eva was standing in the doorway. The sunlight outlined her, making her look like an avenging angel. The gun in her hand certainly added to the nuance. She held it at waist level and pointed it toward Mishka.

"You would not dare shoot me," he declared. "Put that away. That is an order."

She responded by raising the gun, aiming, and firing a shot. The bullet took off a piece of his right ear. Blood spurted out. His facial expression registered not pain, but surprise. He slowly put a hand to his injured ear and then pulled it away, inspecting the blood on his hand. I don't know if he thought what I was thinking; was she that good of a shot or was she aiming for his head and missed? She said something to him in a foreign language and they engaged in a brief conversation. After a moment, Mishka turned to me with a bemused expression.

"She has instructed me to free you from your bonds, or else she promised to shoot me again."

"You better get to it then," I advised him.

He seemed to think it over for a second and nodded. He picked up a razor blade and began cutting the zip ties. I waited patiently as he worked through them. When he was finished, I grabbed my handkerchief out of my back pocket with my good hand and wrapped it around my finger.

"I apologize for this misunderstanding, Thomas," he said.

"Not a problem," I replied.

He was standing in front of me, like we'd been doing nothing more than shooting the breeze. I launched a short right jab. It connected squarely with his chin and knocked him on his ass.

"Yeah, not a problem," I growled.

While he was addled, I stood and quickly retrieved both my gun and his. When I did so, I became lightheaded and almost collapsed to the ground. I reached back, found the chair, and dropped into it. Eva walked over, stared at Mishka a moment, and then gazed at me.

"How are you?" she asked.

"Weak," I replied and gestured at my left wrist. "Help me get these rubber bands off, please."

She stood to one side, no doubt to keep from getting messy, took one of Mishka's razor blades, and deftly began cutting. The rubber bands popped at the sudden release of tension. For some reason it amused me, but only for a minute. I rubbed my wrist to get the feeling back, which happened, but it also brought another wave of nauseating pain, and my finger now soaked my handkerchief. When she had finished, she set the razor blade down and looked over at Larry, who was lying crumpled on the floor.

"Mishka shot him," I explained.

If she had any thoughts about it, she did not voice them. Instead, she pointed down at my hand. "You need medical attention," she said, and then glanced over at Mishka. His eyes were open, but he still seemed addled. "What will you do with him?"

I shrugged. I needed to turn him over to the police, but what I really wanted to do was strangle the life out of him. "The best thing to do is to turn him over to the police."

"Yes, certainly," she replied. She then turned and walked out of the shed.

I was still feeling the effects of the injury to my finger and whatever shit Mishka had injected into me, but an unintended consequence was the pain from the cuts made me more alert.

I stood and was hit with another wave of nausea. I sat down again and kept my handgun aimed at Mishka. "If you even look like you're going to do something, I'm going to unload on you."

Mishka stared but did not reply. After a minute, the lightheadedness subsided enough to allow me to unload his handgun. I tucked it into the back of my waistband and then stood slowly. I was still a touch lightheaded, but the nausea was gone. I stepped over to him and dropped to one knee. I then pointed my handgun at his knee.

"I'm going to search you, Mishka. Don't try anything stupid, or else you'll never walk normally again."

"I understand, Thomas," he said and did not move as I leaned closer and searched him. He had nothing on him. No phone, no wallet, no car keys, nothing. I stood and backed away.

Looking around the shed, I spotted my smashed phone. I grunted, wondering if my insurance was still good. Having a thought, I went over to Larry. He'd called me earlier and it made me wonder. Sure enough, I found a cheap flip phone in his pocket. Opening it, I found it was password protected, but it had the emergency call function. I hit nine-one-one and waited. I caught Mishka eyeing me. I came up with an idea, subtly turned the volume down, and then stared at the phone in seeming frustration.

"Damn it," I grumbled.

"Is something wrong, Thomas?" Mishka asked.

I looked over at him. He was eyeing me curiously. Blood was running down the side of his head and staining his white shirt. He did not seem to notice. I gestured at Larry's phone.

"Damn thing isn't working. I was going to try to call the cops to come get us, but it looks like we're stuck out here by ourselves." I gestured around. "Did you know there is an old fort less than a hundred yards from us? Fort Negley is the name. It was built during the Civil War." I hoped the 911 clerk understood I was dropping clues to our location.

"It wasn't so civil, was it, Thomas? The war, that is," he quipped.

"No, it wasn't. Kind of like when you killed Larry. That was not civil at all."

"But necessary, as I said."

"Most people would call it cold blooded murder. Anyway, he's beyond help. Since it seems we're going to be here a while, I have some questions for you," I said.

He chuckled without humor. "You did not answer any of my questions, why should I answer yours? In case you haven't noticed, I've already had some fingers taken. Whatever torture you intend to perform, it will not work on me."

"Nothing like that. I was thinking more of a quid pro quo."

He stared and straightened his glasses. "Go on," he urged.

"You answer a few of my questions, and I'll answer that one question that brought you to Nashville in the first place."

"Are you saying you know where the location of the artifact is?"

"Yes, I do, and I'll tell you where it is. I'll even give you a hint; there are two of them."

His eyes widened, the lenses making them into two orbs. When he spoke, there was a note of lust in his tone.

"Two? You would not lie, would you, Thomas?"

"I'm telling the truth. Do we have a deal?"

He thought about it for five seconds before speaking. "Very well, proceed with your questions."

The first thing I wanted him to do was confess to his latest murder. "First, why did you kill Larry? He was a harmless drunk."

"He was expendable. A ruined soul long before I ever met him. I did him a favor."

It was true, Larry-T-as in-Thomas Boles was a lost cause, but Mishka Abramovich was not God, he didn't get to choose who lived and who died. Now, I was going to try to get him to admit to the other murders.

"So, you believed he was expendable. What about the grave robbers you hired? Were they expendable too?"

"Their arrogance toward me cost them their lives," he said with contempt. "And yes, they too were expendable. I suppose you now want to know about the fat policeman."

"Richard Tomey was not expendable. He was a good man."

Mishka snorted. "He was a pathetic fat American. He squealed like a pig when I began cutting. Sadly, he died before I could elicit the necessary information out of him. I can only assume his heart gave out."

"Did you drug him like you did me?" I asked.

"Yes, I did. The process was necessary. You may not believe it, but it was not my intention for him to die. In any event, I did the city of Nashville a tremendous favor."

I was sorely tempted to put a bullet in his head, right then and there, but I knew I had to go by the book on this one. Bringing him in alive was going to be the only way to clear my name in all these murders. Besides, people like Abby would not approve if I killed him. I liked the girl and I wanted her to look up to me.

"Alright, Mishka, we're going to walk out of here, find a road, and wait on the police. I'm not going to kill you, but I will shoot you if you try anything stupid. Do you understand?"

"Are you proficient with firearms, Thomas?" he asked.

"I've been around firearms most of my life. If you don't think I can hit what I'm aiming at, by all means, make a run for it."

He considered my answer before offering a small nod. "Very well."

I shoved Larry's phone into my pocket and directed him to the door.

# CHAPTER 46

The man moved slowly and kept messing with his ear. Once outside, I looked around for Eva. Not seeing her, I called out. Mishka made a clicking sound with his teeth.

"She has left, it would seem," he said.

"It certainly looks that way." I tried to keep the disappointment out of my voice, but Mishka heard it.

"You were hoping otherwise. You seem to have an attraction for her, no?"

I ignored his implication and looked around, getting my bearings. I saw the trail leading back to the cemetery and debated on going back that way, but then I heard the sounds of a truck travelling down the road. The tall weeds blocked my view, but it sounded close. I pointed.

"There's a road in that direction. Start walking," I directed.

"As you wish," Mishka said. "But before I do so, it is time for you to honor our agreement, yes?"

I paused and stared at him. "You're right, and I'm a man who keeps his word. But I'm surprised you haven't figured it out by yourself."

He frowned in puzzlement. "How so?"

"It's the bells."

He absently rubbed his wounded ear. "The bells?"

"Yes, the bells. There's one mounted on top of that boulder on Sadie's grave, and there's one at the entrance to Methuselah's mausoleum. Those are the artifacts, Mishka."

He continued to frown. "How are you certain?"

"Because each bell has an inscription etched onto them. The inscriptions are what you are seeking."

He stared in stunned surprise. It was probably the most emotion I'd seen from the man. "Are you certain?"

"Yep."

"What do the inscriptions say?" he asked.

"I don't know. Some kind of foreign script. Hebrew maybe, I don't know."

"Then how do you know the bells are the artifact?" he asked.

"I can't sit here and articulate how I know, but I'm convinced of it. What do you think?"

He rubbed his ear again as he pondered what I said. His hands were now covered in blood. After a moment, he spoke.

"I find myself agreeing with your intuition. Do you now have possession of them?" he asked.

"Nope. I left them where they have been for the last hundred years or so."

He made that clicking noise with his teeth. "Thomas, we must retrieve those bells immediately. Let us retrieve them together."

"You drugged me, tied me down, and carved up my finger. Now you expect us to be buddies? Are you nuts?"

"My actions are regrettable. I don't expect you to understand, but I will compensate you for your troubles."

My first instinct was to slap the shit out of him, but I had another idea.

"Perhaps we can, but first I must ask you. Who helped you?"

"Other than the drunken Mister Boles? Nobody."

"I'm talking about the murders of the two grave robbers and Richard Tomey. Be honest, it was Eva, right?"

"I needed no help."

"You needed help with me," I remarked.

He gave a thin smile. "The two men I hired were smug, arrogant. Former Spetsnaz, did I mention that? They intended to betray me. It cost them their lives."

"And Tomey?" I asked.

"He was fat and slow, easy enough to handle. You are different, Thomas. You are not a man to be underestimated. I saw that the first time I met you."

"Well, thank you for the compliment, I guess," I said.

"It is sincere," he said.

"I'm not sure I believe you about Eva. I believe she is working with you."

"No, Thomas, she did not help me then and she certainly has not helped me now. Considering the predicament I am now in, you would most certainly agree, no?"

"Maybe so, but whenever you're around, she seems to be nearby, no?" I countered.

"So it would seem," he said quietly. His features darkened momentarily and then he changed the subject. "Now, let us go back to the cemetery and pay a visit to Sadie Sartain's grave, yes?"

"I've got a better idea. We are going to walk out to the road and wait for the police. The detectives are going to have a lot to talk to you about," I said.

He clicked hit teeth again. It was beginning to annoy me. "Thomas, we must retrieve those bells immediately. The longer we delay, the greater the risk of them being taken from us. Besides, there is something you may not be aware of."

"What's that?" I asked.

"Once my people are made aware I am in custody, they will come to collect me. You see, Thomas, I have diplomatic immunity."

I stared at him. He gazed back, waiting for my decision. "I don't know if that's true or not, but if I don't turn you over to the police, the suspicion that I have aided and abetted you will be even worse than it currently is. I'm not going to let that happen."

He rubbed at his ear again. Now he had blood all over his hands. He seemed to reach an internal decision and gave a curt nod. "I understand. Let us proceed then."

We started walking again, but I was not through questioning him about Eva.

"What is it with you two?" I asked. "Why did you marry such a young girl?"

"Marry? Is that what she told you?" He chuckled. "That is a new one. No, Thomas, we are not married. My wife and I adopted her when she was a young orphan child."

Now it was my turn to frown in puzzlement. "She's your adopted daughter? Why would she lie about something like that?"

"I wish I could give a logical answer to that question. She has always told lies. My wife and I provided her with everything. A loving home, the best schooling, everything."

I could not decide if he was lying or telling the truth. At the moment, it wasn't important. A police helicopter had buzzed over us, circled back, and was now hovering over our position. I looked up, waved, and gestured toward the road.

"Alright, they've found us, let's keep walking," I directed. I could sense Mishka getting apprehensive, but to his credit, he didn't try anything and kept walking toward the road.

"Are you being honest about the inscriptions? You don't know what they say?" he asked.

"I don't even know what language they're written in. Hebrew would be my guess. I took pictures, but since you smashed my phone, I guess I can't show you."

"Unfortunate," he muttered.

The cops had their handguns trained on us as we approached. I was reluctant to simply toss my gun to the ground. I holstered it, hoping they wouldn't object. One of them was a sergeant. I glanced at his nametag,

G. Young. It'd been a couple of years and I was still woozy from the drug and loss of blood, but I realized I knew him.

"You still had hair the last time I saw you," I said.

He smirked at me. "Still a smartass, I see."

The younger officer, he had to be a rookie, looked like he was still too young to shave. Even so, he did not wait for an order. He directed Mishka down to his knees and handcuffed him before standing him up and walking him back to his patrol car. I could hear the sounds of multiple sirens.

"Sounds like a lot of people are heading this way," I remarked.

Sergeant Young chuckled. "Half the department, at least." He gestured at my hand. "What the hell happened?"

I briefly explained. The sarge grimaced.

"He did that to you? He did the same thing to Tomey, right?"

"Yeah."

The sergeant glowered. "That sonofabitch. I hope they give him the death penalty."

"Yeah." I didn't tell him about Mishka's claim of diplomatic immunity. We'd find out soon enough if it was true.

"You're going to need medical attention. I'll go ahead and get an ambulance dispatched," he said.

I made a head nod toward Mishka. "All that blood on him is from an injury to his ear. I'm sure it'll need stitching up as well."

I was about to say more, but several things happened in less than a second. Sergeant Young's eyes widened, and he pushed me aside as a gunshot rang out. He then drew his duty weapon and fired two quick shots as another gunshot rang out.

I had instinctively dropped to one knee and turned toward the direction he fired at, drawing my handgun in the process. Mishka and the other officer were on the ground. We were approximately thirty feet away from them. Instinct urged us to run up to them, but neither Sergeant Young nor I were that foolish. The two of us tactically approached like we'd been working together for years. There were two holes in the middle of Mishka's shirt that were oozing blood.

"Cover me," Sergeant Young directed as he kicked the gun out of Mishka's hand and cuffed him before checking his carotid artery for a pulse. The sarge glanced up at me and slowly shook his head.

I put away my handgun and focused on the rookie. He was on his back, gasping for air, and staring in near panic. I squatted down beside him and observed a singular hole in his uniform shirt, a half inch above his sternum. I touched it and found no blood.

"How are you doing, Officer? Are you wearing your vest?" He nodded. "Good man. Let me get it off and have a look at you."

I undid his shirt and pulled at the Velcro straps of the vest, releasing the front panel. Carefully removing it, I set it aside and raised his tee shirt. There was a welt forming, but the skin wasn't broken.

"Yeah, he got you, but you're going to be alright. They'll transport you to the ER and check you out."

Sergeant Young squatted beside me. "What happened, bud?" he asked.

"He slipped his cuffs somehow and punched me in the throat," the rookie explained.

I realized now why the evil little bastard was purposely getting blood all over his hands. He was making them slippery. The shortage of all his fingers probably made it easier to slip the cuffs. The rookie looked over at his handgun lying in the road. "He got my gun from me."

I nodded in understanding and moved close to his ear. "Listen to me," I whispered. "You're going to be okay. There will be a couple of knuckleheads that'll criticize you for this, but don't be doubting yourself. This man was a pro. A cold-blooded killer. He's probably been killing people since before you were born. Don't let anybody make you think you're a screw up."

His expression was doubtful, but he nodded. I straightened. "Now, you be sure to tell them you're traumatized, and you need at least two weeks of paid vacation to recover."

I winked at him. He responded with an uncertain grin.

Sergeant Young and I stood together. He gave me a nod of approval at my advice. I pointed at Mishka.

"Good shooting, Sarge," I said.

He sighed. "That's all I need, another incident in my personnel file. I'm already getting heartburn just thinking about the shooting review board."

I started to laugh, but then saw blood on his shirt sleeve. He saw me looking and glanced down at it.

"Yeah, he winged me," he said. "It doesn't hurt that bad but I'm afraid to look at it."

Before I could even check on him, we were suddenly swarmed by at least a dozen officers. They seemed to have come from nowhere and everywhere. One of them had a first aid kit and began working on Sergeant Young's arm. There were more sirens, and after a minute an ambulance arrived. Sergeant Young and the rookie officer were hurriedly whisked away. Someone finally noticed I was injured and called for another ambulance. Soon, I was being tended to by EMT personnel. They took one look at my finger and swapped a glance with each other.

"We need to take you to the emergency room and let a doctor take a look at that mess," one of them told me.

# CHAPTER 47

The nurse, a woman who looked like a mom with a house full of kids, held my good hand while the doctor used a small syringe to inject Novocain or something similar into my finger.

"This will be a little tricky," he said, as much to himself as to me. He then seemed to notice I was paying attention to him. "Don't worry though. I'll get it fixed up."

Percy and Jay came to the ER and watched as the doctor worked. He made some small talk as he worked, using a combination of surgical glue, which smelled a lot like super glue, and small sutures. It took him about twenty minutes. When he finished, he admired his work with stoic satisfaction.

"Alright, my work is masterful, as usual, but you will need follow up treatment. I am going to refer you to a specialist." He gestured at my finger. "I'll have a nurse finish up and give you some clean bandages. Change them out daily. If you see signs of infection, come back here immediately. I'm also going to write you a script for the pain."

"Thanks, Doc," I said.

"Alright, once the nurse is done, we'll get you discharged."

He walked out without waiting for a response. I eyed Jay.

"I'm not going downtown. If you want to interview me, we can do it here, in the car, or you can wait until another time."

"I've already got it worked out with the Vandy police," he said. "They have an office here in the ER we can use, and the sergeant has assured me we'll have privacy."

I nodded in agreement. The nurse had me discharged a short time later and we walked back to the office. The Vanderbilt sergeant gave me a curt nod and closed the office door behind us.

He did not need to ask me many questions. I voluntarily gave a mostly complete statement while he recorded me with his phone. I left a couple of things out and waited until Percy and I were alone before telling him Eva's involvement and the bells. He listened as he drove me back to my Explorer and waited until parking before responding.

"Who else knows about the bells?" he asked.

"I have a strong suspicion about one particular person, but other than him, I think anyone else that knows about them is long dead."

"What about this Eva woman? Is she a friend or an enemy?"

I sighed. I was tired and the Novocain was wearing off, causing my finger to start throbbing. "I don't know, Percy. I honestly don't know."

He nodded in understanding. "It's an interesting story. Definitely intriguing. Are you going to follow up on it?"

"I'm not sure yet." I held my left hand up. "I'm limited on how much I can do until this thing heals up a little. Maybe it'd be best to park my ass at the house for a few days."

"Good idea. I'll tell Anna to bring you some groceries," he said.

"I appreciate that," I said.

When I lowered my hand, I absently let it drop into my lap, causing me to wince in pain. Percy noticed.

"You okay to drive? We can leave your car here and pick it up tomorrow."

"I don't want to leave it here. It'll probably get broken into."

"Yeah, maybe. I can call for a two-person car and have them drive you."

I started to say no, but then I thought of something. "See if Officer Severns is working. She can drive me."

Percy gave a small grin. "You like her I'm guessing."

"I do, but not like you think. She's a friend. Kind of like Anna, I guess."

Percy nodded in understanding and called dispatch. Abby was indeed on duty. She and Officer Clark drove into the cemetery's parking lot ten minutes after Percy had requested them. She had a concerned expression on her face when she saw my bandaged hand. I minimized the extent of my injury and soon she was driving me to my house.

"You're going to have to tell me everything," she urged.

"Briefly, Mishka kidnapped me, drugged me, tied me to a chair, and began cutting on me with a razor blade because he felt I was withholding information from him."

"Wow. How did you escape?"

"Do you remember me telling you about Eva?"

She nodded.

"Yeah, I don't know where she was during the whole kidnapping part, but eventually she shows up and makes him stop. If not for her, I'd probably be missing a few fingers by now."

"That was nice of her. I still don't like her though," she said. I would've chuckled, but I wasn't feeling all that great.

When we arrived at my house, Abby insisted on walking with me to make sure I didn't faint or something. I was about to walk in when she stopped me.

"Stand here a minute and don't move," she directed and then went inside with her weapon drawn. I smiled as I realized she was clearing my house of any possible hostiles. After a minute, she reappeared in the doorway, waved me in, and directed me to sit in my chair.

"Make yourself comfortable. Are you hungry? I can make you something."

"No, but I could do with something to drink," I said.

She went into the kitchen and fixed me a glass of water with a couple of cubes of ice. I thanked her and drank almost all of it. I didn't realize how thirsty I was. She hurriedly refilled it.

"You're a little pale," she observed. "How's the pain level?"

"I'd say moderate, but I'll be alright. A good night's rest will help."

"I can come back after my shift is over," she suggested.

I managed a smile. "That's okay. As soon as you leave, I'm going to bed. I'll be sound asleep by the time you get off."

"Oh, okay. How about I come by in the morning? I can bring breakfast."

I thought it over for all of one second. "Yeah, that'd be nice."

She started to say something else but was interrupted by her partner honking the horn, causing her to groan in exasperation.

"I'll see you in the morning," she said, gave my shoulder a lighthearted squeeze, and then left, making sure the door was locked behind her.

Tommy Boy came out from wherever he was hiding and jumped up on my lap. He plopped down and began purring within seconds. I made myself comfortable and dry swallowed the two pain pills the doc gave me. I turned on the TV with the remote and caught a couple of minutes of the late news. Mishka was the headline and, as usual, the media only had a small snippet of correct information, the rest they speculated on. One would think they'd wait until the official press conference before trying to guess what happened. Fortunately, my name was left out.

I contemplated moving my tired ass to the bed, but I realized the armrest of my chair provided comfortable support for my hand and would keep me from rolling onto it while I slept. So, I didn't move.

While I sat, I started getting a touch of stress induced heartburn. I needed to relax and decompress. I found my remote lying on the floor beside the chair and turned on the local news. As I watched, I had yet another epiphany. I'd told the rookie officer that Mishka was a pro, yet he shot the young man point blank in the chest. If he was a pro, he would have known the rookie was wearing a bullet proof vest and he would have shot him in the head. Mishka wasn't trying to kill the rookie, only incapacitate him so he could kill his intended target. The reason Sergeant

Young was shot in the arm is because it was in the spot where I was a microsecond before he pushed me. Mishka was trying to kill me.

"That bastard," I growled, but I knew instantly why.

Because I knew about the bells. He wanted to be the only person alive with that information, and he was probably counting on being able to kill me and then surrender before anyone could return fire. He underestimated Sergeant Young. Most people did. Balding, with a paunch and a chronic hangdog expression, he looked more like a door greeter at Walmart. Those who knew him knew he was an expert marksman and a decorated Marine veteran who had been involved in at least three shootings during his career.

He had almost succeeded in killing me. I found myself saying a prayer, thanking the big man for letting me live on his Earth for a day or two longer.

I turned the TV off, readjusted myself into a more comfortable position, and closed my eyes. A part of me expected, hoped, that Eva would show up. I fell asleep while I was waiting.

# CHAPTER 48

Abby called at nine the next morning asking me what I wanted for breakfast. She was knocking on the door thirty minutes later with Burger King croissant sandwiches in hand. I'd dressed in Levi's and a casual Polo shirt. She was wearing black shorts showing off her muscular legs and a bright pink shirt with a popular brand name emblazoned across the chest. She was a good-looking girl. I was surprised she didn't have one or two boyfriends.

"I have assorted beverages in the fridge, help yourself," I said.

She directed me to sit before looking in the fridge and pouring herself a glass of OJ. She then poured me a mug of coffee before sitting.

"How are you feeling?" she asked.

"Good, except for the finger. It hurts like hell."

She nodded, sat, and pulled the croissants out of the sack.

"In case you're wondering, I'm not wearing a wire. I'm done with that," she said.

"Good. How did they react when you told them?"

She made a face. "I haven't told them yet. One of them called me this morning. I let it go to voicemail."

I chuckled. "Don't let any of them try to intimidate you."

"I won't," she replied with a smile. "I have to admit though, I'm dying of curiosity."

I proceeded to tell her what happened. She listened intently, her expression a combination of disbelief and fascination. I told her almost everything, except for the bells. I'd probably tell her about them eventually, but there was someone I wanted to speak to first.

"That is incredible," she said when I'd finished. "So, what happens next?"

I shrugged. "The feds will try to follow up on Mishka's other activities. His trip to Miami was not a vacation. He had something going on down there. As far as the murders go, if I know Poston, and I do, he'll slow walk it as long as possible."

She frowned. "What do you mean?"

"If you or I were the lead detective, we'd clear all four murder cases. The official phrase is cleared by exception due to the death of the suspect. Having four murder cases cleared would look awesome on the books, right?"

"Yeah, you could probably even get an award for it," she said with a grin.

"Exactly, but Poston is too conniving. He won't clear the cases immediately. He'll keep them open as long as he can."

She frowned now. "Why would he do that?"

"You see, he thinks he is of a higher caliber than the average detective and therefore he feels he should not waste his time on the run of the mill murders. He only wants to be assigned to high profile cases, the ones that get him in the news. So, he's going to tell Commander Bartlett there are still leads to follow up on that may prove there are others involved. By convincing Bartlett of that, he'll be off rotation. In other words, he'll have his days free to do whatever he wants while the other detectives pick up his slack."

"Will he really do that?" Abby asked.

"He did it when I worked there. I doubt he's changed," I said.

"Wow, that is wrong in so many ways, and unfair to the other detectives," she said.

"Yes, it is. But, as soon as another high-profile case comes along, he'll suddenly be available. Oh, and he'll usually have a lackey with him to do all the grunt work. That's what Kettleworth is for. And he'll still take all the credit for clearing the four murders."

"Does Kettleworth realize she's being used?" Abby asked.

"Probably not, but if she does, she's not complaining. She's got it made."

"Why would he behave like that? I mean, I know he's arrogant, but that's not professional at all."

I shrugged. "Because that's the kind of person he is."

Abby seemed to be thinking over what I said while we ate our croissants. When we were finished, she stood and cleaned off the table. After refilling my coffee mug, she sat back down and gazed out the window. The sun had been out, but it had clouded up again and a slow, drizzling rain had begun.

"It looks like it's going to rain all day," she remarked.

"Yeah, it'll be good for my grass though."

"So, what's next for you? Are you closing this case on your end?" she asked.

"Not yet. There is a person I want to talk to before I can do anything else," I said.

"Who?"

I considered my answer and absently flexed my hand which sent a jolt of pain up my arm, causing an involuntary spasm.

"Still hurting, huh?" she asked.

"Yeah. It's going to take a little bit before I'm back to normal."

She nodded and gave me a motherly stare. "Be careful with it. And be careful with those pain pills. They're easily addictive."

I had to smile. "Yes ma'am," I replied.

"So, who do you need to speak to?" she asked again and stared expectantly.

"It's an elderly gentleman. Do you have to work tonight?" I asked.

"Yeah, why?"

"I'm going on a road trip. I was going to invite you to come along, but I don't think I'll be back before your duty shift starts."

It was going to be hard to drive for seven hours straight and honestly, I could use the company. I was mentally thinking of who else I could invite to go when I noticed her frowning.

"Where are you going?"

"New Orleans."

Her eyes widened in puzzlement. "New Orleans? Why?"

"The person I need to speak to lives there."

"Can't you simply call him?"

"I wish it were that simple, but I have to speak to him in person." I thought a moment. "I'll give Anna a call and see if she's available."

Abby sat and watched while I made the phone call. Anna answered after a couple of rings and listened to my request.

"I'm sorry, Thomas, but I'm going to be with Rochelle for a few days in court."

I told her I understood and hung up. I thought about calling Ronald, but my buddy was high maintenance, and I wasn't feeling up to coddling him. Abby drummed her fingers on the table.

"Can't you wait a few days? You're going to be miserable driving that long," she asserted.

"I think I'll be alright," I rejoined.

"Men are so stubborn sometimes," she proclaimed with a scowl and fished her phone out of her pocket.

After a moment, she began speaking to someone. It sounded like a supervisor. They were reluctant to give her a day off, but when Abby pointed out that rookies were considered nonessential personnel, she got her request. Hanging up, she gave me a look.

"I'm burning a vacation day, and I've only got a couple, so this better be worth it. When do we leave?"

"The sooner the better. I've got a full tank of gas. I can fill a couple of water bottles and I think we're ready to go. There's something I need you to do first."

"What's that?"

"Help me tie my shoes."

It took us an hour to get on the road. Abby insisted on driving, which I was grateful for. It's amazing how an injured pinky finger can limit one's physical activity, but I knew if I tried to drive to New Orleans by myself, I would be beyond miserable. Abby typed in the destination in her app on the phone and we were soon underway.

"I appreciate you doing this," I said to her when she'd merged onto the interstate.

"Well, we have seven hours for you to tell me why this little trip couldn't wait," she responded.

I debated on what I was going to tell her. I'd blindly trusted Eva and I was wondering now if that was going to come back and bite me in the ass. I chose my words carefully.

"Mishka had hired me to locate a religious artifact, remember?"

She blew a tuft of hair out of her face. "Yeah, and he thought either Richard or I had stolen it."

"Right. And you know everything that happened next," I said.

"Yeah, so why are we going to New Orleans?"

"The woman's grave in Nashville? Her husband is interred in a cemetery in New Orleans. That's where I was when Tomey was murdered."

"Okay, I remember Poston saying you claimed you were in New Orleans. So, what were you doing there?"

"Mishka sent me there to see what I could find out. It turned out to be a wild goose chase, but I spoke with a priest while I was down there. He was a nice enough fellow, but he didn't tell me much and I feel like he knows more than what he told me. It's a little complicated."

"You think he'll talk to you now?" she asked.

"I think if I am face-to-face with him, and I tell him about Mishka's death, he'll be more forthcoming."

"What if he isn't?" she asked.

I shrugged. "If he isn't, there's not much I can do."

She pestered me for details, but I refused to say any more. Eventually, she changed the subject and soon we were talking about our respective police academy experiences and how it was when I was a rookie. The miles rolled by as I regaled her with humorous stories and some of the more interesting cases I'd had both as a homicide detective and a private investigator. She was fascinated about the two rogue officers I'd investigated - Smith and Sweet.

"If you had not discovered them, they could still be on the force and still killing people," she commented.

"They would have been caught eventually," I said.

"But still, you probably saved some people from being murdered. That's the kind of person I want to be remembered as."

"I've no doubt you're going to have an exemplary career," I replied.

"I hope so."

We arrived at the church a little before six in the evening. It was a humid evening in New Orleans, and I felt myself sweating almost as soon as I exited my SUV. I expected Father Anthony to be at dinner or back in his room, but surprisingly, he was sitting at his bench, reading a book. I instructed Abby to sit in the Explorer and wait on me. She didn't like it but did not complain.

He looked up at my approach, removed his bifocals, and I saw a hint of a smile hidden under his beard.

"Welcome back, Thomas," he said, and then frowned when he spotted the wrapping around my hand. "Are you alright?"

I sat beside him and made myself comfortable. "I had a little run in with an unpleasant person. The name he'd given me was Mishka Abramovich. Have you heard of him?"

"I have not," he said.

"He was the person who hired me," I said.

"Interesting. Are you still under his employ?" he asked.

"No. He's now dead," I said.

"Oh?"

"Yeah. He had a run in with the police and was killed." His reaction was only to give a small nod. I pushed forward. "I get the impression you were expecting me to return."

"That I was, Thomas, that I was."

I had some papers with me that I'd folded in half to keep Abby from seeing. I unfolded them now and handed them to Father Anthony.

"The first two are pictures of the bell on Sadie's grave. The others are the bell hanging on Methuselah's mausoleum."

He donned the pair of bifocals that were hanging from his neck and inspected the photos closely. After a couple of minutes, he took the bifocals back off and let them dangle on his chest.

"I presume the language is Hebrew?" I guessed.

"Aramaic, to be specific," he said. "An old language. It took me almost three years to learn how to read it. It is an interesting story. Would you like to hear it?"

"Yes, I would," I said.

"I have been living here for twenty years or so. I often found myself wandering the grounds of the cemetery and marveling at the artistry of the mausoleums. One day, I happened upon Methuselah's final resting place. There was nothing extraordinarily significant about it, and yet, I dreamt of the bell that night, and the night after. I made a closer inspection of the bell and found the inscription. I cannot say why, but I did not tell anyone else of my discovery. Once I had determined what language the inscription was written in, I decided to learn it myself rather than rely on an interpreter. As I said, it took me three years to learn. Oh, I took parts of it and sent them to interpreters, only to confirm I was properly translating." He tapped the picture of Sadie's bell. "This one says essentially the same thing. There seems to be an additional description, but I would have to study it further."

"May I ask what they say?" I asked.

"I'll summarize, Thomas. It says that after Jesus was crucified and placed in the cave of Joseph of Arimathea, Pontius Pilate recruited two trusted family members to remove our savior's body and entomb him in a secret location." He saw me staring wide-eyed. "This is not a new claim. There have been several similar stories, or claims, whatever you want to call them."

"Alright, if it's not a new claim, what makes this information so special?" I asked.

"That's the rub, Thomas. These inscriptions give specific details to the location where the body of Y'shua lies at rest. Now, bear in mind, there is no street address or GPS coordinates, but the details are specific enough where someone knowledgeable of the history of the particular area would have an excellent chance of finding it."

When it sunk in, my mouth went dry. He stared solemnly.

"As you can see, if it is true, there are people that would proclaim that Jesus was not resurrected, as it says in the scripture, meaning he was merely a mortal man, and not our Lord and savior. My people would go to great efforts to debunk it, or they would simply destroy those seemingly innocuous bells and anyone who got in their way."

"Do you think it's true?" I asked.

A large leaf had fallen onto Father Anthony's lap. He picked it up and studied it for a moment before responding.

"Many years ago, a terrible accusation was made against me. I felt that I made an adequate defense of the accusation and proved my innocence. Even so, I was removed from the Holy See and exiled here to live out the rest of my life. The accusation was without any corroboration. Their word against mine. It didn't matter. The damage was done. It will be the same if this is ever made public, Thomas. It could potentially cause unfathomable damage. Especially if the instructions are followed and human remains are indeed found."

I swallowed a couple of times and gazed out at the cemetery. When I focused back on Father Anthony, he was still staring at me.

"I am an old man in frail health. I have made my peace with our Lord." He saw the questioning stare and smiled. "Yes, I still believe he is our savior. All I want now is to be buried here, in this holy ground. And now I ask you, what do you want, Thomas? Do you want me to read this to you, where you will now know where the remains of Jesus may possibly lie at rest?"

"Honestly, Father, I'm not sure I'm worthy enough to know that information."

He nodded. "Then what do you want, Thomas?"

Father Anthony did not wait for my answer. He stood, stretched out the stiffness in his joints, and slowly walked away, leaving me with his bench. I sat there, alone with my thoughts. After several minutes, someone sat down beside me. I turned to see it was Abby. She stared questioningly.

"You were a million miles away. What did the priest tell you?" she asked.

"Remember that I told you Mishka was in Nashville seeking a religious artifact, right?" She nodded. "Well, I found it."

She stared in confusion. It only took me ten minutes to tell her about the bells and the inscriptions. It both confused and frightened her.

"Can I see it?" she asked.

I looked around to see if we were being watched. This whole case was making me paranoid. I didn't see anyone, stood, and led her to Methuselah Sartain's mausoleum. I made a head motion toward the bell. She stared at it in wonder.

"Are you taking it back with us?"

"Nope. We're going to leave it here and we're not going to tell anyone about it."

I'm sure I added to her confusion, but she did not question the logic behind my decision and simply nodded.

"Alright, unless you want to stick around and tour this place, we should get going," I said.

"No, I'm ready to go."

We walked back to my SUV. I got the map application going and then looked at the time.

"You've been driving all day. Do you want to stay the night? There's a hotel nearby. I can get us two rooms and find a nice restaurant."

She smiled. "It's tempting but I only got one night off. Maybe when I build up some vacation time we can come back and be tourists." She was about to say something else, but suddenly let out a yawn.

"I can drive a little while," I suggested.

She refused, and insisted on driving, but after an hour, she finally relented. We exited the interstate, had a quick bite, and freshened up before getting back on the road. She made me promise to wake her after an hour. I agreed, and then let her sleep almost the entire way back. She was not happy when she awakened and realized what I had done.

"It's fine," I told her. "I positioned my arm in my lap and hardly felt a thing."

"I don't believe you," she retorted.

I shrugged with my right shoulder only. It didn't matter. We were almost home.

"So, what are you going to do about this?" she asked.

"I'm not doing anything."

"Shouldn't we tell someone?" she pressed.

"Who would we tell, Abby? And think about it. What if we held a press conference and told the world? What happens then?"

She thought about it, and I could see she was conflicted. Finally, she glanced over at me. "What if it's true?"

"I don't have a good answer to that question," I said. "If you're asking me if you should believe it and therefore turn your back on your faith, my answer is don't do it. I'm not a good Catholic. In fact, I have a lot of issues concerning my faith, but I'm not going to denounce it. I was baptized a Catholic and I'll die a Catholic."

We rode the rest of the way in silence. Parking, I killed the engine, got out, and slowly stretched. Abby watched me.

"I almost wish I'd never gone on this road trip," she said. "Don't get me wrong, I enjoyed my time with you, but I already know I'm going to spend a lot of nights losing sleep over this."

"Me too," I agreed.

"How's your finger?"

"Honestly, it's killing me. I can't wait to take a pill or two."

She frowned at me. "You should've woken me up."

"Yeah, I should have, but I wasn't tired, and you were."

"And now you're paying for it."

I chuckled. "Yes, I am."

We talked a few minutes more before she left. As soon as I walked inside, Tommy Boy greeted me and began yammering like he was on the brink of starvation.

"You're not fooling me. I know Anna came by earlier and fed you. She sent me a text confirming it," I said to him.

The little shit looked up at me with a pitiful expression and responded with another long meow. I knew he'd keep it up all night, so I gave in and put some dry food in his bowl. He attacked it immediately.

I fixed a tumbler of Scotch and used it to wash down a pain pill. Turning on the eave lights, I walked out back and inspected the progress of the new garage. My buddy Fitz had been busy. It was bittersweet. Yes, I was going to have a new shop, bigger and better than the old one. Eventually, I'd have an inventory of new tools, but it still saddened me. Everything could be replaced, but those old cars had a piece of my soul in them.

Going inside, I locked up, left the eave lights on, and sat in my easy chair with my laptop. I knew I was too keyed up to sleep, so I thought I'd do a little research. Logging on, I began variously worded searches regarding the burial and resurrection of Jesus. The closest thing I could find was something called the stolen body hypothesis. The hypothesis has been around since his body disappeared. The apostle Matthew is said to have claimed it was a lie spread by the Jewish priests.

After a while, I closed my laptop in exasperation. The only real thing I learned is that, like Father Anthony said, there were many similar stories. So, like Father Anthony said, the only difference here was the location given. I could almost envision all the scholars and opportunists going on a wild treasure hunt.

I thought about the inscriptions and maybe wished I'd gotten Father Anthony to write down the translation. Ultimately, it didn't matter. Now that I knew the language, I could find a way of translating the inscriptions, if I felt the need. The fact is, I doubted I would ever feel the need.

So, what was I to do? In the end, the decision was easy. I was going to leave the bells exactly where they were, like I said to Abby. Maybe, one day, I'd do more research and perhaps tell someone about it. Maybe even go on an expedition to find the remains of a man who was known as our Lord and Savior. A thought flashed through my mind of doing it with Eva.

"Don't even think about it," I muttered to myself.

I brushed my teeth and changed out of my clothes. I stared at my bed a moment but opted to sleep in my chair again. I turned the lights out and sat. I was so tired, I barely remembered pulling the blanket over me.

# CHAPTER 49

They'd used Percy to arrange a meeting for nine the next morning. He'd texted me the details while we were on the road, and I said it'd be okay. It was to be a Zoom conference call. That was fine with me. If anyone started running their piehole, I'd turn my laptop off and end the interview. Percy and Anna had come to the house an hour earlier with Gracie in tow. When she jumped out of their car, her tail was wagging so hard I thought she was going to dislocate it.

"I hope you two are hungry, I've made Spanish omelets, and croissants," I said. "I was going to make hornazo, but one of the ingredients is pork loin."

"Yeah, no on the pork loin," Anna said. She'd recently decided to stop eating meat. I caught a glance from Percy. He gave a small smile but said nothing.

We ate heartedly, and I admit I gave a few bites to Gracie, even after Anna chastised me. We discussed details of the whole debacle, although I left out the part about the Gypsy curse.

"What is the real relationship between Mishka and Eva?" Anna asked as she put the plates down on the floor for Gracie to lick.

"She's either his wife or adopted daughter. I'm not sure which one is the truth."

They pitched in and helped me clean up after breakfast. Anna then went for a walk with Gracie while Percy sat on the opposite side of my laptop. I logged in precisely at nine. Jay was already online.

"Good morning," I said.

"Good morning," he replied. "The rest will be here in a few minutes."

"I'm not waiting. My time is valuable, and I have a lot to do today. Let's get started or I'll log off."

Jay's distress was visible on the screen. He knew I was serious. "Okay, excuse me a moment." His image disappeared from the screen. At about that time, Special Agent Carter Pike came online. When he spotted me, he gave a small wave.

"Good morning, Thomas," he greeted.

"Back at you. I didn't know you'd been invited to this shindig."

"We've been collaborating together for a few days now."

Jay's image reappeared and he sat. "I advised them, Thomas. They said to wait until everyone is present."

I shook my head at the arrogance. I knew who was late. I focused on Carter.

"Carter, if you have any questions, you have the floor."

"Very well. I only have a few. Did Mishka Abramovich ever discuss the fraud scheme with you, and if he did, will you tell me what was discussed?"

"He never mentioned it and I never brought it up. I'll answer your next question. The woman who gave me the storage drives told me she's married to Mishka. Her name is Eva Abramovich."

I watched Carter jot a note, and then a couple of additional faces on the screen popped up.

"Who is this Eva woman again?"

I focused on who asked the question. It was good old Detective Kettleworth. I stared at her in contempt.

"For those of you who lacked the professionalism to come to this meeting on time, I'm not going to waste my time repeating myself."

"You don't dictate how this meeting is run," Kettleworth retorted.

I sighed and slowly shook my head. I had the urge to throw out an insult, instead I used my finger on the pad of my laptop before speaking to the rest of them.

"I've muted Kettleworth so I don't have to listen to her nonsense anymore. If anybody else behaves unprofessionally, I'll log off and this will be our last conversation. That includes you, little man," I said. It wasn't possible to pointedly stare at Poston on the computer screen, but he knew I meant him. "Alright, Carter, before I was so rudely interrupted, I was about to tell you that Eva was once in the Olympics. I forget which one, but if you give me a minute or two after this meeting is over, I can send you a link."

"I appreciate that, Thomas," he said.

"Alright, anyone besides Poston and Kettleworth have any additional questions?"

Poston glared at me through the computer screen. His loathing of me was palpable, but he gritted his teeth and remained silent. Everyone was silent now. After a couple of seconds, Commander Bartlett spoke.

"Detective Sansing, why don't you continue with your questioning."

Jay nodded, cleared his throat, and led me through a series of questions starting with how Mishka hired me. All of it was repetitive. When I told Carter about Valkyrie and her identity, I wasn't concerned about breaking any kind of oath with Eva. She was beyond their grasp and undoubtedly had a new identity established by now.

"Do you concur that Mishka Abramovich acted alone?" Jay asked.

"I only interacted with him. During one conversation, he claimed to be working for a larger organization, which he never named, but like I said, I never interacted with anyone but him."

I saw Jay glance to his left and give a slight nod. Although Kettleworth was muted, I could still see her image and could see she was jabbering about something. Jay was listening and waited until she was finished before speaking.

"Where is the location of the treasure?" he asked.

"There is no treasure," I replied.

"Are you certain?" Bartlett questioned.

"Yes."

Poston decided he needed to chime in. "So, you're claiming this man wasted an enormous amount of time and resources, not to mention murdering four people…"

"Five people," I interrupted. "Don't forget about Larry Boles."

"Alright, five people," Poston conceded after a moment's hesitation. Percy had informed me that Bartlett had a conference yesterday to discuss the murders. Poston had used the opportunity to suggest it was in fact I who had killed Larry. His reference to four murders committed by Mishka instead of five was a subtle play at continuing the theme, but I wasn't concerned. He continued.

"You're claiming your client, a man who hired you and paid you cash money, was seeking something that, in fact, does not exist?"

"Yes," I said.

"How do we know that you haven't found this alleged treasure and you are keeping it for yourself?"

"You don't," I answered, and then winked at him. Percy chuckled.

"I heard that. Someone is listening. Who is it?" Poston demanded.

"None of your business," I answered. "Now, if the questions are over, I have a few of my own."

"Ask your questions," Commander Bartlett said before Poston could interject.

"Is my phone still being tapped?"

"What makes you think it's being tapped?" Poston asked.

"By answering a question with a question, you not only revealed it's being tapped, it's also a subconscious indicator you have a proclivity for sex with farm animals," I said. Poston looked like he wanted to jump through the computer to get at me.

"All surveillance activity has ended," Bartlett said.

"Have the murders been officially cleared?" I asked.

"Tentatively, yes," Jay replied.

Poston spoke up. "Detective Sansing is not entirely correct. There is an ongoing investigation to identify individuals who may have aided and abetted Mishka Abramovich."

"I see you haven't changed much, Poston. You're going to ride these cases as long as you can."

Poston smirked before leaning toward Commander Bartlett and whispering something. Bartlett acknowledged whatever Poston said, but his expression remained deadpan. I know the man would have liked nothing more than to implicate me in any of this. The man plotted and schemed. It was his modus operandi. I'd seen it firsthand more than once. Whatever he whispered to Bartlett, I had no doubt it was something self-serving. He made eye contact with me through the monitor and gave a small, knowing smirk. I ignored him and focused on Special Agent Pike.

"Carter, what is the disposition of your case?"

"Four indictments have been obtained. We are currently working with INTERPOL and Russian law enforcement in obtaining their apprehension."

"Will Eva be indicted?" I asked.

Carter's expression tightened. "No, but there is a material witness warrant pending on a Jane Doe. It will be amended to list her full name before the day is over." He saw my hard stare. "It wasn't my call, Thomas. I hope you understand." He waited for me to comment. When I remained silent, he continued. "Do you know where she is currently located?" he asked.

"I do not. I've not seen nor heard from her in several days. The only number she gave me is no longer in service. I did a little checking and found it's a burner phone that was purchased here in Nashville a week ago."

My finger was beginning to throb. I started gently massaging my hand in an attempt to alleviate the pain. I don't know if this could be seen by the others, but Commander Bartlett spoke up.

"If there is nothing more, we will conclude this meeting. Thomas, if there is a need for a follow-up interview in the future, I hope you are agreeable."

"Certainly, but in the future, I only care to speak with Percy Trotter or Jay Sansing."

Sory Bartlett gave a small, knowing smile. "Of course."

"Before you log off, I want to speak with you privately," I said.

He arched an eyebrow, but then dismissed everyone. After everyone else had logged off, Sory stared in expectation.

"Are you alone?" I asked.

"I am."

"Alright, I'm not saying you owe me anything, but I have a favor to ask," I said. "Two favors, actually."

He stared a moment before speaking. "What kind of favors?"

"The first favor has to do with Poston and Kettleworth. I'm through with their nonsense. Tell them I am off limits. If I am still under investigation, assign the case to someone who is professional and unbiased. The same for any possible future investigations. Otherwise, there's going to be hell to pay."

He smiled slightly. "I've no doubt you'll get yourself in the middle of some other mess and we'll have to investigate you."

"Yeah, well if that happens, you should keep those two out of it." He picked up a coffee cup and took a sip before speaking. I saw a gold cufflink and wondered how much he spent on his wardrobe. "Alright, what else?"

"I recently met a young rookie by the name of Abigail Severns."

"I've met her. What about her?"

"I think she has a lot of potential, as long as she's not ruined by someone like Kettleworth or Poston. We've both seen this happen in the past."

Sory gave a slow, knowing nod. It had indeed happened before and Sory, who'd spent several years in the Office of Professional Accountability, had seen it firsthand.

"I've met Officer Severns. So, what do you want?" he asked.

"Just keep an eye on her, make sure she's not mistreated."

He slowly nodded and took another sip of coffee.

"Don't worry about Poston and Kettleworth, I'm about to have a sit down with them and go over their work product. As far as Officer Severns, I have a lot on my plate already. Babysitting a rookie cop is a little much to ask."

"Anything you could do would be appreciated," I said.

Sory grunted. "Well, we'll see. Alright, I have a busy day ahead of me, so if there is nothing else, I'll end this conversation."

I closed my laptop and faced Percy, who had a slight grin. "Those two idiots are going to be pissed for weeks," he said.

"I hope so. Do you think Bartlett will do anything to them?"

"The rumor is, Kettleworth is going to be transferred back to the domestic violence unit. Poston will get a stern talking to, but that's probably about it." Percy stood and stretched. "I better get going. I've got a few leads to run down on a missing person case."

"Anything serious?" I asked.

Percy scoffed. "Adult son borrows mommy's car to go buy a pack of cigarettes. That was yesterday. He's nowhere to be found and his phone goes straight to voicemail."

"Let me guess, he has a history of drug abuse," I surmised.

"You got it. He'll turn up when he runs out of money, but in the meantime, I have to go through the motions. Hey, why don't the three of us go out to dinner tomorrow night? Anna has been dying to try out a new restaurant on Music Row. Bring a date."

I held up my hand. "If it's feeling better, you're on. I'll let you know."

After Percy left, I went into the restroom and carefully removed the bandages. My whole hand was swollen and had a funny color to it. The finger was still throbbing, and I knew there was going to be a lot of scar tissue. I had an appointment with a specialist in a couple of days, but I was doubtful he could do anything. He'd probably stare at it, maybe poke it a little bit before telling me there would be scar tissue and permanent nerve damage.

I put on fresh bandages, fixed a mug of coffee, and walked out back. The masons were busy with cinderblocks, creating walls with the skill of veterans. They both had air buds stuck in their ears, but they worked in harmony without having to speak to each other and were doing the work of four men. Not a wasted movement between them. It was satisfying to watch. I brought them two large glasses of iced tea before going back inside.

I was restless and decided to call Wes Tilford. He answered, which was a surprise, and advised me he had two motions on Flaky's case which were scheduled to be heard next week, and as far as he knew, there was nothing for me to help him out with.

I'd grown used to his dismissive nature, but honestly, I didn't think there was much he could do. The bikers weren't going to cooperate, Turk's bike was no longer an issue, and the only known witness had died of a heart attack. Besides, any type of physical activity triggered painful throbbing in my whole hand.

Nope, I was out of action for now. This was going to be a day of rest and rehabilitation. I fixed myself a glass of tea and made sure there was fresh food and water for Tommy Boy. I parked myself in my easy chair with my laptop and Springfield. I performed a quick press check on the handgun before placing it in my lap. Mishka was dead and I'm sure Eva had left the country, but I had no idea if there were any associates who believed I needed to be dealt with. If that was the case, I wasn't going to make it easy for them.

I opened my Kindle reader app, downloaded a biography of Theodore Roosevelt, and spent the rest of the day reading about the greatest president this country ever had.

# CHAPTER 50

It was late afternoon when hunger pangs caused me to stop reading. I stood slowly and stretched the kinks out. I wasn't in a sociable mood, so I sent Percy a text declining the dinner invitation. I was in the middle of trying to make a sandwich with one hand when my phone rang. The caller ID indicated an international call. I smiled, thinking it was Special Agent Hope Delmonico.

"Hello?"

"Hello, Thomas." It was Eva. My smile went away.

"Where are you?" I asked.

"I am currently in Vatican City."

It took a second or two before I understood. "You work for them."

"Yes."

"I see."

"Does that surprise you?"

"I knew you were keeping secrets from me, but yeah, you got me. I never suspected it," I said.

"I have more to confess," she said.

"Alright, let's hear it."

"I have hacked into your phone and computer. That includes the computer that Ronald uses as your cloud drive."

"I'm impressed, but there wasn't much to find," I asserted. She wasn't fooled.

"On the contrary, there were so many interesting files. Did you know that Ronald keeps a running biography of your accomplishments? It is a fascinating read. He was vague about your time in the military though. Perhaps one day you can tell me all about it."

"Perhaps," I said.

"You also had many interesting pictures. Particularly the pictures of the bells."

"Don't forget the closeups of the inscriptions," I countered.

"Yes, the inscriptions. Do you understand the meaning of the inscriptions, Thomas?"

"I can't read a word of it," I said.

"That is why you paid a second visit to Father Anthony, to find out what the inscriptions say."

"If you say so," I said, wondering how she knew that.

"Yes, I say so. Father Anthony told you exactly what the inscriptions said. What do you intend to do with this information? My superiors are interested."

"I'm not going to do anything with it. That doesn't mean someone else won't eventually find them and figure out what they say."

"Have you told anyone else?" she asked.

"Yeah, I told Mishka, but he was killed only a few minutes after I told him."

There was a moment's pause before she spoke again. "Who else have you talked to about the bells besides Mishka?"

I had a sudden, bad feeling about that question. The way it was phrased made me suspect she was being told what to ask, so I chose my answer carefully.

"Nobody. I tried calling you, but you didn't answer." Okay, so I didn't tell her I had told Percy and Abby, and I wasn't going to. It was none of her business.

"That is what I told them. Unfortunately, this leads to more of my confession. I have deleted the pictures from your files," she said.

"That wasn't nice."

"The computer data shows you have printed copies of these photographs. You must destroy them, Thomas. It is for your own good."

"Yeah, well, I'll decide what's good for me and what isn't, but it doesn't matter. They've already been destroyed. What about the bells? Did your people steal them?"

"They have been confiscated," she said.

I sighed at the arrogance. "The correct word would be stolen. The Catholic Church is infamous for such acts, no?" I mocked.

"There are those who would agree, but I have no wish to argue. There is something else we need to discuss," she said and paused.

"Yeah, go ahead," I prodded.

"Father Anthony."

Red flags were flying in my face. I tried to be nonchalant.

"Yeah, Mishka sent me on a wild goose chase down there to check out Methuselah Sartain's grave. That's when I met Father Anthony."

"And then after the unfortunate incident with Mishka, you went back to New Orleans specifically to speak to him. This is when he told you what the inscriptions said," she declared. "How did you figure it out, if I may ask?"

"Surprisingly, the pain from the torture somehow made my brain put it all together. I would have thought of it eventually, but Mishka achieved his goal."

"I have heard of this happening. So, you figured out the bells were the treasure, but you did not know what language the inscriptions were in."

"Yep. I went back to New Orleans and asked Father Anthony. Turns out he's known about the bells and what they've said for a few years now." I knew it was pointless to lie about it and only hoped my seeming honesty would work to my advantage at some point down the road.

"And he told you?" she asked.

"He summarized it. I don't see the big deal though. There have been several similar claims. I think I found five or six when researching the internet. I'm sure there are more."

"This one is different, Thomas," she said.

"How?"

There was a moment's hesitation before she spoke. "This one gives a detailed description of the location. Detailed enough so that a focused search can be conducted."

"I see."

"It is hoped that you will not try to interfere."

"You don't have to worry about that," I said.

"Good. That is what I told my superiors. And now, there is one additional thing I must tell you."

"What's that?" I asked.

"Father Anthony died peacefully in his sleep last night. A beautiful mausoleum will be built for him."

The implication and magnitude of what she'd said hit me like a meteor.

"Damn all of you," I growled. "He loved the church. He wasn't going to do or say anything that might harm it."

"He said something to you, yes?" she said.

"Didn't I just tell you he's known what the inscriptions said for years now and has kept it secret? Who do you think convinced me this is something that should stay a secret, huh? It wasn't you or Mishka, and it damn sure wasn't the Pope. It was him, Eva. An old man who stayed out of the way, said his prayers every day, and waited for his salvation."

I realized I was yelling. The foreman, a bald man around my age, paused in his work and looked over at me in puzzlement. I stood and walked inside while Eva spoke to me.

"It was not my decision, Thomas. I hope you believe that, but it was for the best," she said.

"Oh, yeah? What happens if one day your superiors tell you it's for the best that I die peacefully in my sleep? What will you do then?"

She did not answer. I changed tact.

"What are your people going to do with this information? Is there going to be a search?"

"Arrangements are being made to conduct an archaeological expedition in Israel," she said.

"You people believe this is legitimate?"

"Yes," she said. "The information has been analyzed and a possible location has been determined."

"If you find him, then what?" I asked.

"I cannot say. Even now I have told you too much. I would warn you not to speak of this to anyone else."

"Yeah, don't worry," I growled. "In fact, consider it already forgotten. Alright, what about you? What's next for you?"

"I will be continuing with my work," she said, which seemed like a vague answer, but I didn't press the matter.

"Mishka told me you weren't actually his wife; you were in fact his adopted daughter."

There were several seconds of silence before she spoke. "He did terrible things to me, and I do not wish to speak about it. I must go now, Thomas. I am glad we have met. I wished we had made love that night. Perhaps, one day."

"No, I think it's in my best interests that you stay far away from me, or else I'll end up like Father Anthony, or worse, like Tomey."

There was a moment's pause before she responded. "Do you think I was involved in Officer Tomey's murder?"

"The thought crossed my mind," I replied.

There was more silence before I heard the soft click of the call being disconnected. I put my phone in my pocket, absently walked into the kitchen, and stared out the back window. Another two men had arrived in a flatbed and had begun unloading sheets of prefab metal. The way Fitz had explained it to me, the walls were going to be concrete blocks up to four feet and the rest would be the metal. I hoped the finished product would look good.

"Well, let's have a look," I muttered to myself.

Pulling out my phone, I typed in the password and then opened my files. It only took a moment to confirm what she said. The pictures of the bells were gone. I knew they had not only been deleted, but she had also probably used some sort of program like Broken Arrow to totally obliterate them.

I emitted a long sigh and wondered if this was the end of it or if I was going to have a late-night visit by Eva or a couple of her co-workers. I was going to be sleeping with my gun for a long time.

I fixed a fresh pitcher of iced tea and took it to the workers. One of them jokingly asked if I had any cold beer.

The older bald one made small talk. "It looks like it's going to be a nice garage. Are you a mechanic?"

"More of a hobbyist," I replied. "I like to work on old cars and restore them."

"Oh, like those TV reality shows."

I forced out a chuckle that I didn't feel. "Those shows are scripted. You can't restore a car from junk and make it showroom quality in only a couple of weeks. Totally unrealistic."

He nodded. "Yeah, I guess so, but they're fun to watch. It seems like it's a dying art though. These young people aren't interested in old vintage cars." He emptied the glass in a couple of swallows. "I guess I need to get back to work. Oh, I was supposed to let you know that Fitz will be here in an hour or so. He's doing a custom house on the other side of town and the owner is extremely demanding."

I watched them work for a few minutes before walking around to the front of my house and sat in one of the rocking chairs. I'd no sooner gotten comfortable when a familiar sight came rolling down my driveway. It was a van festooned with the logo of one of the local TV news stations. The driver and passenger spotted me, which caused them to fix their mugs with big shit-eating grins and wave at me like we were old pals.

The passenger exited like she was stepping off a yacht. She was a sultry auburn-haired beauty, fairly new on the evening news but already popular. Shelly something or the other. She walked up while continuing to smile, showing off a perfect set of straight, white teeth. The driver, an overweight guy who was in his fifties, came hustling up with a camera.

"Hi, Thomas," she greeted.

"Have we met?" I asked, even though I knew we hadn't.

Instead of answering the question, she instead saw it as an opening and continued walking closer. I had to admit, she was a stunner, but I wasn't going to fall for her charms. I held up my good hand.

"I know why you two are here. I'll save you a lot of wasted time. I'm not going to give an interview."

Her smile faltered. "But this is an incredible story. A mysterious man comes into town and murders four people in search of some kind of treasure. And you play an important role."

I gave a single syllable chortle. "Good looks and a way with words. You'll go far in journalism."

Her smile brightened again. "So, it's agreed then. I think this spot is a good place for an interview. Jimmy, do you want to set up here?"

I cut her off. "No, there will be no interview."

The cameraman, I guess his name was Jimmy, spoke up. "Are you sure, big guy? You know, this'll be good publicity for your PI business."

They threw out a few more compliments in an effort to coax me into it, but I was adamant. Jimmy was probably right, it'd be good publicity, but I wasn't interested. After a couple of minutes, they conceded defeat. I expected to see Shelly's personality change from flirtatious to scornful, but she didn't. Instead, she gave me a disheartened smile before handing me a business card.

"If you change your mind, please give me a call."

I watched them as I sipped my tea, ensuring they left and then texted Fitz, informing him I wanted a security gate installed as soon as possible.

I did not have any incentive to move and remained on my porch, absently rocking back and forth. My mood was glum. The injured finger and Eva's phone call had done a number on me. Even though she had saved my life, I felt that she had betrayed me and now I found myself questioning everything she'd told me. Did she really work for the Vatican, or was that a lie too? If it was the truth, did Mishka in fact work for them as well?

I had more questions than answers, but it was my own fault. I'd blindly trusted Eva and did nothing to learn more about her. Yet another reminder that I was always too naïve when it came to women. My gullibility had come back on me and bit me in the ass more than once. Let's see, there was Marcia, my wife. Lilith, Al, and now Eva. There were others from my younger years, but Eva was the latest, and it left me feeling bitter. I guess it could have been worse. After all, I could have ended up like Father Anthony. In fact, she'd reaffirmed a valuable life lesson that I'd learned long ago but seemed to have forgotten. A lesson that I vowed to never forget again.

What was that lesson? Don't trust anyone.

# CHAPTER 51

"Eva's gone," Ronald said.

"Yeah, no shit," I replied with a yawn. "Is that why you felt the need to call me at five in the morning?"

"I mean, she's gone gone."

I was tempted to hang up. Ronald and I were friends, but sometimes he was a pain in the ass. "You're not making sense, buddy."

"She's gone from the internet. Completely gone," he said. "The pictures from the Olympics, her email account. All of it has been deleted."

I sat up in bed and stretched before responding. "Is that easy to do?"

"If you mean being able to wipe all traces of your existence off the internet, no, it's not easy. I mean, it can be done, but it's not easy. You need to have some high-level internet access to do that. She doesn't even exist in the dark web."

"That is odd," I said and thought for a minute. I instantly became worried. "Look, maybe it's best if you stop searching around for her."

"Why?" he asked.

I sighed. I'd been keeping it from him, but I guess it was time for him to hear the truth.

"Do you remember me telling you about Father Anthony dying?"

"Yeah, that was sad. I kinda wanted to meet him," Ronald said.

"You would've liked him. The thing is, he didn't die a natural death. The last time I spoke to Eva, she practically told me her people killed him to keep him quiet."

There was a long pause before he spoke. "You're not saying Eva would kill me, are you?"

"I don't know, buddy, but she's not what she seems. I totally misjudged her."

"So, I shouldn't keep looking?" he asked.

"No, I don't think so. She knows we're not a threat to her, but the people she's associated with might think otherwise."

"Okay."

His voice was quiet, almost childlike. "Listen, buddy, Eva liked you, but leave it alone. I'm betting she'll be in touch again one day and the two of you can have a nice long internet chat."

After hanging up, I tried to go back to sleep, but that wasn't going to happen. Even if I could, Tommy Boy was now awake and pestering me. I fixed him some food before showering and starting the day.

I sat at the kitchen table and thought about what Ronald said while sipping my morning coffee. I'm sure it took a lot of effort to totally wipe her existence from the internet. No doubt it had something to do with the material witness warrant the FBI had on her. I debated on leaving a voicemail on Agent Carter Pike's office phone, but my paranoia made me wonder if my phone was being monitored by Eva's people.

A bolt of lightning flashed outside, soon followed by a crack of thunder. In Tennessee it was not uncommon for a squall to come through and the sun would be out an hour later, but this one looked like it was going to be here for a while. Glancing at the clock, I wondered if Percy was awake. I decided to text him.

Breakfast?

The old hangout. 30 min.

The old hangout was a Waffle House restaurant we frequented back when we worked in the homicide unit together. I responded with a "10-4" and was waiting on him when he arrived.

"Anna's going to take that job," he said as he sat.

"It's a good job, if Rochelle doesn't take advantage of her," I said.

"Yeah, we talked about it, and even though I can't stand that bitch, I told Anna she had my full support."

"Good man," I said. "Are you two going to get married?"

Percy smiled slightly. "We've talked about it, and let's just say it is a distinct probability we'll do it. Enough about me and Anna. What's on your mind?"

I filled him in about Ronald's discovery. "Pike should be made aware of it if he hasn't already discovered it. I would have called, but I'm worried I might still have bugs."

Percy frowned and gave a slight shake of his head. "Unless there's something else going on, they've shut down the wiretap on you. In fact, Bartlett made it clear that when it comes to you, nobody is allowed to do anything without first clearing it from him."

"I didn't know that," I said, nodding in appreciation. "But I think Eva's people may have an interest in me, and they may even be surveilling my phones and computer traffic."

"You think?" he asked.

"I may be paranoid, but if they are, I want them to think Eva is the furthest thing from my mind."

"I can pass along the information, if you'd like," he offered.

"I appreciate that."

Our meals arrived and we ate mostly in silence. After, we walked out to the parking lot. I watched and listened while he called Carter. The conversation only took five minutes. Percy ended the call and nodded.

"I like the man. You don't have to spell everything out for him. Alright, what's next on your plate? Do you have any new cases?"

"Nothing all that interesting. I've been serving some subpoenas and I have a client who was adopted at birth. She submitted her DNA on one of those ancestry websites and she's got a hit on a first cousin. She's hired me to find the cousin and initiate contact."

"She's paying you a grand for that?" he asked.

I smiled. "She's a nice person, a single mom, so I cut her a break. I'm going to do it today, but after that, I think I'm going to take a break for a while and get my shop put together. Maybe I'll find a car that strikes my interest."

"Sounds therapeutic," he said.

"Do you have any hobbies?"

"Other than martial arts? Not really. I enjoy reading, like you do, but I don't seem to have time for anything lately. And I don't know if you're aware of it, but Anna requires attention, lots of attention. Don't get me wrong, I'm not complaining, but she consumes most of my free time."

I chuckled. Between Anna and his daughter, I doubted he had any free time at all. We spoke a few more minutes before Percy said his goodbyes. He had to go to work, and I was going to visit the address for this first cousin.

The lady lived in a large house located in Brentwood. I was greeted via one of those security doorbells that also acted as an intercom. After introducing myself and explaining the nature of my visit, a middle-aged woman opened the door.

"I'm not sure I want to meet her," she said. "I know her mother. She's a piece of work. Over the years she's hit me up for loans more times than I can count. I know I'll never get the money back, and I know she'll never straighten her life out. You should tell that to your client. Tell her to go live her life and stay as far away from her mother as possible."

We spoke a few more minutes. I ended up giving her my client's phone number and email. She thanked me, wished me a blessed day, and closed the door. The second wave of heavy rain hit me as I was walking to my car.

It was all I could do for my client. I called her and filled her in. The rest was up to her. She didn't seem happy about the news but thanked me anyway. Heading home, I got caught in a traffic jam on Hillsboro Pike. The blue lights of a cop car passing me indicated a wreck up ahead. My GPS confirmed it a second later. I hit the icon that would provide me with a route home. I didn't need directions, but I was curious about the time. On a normal day, it would've taken about twenty minutes from my current location. Today, the GPS showed an estimated time of arrival at forty-seven minutes. What was worse, it was raining too hard to crack open my window and smoke a cigar.

"It's going to be one of those days," I said with a sigh.

The traffic was agonizingly slow. We'd move forward ten feet and stop for a minute before repeating the process. I turned on the radio and tuned in to a local news station. I missed the first few seconds of a breaking announcement but caught enough to know that several members of a local outlaw biker club were being rounded up and arrested for a variety of crimes. The arrests were being made by an ATF joint task force, which meant the charges were going to be federal.

"That's not good," I muttered and continued to listen. They eventually got around to naming the club. As I suspected, it was the Satan's Dogs. I wondered how many of the Baroques had been taken down with them.

As I pondered it, I couldn't help but wonder if my name had been mentioned in their investigation. And then I thought of the curse and wondered if it had anything to do with the Satan's Dogs troubles. I had a sudden ironic epiphany.

"That's it. All I have to do is hang out with my enemies and the curse will make bad things happen to them."

# CHAPTER 52

"Are you sure about this, brother?" I asked as I stared at him through the thick glass. I can't say the orange prison clothing was a good look, but he was finally wearing a set that fit him.

"Absolutely sure," Flaky answered. He gestured around. "They've agreed to let me serve out my sentence here and be a trustee. With good behavior, I'll be out in four years. Maybe less."

I found myself shaking my head. "It's not right. You shouldn't be serving time for something you didn't do."

Flaky stared at me a moment and casually glanced around to see if anyone was paying attention to us. He then set the phone down before pulling out a small piece of scrap paper and the stub of a pencil. He hastily wrote something on it and looked around again before pressing the paper up against the window.

I looked at it for several seconds before making pointed eye contact with him. He stared back impassively. I said nothing. Instead, I hung up the phone, stood and walked out. My phone rang as I merged onto the interstate.

"Hello, Thomas," Sherman greeted.

"Hello, old man," I greeted back. "I've been meaning to call you and get an update on our investment."

"Yes, that's why I'm calling. I'm afraid that I am the bearer of rather somber news," he said.

"Sounds bad," I said.

"Indeed. Don Slocum killed himself yesterday. He failed to appear at the hearing and when the deputy sheriffs arrived at his residence to evict him, he shot himself while standing on the front porch."

"Damn, I hate to hear that," I said.

"I did as well. There is a bit of irony to this though."

"Yeah, what's that?" I asked.

"An unintended result of this is the contractor can finally proceed forward. We had a meeting not more than thirty minutes ago and he has assured me he can get back on schedule within the month."

"That's good, I suppose," I said, not knowing how else to respond.

"I feel the same as well, although Mister Slocum's death is quite sad. I will say a prayer for him," Sherman said.

"He would not have appreciated it, I'm thinking," I replied. For some reason I thought that Don Slocum was one of those people who blamed the Jews for everything that was wrong in the world.

"Even so, I will offer a prayer and rely on God to do what is right."

Sherman then went on about projected dividend payments and other things before suggesting we get together for a round of golf one day next week. I agreed and said I'd text him on a date.

The news of Don Slocum's demise left me in an even gloomier mood. The man had issues and most assuredly it was too late for him to turn his life around and start over, even with a nice fat check for the sale of his house. Still, it depressed me that he ended his life and I admit, the fact that his death meant my investment was going to reap dividends much sooner than expected made me feel guilty as hell.

It took me forty minutes to arrive at my destination, and during that time, my phone rang several times. I ignored all the calls and drove in silence. When I walked in the door of Mick's Place, I still had not completely decompressed and was looking forward to a cigar and beer.

"Hi, cutie pie," Marti greeted when I walked in. She was wearing Daisy Duke shorts which showed plenty of cheek and a tight-fitting black tee shirt that left little to the imagination. In the brief time she'd been working at Mick's, the number of male patrons had increased two-fold. No surprise.

"Hi yourself," I replied, went over to my locker, and got out a Padron. Marti took it from me as I sat, cut it, and even lit it for me.

"You look like you've had a rough day," she said as she handed over my cigar.

I nodded. She held up a frosted glass. "Nashville Lager?"

"Yes, and thank you," I said.

She made a perfect pour and handed it to me with a smile.

"You're in a good mood," I remarked.

"It's been a good day," she said and smiled. "Plus, seeing you always brightens my day."

I gave her a halfhearted smile. It was the best I could do. I took a big swallow and looked around. It was still early in the afternoon. The only other person present was Horace. He was an older retired firefighter from New York. Nice enough, but he'd talk your ear off if you gave him a chance and I wasn't in a talkative mood.

"Where's Mick?" I asked.

"He's back in his office. He's been there a couple of hours, so he's probably taking a nap," she replied.

I nodded in understanding and worked my cigar. Marti leaned over and rested her elbows on the counter, giving me a nice view of her cleavage. She was doing it on purpose. I didn't mind.

"You want to talk about it? That's what bartenders are supposed to do, right?" she asked and gave a sweet smile.

I smiled back. "Oh, it's nothing. We all have bad days, right?"

"Suit yourself," she said and then lowered her voice to a whisper. "Maybe I can work it out of you later." She winked this time before walking away and tending to Horace.

I was polite, but the truth was, I had no intention of talking to her about it. I did not want to discuss how a man who I thought of as a friend and an honorable man shook my faith with seven heartbreaking words scrawled on a scrap of paper.

The case was looking good. The DA, sensing his case was tenuous, made a ridiculously generous offer. To my surprise, Flaky accepted it. Now I know why.

I never said I didn't do it.

Flaky was right. He never said he didn't do it. His lawyer did, but he didn't. I only assumed he was innocent. I drained my beer and motioned to Marti. She poured one in a fresh glass and placed it in front of me.

"I'm going to check on Mick. Be back in a sec."

I watched the rhythm of her hips as she walked toward the back and began idly wondering about that supposed Gypsy curse. They called it an Amriya, and since learning about it, it seemed like I'd been in the middle of multiple misfortunate events.

Could the curse include becoming good friends with a man who turned out to be a coldblooded murderer? I'd killed before, true enough, but shooting someone in the back of the head for nothing more than ensuring a successful patch-over? No, I'd never do something like that.

Marti emerged from the back office, and from her expression I could immediately sense something was wrong. Her face had drained of color, and she stared at me like a deer caught in the headlights of a semi. I set my beer down.

"What is it?" I asked.

Her voice quivered when she answered. "It's Mick. I think he's dead."


The End

www.ingramcontent.com/pod-product-compliance
Lightning Source LLC
Chambersburg PA
CBHW060421180626
46817CB00007B/2607